Hypnotic Voices

I started to take off the necklace, but it was as if there was someone standing behind me grasping my fingers to stop me. I stared at myself in the mirror. I was totally naked except for the necklace. Although it wasn't tight, it felt very warm against my skin.

I heard my voices telling me to leave it on, but then, for the first time, I heard another voice, a different-sounding voice, deeper, darker. It was coming from the far right corner of the room, where there was a shadow that shouldn't be there because it was so lit up.

"Take it off," the voice whispered. "You'll never know the truth about yourself if you let them control you. Take it off."

There was something hypnotic about the voice.

"Take it off. Don't wear it all the time."

I started to reach back and stopped. And then, as if a spotlight had hit it, the shadow evaporated, and the room was silent.

I went to bed with the necklace on, but I couldn't help but wonder if the voice in the shadows was the one I should have obeyed.

V.C. Andrews® Books

The Dollanganger Family Series
Flowers in the Attic
Petals on the Wind
If There Be Thorns
Seeds of Yesterday
Garden of Shadows
Christopher's Diary: Secrets of
    Foxworth
Christopher's Diary: Echoes of
    Dollanganger
Secret Brother

The Casteel Family Series
Heaven
Dark Angel
Fallen Hearts
Gates of Paradise
Web of Dreams

The Cutler Family Series
Dawn
Secrets of the Morning
Twilight's Child
Midnight Whispers
Darkest Hour

The Landry Family Series
Ruby
Pearl in the Mist
All That Glitters
Hidden Jewel
Tarnished Gold

The Logan Family Series
Melody
Heart Song
Unfinished Symphony
Music in the Night
Olivia

The Orphans Miniseries
Butterfly
Crystal
Brooke
Raven
Runaways

The Wildflowers Miniseries
Misty
Star
Jade
Cat
Into the Garden

The Hudson Family Series
Rain
Lightning Strikes
Eye of the Storm
The End of the Rainbow

The Shooting Stars Series
Cinnamon
Ice
Rose
Honey
Falling Stars

Virginia ANDREWS

SAGE'S EYES

SIMON &
SCHUSTER

London · New York · Sydney · Toronto · New Delhi

A CBS COMPANY

First published in the USA by Gallery Books,
an imprint of Simon & Schuster Inc., 2016
First published in Great Britain by Simon & Schuster UK Ltd, 2016
A CBS COMPANY

1 3 5 7 9 10 8 6 4 2

Simon & Schuster UK Ltd
1st Floor
222 Gray's Inn Road
London WC1X 8HB

www.simonandschuster.co.uk

Simon & Schuster Australia, Sydney
Simon & Schuster India, New Delhi

A CIP catalogue record for this book
is available from the British Library

Hardback ISBN: 978-1-4711-3384-8
Trade Paperback ISBN: 978-1-4711-5473-7
eBook ISBN: 978-1-4711-3386-2

Printed and bound by CPI Group (UK) Ltd, Croydon, CR0 4YY

MIX
Paper from
responsible sources
FSC® C020471

Simon & Schuster UK Ltd are committed to sourcing paper
that is made from wood grown in sustainable forests and supports the Forest
Stewardship Council, the leading international forest certification organisation.
Our books displaying the FSC logo are printed on FSC certified paper.

For Gene Andrews,
who so wanted to keep his sister's work alive

SAGE'S EYES

Prologue

The long, dark pathway to the end of my dream was lined with hemlock, branched and graceful, with its white flowers and smooth stems marked with red. History and philosophy students probably know that Socrates was forced to drink it to carry out his own death sentence. I know that my ancestors recommended mixing it with betony and fennel seed to cure the bite of a mad dog.

I cannot tell you exactly how or why I know these things. I don't even know for sure who my ancestors were or where they lived. I don't know if I'm English, Italian, Dutch, or some combination. However, even when I was a young girl, probably no more than four years old, memories like these would come over me when I was least expecting them, but usually back then only when I was alone. Often that would happen when I was sitting outside on my small redwood bench on the rear patio, playing with a doll or some other toy my adoptive parents had given me for my birthday or when my father returned from a work trip.

My father was a commercial insurance salesman and often visited companies more than a hundred miles away. I was sure he could sell anyone anything. He was handsomer than anyone else's father I knew and had a smile that could radiate enough warmth to heat an igloo. With his perennial suntanned complexion, his green-tinted ebony eyes, his rich, thick licorice-black hair, always neatly styled, and his perfect facial features, he could have his picture next to the term *movie star* in the dictionary.

Whenever I was alone because my mother was doing housework and my father was away, I could lose myself in my own imagination for hours and hours. During that time, images, faces, words, and sights I had never seen in real life, in books and magazines, or on television would appear before me as if they were being beamed down from a cloud. I had always heard voices, and although I would never tell anyone, especially my parents, I still do.

The voices seemed to ride on the wind and come at me in waves of whispers clinging to the underbelly of the breeze, swirling about my ears. I often heard my name first and looked to see who was calling me from behind trees and bushes or around corners. There was never anyone there then, and there still isn't now. Sometimes the whispering trailed in the wake of a flock of birds flapping their wings almost in complete silence above me. And sometimes I would awaken suddenly at night, the way someone who had heard their bedroom door just open might awaken, and I would hear the whispering coming from the darkest corners of my room.

It never frightened me and still doesn't. There was always a strong feeling of loving warmth in the voices, which, if they did anything, comforted me. When I was a young girl, I never had to call for my parents after a bad dream. The whispering reassured me. My ghosts protected me. I could close my eyes again without any trepidation, turn over in my bed, and embrace the darkness, snuggling safely like a baby in the arms of her mother.

Back then, whenever I mentioned any of this to my father or especially to my mother, both would scowl. If they were together at the time, my father would shake his head and look at my mother as if he was about to throw up his hands and run off. She would kneel down and seize my shoulders tightly. If she was wearing her fake fingernails, she would dig them into me enough to make me squirm and bring tears to my eyes.

"Control your imagination, Sage," she might say, and then shake me so hard that she rattled my bones. Her startlingly gray eyes seemed to harden into marbles and look more like icy ash. "I don't want you saying things like this out loud, especially when strangers are among us. You're old enough to know the difference between pretend and real."

I saw no difference, I wanted to say, but I didn't. Maybe I wasn't old enough; maybe I would never be. I knew it would only make her angrier to hear this. She would want to know why, and I would have to tell her that what I saw in dreams I often saw in the world when I woke up, whether it was the shapes of shadows, faces in crowds, or the actions of birds, dogs, cats, and rabbits. If I could walk up and touch a squirrel in a dream, I could also do it when I was awake. Birds landed on my open hand and trotted around on my palm, and rabbits would hop between my feet when I walked on the grass. They still do that, but they seem a little more cautious.

Even when I was only four or five, I really did try to keep my thoughts and dreams more to myself, but despite my efforts, they had a way of rising out of me, pushing to the surface like air bubbles in a pond and then exploding in a burst of excitement so intense that my tongue would trip over my words in an effort to get them completely out. I didn't tell my mother or my father, but I felt a sense of relief when I didn't keep my visions under lock and key. They fluttered around my heart until I freed them, like someone opening her closed hands to let trapped butterflies fly away.

My mother was always frustrated about it. One night, she came to my bedroom and tied a rock to the bedpost. The rock had a hole in it, and she could run a thick cord through it.

"What's that?" I asked.

"Never mind what it is. You don't ever touch it or take it off. Understand?"

"How did a rock get a hole in it?"

She stood there thinking. I knew she was thinking whether she should answer me, and then she said, "Water can work a hole into a rock. That makes the rock special. Think of it as good luck. It can stop you from having nightmares."

"I don't have many nightmares," I said. "I'm never frightened by a dream."

"Well, I do," she said, raising her voice. "And I don't want to hear you describe any of your horrid dreams to me or your father or anyone else who comes into this house," she added, and left, her thick-heeled shoes hammering on the wooden hallway floor as her anger flowed down through her ankles.

My dreams aren't horrid, I thought. I never said anything to make her think that. I never wanted to stop them. The rock didn't make any difference anyway. When I disobeyed her and touched it, I felt nothing unusual. Maybe it was too old or something. Eventually, because I didn't stop talking about my dreams and visions, she came into my room and took it away. She looked disappointed and disgusted.

"What are you going to do with that?" I asked.

"Hang it on my own bed," she told me. "I need it more than you do, obviously."

I wasn't sure if she was kidding or not. I knew she and my father were still upset about the things I said, even if they hid that disapproval from other people. If my images and unexplained memories sprouted in my mind while I was in public and I mentioned them, either my mother or my father would quickly squeeze some laughter out of their disapproving faces and then either would say something like "What a vivid imagination she has. We're always amazed."

"She'll be a great writer someday," my mother might say.

"Or a great filmmaker," my father would add, and whoever was there would nod and smile. They might talk about their children and their imaginations or even themselves when they were my age, but they would always add, "But I never was as imaginative as Sage. And I certainly didn't speak with such confidence and authority when I was her age. Even older!"

As odd as it might seem, these compliments didn't please my parents the way they would other parents. The moment she could do it unseen, my mother would flash a reprimand my way and then quickly return to her mask, her forced smile. Afterward, she would put her hand gently on my head but ever so slightly catch a few strands of my hair between her long, firm fingers and twist them just enough to send a sharp sting into my scalp that would shoot down into my chest and burn my heart.

I knew what message she was sending, but no matter what she did or what she or my father said to me, I couldn't stop revealing what I had seen behind my eyes. There was no door, no lock, and no wall strong enough to shut up my visions or hold them back. It was like trying to stop the rain or the wind with your two little hands pressed palms upward at the cloudy sky.

Sometimes when we had company and the guests spoke to me, I might recite something I had envisioned or remembered without any explanation for it. Most of the time back then, the guests thought it was amusing. Some of them, to my mother's chagrin, would encourage me to tell them more.

"I once had a pair of black leather shoes with low heels and round toes," I told the two couples who were at our house for dinner on my father's thirty-eighth birthday. One of the men was Samuel Black, who worked with my father at the insurance company. They all had just praised my new dark pink dress and light pink shoes. "I had to keep them spotlessly clean, or I might get a paddling," I added, lowering my head like some errant sinner full of shame.

"What?" Mr. Black's wife, Cissy, said.

She looked at my mother, who smiled by tightening her lips until they looked like a sharp ruby slice in her face. She shook her head slightly and sighed to attract sympathy for herself and my father. Oh, the burden they carried having a child like me.

"A *paddling*?" Mrs. Black continued. "I don't think I've heard that word used, but I know what it was. Did she really have such shoes that she had to keep spotless?"

My parents laughed. Apparently, only I could tell how forced and phony that laughter was. To me, it sounded more like the rattling of rusty old bells on a horse's harness at Christmas. I could remember that sound, the sled, and being bundled up in a blanket, but when or where that memory came from I did not know. Like all other similar memories, it came and was gone as quickly as the snap of fingers.

"No, and we would never paddle her for getting her shoes dirty," my mother said. She turned to me and put on a stern face. "You know we wouldn't, Sage. We don't paddle you for anything. Don't tell people such a thing," she ordered, with her eyes wide and her jaw tight. I could even see the way the muscles in her neck tightened.

"She's so convincing," Mrs. Hummel said, looking at me with admiration. "I never saw a little girl who could be so convincing. You can't help but wonder how a little girl could make things up so vividly."

"Why did you say you had those particular shoes?" her husband, Michael, asked me. He sat back with his arms folded over his narrow chest and looked very interested. He was a man who always had to push his glasses back up his nose because his nose was too narrow. "I mean, why round toes?" he followed, his brown eyes growing darker and more intense, as though he believed his question and my answer would solve some important puzzle.

I shrugged. "I remember them," was all I could think of saying. "I remember how uncomfortable they were, but no girls my age had any different kinds of shoes. We were all made to wear them, and we all thought they were uncomfortable and ugly."

"Girls your age? What girls your age? Where was this?"

I didn't answer. A silence fell around everyone for a moment. I looked down at my feet and held my breath.

Whenever something like this happened, my mother would feel it necessary to go into some sort of explanation about me, about who I was, as if that would help people understand why I said these things.

"We got Sage when she was just eight months old, so she has no past from which to draw these ideas," she told them. "Mark and I certainly had no past like the one she describes, nor have we ever made up stories about ourselves and filled her mind with fantasy."

My parents never hid the fact from me or anyone else that I was adopted. My mother told everyone that she had read many articles about how to bring up an adopted child and had spoken to child psychologists who agreed that honesty was the best approach. They said it was too traumatic for a child who was already nine or ten, and especially older, to suddenly learn that he or she was adopted.

"It's all a child's wonderful imaginative powers," my mother concluded. "Nothing more or less."

"She reads a lot, too," my father quickly added. "And she often talks and acts like a character in a book. She's good at pretending. She's always had imaginary friends." He looked at me and nodded. "You can leave her alone for hours and hours, and she won't complain. Maybe she'll be an actress."

"Or a politician," Mr. Black said. "If she's good at pretending."

Everyone laughed.

"What about her name?" Mrs. Black asked, sweetening her smile. "It's so unusual. But so beautiful," she quickly added.

My parents looked at each other as if to see if either one objected to the explanation. Neither ever did when anyone asked about it, but they were always careful about hurting each other's feelings, so they checked first to see who would begin. If they ever had an argument, often about me, they would quickly find a way to smooth it over and seal their apologies to each other with a sharp kiss that sounded like the snap of a rubber band and seemed more like a stamp of approval than the soft brush of something loving and romantic.

"That was the only request her birth mother left with the orphanage, that the name she gave her be kept. We promised to do so. Actually, Felicia and I liked her name right from the get-go," Dad replied.

Sometimes my mother gave the whole answer, but it was usually almost the exact same words. She even said "get-go."

"Do you still have those shoes with the rounded toes?" Mrs. Black asked me. "I'd like to see them."

"No."

"What do you think happened to them?" Mrs. Hummel asked. She was smiling, but I could tell that my casualness about one of my stories intrigued her. It was easy to see that some of my parents' guests weren't just amused. They were fascinated with me. Usually at that point, my parents would find a way to end it and send me off to my room. My mother would hug me too tightly, her arms crushing my ribs, and she'd whisper, "You'll get no breakfast for doing this again and embarrassing us, Sage. Stay in your bed until I come for you."

No matter how many times my parents punished me, I didn't stop talking about my dreams and visions. I was more than happy to be doing it this time, too, at Dad's birthday dinner.

"My shoes got worn out," I said. "They were buried with everything else of mine that got worn out."

"What?" Mrs. Black said, her right hand fluttering up to her mouth like a small bird. "Heavens, why would your things have to be buried?"

The faces of all the guests were framed in half smiles. My parents held theirs that way, too, but their eyes were stained with disappointment and anger. My mother's were full of fiery warning, afraid of what I might say next. Sometimes my mother would tell me afterward that they were seriously thinking of giving me back to the orphanage. She'd say there was no guarantee for me, but there was one for them. I could be turned back in like so much broken merchandise, "stored in a cage in a warehouse for damaged children no one really wanted. They are fed through bars and kept in the dark most of the time, without any television or books or any toys, the way some exotic birds are kept."

"Yes, why did they have to be buried?" Mrs. Hummel asked now. She leaned toward me, her dark mint-green eyes wider, the corners of her mouth tucked back. Her face was full of anticipation.

I didn't look at my mother. "Because they were mine," I said. "If someone else put them on, they would go up in flames."

Usually, there would be gasps when I said something like that, at least from the women. The men might just stare at me and shake their heads. This time, both Mrs. Hummel and Mrs. Black just stared at me, too. Mr. Hummel finally laughed, but it sounded more like he was clearing his throat. Mr. Black was the only one who shook his head and cast a look of sympathy at my father.

"Why don't you go to your room now, Sage?" my father said. "You have that new video game you asked for. We know you want to play with it. You can be excused."

Since we had already had his birthday cake, I thought that was all right.

"Very well," I said, and I slipped off my chair, said good night to everyone, curtsied, and walked out.

I heard the soft laughter. "What a polite little girl!" Mrs. Hummel exclaimed. "I love the way she curtsied like a little princess. How did you get her to do that?"

"We didn't teach her to do that," my mother said, and then she realized she had said it too quickly. "I mean, she surprises us every day."

"Like I said, she picks up a lot from reading," my father added.

"What a delight," Mrs. Black said. "You're very lucky."

"That's what we think," my mother said, but there was something about the way she said it, some underlying note in her voice, that only I could hear. It was getting sharper and sharper every passing day, every passing year.

I carried her words up to my room, twisting and turning them over in my mind like a jeweler inspecting a gem for some imperfection. I was sure there was something there, something I didn't see or understand, and it was all because of who I was. No one was more of a mystery to me than I was to myself.

However, I imagined all adopted children had that problem, because they didn't have their biological parents to measure themselves against by comparing their height, their facial features, and, most important, their personalities. I looked constantly for clues in the way my parents spoke about me and the way they looked at me to see if they knew much more than they were saying, especially when they thought I didn't notice or couldn't hear them. If I asked, they would always remind me that they had never met my mother, much less my father. They were just as much in the dark about who my biological parents were and what they were like. Naturally, I wanted to know why my real mother had given me away. Didn't real mothers love their children with all their hearts the moment they were born?

"What we do know is that she wasn't married and her parents were too old to help raise you," my mother had eventually told me, and left it for me to make the right conclusions. Of course, I knew other girls and boys who lived only with their mothers after a divorce, but children of divorced mothers were different from orphans like me. At least the children of divorced parents could see themselves in their fathers and mothers.

This was constantly on my mind. I spent a great deal of time studying myself in a mirror, but not like someone looking for flaws in her beauty. It was more like I was looking for a sign revealing who was inside me, who I really was. Using my own features, I tried to imagine what my real mother must have looked like.

One day, I drew a picture of her and showed it to my parents. After they looked at it, they looked at each other, their eyes wide and full of surprise. Neither said anything. They didn't tell me it was awful or that it was wrong to have drawn it, but they wouldn't let me pin it on the wall or show it to anyone else. I finally did hear my father whisper, "Remarkable," more to himself than to my mother. My mother took the picture, telling me to forget it, and I imagined that she hid it somewhere or maybe destroyed it, as if she was afraid I might see someone who resembled this woman on the streets of our city. I supposed that was possible. I didn't know where she came from or where she lived.

We lived just outside of Dorey, Massachusetts, a town of about twenty thousand residents, only fifty miles from Cape Cod, a place they had yet to take me to visit. Our house was a Tudor, with half-timbering. The space between the timbers was filled with white stucco, so my parents referred to their home as a black-and-white house. It had decorative woodwork, which my father explained was really false half-timbering, diamond-pane windows, and a steeply pitched roof with arches and bay windows. My room was upstairs, two doors down from my parents' room, and it looked out at the section of woods between our property and a small lake that was only a half mile long and wide. It was on an empty plot of land tied up in some family feud regarding its deed.

For me, it was like having our own private lake and park next door. We had barely more than one acre, so I was eager to step off our property and spend time next door exploring, especially around the lake. I wasn't permitted to go there by myself until I was ten and always with a warning to be careful around the lake, as if something in it, some lake monster, might jump out and pull me under the water. Often I did sense something shadowy moving in the woods nearby. I would pause and search among the trees. Sometimes I would hear the rustling of leaves and branches, even the sound of footsteps, but I never saw anything or anyone.

I did hear the breeze whisper, "Be careful. Always be careful."

My father made sure that I learned to swim when I was five. He took me to his sports club in Dorey on Saturdays, when children of members could have lessons with a certified swimming instructor. My instructor was amazed, because I was swimming well after only a half hour of instruction.

"You sure she never swam before?" he asked my father.

"Never."

"All my students should be like her," the instructor said.

Dad nodded and looked at me as if he had expected no less. He stood back and, without any surprise, watched me swim across the pool, unafraid, unhesitant, and confident. Later, at dinner, he reported how I had done. I watched for my mother's reaction. She seemed more disappointed than proud. Both of them did, in fact. I didn't understand it. It was as if I was confirming some evil suspicion they had of me.

But swimming seemed natural, something I remembered having done.

"I swam in the ocean, which is more difficult than a pool," I blurted.

They shook their heads, but I could sense the seeds of concern were planted again, this time even deeper.

"We never took you to swim in the ocean, Sage," my mother snapped back at me with her teeth clenched. "Don't dare tell anyone that. Are you listening?"

As usual back then when I was so young, I just shrugged. I never argued with anyone about what I knew and what I saw. It was as if I understood that they wouldn't understand. However, I think my self-confidence when I spoke was eventually even more of a concern for my parents than the things I said. They could see I wasn't ever going to admit that I was making something up.

"I'm afraid she really believes what she says," I heard my mother tell my father once when I was nearly eleven. "You can't blame it on a wild imagination anymore or talk her out of it or stop her from saying these things."

"Maybe she'll grow out of it," he replied. "She's still quite young. The older she gets, the further away she might get from these visions and imaginings. Some of it is simply what all kids do. It's still too soon to tell."

"No sense in fooling yourself. I'm afraid she won't stop, Mark. I'll admit, it's more difficult to predict what will happen with her, what the end result of this will be. She's not like the others."

"That's why we have to be patient. Let's wait and see," my father told her. "We promised."

"We promised to try."

"And we will," he said firmly. "We have to, for her sake."

I wanted to ask what he meant by "the others" and "for her sake," but I was afraid to start them talking about me again, warning me, practically begging me to shut myself up tightly and bury my thoughts and dreams so deeply that they would be smothered and die. I thought I might die, too. If I kept everything locked up, I wouldn't be able to breathe because of the weight of it all on my chest.

Finally, when I was twelve and still telling them and other people about things I remembered, things they knew I hadn't done while I was with them, which was basically forever, I heard them discussing me very intently one night in the kitchen after dinner. Both of them raised their voices at times. They decided that maybe it would help for me to speak with a child psychologist. After all, besides others my age in school, I was also telling my teachers things that my parents couldn't validate when they were asked about them.

"We can't ignore her, ignore the things she is telling people, anymore, Mark. Everyone will wonder why we're not trying to do something about it, especially her teachers. I hate doing this. It's basically admitting failure, but it's getting out of hand," my mother said. "This is another one that might very well be beyond us."

What did she mean by "another one" and "beyond us"? I wondered. That was the same as saying "the others," but, just like before, I was afraid to ask.

"I agree," Dad said. I heard him sigh deeply. "But

who knows? Professional help might slow it down and give us a real chance to evaluate her properly."

"I have no illusions about this, Mark. It won't stop her if it's in her to be what she is. We can only hope it's the right sort. I hate to think of what it means if she's not."

Now I was full of new questions. "Be what she is"? "The right sort"? The right sort of what? What would I be? Something she hated to even think about? Perhaps I did have serious mental issues. No one was more eager to get the answers than I was, and if seeing a therapist would lead me to them, then I was all for it.

Shortly afterward, I met with the child psychologist, Irma Loman, a forty-two-year-old woman with graying dark brown hair and hazel eyes with tiny black spots in them. She didn't sit behind a desk or have me lie on a couch or anything. She said we were going to be just like two friends talking.

"You can even call me Irma," she said. "I'm not worried about protocol or formalities. Honesty, honesty. That's the only important thing."

She settled on her chair across from me like a hen sitting over newly laid eggs. Her thighs seemed to inflate beneath her knee-length dark gray skirt. She wore a white blouse with a frilly collar and frilly cuffs. Her straight hair was trimmed just below her cheekbones, which made her eyes and lips look bigger. She was only five foot four, with thick ankles and shiny rounded knees that looked like large Mason jar caps for homemade jelly, something I had never seen in our house but could easily envision.

"People who have spots in their eyes were touched

by the devil's tears when they were born," I told her before she could ask me a single question.

She smiled, her cheeks bubbling and her small nose sinking. "What? Where did you learn such a thing?"

"A fortune-teller told me. She was blind and had a dog who led her around. He had silver fur and silvery gray eyes that glowed in the dark."

"Blind?"

"She wasn't always blind. She had been cursed," I explained.

"Why was she cursed?"

"Not everyone likes to hear about his or her future, especially when it's bad. Gypsies don't make the future; they just see it faster than anyone else, and in this case, she tampered with the wrong person."

"Tampered with the wrong person? What do you mean?"

"She annoyed someone with more power, someone who could put a curse on her."

"If she could see the future, why didn't she know that would happen to her?"

"Fortune-tellers can't tell their own fortunes, only the fortunes of others," I said, making it sound like something very obvious, something everyone should know.

She stared for a moment and then smiled again, this time with a slight nod, as if I had just confirmed something she had thought about me from the first moment she set eyes on me. "That doesn't make sense from the start, Sage. Think about what you're saying. How could she see if she was blind?"

"She had eyes behind her eyes," I said.

Irma tightened her pale thick lips and scrunched her nose even more, like someone who had just smelled something horrible. She glanced at her notebook, sighed deeply, and began to ask me questions about my dreams. I tried to answer everything as truthfully as possible, because she had emphasized honesty.

"What's wrong with me?" I blurted before my session was over. "I know my parents are growing more and more upset about it."

"Now, stop your worrying," she ordered. She told me that some people don't stop dreaming just because they wake up, and maybe I was one of those people. "It's not bad," she said quickly. "But maybe we should work on helping you leave your dreams behind when you wake up in the morning."

She asked me more questions about my daily life, what I liked, what I thought of this or that, even colors and shapes. I saw her fill pages and pages of her notebook.

In the end, after two more sessions, she told my parents that I had a delusional disorder, a mixed type, but she felt I might outgrow it. She thought regular therapy sessions with her over time would quicken my recovery.

My mother wasn't as enthusiastic about it as my father was, but I told them I didn't mind seeing Irma now and then.

"I might even be able to help her more than she can help me," I said.

My mother gasped and brought her right hand to

the base of her throat, something she always did when she was a little shocked or surprised. "Why do you say that?" she asked. She looked at my father, and they both waited for my response.

"She has tiny black dots in her eyes," I explained. "She's going to do something very bad someday if no one helps her."

"How would she know something like that?" my father asked my mother. "You can see."

She shook her head. "No. Obviously, she's not going to do Sage any good," she concluded. "This is going nowhere, and it might even take her in the wrong direction altogether."

Eventually, things settled down enough for them to stop sending me to Irma anyway, but I felt bad for her. A year later, she drank too much at a party and, driving home, hit a woman and a man crossing the street at night. The woman died, and Irma was charged with vehicular manslaughter. My father was the one who read about it and remembered what I had predicted.

"Did you ever tell anyone about Irma Loman?" my father asked me. "About what you thought would happen to her?"

"No. I didn't tell anyone anything about her at all, not even that I had seen her."

"Thank heavens for that," my mother said. "Finally, at least this once, anyway, you listened to us." She looked relieved.

But by then, it was too late for lots of reasons.

1

Our house had a wide but short entryway with a narrow closet for hanging up coats and jackets. The floor was a grayish white slate, and there was a large hanging lamp of clear hammered glass in a detailed black finish. The two curved metal hooklike decorations at the base of it always seemed like two cat eyes to me, especially when the lamp was on and the yellowish glow bounced off the light brown front door. They looked like frightened eyes, hinting of danger and not suggesting any of the warmth and security I should find in the house that was my home, something everyone should find in his or her home.

Periodically, my mother would hang a small garland of garlic just to the right of our front door. She would dress it up with some artificial flowers. I never thought it was that pretty. In fact, I hated looking at it and wondered why it was so important to her to do it. When I asked, however, she grew very angry.

"Don't you ever touch it, and don't ask me about

it again," she said. Then she paused like someone who had just thought of something important, narrowed her eyes, and asked, "Why? Does it bother you? Make you feel sick?"

"No," I said, and shrugged. "I just wondered. There are nicer things to hang outside a house."

Her shoulders and neck seemed to inflate with rage. "When you have your own house, you'll hang what you want. That's what I want," she said, and walked away.

The garland of garlic wasn't the only odd thing that drew my curiosity. I remembered, one afternoon when I was seven, seeing my father go out to the front stoop, loosen one of the steps, and slip a knife under it. He saw me watching him and said, "Don't ever tell anyone about this, Sage. Understand?"

"Yes, Daddy," I said.

He nailed the step down, gave me another look of warning, and went into the house.

I never forgot it, but I didn't mention it again, either. There were too many things like that around our house and too many other strange things my parents did to concentrate on just one. The doorbell button outside, for example, was housed in a circle that had a black side and a white side, with the button in the white side. I think few people who came to the house and pressed it understood they were pressing on yang, for the circle was the symbolic yin-yang, yin being the black side and yang the white.

My mother explained it to me when I came home from school one day and remarked that our front doorbell button looked like a yin-yang picture we had been studying in art class.

"That's exactly what it is," she told me. "Yin and yang are the two energies believed to exist in everything in nature and in human beings."

I nodded, eager to show off my new knowledge. I was just thirteen at the time, a year away from entering high school, and despite everything, I wanted my parents to approve of me. "Yin is the female energy," I said, "cold, passive, and wet, and it's associated with the night, the winter, and the moon. Yang is male, hot, active, and fiery, associated with daytime, the summer, and the sun."

"Exactly," my mother said. "And you understand one cannot exist without the other. Light can't exist without darkness. They are always moving energies, and neither is good or bad in and of itself."

I wanted to ask why she had never explained the doorbell button before, but there was really nothing unusual about her withholding information. It seemed she always waited for me to bring home something that would permit her to tell me more, and until I did, it was better if I lived in the darkness of ignorance. It was almost as if knowledge was dangerous for me, especially if it had anything to do with good and evil.

I was even more afraid to ask questions about such things when I grew older. My questions usually caused my mother to look at me more intensely, just as she had done when I had asked about the garland of garlic. Her eyes would search my face, looking for some underlying evil reason for why I would dare to ask, no matter how innocent the questions were. She would often follow one of my questions with "Why do you want to know that? Why did you ask? What gave you the idea to ask?" Or she might ask, "Did you dream about this?" This was especially true for any questions about her or my father, their families, or their pasts. They never seemed to want to talk much about those things, so I stopped asking years ago. But wasn't it normal to wonder about your own family?

Although I rarely heard them talk about their families even when they were with dinner guests, I couldn't help wondering why we didn't have pictures of their parents or grandparents on our shelves and walls like other people had. Whenever my parents and I went to their friends' homes, that was the first thing I looked for and asked questions about. In the house of one of my classmates, her family had two rows of pictures of her grandfathers going back generations, with one picture taken around the time of the Civil War.

How different we were. Wouldn't you think so if, from the day you could talk, comments and questions about almost anything brought intense scrutiny, if not some sharp reply, a warning to you not to think about something or ask about something? Surely, like me, you would tend to go elsewhere for answers, even about the most common things. Maybe that was why I became such an avid reader. There were times when I felt the air go out of the room after I had asked about something, times when I would find myself tiptoeing around my parents and retreating to the silence in my own room to read and to learn.

I used to wonder if maybe I was too inquisitive after all, whether there really was something wrong with me for thinking so much and wondering so much. However, it was pretty obvious that my classmates and friends knew a great deal more about their families than I knew about mine. Of course, almost all of that mystery could be attributed to my being an adopted child and that I knew nothing about my biological parents, but the truth was that I didn't know all that much more about my adoptive parents, either.

I could summarize what I knew about them on a single page. Both of them had lost their parents years ago, but I wasn't sure exactly when. To explain why their parents were gone even though they were still so young, they told me their parents had married late in their lives. They made it sound as if their mothers had them at the very last possible minute.

They both said they had lived in Massachusetts all their lives. My father was from Boston, my mother from Salem. My mother was an only child, so there were no aunts or uncles on her side, but my father had a younger brother, Wade, who fascinated me. He was a professional magician who went under the stage name the Amazing Healy. He lived in New York City, but he traveled a great deal because of his performances, not only in America but also in Europe and even Asia, and he always managed to visit us when he was anywhere nearby.

Uncle Wade had a reason for not answering my questions about himself, a reason I could accept and understand.

"A good magician never reveals the secrets of his tricks, Sage, nor should he tell too much about himself. He must guard the mystery as he would guard his life. One can't be separated from the other when you're a magician. There's an aura about you that enables you to say, 'Now you see it; now you don't.' And people are hooked, amazed, and fascinated. That's how I earn a living. You wouldn't want to hurt my doing that, right?"

His eyes twinkled when he said it. Of course, I wanted to ask why I had to be like everyone else. Wasn't I a little special? I could keep secrets so locked up that they'd gather dust in my head. We didn't have a blood relationship, but I was his niece. I should be trusted.

When I muttered something about this to my parents, my mother said, "Even we don't know all that much about Wade. He wants it that way, and you should respect his wishes. Don't go poking that nose full of curiosity into everything and everyone you meet. Some people want their privacy respected." Her words were sharp and hard.

I didn't argue with her. I never would. I certainly didn't want to do anything to upset Uncle Wade. I just wanted him to like me, to love me at least like any uncle loved a niece. I thought he could. He didn't seem as uptight about everything I said and did. There was always an amused twinkle in his eyes when he was with me. Shorter than my father and just a little stouter, he had light brown hair and vividly electric blue eyes. He never visited us without amazing me with the way he could make things disappear, move them from one place to another just by staring at them, or change colors and shapes and make things float by moving his hands a certain way.

Supposedly, he was also a great hypnotist, but he could never hypnotize me. I loved the soft sound of his voice, and I did see twirling snowballs and multicolored drops fall out of a rainbow, but I never lost awareness. He laughed at his failure, claiming I had too strong a mind, but I did notice that when he looked at my parents afterward, they would all seem to nod and agree about something—something else they would never tell me, of course. That list of secrets seemed to grow as I did. If it continued, I was sure I'd be covered in mysteries as thick as tar.

So because of this and so many other things, I sensed that we weren't alone in the house, that living alongside us were gobs of secrets caught like flies in a spider's web, struggling to break free to reveal themselves. I dreamed of sleepwalking through them, shattering them, and releasing them all. The secrets fluttered about me, whispering the answers to one mystery after another in my ears until I knew everything I should know about myself and my parents.

I suppose that was why I was so excited, one afternoon when I was fourteen, to discover the dark gray filing cabinet in my father's office slightly opened, a cabinet that I had never seen unlocked. Like everything else that was locked, it was surely full of answers. But I was forbidden ever to enter his office without him present and especially warned not to touch anything, move any papers, or look in any drawers. When I was little, my mother had convinced me that if I did try to open a forbidden drawer anywhere in the house, the handle would burn my fingers.

Sometimes I would tempt myself. When neither of them was looking, I would bring my fingers inches from a forbidden drawer handle. Almost always, I felt some heat and pulled my fingers back quickly. What would I do if I did burn my fingers and my mother saw it? She would know I had disobeyed a very strict order. It wouldn't be pleasant. She could lose her temper over lesser things and go into a small rant if I decided to wear something other than what she had put out for me, pummeling me with questions. Why had I chosen that? Why did I want to wear that color today? What made me decide? Did I look into a mirror and see something unusual? Before I could answer, she would rattle off, "What? What?" Even if I swore there was nothing, she would look at me suspiciously. It got so I was nervous about turning left when I thought she might want me to turn right.

Now here I was with a chance to disobey again, but in a much bigger way. And I was fourteen, so I couldn't fall back on the excuse that I was too young to know better, not that that excuse ever worked for me. It was as if my parents expected me to be ages older mentally than I was chronologically. When they said, "You should know better," they meant it, even when I was only five or six.

I looked back to the front door with trepidation

but also with excitement. If someone came through the entryway and didn't walk into our living room on the right, he or she would reach my father's office on the left before turning the corner to get to the dining room and the kitchen. The bottom of the stairway was just between the living room and my father's office. The office door was rarely open when he was away. This particular Saturday afternoon, it was, and no one but me was home.

I had glanced in as I was passing, and that's when I had seen the opened filing cabinet. For a long moment, I just stood there looking with fascination and curiosity at it. I didn't think this overwhelming attraction to an opened but forbidden file drawer was that unusual. My mother had told me people were born this way. She told me that all we had to do was read about Eve in the Garden of Eden to see it was true. *Don't do this* and *don't do that* only made you want to do those things more. She said most religious leaders believed that was our fatal flaw and that God put flaws in us so we would have something to overcome, some way to prove to Him that we were good and deserved a place in heaven.

"Which makes no sense to me," my father quipped. This conversation occurred during one of those evenings when the three of us were reading in the living room together without the television on. "If God is God, why can't he know in advance who will be bad and who will be good?"

"Maybe that's his flaw," my mother replied.

My father laughed. "Blasphemy," he declared. He

pointed at her and playfully twirled his right fore-finger in small circles the way Uncle Wade did when he was going to make something move magically.

"Stop that," she demanded. I saw she wasn't kidding. "I mean it, Mark."

His smile fell off his face, and he pulled his hand back quickly. Why was that so terrible? He wasn't aiming a gun at her. I think I moaned, and the two of them looked at me as if they both just realized I was there. They didn't look embarrassed so much as suddenly frightened. I quickly returned my eyes to the book I was reading.

The most intriguing thing in my life at this time was listening to them when they spoke as if I weren't in the room. Sometimes it seemed they actually did forget I was there or, worse, wanted to ignore me. Maybe that gave them some relief. They were both so nervous and intense about every move I made and every word I said. I knew from listening to my classmates when they talked about their parents that mine were on pins and needles more than most parents. But why? What had I ever done to cause them to treat me this way? Was it simply because I was adopted? Did that really make everything so different from the way it was for my friends? Was this true for most adopted children?

I had read stories about parents who regretted adopting a child after a while or couples who would never consider it because they didn't know enough about the child's family background. Maybe the child had inherited some evil tendencies or something. In a way, it made sense. The adoptive parents might not know enough about a child's genetics. It was natural for them to be nervous about that, but if all of them were as intense about it as mine were, no one would ever be adopted. Why did my parents decide to adopt me anyway? I wondered more and more.

Why, why, why echoed in the house. It dangled off me no matter where I was, like some loose thread, but something much stronger than just curiosity was drawing me to the open cabinet that day. It was almost as if the winds that brought the whispering voices were at my back, urging me forward. My heart began to thump as I stepped deeper into my father's office. All of the figurines he had on shelves—the owl, the eagle, and the bat in particular—seemed to turn toward me, their eyes tracking my every move. I paused. The silence in the house seemed to pound in my ears. It was as if everything in it was holding its breath. Would I dare?

I glanced at myself in the antique mirror on the wall to my left. An image flashed across my eyes. It was quick, but I couldn't help gasping. I saw a woman, dressed in clothes from colonial America, suddenly burst into flames. Around her, men and women were all smiling. The image disappeared as quickly as it had come, but I almost turned and ran out of the office. I caught my breath, and the chill that had washed over my chest dissipated. Whenever an image like that occurred, I was frightened or shaken for a moment but always recuperated quickly.

There was no getting away from how wrong it felt

to be spying on my father. However, I told myself that this wasn't simply disobedience; it was defiance strengthened with the belief that I had a right to know everything. Why should there be such a cloak of mystery around things that others my age clearly had spread out before them, especially children who were part of the family? Cabinets weren't supposed to be locked to keep them out. They were supposed to be locked to keep out strangers and thieves.

Determined now, I knelt beside the open cabinet and began to sift through the files in the bottom drawer, the one that had been pulled open and left that way. In front of the files was a small wooden box. I took it out slowly and set it on the floor, where I turned it around and around, because at first, I couldn't see how it could be opened. Then I realized there were two small indentions for fingertips, one on each side. I pressed into them, and the box snapped open.

What strange contents, I thought. There were what looked like human bones, fingers and the nose portion of a small skull, maybe a child's skull. Mixed in with them were tiny leaves of shrubs and a piece of frankincense. Why was that in there? What did it mean? I closed the lid softly and put the box back. I thought I could feel two strong hands gripping my shoulders, trying to pull me away, but I resisted and looked at the first file that seized my attention.

The file had a college logo at the top of the first page. It was a bachelor of science diploma from a liberal arts college in Boston. This was no special

discovery, I first thought. I knew my father had gone
to college, but I believed he had gone to a business
school. I shrugged and started to put the page back
into the file when I noticed the date. It made no sense.

This diploma had been issued in 1908. How could
my father have been in his early twenties in 1908? Was
this his grandfather's diploma? Did his grandfather
have the same name, Mark Healy? That was obviously
the only answer, but why keep something like this
under lock and key? Why wasn't it framed and on his
office wall? Wasn't he proud of his grandfather?

I took out another document in the same file. It
also had a university logo at the top of what was another diploma, a juris doctor degree from Cornell Law
School in New York State. This, too, had the name
Mark Healy, but the date was 1925. That couldn't be
my father, either, and the date was wrong for it to be
his grandfather. Maybe it was his father's, I thought.

But my father and my uncle had told me their
father's name was Evan Charles Healy. This was all
very confusing. I dug deeper and found pictures, old
sepia photographs that were very faded, but the first
one was clear enough to reveal a young man who resembled my father enough to be his twin. I saw classic
automobiles in the background, too, one that had a
stick for a steering wheel.

The second picture was clearer and was so surprising that it sent me moving backward to sit on the floor.
It was the same man, and a woman with a close resem-
blance to my mother was standing beside him. Behind
them was what looked like an old farmhouse, and

another very old automobile was on their right. The woman wore something around her neck. It looked familiar.

I went to my father's desk and found his magnifying glass. It helped me see that the necklace had a pendant of what looked like seven blossoms. I thought for a moment and remembered that I had seen my mother wearing this pendant, but not for some time. Who was the woman? Was it my mother's mother? Had she given the pendant to my mother? How could all these relatives look so much alike? Why were all these pictures locked away?

I put the picture back. There were many photos with the same two people, but as I sifted through them, the pictures got better; they were clearer, and the backgrounds were more modern, suggesting that they were taken no more than ten or fifteen years ago. The strangest thing about them was that neither the man nor the woman looked a day older in any of the pictures.

I noticed some additional pictures, one of a young boy and another of a young girl. Behind these was a picture of me when I was much younger. Who were the other two? Neither looked anything like me. The boy had much darker hair and almost coal-black eyes. The girl had light brown hair and blue eyes. Both of them looked older than what I imagined their ages really were. They had adult faces on young bodies, I thought, faces that looked troubled, pained. Why were we all in this one folder with the other pictures?

The more I discovered, the deeper I fell into confusion. I almost didn't look at anything else, but the top of one paper looked familiar, so I dug into that file and found the picture I had drawn years ago of how I imagined my birth mother looked. I sat there staring at it, remembering the day I had shown it to my parents. So they hadn't torn it up or thrown it out after all, I thought. I should be happy about that. Maybe they were proud of how well I drew at so early an age, but why keep it hidden away?

I couldn't take it up to my room and keep it, because that would reveal that I had been in the forbidden cabinet. I started to put it back but stopped. There was something else in the file with my drawing. It was a photograph of a woman who looked very much like the woman I had drawn, but she looked sad, as if she was moments away from crying. There was nothing written on the backs of any of the pictures, nothing to help me identify whoever it was.

I pulled out an envelope and opened it. It contained my birth certificate. My name on the certificate was Sage Healy. My father and mother were listed as Mark and Felicia Healy. Attached to it were the adoption finalization papers. This wasn't a surprise. When I had done some research on adopted children, I learned that a new birth certificate would be issued with the adoptive parents' names on it. Nobody looking at a birth certificate would know if a child had been adopted.

The birthdate was correct: September 15, 1999. I was born in a clinic in Dorey, so I always had lived here. My parents told people that they didn't adopt me until I was eight months old, so maybe the original birth certificate with my birth mother's name on it was still somewhere. Would there ever be a possibility of my finding it and discovering her?

I paused when I saw something to the side of the files. It was a piece of dark brown leather. There was an emblem on it that looked like a family crest with three trees. Under it was the word *Belladonna*.

Suddenly, just like when a heavy cloud moves over the sun, the room darkened. I didn't hear thunder, but there was a rumbling in the floor. Maybe I imagined it, but I quickly put the strip of leather back and got up. I studied the cabinet drawer to see if it looked in any way different from what it looked like before I had delved into the files. I thought it was fine and hurried out of the office and into the living room. My mind was spinning with all sorts of questions and thoughts, and I felt a little dizzy. I sat quickly on the settee and closed my eyes.

This could be what my mother meant when she told me that a little knowledge was a dangerous thing. Too many questions and too many answers could clog your brain, but what was worse, they could upset you and make you want to know more than you could or should. What did I gain from peeking into the forbidden cabinet? Only more questions, more secrets to be caught in spiderwebs.

I knew that it was going to be very hard to keep what I had seen and done a secret. Both my parents were very good at looking at me and almost reading my thoughts. Was it because I was so revealing, no matter how hard I tried not to be, or was it because they were perceptive enough to read anyone's dark thoughts and not just mine?

Lying to them seemed impossible. I hated the thought of having to lie to anyone. Besides, my parents were already sensitive to anything wrong or even slightly defiant that I might do or say. A lie would simply reinforce all that. Maybe it was better to simply confess what I had done. Now I wished that filing cabinet had not been left unlocked. I could almost hear my mother, her face twisted with rage, shouting, "That drawer being opened is no excuse for what you did. Why did you go in there? Don't you know that curiosity killed the cat?"

If only this had never happened. If only my father had not left that cabinet drawer open. I sat there with my eyes still closed and wished and wished that when I had walked by the office and looked in, the filing cabinet had been closed and locked. I wouldn't have entered the office. I wouldn't be feeling so guilty and afraid right now. One thing I always found easy to do was create a vivid picture in my mind of anything I wanted to see, and that's what I did now with all my might.

Suddenly, I heard the slam of a filing-cabinet drawer. My eyes popped open. I listened carefully. Had my parents come home and one of them discovered that the drawer had been left open? I didn't hear their voices or their footsteps in the hallway, so I rose slowly and peered out toward my father's office. There was no one, no other sounds.

Gingerly, I walked back to the office. The door was still open. I peeked in carefully and saw there was no one there, but what shocked me was that the cabinet drawer I had searched was closed. How could that be? I had left it the way it had been, hadn't I? I was sure of that. I listened again and then approached it and tried to open it, but it was locked, just the way it usually was. For a moment, I just stood there amazed. Could I have imagined I had left it open but really have closed it? After all, my dreams were usually so vivid that it was impossible sometimes to distinguish them from what was real. I was the first to admit that. This could be the most frightening instance of all, because it could mean that now I could not be sure of what I had or hadn't done.

I backed away and started to flee the office but then stopped in the doorway and looked back at the filing cabinet. No, there was no doubt. I was sure I hadn't imagined leaving it open. After all, that was how I had found it. How could this be? Obviously, I couldn't tell my parents anything about this. I couldn't mention any of the things I had seen in the drawer.

My heart was pounding with both fear and excitement. There was another possibility. When I pictured the drawer closed, had it closed? Had I really done that? Had I willed that cabinet closed? That was something Uncle Wade could do in his magic act. Even if he had some sort of magical power, I couldn't have inherited it. I wasn't blood-related to him. I shook my head. This was all too confusing. There had to be a sensible explanation. Either I had closed it without realizing it or the drawer had just rolled closed and automatically locked. Maybe there was a very small earthquake, or a large truck had rumbled by and shaken the ground enough.

I hurried up to my room and sat at my vanity table, staring at myself in the mirror. *Sage*, I told myself, *you must erase the memory of what you did and saw today, all of it. Push it so far back in your mind that it will be thinner than a distant childhood memory, and no one, especially your parents, will be able to read your face and see your sense of guilt.* I concentrated on my eyes and willed it to be true.

I didn't break out of the concentration until I heard footsteps on the stairway and my mother called to me. When I looked at my watch, I realized I had been sitting at the vanity table for nearly half an hour. I must have hypnotized myself or something, I thought. The next time he came, I'd have to ask Uncle Wade if that was even possible. Although he would think it was a strange question to ask, he might still answer it. Of course, I wouldn't dare ask my mother or father. It would lead to another severe cross-examination.

"Yes?" I called back.

She stepped into my doorway. "What were you doing while we were shopping?" she asked. As was too often the case, her voice was full of accusations.

"Just my homework," I said. "I had a lot to do this time. All our teachers gave us more than usual for the weekend. Everyone in my class is complaining."

She continued to stare at me so intensely that I felt uncomfortable.

"What?"

"Did you go into your father's office and snoop?"

My father must have remembered that he hadn't closed and locked the filing cabinet, and they had found it closed and locked.

"No," I said. "I've been up here practically the whole time you were away. Why?"

She stepped in and narrowed her eyelids. Whenever she looked at me this hard, I felt more than naked; I felt as if she could explore my very bones and nerves, maybe even examine my brain. "Children shouldn't spy on their parents and snoop in their things," she said. "And they should never lie to their parents."

I waited as she gave my face more of her usual close study. Apparently, nothing popped out at her.

"You had better be telling me the truth. Eventually, I'll know if you're not. You know that."

"Yes, I do, Mother," I said.

"And if that happens, you'll be severely punished. You understand?"

"I do, Mother."

She relaxed a little. I breathed in relief. For the first time ever, she really wasn't sure whether I was telling the truth. Whatever I had done in my self-hypnosis had worked. She put a bag on my bed and took out a new sweater.

"I thought this would look nice on you," she said. "Violet is your color. You have violet eyes," she added.

"Thank you." I was really surprised. It was not that often that she bought something for me spontaneously.

"Try it on," she said.

I rose, took off the blouse I was wearing, and put on the violet sweater. I looked at myself in the mirror.

She came up behind me and put her hands on my shoulders as she looked at me in the mirror. For a long moment, she was silent. I could feel the heat in her fingers penetrate my neck and shoulders.

"How does that make you feel?" she asked in a voice that was almost a whisper, a voice I didn't recognize.

"It's very nice. Thank you."

"How do you feel when you see yourself in this color, Sage?"

"What do you mean?"

"Do you feel any different wearing violet?"

I studied myself again. Still looking in the mirror, I gazed at her standing behind me, waiting for some significant reaction. She looked anxious. What was she expecting me to say? "It fits well," I offered.

I couldn't tell whether she was relieved or disappointed. "Yes, I'm glad it's the right size. I want you to wear it for the rest of the day, and I want you to tell me if you have any new feelings about yourself," she said.

"Okay, but how should I feel?"

"You'll tell me," she said.

"I think it's pretty," I offered. "It looks nice on me."

As if I had said something obvious and simple, she smirked with disappointment. "You would look good in any color, Sage. You are a very attractive young girl. But different colors have different effects on us, and in a way, how we react to them tells us something about ourselves."

So that was what she was still doing, I thought, trying to discover who I really was again. I looked at myself. Was there something about this color that would be more revealing? Would I discover that, too?

She stared for a moment more and then left my room. I continued to study myself in the mirror. Violet was my color, she had said. Choosing colors revealed something about us. Did she mean something more than just complementing my complexion and my eyes?

I turned on my computer and searched the meanings of colors. Violet was associated with the crown chakra, I read, which linked the individual and the universal. It symbolized magic and mystery and also royalty. The advice was to put some violet in your life when you wanted to use your imagination to its fullest and remove obstacles.

Surely, then, this gift from my mother was another test of some sort. But really, how did the color make me feel? Did I feel more powerful, with an imagination that knew no boundaries? At first, maybe because I was trying so hard to feel something, anything, I felt nothing. And then, suddenly, I did feel wiser, older, and even stronger. Was this something else I was imagining? As I studied myself, I thought I saw myself mature physically. My breasts looked slightly larger and shapelier, my face seemed to lose all its youthful chubbiness, and my eyes were filled with wisdom beyond my age. It was as if the new sweater had the power to make me fully aware of my developing figure, helping me envision where it would take me. I had been aware of the changes in my body, of course, but I suddenly felt even more mature. My face flushed a little. Should I, could I, dare think of myself as beautiful? I imagined the admiration of boys and the envy of other girls as I walked through the school halls wearing this sweater.

It was as if I had leaped years ahead and a curtain had been opened. *I can't tell my mother this*, I thought. *Can I?*

But something told me this was just what she wanted to know.

When she asked me again that day, I shrugged and said, "I think I look nice in it, and it's comfortable. Thank you, Mother."

"Nothing else?"

"No," I told her. "What else should I feel?"

She looked at my father. He smiled, but she looked at me suspiciously. Did she realize I wasn't telling the truth? Was there a reason she wasn't revealing that, or had I grown stronger, better at hiding something from her? Upstairs, I had gotten away with lying about the cabinet drawer, and I didn't feel as guilty about it as I'd thought I might. After all, there was so much they were hiding from me. That wasn't fair, was it? Why were they afraid to tell the truth about me? Why did they hide the picture I had drawn of my birth mother? When would I know the reason for all this mystery about myself?

And when I did finally find out, would it frighten me as much as it seemed to frighten them?

2

I was always suspicious about my birthdays, even before I had seen my birth certificate and wondered if there was another, an original one. Despite what rights adopted children supposedly had when they reached a certain age, I suspected that in order to keep me from discovering my birth mother, my actual birthdate was different from the one my parents celebrated with me. It could easily have been my birth mother's decision that her identity never be made known to me. Maybe I was younger or older than my parents told me I was, or they really didn't know themselves. There was only one person who was certain about my age, and that was my birth mother.

When I once asked to see my birth certificate, my parents told me they couldn't find it. They thought it was just misplaced. They promised that if they didn't find it, they would help me get a new one. I had never questioned that, but now I knew that my birth certificate had been in my father's filing cabinet all this time.

They had to know that. Why all these lies and secrets? It made every corner of the house seem darker and every whisper even more forbidden.

Unlike other children, I didn't look forward to my birthdays. Whenever I had one, my parents studied me even more intently, analyzing with more intensity every word I said and everything I did. What were they watching for as I grew older? Every birthday since I was ten made me aware that they were looking for some sign, something to confirm a suspicion or a fear. Age was slowly uncovering what was inside me and who I really was. I felt like some bird emerging out of a shell.

Because of the way they acted, I would wake up the morning of my birthday and immediately look in the mirror to see if my face had changed in any way. Were my eyes a different color, a different shape? Did my hair, my ears, my mouth, any part of me, look so unlike the Sage Healy who had gone to sleep the night before? I even talked out loud to myself to see if the sound of my voice was different. Then, when I rose, I checked my body, not for the small, subtle differences every young girl might find as time passed but for changes so dramatic that I might have trouble fitting into the clothes I owned, as if I had suddenly returned to the body I was supposed to have.

There was one terrifying thought that gave me a nightmare even my soothing voices couldn't stop, and that was my looking into a mirror one day and seeing an entirely different person. In the nightmare, as time passed, I would not only look different, but I would act differently, and soon I would forget who I had been. My adoptive parents wouldn't know who I was, either, and I'd be out on my own, a stranger even to myself, wandering about, looking for some nest to crawl into like an orphaned bird whose mother had cast her out.

How I wished I had a close friend who was also adopted so I could compare his or her life to my own. Was my parents' behavior normal for adoptive parents, especially if they had never met their child's biological parents, which was what my parents claimed? If that was true, I guess it was only natural for them to wonder almost daily about what their adopted child was turning into, looking like, sounding like, and behaving like.

I tried to convince myself that I shouldn't criticize them for their anxiety about me. Yes, they were much stricter about what I could do than the parents of almost every other girl my age whom I knew. But maybe I shouldn't dislike them for that, I told myself. Maybe I should be more understanding. After all, they had been willing to take me in and make a home and a future for me. They were willing to take risks, to invest in someone unknown. Also, I had to consider that I was, after all, an only child. I did see that parents of only children were more controlling, more nervous and concerned about everything the child did.

All of my parents' friends and the students I knew at school who had met my parents seemed to understand. However, my school friends let me know they wouldn't like it if their parents treated them that way.

They would say things like, "Your parents are just obsessed with worrying about you. They should have had more children. My parents even forgot to ask me how I did on my recent report card. Tell them to get real!"

There was no question I was always on a tighter leash than the other girls in my class. Almost all of them had slept over at other girls' homes. It was no major thing to meet somewhere and go to a movie or just hang out at the shopping mall. Whenever one of them was there to do actual clothes shopping, a group would be accompanying her.

But not me.

I never went shopping without my mother, who made all the decisions about styles and colors for me, and even though I was invited a few times to join some of my classmates at the mall on weekends, my mother and father didn't approve of it.

"You're too young yet to be in places like that without adult supervision," my mother said, right through my fourteenth year.

Maybe my parents would grow out of their intense concern and worry about me as I grew older and became more of an adult, I hoped. When I crossed over that line into what everyone would consider adulthood, having to take more responsibility for myself, they would ease off, relax, and we'd be able to enjoy ourselves and each other more. Was that just a wish, a dream?

Meanwhile, there was a limit to how many times I would be invited and not accept. Before the end of my ninth-grade year, the girls stopped inviting me not only to join them at the mall and for movies but also to their parties. To be sure, not all of them were very upset about it. Some of the girls in my class never liked me or simply didn't want me around, especially when they were trying to attract the attention of a boy. One of the girls, Patricia Lucas, told me they were jealous of me.

"Why?" I asked.

"You already have a body," she said. "You're too much competition."

"Excuse me? We all have a body."

"Not like yours. You have a mature figure, and you have beautiful hair and eyes, not to mention an unreal perfect complexion. I never saw you have a pimple. Don't tell me you haven't noticed how the older boys drool over you."

I didn't say it, but of course I had noticed. Besides the fact that many of them approached me in school, either in the hallways or in the cafeteria, I could actually feel their eyes on me, and I could hear them whispering behind my back. Some of the things they said made me blush, and later, when one of those older boys, Shelly Roman, approached me, I drove him off the way you might swat a fly. It was easy to do. Whenever he said anything, I asked him why he had said it, which began to annoy him, and then I told him I knew something about what had really happened between him and a girl named Sidney Urban. I said I could never trust him because of that.

"What did I do?" he demanded.

"You lied to her when you told her the drink you gave her at a party recently had nothing alcoholic in it. You didn't know she had a serious alcohol intolerance and it would affect her."

"She had something else wrong with her, some other allergy," he whined in self-defense.

"No. You didn't believe her. You thought she was just afraid of drinking. You hoped she would get drunk so you could take advantage of her."

"Did Sidney tell you that?"

"No, she doesn't know me," I said.

"So who told you that?"

"No one," I said. "I just know."

He squinted at me and stepped back. "What are you, the school psychologist or something? Get a life," he said, and walked off quickly. After that, every time he saw me, in a hallway or outside the building, he avoided me like the plague.

I didn't lie to him, although I didn't know exactly how I knew. I just knew. I had looked at Sidney after that party, and it all came to me, rolled out in my mind so vividly that it was as if I had been there. When the words came out of my mouth, however, I was just as surprised as he was. It was the first time I had ever done anything like that. It was actually a bit frightening. I felt like a small bird that had leaped into flight for the first time, full of trepidation but soon after elated. I felt like I had taken some drug that would make me high. It was as if I was rising off the floor.

A few days after I'd talked to Shelly, Sidney, who was in the tenth grade, approached me in the cafeteria.

I was sitting at a table with some of my classmates. Everyone was surprised at how angry she looked. She stepped right up beside me, practically pushing me out of my seat.

"I want to talk to you," she began.

"Here?"

"Anywhere. It doesn't matter. Why are you spreading stories about me?" she demanded.

Sidney was a good two inches taller than I was and had reddish-blond hair cut in a bob. She had delicate facial features and striking green eyes. The only feature that detracted from her good looks was that her neck was a little longer than normal. I thought she'd look better with a longer hairstyle because of that, but I wasn't about to suggest anything to her now or ever.

"I'm not spreading any stories about you."

She glanced at the other girls at the table. None of them was particularly close to me. None would ever defend me. In fact, they looked amused, happy to see me being dressed down.

"You told someone I had an alcohol intolerance and became seriously ill at a party."

I shrugged. "Isn't that true?" I asked. "It's nothing to be ashamed of."

"I'm not ashamed of anything, you nit. Who told you to say that?"

"Nobody."

"You're a liar. I ought to pull your hair out, you and whoever put you up to it."

"No one put me up to anything."

"Right. You just came up with that out of thin

air. Don't make up any more stories about me, or I'll come looking for you," she said.

She marched off to join her friends, who all looked back at me, trying to outdo one another with expressions of rage. I looked at the other girls at my table. The silence felt like the inside of a tornado.

"Who told you to tell that story about her?" Susan Mayo asked me.

"No one."

"Then where did you get it?"

"I just knew it. She's lying about it, but worse, she's lying to herself. She's going to get into bigger trouble."

I actually envisioned funeral wreaths, but I didn't say it. I must have had a shocked expression on my face. No one spoke. They stared at me.

"It's true. It's not a lie," I said. "She's just embarrassed about it."

"How do you know all that?" Susan asked. "You don't hang out with her friends, so you wouldn't hear them talking. Did you sneak into the nurse's office and read some private stuff or something? Well?"

"No. I just know," I said.

"You're hiding someone," Marge Coombe said. "They're going to find out eventually. You're stupid to protect them. Is it a boy, someone you like or who likes you?"

"No. I'm telling you all the truth. No one told me that story."

"No one told you? You just knew?" Susan asked.

"Yes."

"Delusional," she told the others.

The word brought back memories of my therapy. Was she right? I couldn't explain to them how I knew. I couldn't tell them about my visions and dreams, about the voices I had heard all my life. Of course they would think I was delusional, just as my therapist had, but deep inside, I couldn't stop believing that I was right.

I didn't think the incident got back to my parents, but I might have been wrong about that. My mother knew some of the other mothers. Maybe that was part of the reason my parents had decided to move me to a new school. Whatever the reasons, it did surprise me when they said they wanted me to leave the public school I was in and attend a charter school instead.

"Why?" I asked.

"This school has a much better reputation. It has smaller classes. You'll get more attention from your teachers, and it's closer," my mother explained.

Either she or my father would still have to drive me there and pick me up after school. "It's not that much closer."

"It's closer," my mother insisted. We were all in my father's office. He sat behind his desk, and she stood beside him, looking down at me on the settee.

"But I like my teachers. My grades aren't bad. I've always been on the honor roll, and my teachers tell me I have top reading scores." Usually, I never questioned a decision they made for me, but I couldn't accept their reasons this time.

My father looked up at my mother. She sighed

deeply but seemed calmer. "You're getting to that age now," she said. "Things are . . . well, things are just more delicate, actions more consequential. We hope you'll make better friends, too."

Better friends? I thought. *Better than what?* I never had what most girls would call best friends at my old school, but I did have some classmates who could have grown into real friends if my parents would have let me do more with them. Now I would never see them much anymore, if at all. I thought I would be even more alone.

There was no more discussion about it. Arrangements were made, and I was moved to the school they had chosen.

If they knew about the incident at my old school, they still hadn't mentioned anything about it by the time we celebrated my fifteenth birthday. Whether my birth certificate was authentic or not, I had always been told that my birthday was on September 15, and what I had seen in the file confirmed it.

I say "celebrated," although I'm sure anyone my age would question whether this was really a celebration. It was just the three of us. Uncle Wade was somewhere in Europe, and they hadn't invited any of their friends. They never did when it came to one of my birthdays. It was as if they had always wanted it kept a secret in a house bulging with secrets. We had dinner, but it wasn't anything extra special. My father liked pot roast with grilled rosemary potatoes. I liked it, too, but there were so many other things I liked more, and they never took me to a restaurant and had the waiter or waitress bring a cake with candles. Neither of them asked me what I wanted for my birthday dinner. My mother did put out the better dishes.

As always, I helped set the table, but just like on all my previous birthdays, it wasn't just candles on a cake. We had a candelabra in the center of the table with four tall white candles like the ones in churches. They were lit at the start of the dinner, and the lights were turned lower. All the window curtains were closed, too. I couldn't help feeling like we were doing something we shouldn't be doing, but what? It was my birthday, but it felt more like we were at a séance.

My mother began with the same questions she had asked at every birthday for as long as I could remember. It was almost like the questions asked of children at religious dinners. They had a spiritual air about them.

"How do you feel tonight, Sage? Do you feel any different? Special?"

"I don't feel that different," I said. I always tried to give her the answer I thought she wanted or to avoid the answer she didn't want, but I was too unsure. This time, I was very matter-of-fact. "I'm hungry, but I'm usually hungry."

She grimaced and turned to my father.

"Your mother means, do you feel any older, wiser? Has something about you changed? Do you see the world any differently?"

What parents asked questions like that on their children's birthdays? None of my friends ever described their parents asking such questions.

"I guess I do," I said. "I'd better. I'm in the tenth grade now. The work's going to be harder, and I'm around older kids more often, so I think I'll act older."

Neither looked satisfied with my response. What did they want to hear?

"Are you going to tell us about another birthday you remember?" my mother asked with a sour look.

"I don't remember any right now, except, of course, Lucy Fein's birthday last year. That was a big party. I was surprised she invited me. We had hardly talked in school before she sent out her invitations."

"You know I don't mean that sort of birthday, Sage," she said. "No dreams, no illusions, no inexplicable memories to plague us with?"

"No," I replied. "I haven't had any thoughts like that."

She looked happy and satisfied about that. The truth was that a few days ago, I did dream about being at a birthday party I could not explain. I supposed it would fit the definition of a nightmare more than just another strange dream.

It took place in a small house. The room was lit by many candles because there wasn't any electricity. There were at least a dozen adults and two other children. All the adults were dressed in black. I could feel them all watching me as a woman who was my mother brought out my birthday gift on a dish. It was an amber necklace. Before I was given it, she lifted it out of the dish and began to recite something in what sounded like gibberish to me. Everyone around the table joined in, but the chant was hard to understand.

When that ended, she turned and brought the necklace to me to put it around my neck. She was behind me, and the necklace was not as long as it had looked. It seemed to be shrinking, tightening around my throat until I gagged and woke up.

That was a dream I was definitely not going to tell them about tonight.

My father cut the roast and served me some. I took some string beans and passed the plate to him. I could see how my mother was watching every little thing I did, anticipating something or waiting for me to say something strange. My attention was centered on the gift package they had brought me. I wouldn't be able to open it until after we had eaten dinner and my birthday cake was brought out. I'd had a glimpse of the cake when I opened the refrigerator earlier. At least it was my favorite, a vanilla cake with an apricot icing.

As we ate, they continued to ask me questions about my new school. I had been there only a week, but they wanted to know if I had met any girls or boys I would like to have as friends.

"Yes, there are a few girls I think I could be friends with," I said.

Nothing terribly dramatic had occurred yet, and the other girls were feeling me out the way girls did anywhere. What kind of music did I like? What did I watch on television? What were my experiences with boys? Stuff like that. I tried to give them answers they liked, but of course, I was vague about the boys I had known. I didn't want to reveal that I had no romantic experiences while they were unwinding spools of dates, parties, and sexual explorations that honestly made me tingle, especially the way they freely described their orgasms, trying to outdo one another.

Now my mother was silent for a moment. She glanced at my father and then asked me a strange question. "When you came out of school today, did you see anyone watching from across the way before you saw me waiting for you? A man?"

"Watching? Watching what, Mother?"

"You, of course."

"No. I don't remember seeing anyone watching me. Who would be watching me?"

"No one, but if you ever do see anyone doing that, you tell us right away. Do you understand?"

"No. Why would anyone be watching me? How do you mean?"

"There are sexual predators," my father said. "They focus on someone, and it's better if you're aware of that sort of thing now, Sage. You're a mature young girl. Clear?"

"Yes," I said.

Why were they suddenly concerned about this now? Why not when I was at my old school? I was sure I wasn't less attractive six months ago. The school I was at now was on a side street, that was true, but there was still lots of pedestrian traffic.

My mother rose, went to the kitchen, and brought out my cake, but there were no candles on it. She saw the disappointment on my face.

"You're too old for candles on a cake," she said.

"We don't have to sing 'Happy Birthday.' You know that's what we're saying with this dinner, this cake, and your gift."

I know, I thought, *but who likes to feel their birthday is just something ordinary?*

My father gave me my gift after my mother cut the cake and put the piece in front of me. I looked at the package and then up at them.

"What?" my mother asked.

"Nothing," I said, but I already knew what was in the package. I had envisioned it. I was afraid to tell them I had done that, so I opened it carefully and took out the amber necklace.

"You don't look happy about it. Don't you think it's pretty?" my mother asked immediately.

I couldn't help my reaction. It was as if I had drifted into my frightening dream. "Oh, yes. It is very pretty."

"Here," she said. "I'll put it on you."

She rose to come around behind me. I looked at my father. I was sure he saw the panic in my face.

"What is it, Sage? You look very nervous, even frightened."

"No. I'm all right," I said. "It's just so beautiful and looks so expensive. I was surprised."

He looked up at my mother. Neither accepted my answer.

She plucked the necklace out of the box and undid the clasp. I closed my eyes. My heart was pounding. Would I choke to death? The necklace settled just below my throat. I reached up to touch it. Then I turned to look at myself in the wall mirror. When I was younger and I looked at the mirror, I sometimes saw other people sitting at the table, people who weren't there. I had stopped mentioning that years ago. I was thankful they weren't here now and hadn't been for some time.

"Like it, then?" my father asked.

"Yes, very much, Dad."

"Good. You know what it is?"

"It's amber," I said.

"Yes, it is," he said.

My mother sat.

"It has protective powers," I told them.

My father smiled a little but didn't speak.

"How do you know that?" my mother asked. I could see she was preparing herself to hear another one of my inexplicable memories.

"I read about it somewhere, maybe in a novel."

"Then wear it as much as you can," my father said. He sat back. "Unless you find it uncomfortable."

"Oh, no. Why would I?"

He didn't reply. They were both staring at me so hard that I did feel a little uncomfortable. I began to eat my cake, and they began to eat theirs.

"I'll make you a cake for your birthday, Mother," I said.

"What would you make me?"

"What you like the best, angel food with raspberry jelly in the center."

She nodded. Whenever she liked something I said or did, she would smile, but it always looked like half her face was trying not to.

Later, when I was preparing for bed, I started to take off the necklace, but it was as if there was someone standing behind me grasping my fingers to stop me. I stared at myself in the mirror. I was totally naked except for the necklace. Although it wasn't tight, it felt very warm against my skin.

I heard my voices telling me to leave it on, but then, for the first time, I heard another voice, a different-sounding voice, deeper, darker. It was coming from the far right corner of the room, where there was a shadow that shouldn't be there because it was so lit up.

"Take it off," the voice whispered. "You'll never know the truth about yourself if you let them control you. Take it off."

There was something hypnotic about the voice.

"Take it off. Don't wear it all the time."

I started to reach back and stopped. And then, as if a spotlight had hit it, the shadow evaporated, and the room was silent.

I went to bed with the necklace on, but I couldn't help but wonder if the voice in the shadows was the one I should have obeyed.

3

I was happier in my new school than I had been in my previous one for many reasons, but the main one was that my classes were smaller, which gave me more opportunity to become friends with others my age. I didn't want to make a big deal of it at my birthday dinner and sound too optimistic. I hadn't been at the school that long, but pretty quickly, there were five of us who were drawn to be with one another. I could sense their positive energy toward me. What I feared was that my parents would prevent me from doing things with them, as they had done with the girls in my old school, and these budding friendships would die on the vine just as quickly.

The five of us girls quickly became like a knot moving along the corridors, eating lunch at the same table in the cafeteria, sharing food, and always sharing homework. By the end of the second week of school, we were already commenting about one another's clothes and talking about our hair, lipstick, and nail polish, and of course talking incessantly about boys, all older than us. Of course, they all knew more about these boys than they thought I could, but once one of them was pointed out to me, it was as if I had known him all my life.

I actually felt a little sorry for the boys in our class, even though I thought a number of them were quite nice. From the way my new friends and others talked about them, dating one couldn't be further from their minds. It was almost as if it would be an immature thing to do. For one thing, none of them could drive or had a car of his own, and few, if any, reeked of the worldly experience that made older boys more dangerous and, therefore, more attractive.

Actually, the more I listened to my four new friends, the more the world outside of my very confined home life came into focus. I didn't want to tell them that I had yet to go to a real party or be with any special boy, even if just to meet at a mall and go to a movie. I was sure they'd be shocked to learn that I had never stayed over at a friend's house, either.

The closer I became with my four friends, the more my mind swirled with visions about them. I tried to keep most of that to myself. Occasionally, I slipped up and said something that amazed them because it was about something they hadn't told anyone else, like when Ginny Lynch found her father's contraceptives in a bedroom drawer and thought they were some balloon toy.

"I bet you were surprised when you learned about

birth control," I blurted when we were having a conversation about our sexual experiences.

She blanched the color of a fresh red apple. "What do you mean?"

"What you found in your parents' bedroom drawer."

"How do you know that?" she asked.

"I thought I heard you mention it," I said, so confidently that she blinked and wondered whether she had. "Weren't you shocked when you learned the truth about them?"

She laughed and then described to the others her discovery and how her parents had reacted. "My mother took me aside and gave me my first sex talk. I was only seven!" she added.

The others all claimed it was the first time she had mentioned such a thing to any of them.

"Who did you hear her telling that to?" Mia Stein asked me, making it sound like I had uncovered a betrayal. How dare she tell anyone else but them? Everyone waited for my answer.

I shook my head. "I don't remember," I said, but covered it up by quickly describing my own first sexual discovery. I hadn't actually seen it, but I had envisioned a girl in my seventh-grade class masturbating in the girls' room at my old school. I described how I had discovered her. That got everyone else back to talking about their experiences, and the incident passed.

But one particular day, I was more aggressive and far more specific about one of my visions because

I wanted my friend Darlene Cork to be happy. I thought that if I could help her, she would become an even closer friend.

"If you really want Todd Wells to pay attention to you, Darlene," I told her as casually as I could at lunch, "then let your hair down. Stop pinning it up so severely, and wear something red all the time, even if it's just a ribbon in your hair."

She froze, a forkful of mashed potato hovering in her wide-open mouth.

"What?" Ginny Lynch said, sitting back with a smile of amazement rumbling through her pretty face. Her almond-shaped, stunning hazel-green eyes brightened. "Wear something red all the time in order to catch Todd Wells's attention? How do you know he likes that color? What do you really know about Todd Wells, Sage? He's in the eleventh grade. When do you even speak to him? You just entered this school. And what does wearing red have to do with any of it anyway?"

All four of my friends waited for my reply. It wasn't the first time I had suggested something for one of them to do, but before this, it was something less interesting for them. Mostly, they were logical suggestions, like what I told Mia Stein two days ago. "Ask Mr. Brizel to change your seat in math class. Becky Potter is cheating off you when we have a test, and she's going to get you in trouble. He'll think you're letting her do it. It's going to happen." I didn't go so far as to tell her that the exact scene had flashed before my eyes recently.

Fortunately, Ginny, Darlene, and Kay Linder agreed with my suggestion. Mia asked Mr. Brizel to change her seat. It was easy to tell that he was already aware of what was happening and had his suspicions. It could have been trouble for her, but in the eyes of my friends, predicting something like that was nothing like this thing with Todd Wells. That was boring classroom stuff. They were all looking at me strangely. Butterflies panicked in my chest. I didn't want to lose my new friends so soon after I had made them.

"I haven't spoken to him at all. You're right," I said. "But things come to me instinctively sometimes. Don't they come to you?"

They all continued to stare at me, and I realized that I had to produce a better answer and produce it fast.

"I do see him occasionally," I continued, "and I noticed that he talks more with girls who have their hair down at least shoulder-length, and whether it's a coincidence or not, every time I saw him looking like he was interested in a girl, she was wearing something red."

"You notice that kind of detail about people?" Ginny asked.

"I guess," I said, shrugging. "Colors have an effect on us, you know. Who would like to have her room painted all black or all red? And we all choose colors we think look the best on us and make us feel the best, right?"

I hadn't been to anyone's house yet, but I knew none of them had a completely black or red room. Faces relaxed.

"Maybe she's right," Kay said. She was probably the best student of the five of us. Tall and stately, with amber-brown hair and blue-green eyes, she looked and acted older than any of us.

Kay's family was one of the richest in Dorey, and maybe because of that, she came off as more sophisticated, even a touch arrogant at times. Her family had attended a private event for the governor recently, and she let us all know it. Her father owned ten different auto dealerships, and she had told us he might even run for public office one day. I didn't need her to tell me. I knew her father would become mayor. The first time I saw him, when he picked her up after school one day, I envisioned him being sworn in. Her older brother, Carey, was already in his second year at Yale.

"I hate orange. I'm indifferent to pink, but I love turquoise," she said.

"I don't see how letting her hair down and wearing red will make that big a difference," Ginny said. "It's like falling in love with a book because of its cover and not what's inside. He has to get to know her first, doesn't he?"

"Love isn't logical sometimes, most of the time," I said. Again, they all stared at me. Kay sat forward. She was focusing on me the way my mother did sometimes. I would be a liar if I said it didn't make me nervous.

"It's one thing to talk about colors people favor. That's logical, but as my father's always asking me, from what well do you draw all this wisdom?" Kay asked me. "Especially when it comes to boys. When you told us about your social life at your old school, you didn't mention much experience with boys. At first, from the way you talked, I thought you had been at an all-girls school, or maybe," she added, batting her eyelashes, "you aren't into boys."

Someone else might have been so shocked that she would either start crying or look like she would any moment, but I simply shrugged. "Things come to me," I said again, and smiled at them. "You know, like I said, instinct. Sometimes I'm wrong, and sometimes I'm right. I'm sure the same is true for everyone."

For a long moment, the staring continued, and then Mia laughed and broke the silence.

"Maybe she has a crystal ball that works," Darlene said. "She did tell us about her uncle the magician," she added.

But Kay wasn't giving up. "Yes, but now that I think about it, you never mention any one boy here you especially like," she continued. "You're always giving everyone else advice about boys. What's your story, Sage? If you're not gay, are you wearing your hair and dressing especially for anyone in particular and not telling us? Did you have your eyes on Todd Wells for a special reason, perhaps?" she asked, rolling her eyes.

They all looked at me in anticipation. I could feel the tension building.

"No, but I know Darlene fancies him."

"Fancies him? You talk like someone from another country sometimes," Kay said. "Well, what boy do you *fancy*? Haven't you picked one out yet?"

"Not yet," I said. "I'm still shopping. I don't believe in buying on impulse."

That broke the mood and brought more laughter, but Kay still scrutinized me more than the others from that day on. She listened more keenly to my every word and began asking me more questions about my family. Of course, they all knew I was adopted. Just like my parents were up-front about that with everyone, I always was. I thought it was best that I revealed it myself as soon as possible and didn't make it sound like a big thing, an emotional thing. I was okay with it.

At first, I was afraid they might not be as friendly, thinking I was different, but because I showed no negativity about it and talked about my adoptive parents the same way they talked about their parents, they didn't make a big deal about it. Naturally, there were all sorts of questions about my biological parents, but I made it clear that neither of my adoptive parents, and especially not I, knew anything specific.

"I think you're supposed to be able to find that out someday," Kay said. "If you want to," she added.

"Not always. It's complicated. You always have access to health records so you can know about inherited diseases, problems, but identities are often closely guarded at the request of the natural parent."

"Do you know if that was true in your case?" Kay asked.

"No."

"So you might still find out."

"I might," I said, but not with much enthusiasm. "I appreciate my parents adopting me and giving me a home. And I guess it bothers me that I had a mother who would give me up. If she was so uninterested in me, why should I be interested at all in her?"

They all nodded in sympathy, but I wondered if I was able to hide just how much I really wanted to know my birth mother. For the time being, at least, that put an end to questions and talk concerning my adoption.

Despite how silly the advice I had given Darlene for pursuing Todd Wells at lunch sounded to the rest of them, she had her hair down and wore a red sweater the following day. Between periods three and four, Todd came up to her in the hallway and started a conversation. We all watched her fall back to talk with him, everyone smiling. Later, at lunch, he was waiting for her in the cafeteria and asked her to sit with him. The four of us sat at our usual table, but all eyes were on Darlene and Todd.

"It's like he was just waiting for her to look like you advised her to look," Mia told me, her eyes wide with amazement. "Really, how did you figure that out? You didn't just observe him accidentally. You knew something, right? You heard he was asking about her or something?"

How could I explain something to them if I couldn't explain it to myself? I realized that just as it was with my parents, my visionary powers wouldn't endear me to my new friends. If anything, that could make them suspicious, almost fearful of me, as though I might reveal some great secret one of them possessed. Everyone has something he or she would rather not have revealed. It would drive them away, and I would be just as alone as I had been in my old school.

"I don't know," I said, trying to make it sound as insignificant as I could. "I guess I did see him looking at her often and sensed he was interested. It was sort of in my subconscious and just came out. She looks better with her hair down, don't you think?" I asked, trying to change the topic.

"If something like that was all it would take to get Jason Marks coming after me, I'd do it in a heartbeat," Mia said.

The words were out of my mouth before I had a chance to stop them. "He's not for you. He's too full of himself. He'd take you out once or twice and then drop you without so much as a 'see ya later,'" I told her. I envisioned this exact scene with her feeling so bad about it afterward.

Describing Jason as arrogant wasn't a big stretch. He was on the school's starting five varsity basketball team, and he was student government president. He strutted like a proud rooster.

"How many other girls has he done that to?" I asked quickly to support my comment. "He thinks he's God's gift to women."

"But how do you know these things?" Kay pursued. "I can see where some of us might have those ideas, but you just started at this school, and I don't recall us talking that much about him."

"I guess I'm just a good listener when it comes to hearing what's between the lines," I said.

She pursed her lips and shook her head. "Maybe

you should write a psychic love column for the school newspaper," she said. "What's in store for me, oh great romance guru?"

I knew what was in store for her. Someday she would start dating her older brother's best friend, Russell Lowe. I saw that when they came to pick her up after school one day. But that romance wasn't going to happen for at least another year.

I closed my eyes and pretended to shape a crystal ball in front of me. "Oh, your future is easy to see. Many broken hearts left in your wake," I said jokingly.

"My wake?"

I opened my eyes. "You know, trailing behind you like car exhaust."

"That I believe about her," Ginny said. Laughter returned, but none of them could take her eyes off Darlene and Todd for long.

After lunch, we learned he had asked her out for Friday.

"Don't stop wearing red," Mia told her, "or he won't take you out again."

She laughed, but I knew she wasn't going to stop wearing something red, at least for a while.

In a school as small as ours, developing a reputation for something was not difficult, and usually when you had, it was nearly impossible to change it. Mine was shaping up quickly. Occasionally, I overheard one of the others in our knot say something like "She seems older than the rest of us."

"I don't mind her giving me advice," I overheard

Ginny whisper to Darlene. "But it just feels funny. It's like I'm listening to my mother or someone like that."

"I know," Darlene replied. "It's like she can see through stuff or around corners."

For a while after that, I really tried to keep my mouth shut and just listen, even though I was dying to say something to help one of them. As if she knew something like this was going on, my mother was constantly asking me about my relationships with my new friends. She seemed to want to know the details of our school chatter. I tried to keep it all sounding innocuous and didn't tell her about giving my friends advice. She would surely come back with "How do you know what advice to give?"

Otherwise, my experience at the new school was going very well. For the first few weeks, my grades were all either As or A-plusses. Nevertheless, I was very nervous about my parents attending the teacher conferences. Obviously, I wasn't afraid that my teachers would have anything negative to say about my behavior or my efforts to do well, but I had some disturbing feelings. It was like static on a radio. When I saw my parents afterward, I thought everything was fine and breathed with relief, but the moment she had the opportunity, my mother told me about a comment Mr. Leshner, my history teacher, had made about me, a comment that obviously troubled her, although I didn't understand why it should.

"He says there have been many times when he could see you anticipating his next question. Your hand is always up before anyone else even thinks of raising theirs. He thinks you're remarkable. Do you always know what he's going to ask, Sage? Your other teachers didn't say that exactly, but they implied it. So?"

"I read ahead," I replied. "That's all."

She wasn't satisfied with my answer. Later, I heard my father and her discussing it. He said, "Ordinary people can enjoy some second sight, Felicia. It's not unheard of. Ask Wade when he comes to visit next week."

"She's too much like I was when I was her age," my mother replied. "And you know in your heart, Mark, that she's just like you were, too. She's developing rapidly now. It won't be long before we discover to what end, and I hope it's not bad."

That seemed to end the discussion but not my curiosity. What was I developing? How was I developing? She wasn't talking about my physical development. Was it simply my intellectual abilities? How could they be developing toward a bad end? Did she think I might become some sort of mad scientist or something?

It all made me self-conscious about everything I said and did. I started to hold back on anticipating questions in class, and when I saw one of my friends doing something or about to do something that would make her unhappy, I clamped down my mouth and swallowed back my vision. I felt like a policewoman unable to stop a crime she knew was about to happen or like a doctor who knew something would make someone sick but couldn't take any action, give any advice to prevent it. Was it arrogant to think of myself this way, to think of myself as someone with powers to help others? Was it my fault I had this foresight?

Mr. Malamud got me thinking about all this when he responded to a question Kay asked about instincts in science class.

"Do human beings have instinct, too?" she asked, looking directly at me when she did.

"We say any behavior is instinctive if it is performed without being based on prior experience. It's a product of innate biological factors. I've given you examples of this with animals and insects. We talk about humans having a maternal instinct or a survival instinct. But these examples don't fit our scientific definition, a pattern of behavior that must exist in every member of the species and cannot be overcome willfully. So I'd say no."

When he paused, I looked at Kay. She was smiling at me as if she had been validated. I looked away quickly.

Most everyone else in the class wasn't very interested in Kay's question. Mia looked thoughtful for a moment but then went back to her doodling. After class, on the way to math, Kay stepped up beside me.

"I guess it's like you say, you're just a lucky guesser," she said. "Maybe you should play poker or something."

"Maybe," I replied, trying to make light of it all. "My uncle Wade the magician is a great poker player. He makes more money playing poker than he does performing. At least, that's what he told me."

"You should be tested by the CIA," she added, but then laughed. She looked relieved that my claim of having good instincts didn't hold water with our science teacher.

"I'll let you know when they call me," I said.

She laughed again and sped up to catch Ginny.

I suddenly saw myself drifting away from my new friends before I had really gotten to do much with them—or, rather, them pulling away from me. It wasn't going to happen today or tomorrow, but it was going to happen, and what I saw for myself was a new darkness, a new loneliness unlike any I had previously felt. There was something else out there, however, something coming that might make all the difference.

When Ginny invited me to a party at her house the following weekend, I hoped my vision was wrong this time and I wouldn't lose my friends.

"Darlene and Todd will be coming together," she said, "and Jason Marks will be there, too. Mia insisted I invite him despite what you said about him and what we all know he's like. Anyone yet you'd like me to invite?" she asked in a teasing tone. "I know there are boys interested in you. Darlene says Todd told her Rickie Blaine has been watching you and asking about you. You know who he is, right?"

How could I tell her that I was always aware of anyone who looked at me more than others did? It was as if I had some sort of radar that picked up on an intense gaze, a whisper about me, or a smile sent in my direction even before I turned and saw it. "Yes.

He's good friends with Jason, but as they say, if you lie down with dogs, you'll come up with fleas."

"What?" She smiled. "Who says that?"

"I heard my uncle say it," I replied quickly. I hadn't. I had no idea where I had heard it, but like so many other quotes I could pull out of some dark pocket in my mind, it was just there on the tip of my tongue.

"At least they're not boring boys," Ginny said. "You're not afraid, are you?"

"No, but I don't like wasting my time. Invite whom you want, Ginny. I'll be fine," I said.

"Probably of all of us, you will be," she replied, which I hoped was prophetic even though I knew that wasn't her sole reason for saying it. The sarcasm dripped from her lips. Still, I thought, maybe everyone had psychic powers and some just had more.

I laughed to myself. What if every high school in America had a fortune-teller in a booth in the lobby? After all, who needed a fortune-teller more than teenagers, people with limited experience, especially when it came to relationships? Teenagers were supposedly more impulsive and more indifferent about the future, believing and acting as though they were invulnerable, if not immortal. They took more risks with drugs and driving. They smoked without worrying about lung cancer and were more apt to drink too much alcohol, and they generally enjoyed disobeying rules and regulations.

Maybe because of how I was being brought up, I really was less of a teenager than my new friends were.

Maybe that was why they thought I acted older, even accusing me of being like a mother. Being aware of consequences made you more cautious. It was worse for me. I not only had more awareness of consequences, but I envisioned them so vividly they made my head spin and my heart race.

We had just finished reading and discussing the play *Our Town* by Thornton Wilder in English class. In the third act, Emily Webb, who has died in childbirth, comes back but at an earlier time, and what's tragic and sad about that, why she was warned not to go back, is that she can see everyone's future and knows what sadness awaits, how old they will become, and who else will die early. It's too much for her to bear.

The whole time we were reading it, I kept thinking of myself and looking at my friends in the class. I had the terrible thought that maybe someone like me shouldn't have any friends and shouldn't invest emotions and trust in anyone. I'd become too attached, and I'd eventually know something sad and tragic about them. I'd be like Emily Webb.

All my life so far, I had seen things others didn't see, I had known things I couldn't explain knowing, and I had heard voices whispering warnings. I had hoped that if I worked harder at making friends and being more of a normal teenage girl, I could put all that behind me. Maybe it would stop; maybe my parents wouldn't be so worried about me; but mostly, maybe I wouldn't be so worried about myself.

When my mother was there to pick me up after school, I told her about Ginny's party.

"Lynch," she said. "Why do I know that name so well?"

"Her father is president of the Dorey First Trust bank."

"Oh, right. Well, what sort of a party is it?"

"Just a party. Not a birthday or anything."

"We'll see," she said.

My heart sank. Wasn't this the sort of thing she wanted for me, making friends and socializing? Were things going to be the same for me in this school as they were in my old school? Did more birthdays for me mean nothing?

"Oh," she added quickly, "your uncle Wade is coming this weekend."

"I'll still see him during the day. The party's at night, Mother."

"We'll see," she said again.

I didn't argue about it, but as soon as my father came home, she told him. I was in the living room doing some reading for history class.

"That's good," I heard him say.

"I'm not so sure."

"Why not? If we want her to be normal, we've got to treat her like she is," he said.

They spoke too low for me to hear the rest of it, but a few minutes later, they both came into the living room. I put my book aside and looked up.

"This will be your first party as a teenager," my mother began. I smiled. They were going to let me go. "We're not going to give you all the warnings your friends get from their parents, I'm sure. We trust you not to do stupid things. There is one rule you must obey, however," she added. "You don't leave the party with anyone. You don't go anywhere else. We'll come for you at eleven thirty. That's more than adequate time."

"Besides," my father said, smiling, "if we wait until twelve, my car will turn into a pumpkin."

I thought that was it. My father turned to go up to shower and change for dinner.

"Is there a particular boy you are going to be with?" my mother asked.

"No."

She nodded, looking satisfied, but then looked at me more intently. "Have you told any of your girl-friends things about themselves that no one else would know? Are you still doing that sort of thing?"

She asked the question so fast that I held my breath for a moment. My father heard her ask it, too, and stopped in the doorway. So they knew about what I had done in my old school with Sidney Urban after all, and here I had done something like that again. She would surely be angry about it. There was no sense hiding it. She could find out just the way she had before.

"I gave one girl advice on how to win the attention of a boy she liked."

"What sort of advice?"

"How to wear her hair, a color he liked, stuff like that."

"Why did you do that?"

"Why?"

"Do you like the boy? Did you do it to keep the boy from liking her more?"

"Felicia!" my father said.

"Let her answer, Mark."

"No. I did it to help her. I don't want the boy for a boyfriend," I said. Even though it was the first time she had accused me of such a thing, it brought tears to my eyes. "She's my friend. I don't want to hurt her."

"And? Did it help her?"

"Yes," I said.

She looked at my father. He wasn't smiling, but he looked happy about my replies.

"How did you know what to tell her?"

"Just a feeling, an idea I had when I watched him with other girls. Lucky guess, I suppose, or maybe it was bound to happen anyway, and nothing I said or didn't say would have made any difference."

She narrowed her eyes. "Take my advice. Don't do that again, Sage."

"Do what?"

"Tell anyone how to get what he or she wants, especially new boyfriends."

"C'mon, Felicia," my father said. She looked at him. "Teenagers giving each other advice is just them being teenagers."

"Never mind what other teenagers do. You be careful. You especially don't start talking about those visions you used to have, understand? Do you?" she demanded, her eyes big, her pupils floating in some unimaginable fear.

I nodded quickly. "Yes, Mother."

"Good. You know how it frightened the parents of other girls at your old school when you warned them about certain things they did, how something could bring them great harm." Then, to drive it home, she added, "That was why you never had any real friends. They didn't want to hear such things."

"That wasn't why," I countered. Rarely did I ever do that. "You wouldn't let me do anything with them."

She stared at me a moment, her eyes darker.

"She's partly right," my father quickly interjected.

"Maybe, but she still frightened their parents," she insisted. "She'd better not do anything like that in this school."

He didn't disagree. In fact, he nodded.

She finally turned to leave.

Don't tell anyone how to get what he or she wants? Don't reveal any visions even if it might help someone? Parents would keep their children from being my friends again? Soon I'd be too terrified to open my mouth or offer an opinion about anything, even homework.

What parent anywhere in this city, I wondered, would tell her child such a thing? And look so terrified about something so harmless?

Or wasn't it harmless?

The cloak of mystery that had surrounded me in my house all my life wasn't opening as I grew older. Secrets weren't being revealed.

If anything, they were multiplying like rabbits.

4

The moment I awoke Saturday morning, I knew Uncle Wade was in the house. From as far back as I could remember, as soon as I opened my eyes in the morning, I could sense the current mood in my home. If something was troubling either my father or my mother, I would feel the tension in the air, no matter how bright the morning was. My senses went beyond the music of singing birds or the richness of a soft blue, cloudless sky. It was as if heavy waves of troubled thoughts flowed under my door and into my room, whirling around my bed.

Most of the time, my parents would not tell me about anything that brought worry or unhappiness to them. The tree of secrets grew more leaves. I could see them in the way they looked at each other, and I could hear them in the deep silences that fell between their words to me and to each other. I was always afraid to ask what was wrong. If I did, my mother's eyes would widen with panic, and I would feel like I had done something to add to their problems just by sensing they were there and that they thought they could hide them.

Perhaps they could—from others, but never from me.

I had never known a time when Uncle Wade's arrival had brought any cold winds or dark clouds. It was always just the opposite. When he appeared, it was as if all the air in our house had been replaced with a fresh new atmosphere in which smiles and infectious laughter could float through rooms with ease. There was a new lightness in my parents' voices, and whatever fears or worries they had about me or anything else could be put away on shelves or stuffed into drawers for the time being.

I always had a new injection of energy when he arrived, too, and that was especially true this morning. I hadn't seen Uncle Wade in months and months, and besides looking forward to seeing him, I anticipated his bringing me some sort of unique gift from somewhere he had performed.

As quickly as I could, I washed my face and brushed my hair. I chose something bright to wear, a sea-blue top with one of my newer pairs of skinny jeans. Lately, I had been wearing my hair down. It had grown to about two inches below my shoulders. Until now, my mother had insisted on having it cut shorter. Every day, I expected her to demand that I do just that, but she had yet to make an issue of it. I put on my amber necklace, slipped sockless into a pair of black and blue Skechers, and practically bounced down the stairs. They were all in the kitchen nook.

"Can this be the little girl I saw here the last time I visited?" Uncle Wade cried the moment I appeared. "Did you two take in another beautiful child?" he facetiously asked my mother.

She grimaced, but she didn't look disapproving.

He rose when I went to him, and he hugged me and kissed me on the cheek. "I have something special for you," he said.

"Let her have her breakfast first, Wade," my mother told him. "You'll get her too excited."

"I'm the one who's too excited," he said, "but right, right, first things first."

My mother rose. "We have your scrambled eggs and cheese," she told me.

It was Uncle Wade's favorite breakfast, too. I started to help her.

"Just sit," she said. "And tell your uncle about your new school and your new friends."

I glanced at my father. He was smiling, but I sensed there was something else going on. They didn't simply want me to pour out my descriptions of the school and the other students. They wanted Uncle Wade to listen keenly, like someone who was here to evaluate every word.

"My classes are smaller, most with fewer than fifteen students. I have very good teachers, and I've made friends with four of the girls in my class, one of whom is having a party tonight," I rattled off quickly.

Uncle Wade's smile widened. "And boys?"

"There are boys invited," I said.

"Anyone special yet?"

"Not yet," I said. "I haven't been there that long," I offered as an excuse.

His smile froze, but his voice changed just enough for me to recognize something more serious behind his words. "Don't be too harsh in judging them, Sage. Everyone has some flaws. Even your father and I, as hard as that is to believe. But we have plenty of good qualities," he added.

"Why haven't you married yet, then?" I came back at him, maybe a little too quickly. His smile became more a look of surprise.

"Sage!" my mother snapped.

"It's all right, Felicia. This girl is growing up fast," he said, turning back to me. "Simply put, I haven't found anyone who would be willing or happy to live the life I lead, but that doesn't mean I won't. I am looking. When I was in France last week—"

My mother cleared her throat emphatically, interrupting him.

"Besides," he said, "you're still my favorite girl."

"I'm too young for you," I said.

"Apparently, your uncle has regressed a bit. Maybe you're not too young for him after all," my father teased.

Mother served my eggs, and I asked Uncle Wade to describe where he had been. He always had a wonderful way of spinning his tales of travels, the people he had met, and the beautiful things he had seen. Whenever he finished, I was filled with a traveler's hunger and vowed to myself that I would go to these wonderful places someday.

After we finished breakfast, Uncle Wade produced a small box wrapped in lavender paper. I saw from the way he was anticipating my reaction that he was just as excited giving it as I was receiving it. In fact, all three of them were interested in my reaction. I began to open the box. Unlike the present my parents had given me on my birthday, this one remained a mystery. I'd had no visions about it. It was as if there was an invisible magnetic wall around it. When the box was open, I looked at a silver and black ring. Carefully, I plucked it out and turned it in my fingers. It looked ancient and very special.

"I found it in a small antiques shop in Budapest," Uncle Wade said. "It called out to me, and I heard your name. Sage . . . Sage," he sang. "I had to buy it."

I studied the carvings on the ring.

"Yes, the dragon of the east, the messenger of heavenly law, facing the dragon of the west, keeper of earth knowledge. The truth that links them involves mind, body, and spirit, also birth, life, and death, all bound together in the timeless circle as one. The ring symbolizes perfection and luck. Do you like it?"

"Yes, very much," I said, and tried it on my right ring finger. "It fits perfectly."

"Of course. It called your name to me. It's very old, a few hundred years."

The way he said it sounded as if he believed I had lived another life and had worn this very ring before.

"Really?"

"Yes. The antiques store owner had no idea what he had. I got a great bargain," Uncle Wade told my parents, but they didn't look impressed with that. Their attention was fixed on me, both of them looking at me so hard I felt self-conscious and took my other fingers off the dragons instantly.

"Is it uncomfortable on your finger?" my mother asked.

What a strange question, I thought. "No. It feels fine," I said. "Thank you, Uncle Wade."

"You're welcome."

Everyone was still looking at me hard, so I rose and began to clear the table. Uncle Wade continued to describe some of the shows he had done and the theaters he had performed in, especially ones in eastern Europe that he described as old movie theaters with pipe organs that accompanied silent films, canopies of lights, great arches, and red velvet curtains. The seats were old but plush, "and you could smell time," he said. It did sound as if he had gone back in time and traveled through ages, not just miles.

After I helped clean up our breakfast dishes, Uncle Wade surprised me by asking if I wanted to go for a walk.

"I need some fresh air," he said. "I've been riding in trains, staying in hotels, flying, and taking taxis so much I forgot what a nice fall day can be like. Let's walk around the lake."

I looked at my father to see if he would be coming, but he continued to read his newspaper. Uncle Wade and I started out toward the lake next to the house. I looked back, anticipating some sort of warning from my mother, but she was still in the kitchen.

The air was crisp but not too cold. Clouds moving west were racing against the light blue sky. Tree branches danced to the rhythm of breezes, and off in the distance, we could hear a mournful car horn, mournful because it sounded like the last desperate cry of a nearly extinct animal. It came from beyond the woods, but all sounds traveled faster and clearer on days like this, I thought. I even picked up the caw of a crow deep in the woods on the south side of the lake.

When we stepped out and walked down the sidewalk, the world around us suddenly grew silent. Looking up, I thought even the clouds had stopped moving. Way off on the western horizon, I could see a jet trailing a thin streak of pure white exhaust. Uncle Wade clasped his hands behind his back and walked slowly, like some ancient philosopher sculpting new thoughts into a grand idea. I smiled to myself because I could feel his struggle to begin our conversation.

"Ask me whatever you want, Uncle Wade, whatever you were afraid to ask in there," I said.

He paused and then smiled as he nodded. His blue eyes were never brighter, never more filled with glee. "I should have realized you would hear more in the silence."

"Why?"

"I've always believed that you have the third eye," he said. "I think you've realized it yourself, but you've been afraid to say it. It's nothing to be ashamed of. Most people who want it spend their lives trying to find it. Many religions recognize it exists. You were born with it, and you're just learning how to use it, but it's like any new skill or talent. If it's not treated well, developed properly, it could end up doing more harm than good, sort of like a brilliant scientist who uses his brilliance to develop a nasty weapon instead of a cure for cancer."

"The third eye? I don't know what it is, so I don't see how I could realize I have it. What is it exactly? What does the third eye give me?"

"Better perception, awareness, ability to envision outcomes and results more than most people."

"Is that what you have, why you are a successful magician?"

"Yes," he said without hesitation. "I'm not being arrogant, just realistic."

"Will I become a magician, too?"

He laughed. "No, no. That's just the way I use my talents. You have many more, I'm sure."

"What could be more than that?"

"Maybe just more wisdom," he said. "Everyone takes a different path to his or her own enlightenment. You'll find your way."

We turned down the road toward the lake. Two crows suddenly shot out of the darker part of the forest, sailed over the lake close to the water, and then turned sharply and headed deeper into the forest.

"Why did they do that?" Uncle Wade asked me. "Why did they change direction so rapidly?" The tone of his question reminded me of a teacher testing to see whether his student really was paying attention or to see just how smart the student was.

"They saw their own image in the water and were frightened."

He smiled and nodded. "That's exactly what you have to avoid, fearing yourself," he said.

"My mother, more than my father, makes me afraid of myself," I revealed. Right from childhood, I found I could always be more honest about my feelings with Uncle Wade. He never wore the cloak of tension that my parents wore whenever they were around me.

He didn't look shocked. "You're still telling stories about things you imagine or remember, things that make no sense?"

"Not as much, no. I know how much my mother hates that, but she's constantly asking me now if I tell people things like I used to. I don't. She doesn't even want me to give my new friends advice."

"I thought that was what was troubling you. I sensed it throughout breakfast. She means well. They both do."

If they meant well, I wanted to ask, why did they keep so much about me and themselves secret?

We followed a path to the edge of the water. The wind paused. The trees were still. The rippling in the surface of the lake diminished. It was the second week of October. More birds had gone south. There were almost no insects. Squirrels and rabbits looked more desperate about finding food. Some of the leaves had taken on more yellow and brown. The tips of winter's fingers were grazing the surface of the world around us like a blind man feeling his way, exploring to find the best path over which to bring in the colder winds and the flurries of snow.

"What is it they're really afraid of, Uncle Wade? What do they think I'll do?" I asked, and immediately held my breath.

Would I finally know?

Did they deliberately send me out here to walk with him so he could tell me something they couldn't tell me themselves?

"Just what you've done, perhaps, sense your power, your abilities, and become arrogant. Arrogant people do bad things to others."

"My power? What power?"

He paused, lowered his chin, and raised his eyes. "Don't try to fool a professional," he said. "You know of what I speak." He pointed to the center of his forehead. "The third eye."

"I've done nothing to cause them to think I was being arrogant," I said. "I'm hardly a snob. It's just the opposite. I practically tiptoe through the house. I rarely ask them any questions anymore."

"No matter what you might think, they want only the best for you," he said.

We started around the lake. As we walked, I debated with myself about whether to confess having explored the files in my father's office. Would he immediately tell my parents and reveal that I had lied to my mother?

"Remember when you were here last time and you put that marble on the kitchen table?" I asked.

"Yes, one of my favorite ways to impress a small audience."

"You just looked at it, moved your hand, and made it roll off the table."

"Now, you're not going to ask me how I did that, are you?"

"No. Maybe I know. Maybe I've done it."

"Oh, really," he said, stopping and smiling. "In that case, how did I do it?"

"Once I saw that my father had left a file drawer open. I knew he always closed and locked that drawer."

"And?" he said.

"I . . . was worried he might think I went into his private things, so I wished . . . I pictured the file drawer closed. I concentrated hard on it."

He was just staring at me coldly now, wearing an expression I had not seen, a face full of just as much worry as my father's, the face of someone who was waiting to hear terrible news. I was sorry I had even mentioned the drawer, but it was too late.

"And?" he asked again when I still didn't speak.

"It closed. I kept questioning myself about it, wondering if I had closed it without realizing it when I was finished looking at the contents."

"So you did go into the drawer, searched the contents?"

"Yes."

"But you're sure it was open? You didn't do anything to open it?"

"No, but like I said, after I pictured it closed, I thought I heard it close. In fact, I thought my parents might have returned, seen it open, and closed it, but when I looked, no one was there. But the drawer was closed."

"And you think that's how I moved the marble, by thinking hard about it?"

I nodded. He continued walking.

"Have you ever heard of telekinesis, the movement of objects with the mind?"

"I did read about it," I said, "after I had this experience, but I didn't get deeply into it."

"Some people have the ability to do that more than others, or they learn to do it faster," he said.

"And you can do that?"

"Don't make me tell you my secrets," he said. "Maybe you can do it, and that's what happened with the file drawer. As I said, there are many people who can do that. It's not voodoo. You didn't ask your parents about this?"

"No!" I said emphatically. "And I hope you don't mention it. I never told them I looked into that drawer. My mother came to my room and asked if I had been snooping in my father's office. I denied it. Everything about it remains confusing to me, but I know she and my father would be upset."

He nodded. "I see how frightened you are of what they think of you, Sage. Is that what troubles you the most these days?"

"It's not just these days," I said. "There have always been too many secrets in our home," I said.

"About what?"

"About me. And about them. They don't tell me

stories about their youth like the parents of other girls and boys my age do. It's almost as if . . ."

"Almost as if what?"

"Almost as if they were just here," I said, and he stopped. I thought he was going to talk about what I had said, but instead, he looked out across the lake as if he saw something. His eyes grew dark, the muscles in his face tightening. I looked in the same direction.

"Do you come out here yourself a lot?" he asked, still concentrating on a portion of the woods. He seemed very worried suddenly.

"I used to, but not lately, no. Why? Do you see something out there?"

"No." He looked around. "My brother found a very isolated place to live. Just be careful."

"Of what?"

"Of everyone and everything. The world looks hopeful and promising to you now, as it should, but let your third eye look into the darkness, too." He shivered as if he suddenly had a bad chill.

"Are you all right?" I asked.

"Yes, fine. Let's go back. I should spend more time with them. I don't see them that often," he added. He turned toward the house.

I looked again in the direction that had captured his attention. The shadows moved, but the wind had started again.

It's just tree branches swinging, I told myself.

But I knew there was something more, something I didn't want to see. I turned and quickly caught up with him. He looked so troubled now. Had I said all the wrong things? Was I wrong to admit lying to my mother and snooping in my father's drawer? Did he think much less of me because of that? He spoke before I could ask.

"You're adopted," he said as we walked. "Your past is a mystery, and with a mystery there are secrets. Right?"

No, I thought. *It's not that simple anymore, not with what I do know.*

"If I tell you something, Uncle Wade, will you keep it a secret, or will you tell them?"

"I thought you didn't like secrets."

"I don't, but I'm not ready to reveal this one to my parents."

"Okay," he said. "When you're ready to reveal it, you will, or you will tell me to."

I reached for his arm. He turned to me, and I looked into his eyes. I couldn't be sure he wouldn't tell them. Maybe he wouldn't be able to help himself. "Forget it," I said. "It was silly anyway." I started to walk away quickly.

"Hey," he said, coming up beside me. "I told you I wouldn't tell them. Look," he added when I didn't stop walking, "if I do, you'll know it, I'm sure, and you won't tell me anything again. You'll lose faith in me, and I don't want that to happen."

I could see he was sincere. I didn't quite understand it myself, but I feared that even if he didn't tell them, they would know once it had traveled through his ears and taken up residence in his memory.

Nevertheless, I realized now that I had to show him that I trusted him, or he would never trust me.

"I think my parents know who my birth mother is. I'm not sure, but I suspect they even know who my biological father is," I said.

From the look on his face, I knew I had penetrated deeply into his mind, maybe even into his soul. He nodded. "You saw something to that effect in that opened file drawer, didn't you?" he asked. "That's why you wanted it to be closed so much. That's why you could do it."

I didn't answer.

"Are you absolutely sure they don't know you were in that drawer?"

I shook my head. "Why? Did they say something about it to you, Uncle Wade?" I held my breath.

"No. Look, I'm not going to tell them. I swear. But for now, I wouldn't push it, Sage. Whatever you saw and whatever they know, they will eventually tell you when they think you're ready to know. Just try to trust them. Okay?"

I nodded, and we walked on, neither of us speaking, but inside I was trembling.

My parents looked up when we entered the room. I saw how they were studying Uncle Wade's face. It was uncanny, like the three of them had a different way of communicating. Their thoughts didn't need to be expressed in words. They traveled in magnetic waves among them, punctuated by a glint in their eyes, a blink, a slight movement in their lips. I felt hearing-impaired. All I could discern was static.

"Your friend Ginny called," my mother said. "She sounded troubled."

Oh, no, I thought. Was she canceling her party? I was so looking forward to it. I went up to my room to call her back.

"Hi," Ginny said. My mother was right. I could sense unhappiness just in that one syllable. Was Uncle Wade right about me, too? I did have the third eye?

"What's happening?"

"Bummer," she said, moaning. "My mother is making me invite Cassie Marlowe."

I stopped holding my breath. Why were all the girls my age so much more dramatic than I was? What was I missing? Practically everything that upset them was a major tragedy.

Darlene Cork sounded like she would commit suicide because she had to travel to her paternal grandparents' house for Thanksgiving this year. "It will be sooooo boring. And it's three days!"

Mia Stein had unknowingly gained four pounds and was going to fast for a week, hiding it from her parents by spitting her food into a napkin when they weren't looking. If she didn't lose the weight, she said, "I'll cut school and walk until the weight is off, even if I walk to China!"

Kay Linder's smartphone went dead, and neither her father nor her mother wanted to spend the time immediately to replace it. She swore she would end up in the loony bin. "It's like being in Communist Russia!"

I asked Ginny now, "Why is your mother making you invite her?"

"She met her with her father in the grocery store and thinks it was terrible that her mother deserted them and now Cassie has to be the homemaker. My mother said she looked so lost. Why do I have to be the one to help her find herself? Why doesn't she just go to the lost-and-found? Damn. And just when I'm having this great party."

"That's okay," I said.

"It's not okay. Cassie is soooo depressing. No one likes being with her for ten seconds. She walks around in a constant state of gloom and doom. She can wipe a smile off your face in a second. I think she sleeps in a coffin."

"Maybe your mother is right. She just needs friends," I said, thinking of how it was for me at my old school.

"I'm not having a party for charity."

"Don't worry about her. I'll keep her busy."

"That's not fair to you, especially with how many boys asked me if you were coming."

"What do you mean? How many boys?"

"All of them, practically," she said. "I told my mother, and she said maybe we need to do what they used to do in olden times, have dance cards. The boys put their names on them and dance with you in the order they're listed."

"Really?"

"Just kidding. We're not going to do that. Girls should be able to choose who they want to dance with. If anyone you don't like asks you, just tell him to bug off and ask Cassie." She laughed. "See you later," she said.

The girl she was talking about had crossed my radar, but, like everyone else, I had avoided her. Now I asked myself why.

"Use your third eye," I whispered to my image in the mirror. "If you dare."

Later I learned that Uncle Wade had volunteered to take me to the party and pick me up at the chipped-in-cement curfew I was given, eleven thirty. I spent a good part of the afternoon deciding what to wear. I was so good at giving other girls advice about what would make them look attractive. Why was it so hard for me to decide for myself? I was reminded of what I'd told my therapist about the fortune-teller. Fortune-tellers could only predict for others, never for them-selves.

Did that make the world more dangerous for them and for me?

There were obviously some things the third eye could not see.

And those things were out there waiting for me, maybe more than they waited for anyone else.

5

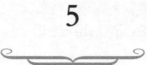

"Wow!" Uncle Wade said when I came down the stairs ready to go to Ginny's party. "I pity the poor innocent young men about to be devastated by this beauty."

I turned quickly to see what my mother thought. Ginny and Mia had spent a lot of time showing me how they used makeup. My mother never wanted me to wear any, not even lipstick. Frightened of her reaction, I just used a little of the lip gloss Ginny had given me. For now, I thought my clothing captured her attention the most.

I was wearing a short and silky black dress under an oversize sleeveless denim jacket, my amber necklace and my new ring, of course, and my highest-heeled black shoes. The dress was something I had chosen and my mother had reluctantly agreed to buy.

"Where did you get that denim thing?" she asked with a severe twist in her lips.

"Ginny loaned it to me. She was wearing it one day, and I admired it, and she just took it off and said,

'Here. You wear it for a while.' All the girls are like that, exchanging clothes and stuff. I thought it looked nice with my dress."

"What stuff?"

"Jewelry, hair clips, things like that." I didn't mention makeup.

"Why do you think what you're wearing is nice? It looks like you just threw some odds and ends together," she said.

"That's the style for young people these days, Felicia," Uncle Wade said. "They're dressing like that in Europe, too." He looked to my father for support.

"I suppose so," my father said. "Fashion changes with every new generation. You remember how people dressed in the nineteen-twenties."

My mother shot him a sharp, angry look.

"I mean, you can see it in movies and pictures from that time," he added.

"At least she didn't choose to wear all black, with that black lipstick, nail polish, and eyeliner, and put rings in her nose," Uncle Wade said. "What do they call them, Goths?"

My mother nodded, looking a little more relaxed.

She was always upset when I chose to buy something to wear that was black. All she would say was "You look better in colors." She herself never wore anything all black.

"If I ever catch her piercing herself or getting a tattoo . . ." she threatened.

"She won't, but you have to let her breathe," my father said softly.

She turned away.

"You look very nice, Sage. Have a good time," my father said.

Uncle Wade smiled and held out his arm to escort me out the door. "M'lady."

I took his arm, and we started out.

"Behave yourself," my mother called after us.

"Not to the point of being boring," my uncle whispered. When we stepped out of the house, he paused and looked up. "Look at this clear sky, and it's a bit warmer than usual for this time of the year. Good night for a party. Makes me wish I was seventeen again."

We continued to his car. He opened the passenger door for me.

"Your pumpkin, Cinderella," he said, standing back.

No one could make me feel as light and happy as Uncle Wade could. How I wished he were here more often, even lived here, I thought, and got in.

He hurried around like an obedient chauffeur. "Give me directions," he said, and I rattled them off.

As we drove away, I looked back and was sure I saw my mother gazing after us from the living-room window. She looked framed in the white curtains, a study of worry and concern as deep as that of a mother watching her child go off to war. I made a mental note to ask my girlfriends if their parents reacted like this when they went to their first real party. However, I hated revealing that this was my first unchaperoned party.

"Was my mother always this nervous, Uncle Wade? Even before they adopted me?"

He was silent so long that I thought he wasn't going to answer, but then he turned and smiled at me. "That's how you know how much she loves you. If you're precious to her, she cares more, worries more."

"You didn't answer my question," I said.

He shook his head. "You're going to be a tough one, all right."

"Tough on whom?"

"Boys, of course, who else?" He laughed. "You'll pin them to every word they utter."

I didn't want to tell him that I was already doing that.

"Just try not to think so much and so hard, Sage. Enjoy what little youth you have left. Once you've crossed over into adulthood, you have to work harder to enjoy yourself. Too much responsibility, too many people making judgments," he added.

We drove in silence for a few minutes. I still couldn't get past the idea that my parents were using my uncle to find out more about me, what I was thinking and perhaps what I had done. That was why they were so eager to have him drive me to the party and pick me up. I hated thinking of him as a spy, but maybe I could play the same game, I thought, and turn him into *my* spy. My earlier conversation with him at the lake gave me the courage to reveal more.

"Did my parents have a child before me?" I asked.

He slowed down immediately and pulled to the

side of the road. "Why did you ask that?" Before I could reply, he added, "You did look all through that file drawer, didn't you?"

"Yes. I saw the pictures of two children, a boy and a girl. Who are they?"

"Look, I said I wouldn't say anything, Sage, but I don't like that you're snooping and spying on your parents."

"Well, they don't want to tell me very much, Uncle Wade. You have no idea how it feels to be in a whirl-pool of secrets and half answers. I feel . . . I feel like an outsider."

He nodded and then surprised me by smiling. "My brother and his wife have no idea how brilliant you are, Sage, but give them time. They'll realize it."

"What about those other children?" I pursued.

"Yes, they had fostered a boy and a girl before you, a brother and sister."

"Where are they? What happened to them?"

"Let's just say it didn't work out. It was before they moved here. They took them on too late and weren't up to the challenge. That's why they wanted an infant—you. They didn't want a child nearly fully baked. They don't like talking about their first experience, so, as with everything else they haven't mentioned, don't be the first to mention it. When they're ready to tell you about it, they will. Felicia wants to be sure you're old enough to understand everything. She's looking out for you. They both are."

He continued driving, but I didn't want to lose my momentum. He was already more forthcoming than my parents had been all year. "Is that why they're so nervous about me—the bad experience they had?"

"Probably. I'm not their therapist, you know," he said, smiling. "They'll be the first to tell you *I'm* the one who needs the therapist."

"Did you know they sent me to one once?"

"I heard about it. I'm sure you really didn't need that. They realized it, too."

"Did they tell you any more about it?"

"Just that you terrified the therapist," he said, smiling. "Put all that behind you, Sage. Dark thoughts corrupt our faces, crush our smiles, and bury our dreams. Have a good time. What will be will be."

"Are you still going to keep my secret about the file drawer?" I asked.

"I don't like your not being honest with them, but I promised I would, so I will," he said.

Usually, it was easy for me to tell if someone was lying to me or telling me something that he or she didn't believe, but Uncle Wade had an impenetrable wall around him when he wanted it, so I couldn't be absolutely positive one way or another. That shouldn't surprise me, I thought. After all, he lived and worked in the world of mystery and magic, a box inside a box inside a box.

I thought that was it for our discussion of the file drawer, but I had opened the door to a room full of secrets, apparently.

"What else did you find in that drawer?" he asked.

"Lots of other pictures, pictures of people who looked just like my parents, but they were old pictures. Did they both look so much like their parents or something?"

"I'd have to look at the pictures to tell you. We all used to take funny pictures, dress in old-timey clothes and such. The photographer could make them look like they were taken years and years ago by vintage cameras."

"I also saw college diplomas that didn't make sense. They had my father's name on them, but he couldn't have gone to college that far back."

"Oh, they're probably fakes, too. We did all sorts of things when we were younger. I have some of those myself. Next time I come, I'll bring my old-time pictures."

"There was a little box full of bones in the file drawer," I said.

He didn't say anything.

"What could that be?"

"Mementos of something, I'm sure. Your father is more of a hoarder than you know. He never likes to throw anything out. I think he was a squirrel in an earlier life."

"Mementos of what? There were bones in the box."

"It's probably something I gave him, something I picked up at a fair in Europe. I should be flattered he kept it, I suppose." He turned and smiled. "I haven't been as loyal to the things he gave me."

"I found my birth certificate."

"Well, that's good. So many people misplace theirs, and then when they need them, they panic."

"That's what they told me when I asked about it. They told me they couldn't find it, and they might have to get another one."

"You mean they're becoming that forgetful?" he asked. He sounded serious.

"I don't know. Maybe."

He nodded. "We're all a bit forgetful at times."

"You don't forget things. You do that wondrous thing with memory, asking an audience of a hundred people their names and then repeating them."

"It's a memory trick. I might show you that one someday."

"Maybe you should show it to my parents."

"Will you stop all this worrying, Sage? I'm beginning to worry about *you*," he said. "I'm serious, Sage. It's all right for a girl to be bright and responsible, even curious, but you've got to let loose sometimes."

"I do try."

"Good, but try harder."

When we pulled into Ginny's driveway, we could see that most of the guests had already arrived. The large picture window in the living room was filled with them talking and drinking.

"I hope that's only soda or juice in those glasses," Uncle Wade said.

"You don't have to worry about that. I don't like anything alcoholic."

"Oh?"

"It blinds me, makes me deaf."

"How do you mean?"

"It closes my third eye," I said, smiling.

He nodded. "Yes, it would," he said. He leaned over and kissed me on the cheek. "I wanted to be the first tonight," he said. "Have a great time, Sage, and try to be more like fifteen than fifty."

"Okay. Thank you, Uncle Wade."

"See you at half eleven," he said in a heavy English accent.

I laughed, got out, and started for the front door. A car full of senior boys pulled up behind Uncle Wade just as he had begun to back out. He had to hit his brakes fast. Jason Marks was driving. From the way they were shouting and goofing around, it looked obvious that they had already begun drinking something alcoholic and didn't even notice Uncle Wade at first. The car pulled back, and then Todd Wells stuck his head out the front passenger window and started to yell for Uncle Wade to back up faster.

"We're getting as old as you waiting!" he screamed.

I had no idea how it happened, but Todd's door flew open immediately after he said that, and he fell out of the car awkwardly. The other boys roared with laughter. Uncle Wade backed out carefully and slowly drove off.

"Are you all right?" I shouted to Todd.

He struggled to his feet and looked at me. He was obviously embarrassed and a little shaken. He rubbed his knees and wiped off the palms of his hands on his pants. "Yeah, sure," he said, and brushed down his clothes as Jason drove into the driveway and the others spilled out of the car, continuing to ridicule Todd. Jason said he was always sticking out too far. They all laughed.

"It was your stupid car, Marks!" Todd shouted back. I couldn't see him in the shadows, but I was sure his face was crimson. "The door doesn't close right, just like your mouth."

"Serves you right for not wearing your seatbelt," Ward Young told him.

They all patted him on the back and headed toward the front door. When I stepped into the light, Jason howled. "Don't anyone go near this girl. She's mine."

He hurried up ahead of the others to put his arm around my waist as we walked through the opened front door and into the cacophony of laughter, shouts, and music piped through the house on speakers in every room. Ginny came hurrying through the living room to greet us. Darlene was right behind her, focusing like a laser on Todd.

"You look great," Ginny said.

"Thanks." I slipped out of Jason's embrace.

"Hey, where you going?" he cried. "I thought we were attached at the hip."

"Sorry. My hip is choosier," I said, and everyone laughed, especially Todd, who hadn't enjoyed being the butt of their humor out there on the driveway.

"You and your hip will come begging later," Jason said. "Take my word for it. Where's the booze?" he cried, and walked into the living room. The other boys followed, but Todd took Darlene's hand first. She smiled from ear to ear when she looked back at me.

"That girl will take a bullet for you now," Ginny said. "What's that ring you're wearing? I never saw it before. It's different."

"My uncle the magician brought it back from Budapest for me."

She brought my hand closer. "Are those dragons?"

"It's a good-luck ring. Very old. Yes, the dragon of the east, the messenger of heavenly law, facing the dragon of the west, keeper of earth knowledge. It's perfection, truth."

She dropped my fingers from hers as though they were too hot. "That's too much for me. I'll stick with diamonds," she said, waving her own ring in front of me. It was the ring she had been given on her last birthday. "C'mon. Get something to drink, and start dancing."

"Do your parents know how many people you invited?" I asked, seeing that it was wall-to-wall on the marble tile area she had cleared for dancing.

"I told them just my close friends. It's not my fault that I made more close friends since I told them," she said, and laughed.

"Where are they?"

"At my aunt Dede's in Boston until tomorrow. Don't worry about it. I've done this before. As long as the house is still in one piece when they return, it's fine."

As I looked around, the question for me was, *would* it still be in one piece?

There were many expensive-looking things here, like the cabinet full of Lladros in the hallway and the large landscape oil paintings. It was quite an upscale home. My first impression was that it was at least twice as big as ours. It was a ranch-style house, with a flow to the rooms, the living room opening onto the dining room, which had just a granite countertop between it and the large kitchen. There were very big, expensive-looking area rugs and a continuous marble tile floor. To the right was a large den with red leather sofas and chairs and a very big television. Kristen Gayle and Curt Bishop were entwined on one of the settees, kissing as if they were on a movie set. On the other settee, Mia Stein was sitting, with Greg Storm sprawled out, his head on her lap. The television was on, but I doubted they could hear the music video. Why would they want it on, anyway, with all the other music? Noise seemed to make everyone more comfortable.

One of the school's football players, Nick Kowalski, stood like a cigar-store Indian, with his thick, muscular forearms folded across his barrel chest, beside the refreshment table in the dining room. He was eyeing everyone like a department-store detective.

"Nick's my bouncer," Ginny said. "And everybody knows it, too."

Nick smiled when he saw me. I knew he liked me. He was important on the football team, but he wasn't good-looking enough to attract many girls at school. Despite his size and aggressiveness on the football field, I sensed he was gentle. He was always very polite with me.

"Hi, Sage. What can I get you?" he asked when we drew closer. I saw the rum and vodka poorly camouflaged on the side of the table.

"Just a Coke, thanks, Nick."

He widened his smile. "Smart girl," he said, and poured me a Coke.

"Boring," Ginny said.

I turned and watched the others dancing. Someone made the music louder just as Cassie Marlowe entered the house. She stood in the hallway looking in at everyone. She looked frightened, mousy, hugging herself like someone about to come apart. No one called to her. She searched with desperation for a friendly face.

"Oh, no. I was hoping she would decide not to come at the last minute," Ginny said.

"She's not that terrible, Ginny. I'll see to her."

"If you hang out with her, no one will ask you to dance or anything."

"I'll risk it," I said.

Ginny shook her head and quickly went off to dance so she wouldn't have to greet Cassie.

I started toward her. "Hi, Cassie. You want a soda, something to eat?" I asked her.

She looked at me suspiciously. "Just a soda?"

"That's all I'm drinking," I said. "C'mon."

I started back to the refreshment table, and she followed, remaining a few steps behind. I signaled Nick, and he poured another Coke and handed it to her. She sipped it cautiously, her eyes full of trepidation. She gasped when Nick reached out to take someone's empty glass for a refill. It set off some alarm bells inside me, but before I could give them any attention, Rickie Blaine stepped up between us, inserting himself aggressively. He was almost as big as Nick and was also on the football team. Cassie stepped back quickly.

"Wanna dance?" Rickie asked me.

"In a while," I said.

"What, ya got to warm up your engine or some-thin'?"

"Somethin'," I replied.

He turned, glanced at Cassie, and then shook his head at Nick and walked away. Off to the right, two other boys, Sam Becker and Adan Fellows, were hors-ing around and bumped into a side table. Nick shot out quickly, seized each one's arm, and squeezed hard and tight enough apparently to terrify them both.

Ginny stepped up beside me. "See, I'm protected. No worries." She looked at Cassie and shook her head before stepping closer to me to whisper. "Get rid of her. You're wasting precious time," she said, and rushed back to the dance floor.

"Why didn't you want to dance with Rickie Blaine?" Cassie asked me.

"I was afraid he'd step on my foot," I said, "and I'd be on crutches for months."

She studied me for a moment to see if I was seri-ous. When I smiled, she smiled. "Isn't there anyone here you like? I mean boys?" she asked.

I looked around, really more for her than myself. "No one I'd pine over. Peter Murphy is a nice boy," I said, nodding in his direction. He was talking with another boy, Danny Cook, intensely as if nothing was going on around them. They were practically insepa-rable in school, and they were the only boys from our class here.

"Everyone calls him a super nerd," Cassie said. "But you're right," she added quickly. "He's nicer than most."

By "most," I could see she meant everyone else.

I took a closer look at her. She was wearing a
sleeveless dress that hung on her body like a hand-me-
down at least a size and a half too big. She had a nice
figure, but she never wore anything that would clearly
reveal it. She wore a pair of dark brown, worn loafers
and no socks. She had no jewelry, just an inexpensive-
looking watch. At first, I thought that her mother deserting her and her father five years ago was probably
what made her so timid and plain. Her dark brown
hair looked unwashed, pinned up clumsily, with split
ends. She was wearing only a touch of lipstick, and
it looked put on too quickly. Her nails were nibbled
down, and she wore no nail polish.

"I was surprised I was invited tonight," she said.
"I'm not really friends with Ginny. I'm not really
friends with anybody."

"Why not?" I asked.

She shrugged.

Jason Marks swaggered up to us. He sipped what
was obviously more than soda and smiled. "How's
your hip?" he asked. "Ready for some hip action?" He
did a disgusting bump-and-grind. Cassie's eyes widened. "Your friend's interested," he said.

"Not interested, revolted, as in turning her stomach."

"Yeah, well, maybe someone should."

"To answer your question, my hip is quite content
as it is," I said.

His smile faded. He looked at Cassie and nodded.
"You're in the right company," he said. "Enjoy yourself."
He walked off quickly and started to dance with Shirley
Jones, even though she was dancing with Ward Young.

"I never liked him," Cassie said. "He was always making fun of me."

"Good judgment on your part," I said.

"You're so pretty," she told me. "You should be out there dancing with someone."

"I'll be out there when I'm ready. Let's go talk to Peter and Danny."

"Really?"

"Sure."

I started to cross the room toward them. Cassie stepped around someone and walked ahead of me, and I noticed a bruise on the back of her right arm. Without hesitation, I reached out and touched it. There was a flash when my fingers grazed the bruise, and what I saw next stopped me from moving.

There were two large male hands on Cassie's upper arms, holding her down forcefully against a pillow on a bed. Her face was rippled with fear. Suddenly, she closed her eyes and held her breath. I saw a head of dark brown hair with a bald spot at the center. It closed in on Cassie's naked breasts. I knew who he was. I had seen him at school.

I saw Cassie turn her head from side to side and open her mouth in a silent scream, a howl that went inward. Her father was moving all over her, mumbling distorted words in a drunken rage. In my ears, it sounded like growls over static. When he was finished, he fell forward on her, breathing hard like a racehorse. Cassie remained unmoving, her eyes still closed, her mouth still open. She was in some sort of state of shock. He raised his head and looked down at her, and then he slapped her, and her eyelids fluttered, just as they were fluttering in front of me right now.

The whole vision had passed in seconds.

"Sage?" Cassie said. She looked at me curiously. Others dancing around us stopped and looked, too. I supposed my face was full of shock and surprise.

"What's with you?" Mitchell Barton asked me. He and Lilly Thomas stood there staring at me. "You look like you just saw a ghost. What, did you get your period or something?" He laughed, and Lilly slapped him on the shoulder.

Cassie bit down on her lower lip. She looked like she was going to cry. Maybe she was afraid I had changed my mind and was going to desert her or something.

"Nothing's the matter with me," I told Mitchell. "But you had better check your pulse to see if your brain's alive."

This time, Lilly laughed.

I nodded at Cassie and moved forward toward Peter and Danny, but my heart was pounding. Peter and Danny looked dumbfounded when it was clear we were coming to talk to them.

"Hi," I said.

Danny put his hand behind his ear. "What?"

"I said hi. How are you guys doing?"

For a moment, neither replied. They looked like they didn't understand English.

Then Danny smiled. "We're all going to need cough drops by the time we leave," he said, practically shouting to be heard over the music.

"They've got quite the sound system here," Peter said. "Did you see the amplifier? It's real high-end stuff, too powerful for this space. They can't turn it up completely, or they'll blow out the walls. I'm surprised they don't have more feedback, and what about that woofer? I wouldn't have placed the speakers where they are acoustically," he continued.

Cassie looked at me to see if I was going to stay there.

"Maybe we should dance," I said.

"Dance?" Danny looked at me as if this was a foreign idea.

"When in Rome," I said, and he laughed.

"Yeah, you're right." He nodded at Cassie. She looked at me as if asking permission, and I smiled.

"Go on," I said.

She followed Danny onto the dance floor. She moved tentatively, but Danny was quite aware of how poorly he danced and made fun of himself. I realized Cassie was laughing for the first time since she had arrived.

Peter looked at me helplessly. I could see Ginny and Mia now standing by the piano looking absolutely incredulous. Jason Marks was glaring my way. I took Peter's hand and pulled him along. Like Danny, he had almost no rhythm, but I wasn't doing much better. My nerves were still vibrating from the image I had seen and what I felt confident I knew as a result.

It was my third eye, and this time, I had used it to look into the darkness, just as Uncle Wade thought I might.

The question now was, what did I do about what I had seen?

6

When I looked at my watch, I realized it was nearly eleven, and I had spent almost all my time at the party with Cassie, Danny, and Peter. We had eaten together, danced some more, and sat talking comfortably about school, our teachers, and books we had all read outside of what was required in English class. I was happy to see Cassie open up and talk. Her timidity dwindled thanks to the way Peter and Danny listened to her and got her to participate. She became more and more relaxed. It was as if we had created an impenetrable bubble around us. No one bothered with us or tried to get us to talk to them, and none of the other boys asked me to dance.

Ginny was obviously not too happy with me. Whenever she looked my way, she shook her head and smirked. She retreated from everyone, however, as she became more and more involved with Ward Young. The night began winding down, at least for me. It was obvious to me that along with Cassie, I was going to be one of the earliest to leave. She announced that she absolutely had to go at eleven.

"And not a minute later. I know it's early, but my father wouldn't have let me come otherwise," she explained to Danny, Peter, and me.

"I'll probably be going soon myself," Danny told her. He had been eyeing some of the cakes and cookies no one else was touching and wasn't going to leave without having some more.

A few of the others had disappeared, but they hadn't left the house. Some, I realized, had gone up to Ginny's bedroom, and another couple had gone to one of the guest bedrooms. More drinks and some drugs were being passed around. The party was becoming more raucous. Nick looked very busy policing the expensive knickknacks and furniture and literally lifted Skip Lowe off a small table he had decided to use as a chair.

I saw how nervous Cassie became as it grew closer to eleven. She was looking at her watch practically every thirty seconds. Just a little after 10:55, she got up quickly and said she had to go out to wait for her father. He'd be coming any minute. Danny took that as an opportunity to attack the desserts again, but before he did, he told Cassie he had enjoyed being with her. He added that he was looking forward to seeing her in school. After he said that, she wasn't just smiling; she was beaming. I had the feeling that laughter and smiles were rare in her house. I knew how mousy she was around her classmates, always lingering in the background and slinking along through every available shadow.

In the back of my mind, I thought that perhaps she was afraid someone would talk to her or just look at her and know what had happened to her and what was probably still happening to her. I was confident I knew what that was. Fear had become her sister, her second shadow.

"Should I go thank Ginny?" Cassie asked me. Ginny and Ward were in the den now, practically glued to each other on the sofa.

"I'll tell her for you later," I said. I could see how nervous it made her even to contemplate going in there and interrupting the love scene. She couldn't look long at any of the couples who were kissing or embracing each other passionately. The sight put fear in her face, every tiny muscle straining in anticipation of something dreadful about to happen to her.

I wanted to walk her to the door and see her father pick her up. She stood out front trembling as we watched for any oncoming automobile.

"Are you okay?" I asked.

"Yes," she said, but I could see her lips trembling. She practically leaped off the front stoop when he drove up.

"Night!" she cried. "Thanks for being my friend tonight," she added, and ran toward the car. I started toward it, too. She stopped. "Thanks," she said again, obviously afraid of my getting too close to him.

I paused. I was close enough, and I didn't like making her any more anxious.

When she opened the door, the inside of the car lit up, and I saw him glaring out, looking past her and directly at me. The flow of dark, negative energy came freely at me and didn't dissipate until Cassie closed the door, shutting off the light. Silhouetted in the glow of the streetlight, she seemed to shrink in her seat. She turned to wave good-bye to me, but he said something that stopped her, and she turned her head away. He drove off quickly. I watched until the darkness swallowed them up.

Peter and Danny were eating cookies and drinking soda when I returned. I stood there, still a little shaken by that flow of dark energy. Todd and Darlene came up to me.

"You did your good deed for the night," Darlene said. "Now, how about coming with all of us and having some real fun? We're going to the Doll House in about forty minutes. It doesn't get good until midnight. Jason knows the owner, and we can get in even though we're underage."

I looked at them both as though I were really from another country, another culture. How could they stay out so late? Weren't they worried about their parents finding out where they had gone?

"You know what the Doll House is, right?" Todd asked when I hesitated.

"It's just a dance club," Darlene said before I could reply. I had heard about it at school.

"Just the best dance club. Good stuff's passed around," Todd added.

"I would have thought you had enough good stuff here," I said.

His smile withered, his face suddenly becoming

a dried-out grape. "Yes, Mommy," he said, sounding like a little boy. "I guess you're not interested in having a really good time tonight."

"I had a really good time here," I said.

"You had a really good time with losers? C'mon," he told Darlene. "We're wasting our time."

"Sure you won't come?" Darlene asked. "It will be fun. I promise."

"I can't, but thanks."

"Okay," she said, and joined the others.

I could see they were all talking about me. They weren't looking at me now much differently from the way they had looked at Cassie. I wanted to talk to the girls, explain how this was my first real party and how worried my parents were, but they all turned away from me. I felt like an iron curtain had come down between us. It was close to eleven thirty anyway.

"I've got to go," I told Peter and Danny. "I had a good time with you guys."

Danny beamed, but Peter considered it for a moment the way he might mull a serious math or physics problem and then nodded.

"Yes, it was better than I had expected it would be." He leaned in to me to whisper. "We got invited only because we do Ginny's homework," he revealed.

"You do her homework?"

"We even found a way to help her on tests," Danny added.

"She can't take you with her later."

"Later?" Danny asked. "What later?"

"Life," I told him.

Peter smiled. "She means we're carrying her on our backs, but when we swim away to follow our own destinies, she'll drown."

He turned and looked at me with obviously more respect. "You're pretty smart, Sage. I bet you'll be successful no matter what you do."

"I don't know about myself, but I know you will be, Peter."

He nodded but not with arrogance. Facts supported predictions. I didn't think I had to be a fortune-teller to read the future for people like him. They were past the point of needing encouragement. They had the requisite self-confidence and, most important, self-respect.

"See you," I said.

I sauntered over to Ginny to say good night and thank her for inviting me. She looked at the others, took my hand, and walked me to the door.

"Everyone is worried about you, Sage. They think you should get out more and hang out with live people. Unless you're interning for social work or something. Todd is telling them that being around you is like having a chaperone or something. Why don't you come with us to the Doll House? You can let your hair down and show them all. We'll only be there another couple of hours. It's an exciting place."

"I bet it is. Look, this is my first time out to a real party. My parents are nervous about it and want me home at eleven thirty. My uncle is picking me up any moment."

"Eleven thirty? Medieval," she said. "Too bad."

I watched her return to the others, shrugging her

shoulders, and then I walked out to meet Uncle Wade. He had just driven up. I hurried to his car.

"Surprised none of the boys walked you out," he said when I got in.

"Most of them will need someone to walk *them* out," I told him.

"Oh?" He looked at the house and then started to drive away. "Didn't you have a good time?"

"Yes."

"But?"

I didn't answer.

"Something's troubling you. What is it?" Uncle Wade could read me just as well as my parents could, I thought.

"What if you knew something terrible was happening to someone in your class, something she wouldn't admit to you or anyone else?"

"How would I come to know it? Someone else told me? I saw it?"

"Yes, you saw it. In a way."

"What way? How can you see something in a way?"

I sensed what he was after, but I wasn't going to start talking about my visions. I was sure my parents were waiting to hear him report something like that. I tried to skate around it. "Sometimes you can just realize something, like when someone is very upset but tries to hide it."

"I'd be careful about what I did if that's all I had to go on, Sage. One thing I wouldn't want to do is accuse someone of something without real proof. It would only come back on me. It's something someone also might do to hurt that person, hurt his or her reputation. Would you deliberately do that? Do you want to hurt someone?"

"No," I said. "Unless he or she deserved it," I added.

He looked at me suspiciously. "Who decides who deserves it and who doesn't?"

"No one would disagree in this case, I'm sure."

"Was it something that involved those boys who were carrying on when I dropped you off?"

"No," I said. "Forget it. You're right. I shouldn't even talk about it."

"I hope you will always feel that you can talk to me, Sage. I know I'm not here that often, but you can always call me on my cell phone, and if I don't answer, I'll get back to you. I mean it," he said.

"I know you do. Thank you, Uncle Wade."

"Well, tell me, then," he said, smiling to change the mood. "Were you more like fifteen or fifty at the party?"

"Depends on whom you talk to," I said. "But doesn't it always?" I asked.

He laughed. "You're going to be fine," he said. "You're going to be just fine."

Was I?

It wasn't only what I believed was happening to Cassie and the way I discovered it that made me feel different from everyone else tonight. While they were all enjoying a carefree time and forbidden things, I was in deep, serious thought. No wonder I was comfortable with Peter and Danny. There was no risk being with them, nothing to distract me from dark thoughts and mature concerns. However, I knew that behaving like I did I was risking new friendships. As Ginny had told me, they would think of me as like a chaperone at a dance or something. I understood why and couldn't blame them.

Girls and boys my age who were doing illegal things or things their parents would disapprove of wouldn't want someone like me around. I wondered if I would ever be invited to another party or even just to hang out with them now. It didn't take a fortune-teller to see that they would be afraid I would betray their secrets and get them into trouble. Promising that I wouldn't do that still wouldn't be enough for them to trust me.

"I have to leave tomorrow," Uncle Wade said, shaking me out of my thoughts.

"So soon?"

"My agent called. I have to go to California and then Hawaii. Poor me, right?" he said, smiling.

"I wish I could go with you."

"Maybe you will someday. What do you think?" he asked, as if I could either confirm or deny the future right then and there.

"I don't know," I said. It would always be a mystery to me why my parents and my uncle were immune to my third eye. They were protected in ways most people weren't. Was it simply because I was too close to them, or was it something else? I felt like I had been brought up in a dark maze and was still trying to figure out a way to the light.

I decided to press on to see what else I could learn from Uncle Wade.

"There was one other thing I found in that file

drawer, Uncle Wade. It was a strip of leather, like a bookmark."

"Oh?"

"There was a word on it, engraved in black. *Belladonna*," I said.

For a long moment, he was silent, and then he nodded and smiled. "Belladonna was the name of the estate my family owned in Hungary a very long time ago. That strip of leather is probably hundreds of years old. Precious," he added. "It has the family crest on it, right?"

"Yes."

"That's it. Something handed down from our grandfathers, most likely."

"I wonder," I said, after hearing his explanation, "when my parents will ever tell me . . ."

"Ever tell you what?" he asked.

"Who they are," I said. "They dole out tidbits about themselves and their families as if every word was solid gold, and if I ask too many questions, which is one or two, my mother takes my head off." I would never let myself sound so upset about it with anyone else but him.

"Look, Sage, I was thinking about all this, all that you told me you found in that drawer and how you've kept it to yourself all this time. I promise, I didn't say anything to my brother or Felicia," he added quickly, "but I think you should. I think when they find out someday, maybe because you'll come out and tell them, they will be disappointed that you didn't tell them or ask them anything back when you looked in that drawer."

"I was afraid to say anything about it, Uncle Wade. My mother especially often makes me feel like I'm on the verge of doing something terrible. If I told her I snooped in my father's things . . ."

"You said the drawer was open, right? You didn't jimmy it open or something, did you? You're not lying about that, right?"

"No, it was open."

"So you were curious and looked inside. It's understandable."

"They told me not to go into my father's office and look at his things. My mother gets very upset when I forget to do something she had told me to do or accidentally do something she didn't want me to do."

"What's worse?" he asked. "Disobeying that rule or lying to them about it? Lying poisons everything. My father used to say it rusts trust."

"Not telling her I looked in that cabinet is the only time I've ever really lied to my mother."

"Well, you'll be able to tell her that. Look, Sage, how can they trust you with things if you don't trust *them* with things? Right?"

I nodded, but it didn't lessen my fear. "Okay," I said. "Maybe I will tell them."

"Get off the maybe, Sage. Make a decision, and be firm about it. He who hesitates is lost."

"Fools rush in where angels fear to tread," I fired back.

He laughed. Then he quickly grew serious again. "This won't make you a fool."

"Should I do it now, tonight?"

"We don't want them to think you're doing it because I told you to," he said. "And if that's your only reason, then you shouldn't do it. Do it when you feel you want to, when you need to for yourself. Okay?"

"Okay. Thanks, Uncle Wade."

"Like I said, you'll be fine."

We rode on in silence, a silence I tried to penetrate to see if he really believed what he had said or if he had said it to help himself believe it, but just as with my parents, it was still impossible to probe beyond where he wanted me to go. There was that invisible magnetic wall that kept me outside with my questions unanswered.

My mother didn't lack any questions when we entered the house, however. Both she and my father were waiting for me in the living room.

"Here she is," Uncle Wade announced, "home safe and sound."

I saw the way my mother and he looked at each other. Pages could be transcribed from what their eyes said.

"Come in and sit," my mother told me. "Tell us about your party."

I sat on the settee. My father was in his favorite easy chair with the thick arms and plush cushions. My mother sat across from me on the matching settee. They had both been drinking their homemade elderberry wine. My father looked relaxed, but my mother looked poised to pounce.

"Well?" she said when I hesitated.

"There were more kids there than I expected," I

began. "Ginny ordered in pizzas and other food from a restaurant. I thought the music was too loud. The house has speakers in every room. You practically had to shout to be heard even if you were standing right next to someone."

I saw my father's lips soften into a small smile. He glanced at my mother, but she had her eyes fixed on me as if she could X-ray every word I spoke to see the bones of truth.

"And were there alcoholic drinks?"

"Yes," I said, "but I didn't drink any. Not everyone did," I added. That was true. Neither Peter nor Danny nor Cassie had.

"There were drugs, too, weren't there?" she followed.

"I didn't actually see any, but I thought there were some drugs being passed around. Only some of the kids did that."

"You didn't do any of it?"

"No, absolutely not."

"Where were her parents?" my father asked.

"In Boston, visiting Ginny's aunt."

"So the party's still going on?" he asked.

"Yes, but others were leaving soon after me."

"And the rest?" my mother asked.

"Some were going to a dance club."

I felt like a spy on my friends. I told the truth, however. Uncle Wade was watching me, and his prediction about lying was still floating in the air between us.

"Did they want you to go, too?"

"Yes."

"Did you want to go?" she asked. "I know I told you not to, but did you want to?"

I hesitated just a second too long.

"Temptation is the siren that calls you to your downfall."

"I told them I couldn't go," I said.

"That's not the same as saying you don't want to go. What kind of dance club permits people your age this late at night anyway? Well?" she demanded.

"It's called the Doll House. One of the boys is friendly with the owner and could get everyone in."

She looked at my father with that "I told you so" expression on her face.

"She didn't go," he said. "She didn't make up some lie and cover up her going."

My mother turned back to me and just stared for a moment until another thought blossomed in her eyes. "Were there any adults at the party during the evening?" she asked.

"No."

"Did you see anyone outside the house?"

"What?"

"Someone, a man, watching the house?"

"Felicia," my father said. She looked at him. He had a stern, unyielding look on his face.

She turned back to me again. "You can go to bed," she said, sitting back.

"Why do you always ask me if I've seen someone watching me, following me? Who is supposed to be doing that?"

"Don't question me," she snapped, her consonants and vowels so sharp I thought she might have cut her tongue on the words. "We told you. There are perverts out there, stalkers just waiting for someone as innocent and trusting as you."

"I'm not innocent and trusting."

"Why do you say that?"

"I'm not stupid, Mother."

"You think you know evil when you see it?" she asked, this time with a strange, wry smile. "Are you that familiar with deception, with all the seven deadly sins? Do you think you could survive on your own in the world out there?"

I looked at my uncle, hoping he might say something to support me, but he looked pensive and said nothing.

"No. You're right, Mother." I rose slowly. "Good night," I said. "Thank you again, Uncle Wade. Are you leaving early in the morning?"

He nodded.

"You'll be gone before I get up, won't you?" I asked him.

He smiled at my foresight. There was no need to put up a wall to protect himself from something so simple. "I'll be back soon. I promise."

"Okay."

He looked at my mother, and then he hugged me and kissed me on the cheek. I turned and hurried up to my room. My heart felt like a balloon bouncing in my chest. I was sure no other girl's parents would be cross-examining her about the party like mine just had, and even if other girls—or boys, even—were asked some of those questions, I doubted they would be as honest with their answers. Yet even though I was, I could see my mother wasn't satisfied. Perhaps she still feared that I was being conniving or manipulative. She was always looking for some evil motive in practically anything I did or said. What had I ever done to nurture that fear in her? Once again, I wondered why, if she was so paranoid about an orphan baby, she would have wanted to adopt one.

But tonight I wasn't going to be able to think about myself even if I wanted to very much.

Almost the moment I closed my eyes and my head settled on my fluffy pillow, that image of Cassie being held down by her father returned, only now, alone in my own darkness, it was even more vivid. The terror in her eyes was sharp. I shuddered and suddenly realized that I wasn't just visualizing something happening to someone else. It was happening to me! I had slipped into Cassie, taken her place in the event. I felt the pressure on my own wrists, the weight of his body on mine, and then the violation. The graphic experience brought a scream to my lips, but just as I had pictured this scene when I confronted Cassie at the party, I swallowed back that scream. It resonated deep inside me.

The most frightening thing was that I couldn't break out of it. I struggled, twisted and turned every which way, but I was trapped in my own vision. Never before had something I saw in my mind's eye, what Uncle Wade called my third eye, shackled me so firmly. I was as completely subdued as Cassie had been, probably many times. It wasn't until it had ended for her that it ended for me.

The moment it did, I sat up and turned on my table lamp. I needed the illumination to burn away the remnants of this horrid revelation. I rubbed my arms and legs as if I were washing off the sweaty lust that had smothered my resistance. I was still trembling inside. I had to stand up and walk around my room to calm myself. I paused at my mirror and looked at myself.

Yes, I saw myself as someone else many times, the most recent time being my birthday, when I envisioned myself being given exactly the same amber necklace my parents would give me, but I had been able to shake myself out of the nightmare. This was the first time I'd had a vision that threatened to steal me away, keep me in it.

Had whatever was wrong with me gotten worse, this condition of delusion? Would it get so bad that the time was coming when I really wouldn't be able to escape one of these visions? I would disappear, literally become someone else, somewhere else, either in the past or now, like someone with a multiple-personality syndrome suddenly trapped forever in one of them.

I had to go into my bathroom and wash my face in cold water. It helped. I felt myself calming down, but then I looked at my wrists in the mirror image and felt like I had stepped off a glacier and slipped into the icy Arctic Ocean. I was freezing from my ankles up, and when it reached the top of my head, I would shatter and fall into shards of myself on the floor of my bathroom.

There, suddenly, on both my wrists were black-and-blue marks resembling those that would come from someone much stronger squeezing me with a fierce, raging pressure as tightly as iron clamps.

I stepped away from the mirror, hoping the sight was just in the glass, but when I looked down, I saw the black-and-blue marks still there. I gasped and put my wrists under the cold running water, hoping that would wash them away. It didn't.

I was in a panic. I turned toward the door, intending to go out to my parents and my uncle for help, but I stopped. How could I explain this, what I had seen, without my mother accusing me of something even more evil? I had to get hold of myself, calm myself down. I swallowed back my terror and retreated to my bed. For a moment, I was afraid to turn off the lamp. Never before had the darkness frightened me like this. Where were my comforting voices when I needed them? I waited, hoping to hear some soothing whispers, but I heard nothing and felt nothing but the pounding of my own petrified heart.

I snapped off the lamp and looked into the darkness, waiting for my confidence to build enough for me to close my eyes. It was finally emotional exhaustion that shut them. Merciful sleep came rushing in over me like a warm ocean wave washing away the fear.

But I had no doubt that the fear would return.

7

The first thing I did the moment I awoke was look at my wrists. I was thankful to see that the black-and-blue marks were gone. I lay back on my pillow and wondered if I had imagined it all. It was something I could ask Uncle Wade, I thought, but then I suddenly felt his absence like a cold draft seeping through the windows. The warm comfort his presence had brought me was gone, and in its place was only this chilling trepidation. The one thing I didn't want to do, however, was reveal my feelings to my mother. I was sure she only would return to the questioning with the same policewoman's intensity with which she had attacked me on my return from the party last night. She might even think my obvious unease had more to do with something I had done at the party or something that had been done to me than it had to do with Cassie Marlowe, no matter what I said.

What could I say about Cassie's situation anyway? I had spent a good deal of the morning wondering

what, if anything, I should do about what I felt certain
I had discovered. Uncle Wade's cautions still echoed
in my ears, but my visions were too real to simply be
ignored. There had to be a way to help her.

Later, in the afternoon, I decided to call her. Her
father answered the phone on the first ring, as if he
was on constant duty to intercept anyone trying to
reach his daughter. She had told my girlfriends and me
that she wasn't permitted to have her own cell phone
or a landline number. She said her father believed that
half, if not more, of the problems with young people
today came from the time they wasted talking and
texting each other about nonsense.

One of the reasons Cassie was not popular with
other girls was the severe restrictions with which her
father had shackled her. It was as if other girls thought
that hanging around with her might infect them with
the same chains and constrict their activities and ruin
their young lives. Their parents might get similar ideas
and employ keys and locks where they had never used
them. Mia Stein said she thought Cassie might be just
the one to get the rest of us in trouble because she was
so envious of our freedom and fun. Jealousy, after all,
came with the territory teenagers inhabited. Celebrat-
ing someone losing an advantage or a privilege was
practically a team sport. I knew that was the main
reason Ginny was upset that she had to invite Cassie
to the party. Ginny feared that Cassie was just the sort
who might get her grounded once she had witnessed
what went on.

"Who is this?" Cassie's father demanded. I could

see him holding the phone the way a Neanderthal would hold a club, readying himself to pound my voice against the wall.

"Sage Healy, Mr. Marlowe. I wanted to talk to Cassie about our math homework, please."

He grunted. "Just a moment."

It took so long for her to come to the phone that I suspected he wasn't going to tell her I was calling and let me wait until I gave up, but she finally said hello in a tiny voice. I could almost feel her trembling through the phone. Was he standing right beside her?

"I thought we had a good time last night," I began. "I hope you enjoyed it."

"Oh, yes, I did."

"Maybe you and I can do something together next weekend. My father would drive us to the movies or—"

"I thought this was about math," I heard her father say. He had been listening in on another phone. My heart sank.

"I was just about to talk about math, sir," I said.

"You can talk about it in school," he replied. "Hang up, Cassie. Now!"

I heard the phone click. He remained on the other phone listening for me to hang up. I could hear him breathing. I decided to wait him out, and finally, he hung up, too. I held the receiver for a few moments, my ear buzzing and the heat in my face making me feel sunburnt. After I hung up, I sat there fuming.

He was destroying her, destroying his own daughter. The man was sick and cruel. I had to do something about this. For the rest of the weekend, I mulled over possible things I could do. Uncle Wade had been right. Without any tangible evidence and Cassie coming forward herself, what *could* I really do? But I wouldn't just give up. Twice my mother asked me why I was in such deep thought. Suspicions came out of her eyes, ears, and mouth like black bubbles.

And then she finally asked what I had expected she might.

"Did you tell us everything you should about that party?" she demanded. "Did you hold something back, something you did that we might find out? Are we going to find out from someone else? Well?"

"What else could I tell you? We danced, we ate, and we talked," I replied. "I told you some were drinking alcohol, and some passed around one of those drugs to make you high and wild, but no one was building bombs. Can't you stop making me feel like a terrorist every time I set foot out of this house?"

The words came out before I could stop them. I was trying to hide my deeper worry about Cassie with the tone of frustration and defiance in my voice. It set her back for a moment and sent her looking for my father. He returned with her, and they both simply stood looking at me as if they saw the early evidence of some Third World disease, a rash, spots, pimples on my face.

"What?" I finally had to ask.

"Your mother tells me you were snippy with her," my father said.

"I'm sorry if I sounded that way, but I don't know

why she's still asking me all these questions about the first real party I've ever gone to with others my age. How am I supposed to make any friends anywhere if I can't go anyplace they go or do anything they do? And then I have to rat on them like a narcotics agent or something."

"Rat on them?" my father said. I didn't think what I had said was so terrible, but they both looked like I had admitted to a murder.

"I can't help it that some of the kids do bad things, but I haven't done anything to give either of you reason to think I'm some kind of juvenile delinquent," I protested, the tears building under my lids.

They both continued to look at me as if I had bloodstains on my clothes and hands and was caught standing over a corpse. Neither spoke, so I continued.

"I don't go anywhere you don't want me to go. I don't get into trouble in school. My grades are very good. I never cheat or steal. I've never been disrespectful to my teachers, and yet I'm so restricted compared with anyone else in my class," I added, not mentioning Cassie, who was obviously chained down more.

"Satan was an angel before he fell," my mother said.

"What's that mean? You think I could be Satan or a fallen angel?"

"When you were little, you were always disrespectful, embarrassing us with those tall tales even though I forbade you to do it," she reminded me. "We had to send you to a therapist, remember?"

"But I'm not doing that now." I looked to my father for some relief, but he seemed unsure of what to say. He continued to study me. "I said I was sorry if I sounded snippy. I didn't do anything bad last night, but it seems I still have to deny it. I'll probably have to deny it for weeks."

I couldn't imagine any of my girlfriends being reprimanded for exhibiting just a little frustration and sarcasm in their voices when their parents spoke to them. In fact, the parents of most of my new friends probably would be grateful to know that was all the misbehavior they exhibited. Most, if not all, of those parents were unaware of how often their daughters smoked pot, took some Ecstasy or something similar, drank alcohol, were sexually active with boys, smoked in the girls' room, and generally lied about most places they went and things they did. Maybe my mother was right. I was so angelic that I had to fall sometime.

"We're not treating you unfairly, Sage. You're hardly old enough to be completely independent and free to do anything you please," my father finally commented in a calm tone. "We're responsible for you and your actions."

Was that commitment more than it was for natural parents? I wanted to ask. Did adopting me come with more responsibility for some reason? To whom else but themselves did they make these promises—some state official, or maybe my birth mother, whom I now believed they knew after all?

More than once, I had heard someone say, "You can't choose your relatives." But my parents could, and now that I thought about it, I could, too. I could decide one day that I'd had enough of them. When I was old enough, perhaps I could walk out that front door more easily than a natural child could. A natural child would still carry the mystery and the power of blood ties. She wouldn't be able to look at herself without being reminded of the parents left behind. Their hair, their eyes, the shapes of their faces, and even the sounds of their voices were indelibly written into her very soul.

But not me. I had no one I knew written on my soul in any way, shape, or form. I was like an offshoot of some meteor sailing independently through space, maybe blazing once and burning out on my descent to somewhere I never intended.

I didn't say anything, even though I wanted to continue to defend myself, to show some defiance. Yes, they had a parental right and obligation to know where I was going, whom I was seeing, and what I was doing, but did they have a right to know what I was thinking, too? Was I completely naked and forever exposed? Didn't every child, adopted or not, need some privacy?

"When your mother or I ask you questions, Sage, it's only out of the deep concern and love we have for you," my father said, filling the void of silence. "It's a parent's job, responsibility, and obligation to do that. It's just something natural for a parent to do. Anyone who doesn't place the welfare of his child ahead of his own is a dismal failure."

I looked down. I wished I were an angel, fallen or otherwise, and wings would sprout out of my back. I'd fly away instantly.

"I know there are parents who conveniently believe their children should sink or swim on their own, almost from the day they can walk and talk," he continued in that same reasonable, calm tone of voice that always made it difficult to dislike him or even argue with him. "Maybe their own parents treated them that way, but more than likely, they are too self-centered. It should be natural for parents to protect and nourish their children in every way possible, no matter how old their children are."

"Wild animals leave their offspring as soon as they can care for themselves," I said. "Some consume their own young. It's called filial cannibalism. Scientists believe they do it to ensure the production of healthier offspring."

I wasn't sure they understood what I was suggesting, but the moment I had learned about this in Mr. Malamud's science class, I recalled my mother's frequent threat to return me to the orphanage. She wasn't threatening to eat me, to kill me, but she was threatening to put me back in a place where I could easily fade away and, in a real sense, die. The very fact that she could conceive of doing that filled me with fear that she could do something even worse to me.

"We're not wild animals," my father said.

I looked at my mother. She didn't seem as willing to say that.

"If you're especially tired or something serious is bothering you, we want to know about it," my father added. He stepped forward to put his hand gently on my shoulder and then patted my hair and smiled.

"We're hoping you will always trust us enough to confide in us, Sage. Your trust is very, very important to us," he stressed. "It's actually our biggest worry. Can you appreciate that?"

"Yes," I said, my same budding tears turning from cold to warm, now coming more from my heart than my rage.

"Well, then?" he asked.

I looked at my mother. How did she do it? How could she look at me and see so deeply inside me, no matter how I tried to disguise it? "I trust you," I said, but I looked down instead of at him.

"No, you don't," my mother said. "You lied to me a while back. We both knew you had lied, and we waited to see if you would correct it, but you still haven't."

I looked up quickly. Uncle Wade had told them after all, I thought. That, more than anything, depressed me.

As if she could read my thoughts, however, my mother added, "No one had to tell us that, either. You're not as good as you think you are when it comes to disguising deceit."

Another girl my age would try to defend herself, perhaps pretend she knew nothing about it. She would twist and turn, looking this way and that, for an acceptable escape. She would feign innocence, act as if she had no idea why her parents would be so angry. Maybe she would turn the argument on her parents and accuse them of something, make them defensive. I'd overheard many girls talking about how they got away with things at home by doing just that. I didn't know if I was capable of doing something similar.

I always wondered if their mothers and fathers did the same sort of thing when they were their children's ages. Why wouldn't they recognize the deceptions and rationalizations? They had walked the same paths, had played the same parts, and were characters in similar stories. Did every young person live with the same fantasy, that their parents were perfect people? Didn't they ever hear their parents' friends say, "I hope my children never do what I did" or "They'd better not ever do what I did"?

My guess was that most of their parents pretended to believe them or let themselves be distracted to avoid a crisis. Was it Uncle Wade who once told me that you couldn't lie to a liar? Someone who's had a history of being deliberately deceptive recognizes the symptoms in someone else. I knew now that my parents hadn't told me the truth about myself or about themselves. That rule surely applied to them, if it applied to anyone, I thought. I might as well confess.

"I was afraid to tell you," I said.

My father stepped back. He looked at my mother, who nodded confidently like someone who wanted to remind someone else she had been right all along.

"Tell us what?" my father asked.

"One afternoon, Mother asked me if I had gone into your office to snoop. When you two were out of the house, I saw you had left a file drawer open, so I went in to look in the drawer. I was going to tell you soon."

"Soon?" my mother said skeptically.

"Yes. I told Uncle Wade about it. He thought I should have told you and that I should tell you soon."

My father's eyes narrowed, not with suspicion as much as with pain. I knew immediately that he was wondering why I trusted Uncle Wade to talk to more than I trusted him. I did feel very bad about it, but what was I going to tell him? The truth? That I didn't go to him because I was afraid he would tell my mother? If I couldn't keep secrets from them, they couldn't keep them from each other.

"Go on," my mother said. "You might as well tell us everything about it now."

I thought about the things that bothered me the most and decided to start with that. "I found the picture I once drew of my birth mother, a picture I gave you and you hid. There was a photograph with it, and the woman looked similar. I don't know how I drew it to look so similar, but is that a photograph of my birth mother?"

"Yes," my father said, before my mother could deny it.

"Then you did know her?"

"Yes."

"You didn't just find me in an orphanage at eight months old?"

"No. We told you that to make it less painful for you when you were old enough to understand. Even a little girl would be upset about it, and you've always been mentally beyond your years. We didn't mean it to be a hurtful lie. We were going to tell you all about it soon."

"Soon?" I fired back, sounding just like my mother.

"Your snooping made it sooner than we intended," my mother said, the corners of her mouth dipping.

"What else did you find?" my father asked, waving his right hand to shove aside that issue.

"There were pictures of two other children. Who were they?"

"Children who needed to be adopted. They had too many serious mental and emotional problems baked into them," my father said. Those were almost Uncle Wade's exact words. "We didn't think we could handle them. That's when we thought that if we were going to adopt a child, it would be better if it was an infant."

"I found my birth certificate. You told me you had lost it."

"We don't have your original birth certificate. We were going to reveal the one you found when we had explained it all to you," he said. "You probably saw diplomas and old photographs."

"Yes."

My mother looked at him sharply, her eyes suddenly two swirling orbs of cold fear.

He smiled. "Just things we did when we were younger, posing, going on movie sets."

"Why are they hidden in a drawer?"

He shrugged. "We have lots of old pictures in closets and boxes. Your mother doesn't like cluttering our house with them."

"I also found a small box full of strange things, bones."

"It was something your uncle brought back from one of his trips. He knows that we're both a little superstitious. It's the way we were brought up. It's not something we like people to know about us," he said. "That's why your mother gave you that amber necklace."

"And that rock with a hole when I was younger, the one she hung on my bed?"

"Exactly," he said.

"That garland of garlic, the knife I saw you put under one of the front steps, all of that?"

"Our superstitions. So you see, we can be foolish, too."

"Is that why you always hated my stories and dreams?" I asked my mother.

"Yes," she said, looking like she hated admitting it.

"And why you worry about me so much?"

"That's it," my father said. "Now, is there anything more you want to tell us?"

I wondered if I should mention anything about how I had closed the file drawer, but since I wasn't sure of that myself, I thought I had told them enough. They looked satisfied anyway. I shook my head.

"I hope this is the first and last time you keep something secret from us, Sage," my father said. "No matter what you do, what you hear or see, we'll be there for you first. Okay?"

I nodded. When I looked up, I saw that my mother was not as confident of it as he was. I couldn't blame her. After all, she had reason not to be. I wasn't telling them everything, and right now, I had no intention to. I was afraid that, like Uncle Wade, they would not only advise me not to think about it anymore but also forbid me to do anything.

And I had a plan I was now determined to follow.

What I had to do was push it as far back in my mind as I could, so that I wouldn't look like a plotter and my mother wouldn't realize there was something more. I avoided them both for the rest of the day by pleading too much homework. I found myself behaving just like any of the other girls by keeping my parents distracted.

"It's like all our teachers knew we were going to a party this weekend," I moaned at dinner.

"I'm sure none of them expected you to leave it to the last moment," my mother said. "You should have done most of it the day of the party."

"Probably," I said.

They both seemed to buy my act this time. But I couldn't help wondering. Were they just playing along to see how far I would go? Even though they told me things they had hidden from me, I still felt there was more, lots more.

I went up to my room after dinner, ostensibly to do this neglected schoolwork, but I had really done just about all of it. I had started to read ahead in my history text when I had a phone call. It was Ginny. I was both surprised and grateful that she was calling me after I had disappointed her.

"You missed a great time after the party," she said.

"Half the time, I found myself defending you, but I think most of the girls bought your excuse for not coming with us."

"It wasn't an excuse. It was the truth. This was the first party without adult supervision I've been permitted to attend. If I didn't obey the curfew, it would be a long time before I would be able to go to another."

"Whatever. Everyone wants to give you another chance, especially the boys. Until now, we've all been impressed with how smart you are. You give good advice, but you should try not to sound like someone's mother or grandmother when you do it. And don't waste your time with that Cassie Marlowe. She's a loser with a capital L."

"I feel sorry for her."

"Yeah, well, feel sorrier for yourself. You have more boys after your bod than any of us. Jason was the most pathetic about it. He was actually crying real tears when he started talking about you. Of course, that might have been the X he took," she added with a laugh. "He claims you're like a bullfighter."

"Bullfighter?"

"A moving target. You hold up promises like a red cape, but as soon as he charges, you pull them away. It was hysterical. He fell asleep the whole way home. Anyway, we're planning on doing something this weekend again. We'll talk about it tomorrow. And remember," she added, "stop being someone's therapist. If you have to give anyone advice, give it to us." She laughed again and hung up.

I lay back on my pillow, thinking. A part of me

wanted to be what Ginny had described, concerned more about myself. It was what Uncle Wade had advised, wasn't it? And I had little doubt it would be what my parents would advise if they knew enough about what I had been planning.

Later, when I started to get ready to sleep, I heard that dark voice whispering. It was that different-sounding voice again, deeper, darker than the voices that would comfort me. It was coming from the far right corner of the room, where there was that shadow that shouldn't be there because it was so lit up.

I was thinking maybe I would listen, but then another voice came from another corner of my room. It was louder, stronger, and more familiar. It was a voice I always had trusted.

And it changed my mind again.

"Everything your parents told you today about what you found in the file drawer," it began, "was a lie."

8

One of the special gifts Uncle Wade had brought back for me after one of his magic tours was a quill pen he had found in another antiques store he had discovered. This time, it was when he had free time in London. He said the quill was from the early nineteenth century, and although there were no identifying letters, marks, or symbols on it, he claimed it had once belonged to Samuel Taylor Coleridge, the famous poet. As with most everything he found in antiques stores, he also assured my parents and me that it was far more valuable than the store owner knew. It was another one of his rare finds.

"Use it only on a special occasion," he told me. "It has magical qualities. Anything this old does."

It didn't take me long to realize that he favored things from way in the past, whether it was furniture, clocks, knives, mirrors, anything, as long as it was at least a hundred years old. Time was full of mystery, and mysteries were full of magic.

Other girls my age probably would laugh at him and put whatever he had given them aside and rarely, if ever, look at it, much less use it. And when they were older and received these presents like I did, they would accept such gifts to be polite, but they would be full of skepticism about their origins and even feel disappointment, maybe even a little foolish. Who my age wanted to brag to her friends that she had a hand mirror once used by some important French baroness or one glove worn by Catherine the Great? What friends of mine would be impressed or even give it a second look, especially my new friends? If they didn't say it, they would certainly think it. "Couldn't your uncle have brought back something contemporary that was pretty to wear?"

But none of them had someone like Uncle Wade, who had an energy about him like no other man I had met, including my father. It was difficult to be skeptical about things he claimed when you could witness him performing acts that seemed to defy the laws of physics. The ability to do these things gave him a wisdom, a real power to convince anyone of anything, most of all me.

I had used the magic quill to write my parents birthday wishes. When I picked up the quill and dipped it in the ink, the right words did seem to come magically, words that impressed and pleased them. But this time, it was going to be very different. I was using it to write something terrible, something that would bring a lot of pain, trouble, and turmoil. Nevertheless, it felt right to use it for this purpose.

One of the magical things it did, I thought, was change my handwriting to such a dramatic extent that no one, no handwriting expert, could compare my regular handwriting with it and confirm that it was I who had written it. I wore the pair of white silk gloves Uncle Wade had given me years ago, too, gloves he also claimed were worn by an Italian countess in the eighteenth century. There would be no fingerprints on the paper or the envelope. For now, I wanted anonymity. Obviously, if my parents found out I had delivered this letter to the school nurse, they would be enraged. I had no doubt of that.

Dear Mrs. Mills, I wrote to the school nurse.

I am writing to you as a friend of Cassie Marlowe. I know that anonymous letters like this immediately raise the suspicion that the author is just trying to cause someone else trouble and embarrassment, but please believe me when I tell you that I am not afraid for myself as much as I am for my family if I revealed my identity.

Nevertheless, I am even more terrified for Cassie Marlowe, because I believe she can't go on much longer suffering what she is suffering. I fear for her very life.

Cassie Marlowe is being sexually abused by her own father. You can begin by asking her about the black-and-blue marks on her arms. If you can win her trust, she will tell you what is happening to her. I am sure she will reveal the truth. She is rarely permitted to have anything to do socially with kids her age, and when it is absolutely impossible to prevent it, she

is severely restricted. She's almost made to avoid hav-
ing friends. There is an ugly reason for this, why she is
practically a prisoner in her own home.

Please look into this before it is too late for her. I
am sure you and the school authorities can help her. It
won't take you long to see that I am right.

A worried friend.

I wrote Mrs. Mills's name on the envelope. I knew
just when and how I could slip it under her office
door at school. I put it into my book bag along with
my gloves to wear when I took it out and delivered
it. Even if nothing came of this, I thought, I would
feel better having tried to help rather than doing what
Ginny had suggested and forgetting about Cassie and
thinking more of myself.

Besides, if Uncle Wade was right and I had the
third eye, I had an obligation to use it. That thinking helped me persuade myself to go through with
it. When I saw Cassie in school the next morning, I
immediately realized she was even more standoffish
and meeker than she had been before the party. Both
Danny and Peter seemed to have the same impression
and said so. She wouldn't talk very much and avoided
the three of us before lunch hour. I noticed two additional black-and-blue marks on both her wrists, the
marks I had seen on myself when I'd had that extraordinary vision experience.

Later, just at the start of lunch when I knew the
hallway in front of the administration offices was
emptier than at other times, I approached the nurse's
office. Careful not to be seen, I put on my gloves, dug

into my purse to pluck out the envelope, and slipped it under Mrs. Mills's door. I fled instantly, my heart thumping. I almost forgot to take off my gloves before entering the cafeteria. I was a little behind everyone else in my class. Ginny and the girls were already seated, and they all looked up at me when I entered. I saw that Danny and Peter were sitting with Cassie, but she looked so afraid I thought she might burst into tears and charge out of the cafeteria.

It was very hard for me to do it, but I went to sit with the girls rather than with them. It occurred to me that the more I was seen with Cassie right now, the more chance there was that the nurse would be able to accuse me of writing the note. For a moment or two, I felt sorry for Danny and Peter. They would come under suspicion more than anyone else, just because they were befriending her, but their denials would be credible because they were truly innocent. What's more, unless Cassie was telling them the ugly truth, which I very much doubted, the entire idea would be shocking to them. Anyone would be able to see that they had no knowledge of anything similar to what was happening to her.

"Glad you're coming to your senses," Ginny said when I brought my tray to the table with her and the other girls. Mia moved over quickly to make a place for me.

"We had a bet that you would go sit with the losers," Darlene said. "I was the only one to have it right. See? I still believe in you."

"Why did you spend so much time with them at Ginny's party?" Kay asked.

"They're not so terrible," I said, buttering my bread and then looking at Ginny. "Actually, Danny and Peter are pretty intelligent. I think some of you know that more than others," I added. "Just ask Ginny."

Her eyes widened and brightened with indignation. "They have big mouths," she said. Everyone looked at her and then at me. I continued to eat.

"What?" Darlene asked her.

"They helped me with some homework," Ginny muttered. "Big deal."

"And tests," I added.

She sent fire at me through her eyes but then shrugged. "God helps those who help me," she muttered, and laughed.

"Oh, so that's why you invited them," Mia said. "We were all wondering."

"One hand washes the other," I muttered.

"What?" Darlene said. "Where do you come up with these expressions?"

I shrugged. "Reading, I guess. It's something you do with a thing called a book."

"Very funny," Mia said, but she was sincerely smiling. "I think I heard my grandmother say that," she added.

"My grandmother is a fanatical Rolling Stones groupie," Kay said. "She'd rather be caught dead than show her age."

"The Rolling Stones aren't kids. She *is* showing her age," I offered.

Mia laughed again.

"What's with Cassie Marlowe? You must know more about her than anyone in the school. You spent all that time with her. Why did her mother leave her and her father?" Ginny asked.

"I don't know all that much about her," I said defensively. "I didn't get too personal with her. At your party, she looked like she would shatter if I did."

"Second that," Kay said.

"Have you ever seen her father?" Darlene offered. "He looks like Boris Karloff."

"Who's Boris Karloff?" Kay asked her. I think she knew but was teasing her.

Everyone turned to Darlene.

"An actor who was in lots of old horror movies," she replied.

"Showing your age!" we all cried together, and then everyone laughed.

It really was fun being with them. I breathed a sigh of relief, thinking they had almost given up on me right from the beginning. Would it always be this way for me? Would I always have to struggle more than anyone else to have friends? Could I blame it all on my parents? Or was there something about me, something I hadn't fully realized yet myself, that made close friendships impossible? I knew I was timid about looking too far into anyone's future, and maybe that was why I was always going to be just a little outside, a little too standoffish.

"Anyway," Ginny said, "let's stop talking about them. There's more important news."

"What?" Kay asked.

"Jason thinks he's going to have his house free this Friday night. His parents and his younger brother are going to Albany to his grandparents'."

"Why isn't he going?" I asked.

"They think he is, but Friday afternoon, he's coming down with a head cold," she said, smiling. "Look, we know you're on a tighter leash than the rest of us. We've all been through something like that, when we were younger. You tell your parents we're all meeting at the mall and going to a movie and then pizza afterward. We'll figure it out this week. Jason won't have the party unless you can come," she added.

All the girls looked at me like I might spoil their fun.

"Unless I come? Why?"

"How come you are so smart about everything but yourself?" Kay asked. "He has a thing for you. You know what a thing is, right?"

Everyone was smiling at me.

"I'll try," I said. "I mean, I'll really try."

"Good."

Everyone looked up when Mrs. Mills entered the cafeteria. I had forgotten that she sometimes ate her lunch in her office and not in the faculty room. I was lucky she hadn't seen the envelope slipped under her door instantly and seen me walking away. She panned the room. Some of the students quieted down, but most didn't pay much attention to her.

"What does she want?" Kay asked. "Someone need a tampon?"

"I hope someone else in this school isn't pregnant. When that happens, my mother goes ballistic every time I go out," Darlene said. "And Todd isn't exactly Donnie Osmond."

"Who?" Kay teased.

Everyone but me smiled, especially when Mrs. Mills's gaze fell on Cassie. It was clear that was who she was looking for. She started quickly toward her, Danny, and Peter. She was all smiles, but she said something to Cassie that made her nod and lower her head quickly.

"Maybe she has some contagious disease," Ginny said. "We'll all have to be inoculated since I had to invite her to my party. Damn. I'll blame my mother."

Mrs. Mills walked out. I watched Cassie carefully. She didn't finish what she had to eat, but Danny said something to her that pleased her, and she rose, gathered her books, and left the cafeteria.

"I forgot to tell you guys," Mia said when everyone returned to eating. "I think we're getting a new student."

"Boy or girl?" Kay asked.

"Definitely a boy. I only saw him for a few seconds, but he looked like he was auditioning for *GQ* or something. He was wearing a dark blue sports jacket and a light blue tie. He had ink-black hair as long as Jason's but not stringy and wild. It was styled. He had the cutest dimple in his left cheek and wore a very expensive-looking gold watch."

"You saw all that in only a few seconds?" Kay asked her.

"When it comes to great-looking boys, I have a photographic memory," she bragged.

"Well, how come he's not here?" Ginny asked, gesturing at the students in the cafeteria. "Maybe you didn't see that well. Maybe he's one of those student teachers we get sometimes from the teachers' college."

"I don't think so," Mia said, but I could see she wasn't positive, and the possibility was upsetting her.

"If he dresses like that and he's not a student teacher, he'll be persona non grata with the boys in this school," Ginny said.

"Excuse me? Persona what?" Darlene asked her.

"Persona non grata. Someone not welcome."

"Who taught you that expression?" Kay asked, turning her suspicious gaze on me.

I shook my head. "Sounds like something Peter Murphy might have taught her," I offered. They all looked at her for confirmation.

She laughed. "One hand washes the other," she said, winking at me. "See? I can come up with Granny expressions, too."

Was that really how I sounded? How did I keep my unexplainable memories from shaping and coloring who I was? Or was that who I truly was, some combination of the old and the new, someone who would never fit in? Right now, I didn't want to think about it. There was a bigger concern.

On the way out, I caught up with Peter and Danny.

"Why did Mrs. Mills come looking for Cassie?" I asked them.

"Something about her health records that might not be correct. No big deal."

"She looked upset," I said. "Was she upset?"

They looked at each other.

"No more than usual," Danny said. "I spent most of lunch hour helping her with the math homework. She said she had forgotten to do it. I couldn't get it all done before she left with the nurse, but I told her I would have it for her before math class."

I nodded. That was what I had told her father when he wanted a reason for my calling, our math homework. Did he make such a big deal out of it that she had deliberately avoided it? Maybe she thought if she got a bad grade for not having it done, she would make him regret forcing her to hang up on me. I could easily imagine the games she had to play to get him to give her room to breathe.

Just thinking about that brought new disturbing images into my mind. I saw him coming in on her while she was taking a bath and insisting that he wash her back but intending to do more. Every lock on every inside door in her house was inoperable. She had no privacy anywhere, anytime. Some nights, he made her sleep with him naked.

All of this flashed before me as I walked through the hallway, half listening to Peter and Danny argue about the meaning of Coleridge's poem *Kubla Khan*.

It didn't occur to me until after I entered my classroom that according to Uncle Wade, I had just used

Coleridge's quill in an attempt to save Cassie Marlowe. Coincidences didn't exist to Uncle Wade's way of thinking and were starting to disappear to my way of thinking, too. Everything was meant to be, had a purpose and a design.

After the flow of those disturbing sexual images I had envisioned, it was difficult for me to concentrate on the lesson in history class. I kept looking at Cassie's empty desk and anticipating her entrance any moment, but it never happened. My curiosity and concern grew stronger. Did she become hysterical when Mrs. Mills asked her about her black-and-blue marks? Did she reveal anything, or was she so terrified of what her father might do that she went into shock? Did they have to take her somewhere else, to a doctor? Could it be that they called the police?

In my heart of hearts, even though I wanted the police to get involved, I couldn't help but feel sorry for her and what she would go through. Of course, I wondered if I had done the right thing. And then I wondered if my letter wasn't magical after all, if somehow my words became more than words. Maybe they became images like they did for me. Maybe they empowered Mrs. Mills so she could picture the horror Cassie was enduring. If that happened and I had succeeded, I wondered if I should ever tell Uncle Wade how his quill lived up to what he had promised. Would he be happy I had that third eye, or would he worry more about me and tell my parents, who would then be enraged that I had kept another secret?

Cassie didn't attend the next class, either. Just

before the last period of the day, Kay hurried up to the rest of us entering the room. She was flushed with excitement and looked like she would burst if she didn't get her words out quickly.

"Cassie Marlowe was taken out of school by a social worker and a policewoman," she reported. "Something really weird is going on."

"Something was always really weird about her," Ginny said. She looked at me. "Right?"

"There have to be reasons for why she is like she is," I said.

"What reasons?"

The bell rang for us to be in our seats.

"Reasons," I replied cryptically. She smirked, and we all sat. I was the only one whose mind was a million miles away when we were told to open our textbooks.

Cassie would be saved from her horrific situation at home, I told myself. That was good, but really, how did I do it? Why was I able to do it? Why hadn't her teachers, the nurse, and other administrators been able to see what was happening to her? Why just me? Sometimes I'd thought Uncle Wade was teasing me with all those references to the mystical third eye, but maybe it was true.

How should this make me feel? I wondered. Did I want this power? Did I want to be so different from everyone else? I was already different from every other girl in my class because I was adopted. I honestly didn't believe anyone thought less of me because of that. Once my classmates got over the initial typical questions like whether I knew who my birth parents were, they never mentioned it again. If there was any complaint about me, it was similar to the complaints I had heard from Ginny after her party. I was too conservative, acting too old for my age. Even Uncle Wade had accused me of that.

That was something I could blame on my adoptive parents. All my life, they had made me so self-conscious about anything I had done that could be thought extraordinary, whether describing some of my visions or asking too many questions. I grew up with my parents expecting me to show signs of misbehavior and my mother especially pouncing on the slightest indication. Why shouldn't I have turned out too conservative for my classmates? How could I overcome that? Go out and do something absolutely forbidden, deliberately get into serious trouble? Would that finally satisfy them?

It wasn't until nearly dinnertime that I learned anything more about Cassie. Someone, perhaps one of the secretaries in the administrative offices, told Kay Linder's mother why Cassie had been removed from school and taken off in a police vehicle. Probably nanoseconds after Kay learned about it from her mother, she was on the phone or texting the other girls. Ginny wanted to be the first to tell me. There was a note of remorse in her voice. Like most everyone else, she had condemned Cassie too quickly, too eagerly, and now felt guilty about it.

"Cassie has been sexually abused by her own father! Did you know about it?" she asked me after she rattled off the headline.

"She didn't tell me, if that's what you mean."

"Yeah, but you seemed to know more. When I said there was something weird about her, you said there had to be reasons."

"People can be shy, but Cassie was more than just shy," I said.

"One of these days, you're going to have to tell me why you're so much wiser than the rest of us. The truth is, everyone thinks there's a lot more mystery to you than you reveal. Did you have different parents before the Healys?"

"Only my biological ones, whom I have never met," I said.

"Did something really dramatic happen to you at your old school? Is that why your parents transferred you to ours?"

"I'm not a veteran of anything that would give me more insight into someone being sexually abused by her own father, Ginny. Nothing like that happened to me."

"Sorry, but we're trying to find out how Mrs. Mills found out about it. Kay's mother didn't know."

"Maybe she was just doing her job well. If anyone should have the ability to spot something like this, it would be Mrs. Mills, don't you think?"

"Maybe," she said, but not with much confidence.

"What's the difference, anyway? Who cares how Mrs. Mills realized it? The main thing is that Cassie's been saved."

"As much as anyone can be after all that. She's going to be in some special therapy. She won't be at our school anymore. Maybe they'll find her mother, and her mother will take her back. I wish I would have known. I would have . . ."

"What?"

"I don't know. Done something. Let's try to forget about it," she added quickly. "It gives me the chills. Her father looks like a cross between a frog and a snake. Thinking about him makes me want to vomit up lunch. I hope they . . ."

"Burn him at the stake?"

"What? Yeah. Something like that. Stop talking about him."

I laughed. "I'm not. You are."

"Concentrate on the weekend and the party at Jason's. Start working on your parents. Say we're all going to a movie and for pizza."

"What movie?"

"Oh. Wait a minute. Let me look on the Internet," she said, and after a minute came back. "*Ruby*, the one about the Cajun girl who's a twin. I actually want to see that. I have the novel. I'll give it to you so you'll know something about the story." She paused. "You're not too good at lying about stuff, are you?"

"Terrible."

"Pretend you're actually going to do it, Sage. Get yourself to believe it, and then it's easier to convince someone else. That's what I do. See you tomorrow. Oh," she said just as I was going to hang up, "that handsome boy Mia saw today?"

"Yes?"

"He definitely is a new student, and he's in our

class. We already know his name. Get this: Summer Dante. And how's this? Just like Cassie, he has no mother. He's living only with his father. No brothers or sisters. One in, one out, but something tells me *he's* not going to be shy," she added.

"You're better than CNN," I said.

She laughed. "And you're better than Dr. Phil."

The conversation that had begun with heavy news turned into laughter and some intrigue.

Who was Summer Dante, and what had happened to his mother?

Put that aside for now, I told myself. *Concentrate on the weekend and being as good a liar as Ginny and the others.* It was almost a requirement to be accepted by them. How they could trust each other knowing that they were all capable of being so false amazed me. Perhaps it was just honor among thieves or something.

Or maybe they really believed in their hearts that everyone was dishonest, that everyone lied. I thought about a reference I had just read to Diogenes, the Greek philosopher who helped create the philosophy of cynicism. Supposedly, he went around with a lantern searching for an honest man.

Was it a fruitless search? Would I look just as foolish if I didn't accept the same rules my girlfriends lived by?

Maybe my mother was right after all by anticipating my doing something evil and dishonest. Maybe once I had done so successfully, I would be addicted to it. I would be better at it than Ginny or any of them.

"Once you take a bite of the apple, it's difficult to avoid eating it all," my mother would say. "If you do and you stop, you're one kind of person, a special kind of person. If you don't stop, you're like most people, and how far you fall depends entirely on how much of the apple you consume."

How much would I consume? Maybe she was right. Maybe that would be the final clue to discovering who I really was.

9

At dinner, when I mentioned going to the movies with my girlfriends and then out to have some pizza, I expected my mother would absolutely refuse to permit it, but apparently, she and my father had discussed my behavior at Ginny's party and how sensible I had been, because she didn't say no before my words were spoken, as she often did. The more my father praised me for how I had handled being at Ginny's party, the guiltier I felt about lying now, even though I had successfully done what Ginny had suggested, rationalized with myself that I might not be lying at all, that this might be all we would do. The party wasn't a sure thing yet. I could lie to myself first and then behave as if that were the truth.

This shouldn't have surprised me. Often it was easier to convince yourself of something than it was to convince others. In the end, everyone believes what he or she wants to believe. Facts and evidence melt away like icicles on the first day of spring under the heat of what you are determined will be true no matter what.

Anyway, neither of my parents seemed to pick up on my deception, and after the way they had picked up on the filing cabinet, I thought they might. Maybe I was just getting better at it. I had made it all sound so casual and ordinary. All my friends were going. It was just something for us girls to do together. My father was nodding, so I added, "It helps bond us, make us all closer friends."

"Sure. Why wouldn't girls enjoy just being with each other sometimes?" my father agreed. "Girls' night out. Show the boys you don't need them around all the time. Female independence." He looked at my mother. "Didn't you want that?"

"Times were different," she muttered.

"Times are always different," he replied.

I looked more closely at my mother. She didn't disagree. For a moment or two, she was really lost in her own thoughts, perhaps recalling her youth and regretting not doing enough with her own girlfriends when she had the opportunities. Maybe she wasn't always as serious as she was now, or she was wishing she wasn't. Thinking deeply about that might loosen her up, I hoped. She might want me to have more fun than she did when she was my age. Before he had left, Uncle Wade could very well have lectured them both, mostly her. I could hear the words as if I had been a fly on the wall.

"Stop worrying about her," he must have said. "Let her be a girl her age. Let her explore and make her own discoveries. She's wrapped too tightly. That usually results in just the opposite of what you intended for her."

I was sure he was convincing. Maybe I didn't have to lie as much as I thought I did. Maybe they would have permitted me to go to another house party if I had been honest and told them what our real intentions were, but it was too late.

"Can I stay out at least until midnight this time?" I asked. "It's embarrassing having to be the first one to go home, especially when everyone else can stay out that late."

My mother looked at me in that intense way she often did, her eyes smaller, darker, her lips tightened with disapproval, and shook her head before she took on that all-too-familiar cold, cynical smile. "You know people don't give the devil his due. He's no fool. He's clever."

"Stop it, Felicia," my father said under his breath.

"How cleverly he uses logic to worm his way into our souls," she continued, ignoring him.

"What does this have to do with the devil? I'm just going out with my new girlfriends, doing what girls my age do. Nobody trusts someone who's so restricted. They think she'll get them into trouble by complaining to her own parents, who will then go to theirs," I added, using the argument the others had used against befriending Cassie.

My mother sighed and sat back, now looking like she was the one overwhelmed. "It's up to you," she told my father.

"All right. I'll drop you off at the mall and pick you up at midnight where I dropped you off and no later. I don't want to have to go looking for you. This is a bigger test, Sage. We're interested in how you handle yourself when you're on your own. You know what's right and what's wrong. You're a very bright young woman. You know there are others who will try to get you to do bad things. Sometimes kids your age do them just to be accepted. It's not worth it if that's the only way you'd be accepted."

"I know."

For a moment, as the reality set in, the two of them looked absolutely terrified, and for the first time it occurred to me that if they failed with me as they had with the first two children they had taken in, they would have to suffer something very unpleasant, that maybe they were looking out both for themselves and for me. Perhaps they were being tested somehow, and it wasn't only me.

I always wondered why they sounded like they had an obligation to someone else. I thought it might even be a deeper sense of responsibility to my birth mother, that they really had spent more time with her than they had suggested and made promises that would make them feel guilty and terrible if they failed to keep them. I thought about what Uncle Wade had told me. Perhaps they hadn't met the mothers of the previous orphans and weren't as emotionally involved with them as they were with me.

How sad for them. They never mentioned them to me because they must have been so devastated.

Suddenly, I was now thinking I was the one who owed the responsibility to them. I could fail them, and that would mean more. This was really unfair, I thought. What girl my age had so much pressure on her to do well, to behave like an angel? It deprived me of the carefree innocence and joy that were so much a part of being young. Yet I shouldn't be so surprised about it, I thought. All my life, they were telling me I was old enough to know better. Simply put, they never wanted me to go through puberty and adolescence. They wanted me to be an adult almost as soon as I could walk and talk.

I couldn't help feeling a little sorry for them. Raising children was like running through a war zone, worrying about minefields and holding your breath whenever your children did anything on their own. News of accidents befalling them and others their age, possibilities of misbehavior, the influence of their peers, exploration of drugs and alcohol to keep up with the crowd, speeding in cars, or being the victims of random violence like what was streamed into homes through television and radio news, newspapers, and telephone calls—it got to the point where parents trembled when they opened their doors and when they permitted any unsupervised activities.

But then again, I thought, what other girl in my group would worry so much about this? If I were even to mention such things, they would shriek at me like angry wildcats. I would be making them all feel guilty, preaching at them.

"Become a nun," Kay or Ginny might say.

And I would be devoured by their total indifference to my very existence. Nothing more was said about the upcoming weekend. This morning, my father drove me to school and surprised me with the news that an uncle and an aunt of his were going to pay us a visit very soon. He had never mentioned either of them. I asked him why he hadn't. I really wanted to ask why neither he nor my mother talked very much about any of their family, why asking questions about them was harder than pulling teeth.

"Uncle Alexis is what is normally called the black sheep of the family. He had little to do with our family after he left home on his eighteenth birthday. My grandfather and he were like oil and water. He and my father got along a little better, but my father usually sided with my grandfather."

"What did they fight about?"

"Uncle Alexis always wanted to have a career in the military. My grandfather wanted him to go into business or some profession like law, but Uncle Alexis went off and enlisted as soon as he was old enough. Even though he rose in rank and became an officer, my grandfather never forgave him. My father got along with him, but he didn't get in the middle of it. Most of the time, Uncle Alexis was stationed somewhere out of the country. I saw him only a half dozen times, if that. No one went to his wedding when he married Aunt Suzume."

"Suzume?"

"She's Japanese. Her name means 'sparrow,' and she's like a sparrow, small, graceful, and very beautiful.

She has a face that belongs on a cameo. They met in Japan when he was stationed there for a while. They have no children," he added quickly before I could ask. "With Uncle Alexis's lifestyle, they decided against it."

"Do they know about me?"

"Absolutely. I always liked Uncle Alexis and kept in touch with him as much as I could. He's a typical army general, but once you get past his snip-snap, as I like to call it, you find a decent chap."

"I look forward to meeting him."

"We'll practice saluting," he said, smiling.

"Really?"

"Just kidding, although I always felt like I should whenever I did see him."

He smiled at me, and for the first time in a long time, I felt sincere father-daughter warmth between us. It should have made me feel better, but it didn't. It made me feel worse, because I was going to deceive him this weekend. I was sure no one else felt so bad about betraying a parent's trust.

Almost as soon as I got to school, I sensed the excitement in the air. All of it was coming from my knot of friends intertwined in one another's laughter and smiles at Ginny's hall locker. I hurried up to them, and they all turned, all with one gleeful face.

"What?"

"Summer Dante made a big point to say good morning to each and every one of us, as if he knew us all our lives or something," Mia said, her breasts rising and falling as she gasped between her words. "He's in our class. He's a sophomore. I thought he was older, at least a junior. He's absolutely . . ." She looked at a loss for words. "Absolute!"

I perused all their faces. How could any boy be so handsome and charming that he struck such a note in the hearts of all of them so quickly? They were behaving as if he was a rock star.

"He wasn't wearing a jacket and tie," Kay said, with audible relief in her voice. "He was dressed really cool in this coal-black shirt and black jeans, with the sharpest-looking black shoe boots I've ever seen. They had splashes of crystals on the back."

"Not just jeans. Very tight black jeans," Ginny added. "He looked poured into them as if they were a mold of him from the waist down."

"They're hip huggers," Darlene said. "So it would be from below the waist down."

"Excuse me," Ginny fired back. "I didn't take his measurements as quickly as you did."

"You mean you wish you did," she replied. "Maybe he didn't give you time enough. Maybe he spent more time with me."

Ginny pressed her lips together and slammed her locker closed.

What was going on here? Were they already competing for Summer Dante, competing so intently that they'd sacrifice one another on some altar of romance? Was all truly fair in love and war? I had been attracted to these girls because they were like a knot, tight, ready to risk almost anything for one another and so in sync that they practically ate and slept simultaneously.

Everyone at school, even the older girls, recognized that there was something special about them, and everyone was jealous of their friendship, a friendship that they wore like dog collars around their necks. It was why I was so intent on becoming one of them and so depressed that I might have failed.

"What about Todd?" I asked Darlene.

"Todd who?" she replied, and they all laughed.

"Wait until you see Summer Dante's eyes. I've never looked into eyes like his," Mia said. "I swear, those ebony orbs were swirling."

"Or yours were swirling," Kay said. "Mine were," she confessed without hesitation or embarrassment. "I felt like I was . . ."

"Like you were what?" I demanded. They were beginning to annoy me. No boy could be this compelling.

"Like I was falling into them, helpless. I think I would have done anything he wanted right then and there. I can't explain it."

They all turned strangely silent, falling into their own memories, reliving a few moments with Summer Dante. For a moment, I wondered if he could hypnotize people as well as Uncle Wade could.

"He doesn't float or something, does he?" I asked. "His feet hit the ground when he walks, right?"

Indignation washed across their faces as if I had spoken blasphemy about a real American hero or a biblical one.

"Wait until you meet him, smartass," Kay said. "We'll see if you don't drool."

"Well, I hope I do," I said, smiling. "You all seem so pleased."

"So pleased?" Darlene mimicked. "Pleased? I don't think that's the word I'd use. It's more than pleased."

"It's an orgasm," Ginny said, finally breaking the intense mood. She laughed. "Practically. I mean, I'm speaking for myself when I say practically. One of you might have had one."

"I won't be the first to tell," Kay said.

"Boys can pop their corks quickly, but girls are better off," Mia said, as though she were the authority on sexual relationships. "We keep popping," she added, and everyone laughed. I did, too.

Good humor returned, and we started for homeroom.

"I thought none of you would go out with a boy in our class," I said.

"Somehow I can't think of him as just another boy in our class," Mia said. "He's too sophisticated."

"And you know this that quickly?"

"I have a sixth sense when it comes to that," she offered. "We all do."

Nobody disagreed.

"How does it look for this weekend?" Ginny asked, stepping up closer to me.

"I'm in."

"How much do they know?"

"Only what I know for sure—the mall, a movie, and pizza afterward."

"Very clever. See, it works. Believe your own lies first."

I nodded, clinging to the idea that it was still not a lie since the party wasn't confirmed.

"Oh, and I have until midnight this time."

"You're a regular Cinderella," she said. "Good work. We'll get you straightened out yet."

Will you? I wondered. *Or will you bring me so far down I'll never get up, not in my parents' eyes?* We sauntered in and took our seats. For a moment, I didn't realize it until I saw where all my friends were looking. Summer Dante was in Cassie's seat. I had the chilling feeling that he was somehow destined to be there, destined to replace her.

He sat with perfect posture and didn't look at anyone. His hands were clasped before him on his desk. I couldn't take my eyes off him, first because his sitting there brought home the reality that Cassie was gone, off into some therapeutic fog, working to bring herself back into the sunshine, and second because there was an aura about him that was both pleasing and dangerous.

Suddenly, he broke his perfect form by turning sharply in my direction and stabbing me with his eyes. I think I gasped audibly. He had turned just the way I might if I had felt someone was looking at me intently. There was that tiny sting at the base of my neck whenever I felt that, and I was always right. Someone was staring at me. Now I was caught doing the same thing. I felt my face flush with embarrassment.

The girls hadn't exaggerated about his striking good looks. His beautifully formed full lips softened instantly into smoothly tanned firm cheeks. I couldn't turn away. He nodded at me, and I rolled my eyes away like a fighter pilot might roll his plane to escape an attack. I was grateful for the relief the day's announcements brought. I could catch my breath.

When the bell rang, we all rose with the same hopeful expectation: Summer Dante would gravitate toward one of us to walk through the halls to our first class. It would be like putting on a valuable jewel, eye candy, evoking green envy from the eyes of every other girl in the school.

Out of the corner of my eye, I saw Darlene shake Todd off. It didn't take a genius to see why she was being cool to him so suddenly, and I knew he was hurt and angry. He glared at Summer Dante and fell back as Darlene, wearing her inviting smile as obvious as a car's front bumper, slowed when she reached Summer first. He barely acknowledged her, made a sharp turn to his left, and fell back to speak to our homeroom teacher. Disappointment fell like a window shade across Darlene's face as she caught up with the rest of us.

"I'm curious," I said. "You were so enamored of Todd Wells that you're still wearing red this morning." I nodded at the red ribbon in her hair.

"So?"

"What happened to your being so desperate for Todd's affections?"

"Summer Dante happened," she replied without the slightest bit of shame.

Everyone but me smiled with approval.

"So you're no longer interested in Todd?"

"Why? Are you going to chase after him now?"

"No. I was just curious about how this works," I said.

"How what works?" Darlene asked.

"Being in love with someone one day and not the next or when someone better-looking comes along."

"Hello! We're not love slaves, Sage. If Todd saw he had a chance with Scarlett Johansson, he would drop me so fast my head would spin. He's always talking about her. We're not committing ourselves for the rest of our lives when we go out with someone, even when we go steady," she said. She looked at the others for support. "Give me a break, right?"

"Right," Ginny said. She looked at me. "Sometimes you do seem like you're out of another time, Sage. Relax. We're all just drooling and enjoying it."

"So are you," Mia said under her breath. "So don't act like Miss Goody-Goody."

"Pardon?"

"I saw the way he looked at you and the way you reacted," Mia said as we continued down the hallway. "The others weren't in position to see, but I did."

"And?"

"I'm not blaming you for anything. I wished he looked at me that way," she said, and walked faster.

Really? I wondered. Was there something special about the way he had looked at me as opposed to how he had looked at each of them after all they had told me? I looked back. Summer was just coming up behind us, talking to Ward and Nick. What had drawn them to him so quickly? Whatever he said to them made them laugh. They looked like they had been friends forever, patting each other on the back and nudging each other playfully for superior position the way boys who were good friends often did.

He obviously made friends more easily than I did. A ton of questions about him cascaded through my mind. Where he came from and what brought him and his father here were at the top of the list, along with what had happened to his mother. Obviously, whatever tragedy had befallen him and his father had eventually made him stronger and never detracted from his personal strength. He looked so centered, self-confident, and determined. How did he get that way? What was his secret, and could I steal it for myself?

He caught me looking at him, his eyes shifting quickly to capture mine as if he was highly receptive to my gaze. He smiled, and I turned away and kept walking. Unlike the reaction to him that my girl-friends had, I was feeling some uneasiness about drawing his attention. A strange black veil suddenly seemed to fall between us. Of course, no one else could see it. I felt blinded.

It wasn't difficult for me to read and handle any of the boys I had met in this school. To me, they were all open books, talking to me with heads made of glass, their thoughts and real intentions written across their foreheads. But Summer Dante looked invincible, like someone beyond me. I didn't tremble, but I told myself to be careful. From where the warnings came, I couldn't say, but they came from someplace deep inside me, a place that existed in my old visions, maybe even one I had yet to realize.

He sat behind and away from me in our first class together. Despite how much I wanted to, how much the urge to do it banged away at my resistance, I did not turn around to look at him. I did have trouble concentrating on the lessons, and when I looked at my girlfriends, I saw how often they were turning to look at him and wink a smile.

After the bell rang to end class, I rose slowly, taking extra time to gather my things. I was hoping he would leave ahead of me. From the way my girl-friends were exaggerating their preparations to leave, I guessed he was still in the room.

Tired of hearing them giggle and fantasize about him, I decided to walk to my next class myself and shot forward. Just as I reached the door, I felt him come up beside me.

"You have extraordinary self-control," he said. "You must be special."

"What's that supposed to mean?"

"I think you know," he said with a smile, and hurried ahead to catch up to Skip and Jason.

He was making friends quickly with every boy in class, I thought. How was he doing that?

"What did he say to you?" Ginny demanded first as the girls caught up with me.

"Who?" I asked, even though I certainly knew. It was important for me to pretend indifference, as if I had an obligation to show them how to behave around boys.

"Don't play games, Sage. We all saw him hurry to catch you, and we saw him talking to you."

I looked at them, all so intent on knowing. "I made no sense of it," I told them. "He babbles."

"Babbles? I wish he'd babble to me," Ginny said.

"Babbles what?" Mia practically shouted.

"He told me I had great self-control. Well?" I followed when they all stared blankly. "Can anyone tell me what he meant by that?"

"You didn't know him from before, did you?" Darlene asked suspiciously.

"No. Don't you think I would have said so?"

"Maybe you would; maybe you wouldn't," Kay offered.

"What's that supposed to mean? Does everyone have to talk in riddles?"

Kay laughed, and everyone kept walking.

"What?" I yelled after them.

Kay paused. "We're all friends, Sage, some of us since kindergarten, but we're all in competition with one another."

"For what?"

"Every good-looking boy out there. Is that breaking news for you?"

I just stared at her. I was afraid to say yes.

For the next two periods and until lunch hour, Summer paid no attention to me. I glanced his way a few times, but he was focused on schoolwork and barely looked up at any of us girls. They were all disappointed; Darlene was the unhappiest, since she had driven Todd away. Between classes, Todd was already talking to one of the prettier girls in the freshman class, Hannah Rose. I saw the tiny but distinct signs of regret in Darlene's face as we gathered around our table to eat lunch. Summer wasn't with any of the boys in our class. He was sitting with Nick, Jason, and Greg, which was strange. He was already involved with older boys. They were talking and laughing. Did boys bond faster than girls? I wondered. Obviously it wasn't such a no-no for older boys to be friends with younger ones.

"I found out something new about Summer Dante," Kay said when we were all settled. She wore a look of self-satisfaction, even superiority.

"How could you find out anything new so fast?" Mia asked, jealousy seeping out of her eyes and smeared across her lips.

"I have my ways," Kay teased. Then she sat forward, as we all did to hear what she had learned. "He was homeschooled for the last five years. That's why he's in our class, even though he's older."

"He's older? How much older?" Mia asked.

"I don't know, exactly. His father is a romance writer. He publishes under the name Belladonna, and his books are supposed to be very, very sexy."

"What?" I asked. I felt the blood rush up through my neck and into my face.

"What what?" Kay asked.

"That name he writes under—Belladonna?"

"So? Why? Does your mother read his books?" she asked, looking at the others and smiling. "Or have you been sneaking them into your room or something?"

I shook my head. "No, I just . . . I've heard that name," I said, fumbling my words.

Ginny was busy working her iPhone and leaned in with her discoveries. "*Atropa belladonna* is a perennial herbaceous plant whose berries are extremely toxic. They can cause delirium and hallucinations." She looked up at me. "Is that where you heard it?"

"No," I said quickly.

She continued to read from her Internet search. "The name means 'beautiful lady,' and the plant was used in a risky cosmetic practice in Italy. The belladonna berry juice was used to enlarge women's pupils, giving them a striking appearance, but it can be poisonous, and many died unexpectedly, chasing their dreams of beauty."

"I love it," Mia said. "I'm getting one of his books today after school."

"That's good. Wait! I have a terrific idea." Darlene leaned in like a conspirator, and we all did the same. "Let's all get one of his books and bring them to school tomorrow and display them in front of Summer Dante," she said.

Everyone but me giggled with anticipation. I was still thinking about his father's pen name.

"I'll take care of it. I'll buy a copy for each of you," Kay said.

"I can't wait to see the expression on his face," Mia said.

"I hope Jason is inviting him to his party this weekend," Ginny said, looking toward the boys.

Kay turned to me. "Who do you predict will hook

up with him first, oh great romance guru? Should we wear any specific colors or do our hair any specific way?"

I looked at Summer and then back at them and shook my head. I wasn't getting any vibes. That black veil had fallen again. In fact, it was almost as if he wasn't there. "I don't know," I said. "Maybe none of us."

They were all quiet for a moment, and then Mia practically growled at me. "Don't dare tell us you think he's gay."

I looked at him again. I still had no visions, no flow of energy coming from him that I could read. "I don't know what he is," I said softly, almost too softly for any of them to hear, "but I can tell you this."

"What?" Ginny pounced.

"He's different, very different."

"You sound like you're afraid of him," Darlene said, smiling. "Afraid you might lose your virginity?"

They were all smiling at me now, waiting for my reaction.

"Maybe she has already," Mia said.

"None of you has," I said.

"How the hell do you know?" Kay asked, as if I was insulting them.

"I didn't for sure, but from the way you reacted, you just told me I'm right," I said.

No one disagreed.

Darlene changed the conversation, probably to avoid any more talk about it. All of them seemed eager to do that. I listened and nodded at some of the comments about hairdos and nail polish, but my mind drifted away constantly, and my eyes, as if under his control, turned toward Summer.

Before the bell rang to send us to class, he looked my way, but he didn't smile.

It was strange. It was as if he was throwing down a challenge, daring me to try to ignore him.

More important, I had no doubt that I would lose that dare.

And even more important, despite the act I had put on for the girls, I didn't care about losing to him.

10

I was the only one in our group of girls who had chosen to take the vocal music elective and therefore the only one who was in the school chorus. It was my next-to-last class of the day. I had just started singing in the chorus in my previous school before my parents had decided to transfer me.

A vision of myself singing in a church choir had haunted me until I had joined the chorus, but when I sang at my old school, even though our choral director, Mr. Hertz, was sweet and gentle, I often had flashes of a dour-looking elderly lady berating us for not putting our lungs fully into it and being stingy with God. I still decided to continue singing at my new school.

The moment I walked into the practice room and saw Summer Dante up front speaking with Mr. Jacobs, I knew all my girlfriends would regret not taking the class. All of us quickly took our places, the girls mesmerized by the sight of Summer and Mr. Jacobs laughing like old friends. Mr. Jacobs wasn't dour, but he usually rationed his smiles and laughter like someone making his way through a desert of depression. He turned to the class and held his hand on Summer's left shoulder.

"Class, I'd like to introduce Summer Dante, who just entered our school today," he began, "and who has joined our team."

Mr. Jacobs also coached varsity basketball and often used sports references when talking about our music class. He was working on getting us special chorus blouses and shirts with the school colors, black and gold. The joke was that they would have numbers on the back.

"As you all know," he continued, "I have to be the piano accompanist during our practices, and then the school hires Mrs. Kerry, who gives private piano lessons, to play for our performances so I can be out front to conduct. I like Mrs. Kerry. She does a fine job for us, but yesterday, unbeknownst to all of you, I auditioned our new team member, Summer. I was very impressed with how well he played the piano, and he's offered to be our new accompanist. So let's all give him a big welcome."

Everyone clapped. The chorus class had sophomores, juniors, and seniors in it. Most had seen Summer in the halls or in the cafeteria today, but a few hadn't seen him at all. I could see their surprise and interest, especially the two senior girls in the chorus, Sandy Worth and Jan Affleck. Neither was very attractive. Sandy had a perpetual acne problem and was a good fifteen pounds overweight for her five-foot-four frame. Jan was tall and skinny, with a figureless body and poorly styled dull brown hair. However, they both had beautiful singing voices, and they took turns singing lead.

Summer didn't look at me. He went right to the piano. Our first number was the Adele song "Someone Like You." Mr. Jacobs liked to intersperse the selections he chose from classical music with some modern music so as to have something for everyone in the audience when we performed our concert just before the Thanksgiving break.

We all took our positions and Mr. Jacobs happily took his in front of the group, or team as he would call us. Summer didn't need the sheet music. He impressed everyone, especially me, but I thought perhaps he liked Adele and had serendipitously memorized this one. Jan sang the opening verse solo, and then we all came in, never more perfectly on key and in sync according to Mr. Jacobs.

"With a pianist like this, you almost don't need a coach," he said.

I had never seen him so filled with enthusiasm and so light and happy. He had always struck me as too intense, as if everything he did in his life was in competition with someone. He was tall and lean, with chiseled facial features and deep-set dark brown eyes almost always soaked in a pool of intensity and determination. The motto he had hung over his classroom door was "Anyone can play, but not everyone can win. Practice!"

Although Summer used the sheet music for the rest of our numbers, I had the feeling he could play every one of them without it. Once he did play a song, I noticed that he didn't refer to the sheet music again. Some people have photographic memories, and some have it along with a special ear for music, I thought. Summer was just one of them.

Or was he more?

We were all doing so well and getting so many compliments from Mr. Jacobs that we audibly sighed with disappointment when the bell rang to end our class. I noticed there wasn't a girl who didn't linger in hopes of walking out with Summer, but Mr. Jacobs kept him back with his compliments and enthusiasm. He was waving his arms and shifting his feet like he was talking excitedly to a team playing in a close championship game.

Before I walked out, I caught Summer gazing at me with his small impish smile. Despite the caution I was feeling, it made me want to linger, and even though I felt a little foolish and obvious doing so, I waited just outside the doorway, fiddling with my notebooks, pretending a reason for my delay.

He was beside me so quickly and silently that I thought for a moment that he really could float. I looked up at him. He did have stunning deep black eyes. Most boys I had met rarely held their gaze on you when you looked intently back at them. Their eyes shifted, and they got a little nervous, as if they had been caught looking at you and thinking about you with lust. Some of the girls I knew liked that and washed away their prospective new boyfriends' nervousness and guilt with their own obvious looks of desire. They would titillate each other with promises of sexual pleasure.

There was no nervousness in Summer's face. He was filled with self-confidence. I wanted to be annoyed by it, to think of him as arrogant, but something restrained me, something pleaded with me not to drive him away. Of course, it had to do with his good looks, but there was more curiosity in me about him than anything else. Why was he so different from other boys I had met?

"Hey," he said.

"Hey yourself. You play beautifully," I said.

"Thanks."

"How long have you been playing piano?"

"Not that long," he said, with the sort of impatience someone would show if he thought the compliment was nothing unusual. "You should be the one singing solo."

I pulled my head back. "Really?" I asked dryly. Because I gave him a compliment, he had to give me one? Did he think I would crumble quickly and maybe become his first female conquest at the school? "And you know this how?"

"It's not a false compliment, Sage, just because you gave me one," he said, reading my thoughts. Usually, I was much better at disguising them, from boys especially. "It's not rocket science. I could distinguish your voice from the others', and you have the timbre."

"Timbre?"

"Your voice has that delicious complexity a good singer's voice needs. I mentioned that to Mr. Jacobs."

"And what did he say?"

"He thought I might be right, especially when I referred to your singing the lead in 'Must Be Santa.' It would sound better with just you singing the questions."

"Oh, so you really have been studying music. Is that your favorite subject?"

"I don't think of it as a subject. Music, art, poetry are ways to extend yourself, grow bigger and touch stars."

"Touch stars?" I asked, smiling.

"I would have thought you knew that yourself, Sage."

"I'm surprised you know my name."

"A little bird whispered it in my ear," he said, and reached for my hand and touched my ring. "Interesting ring. Those are dragons, right?"

"Yes. You know what it's supposed to mean?"

He studied the ring, still holding my hand. "I believe one is supposed to be the dragon of the east, the messenger of heavenly law, facing the dragon of the west, keeper of earth knowledge."

"How do you know that?"

"Didn't you see it? That same bird whispered in my ear."

"Very funny."

He shrugged. "I'm into that spiritual stuff. I guess you are, too, if you're wearing this ring."

I finally took my hand back. "My uncle gave it to me. He bought it in an antiques shop in Budapest."

"Oh. Well, it's a beaut," he said. He was looking at me so intently I had to shift my gaze away.

"Got to move on," I said.

"We have history now, right?" he asked.

"Right," I said, and started down the hallway. He was right beside me.

"You haven't been here that long, either, correct?" he asked.

"No, I haven't."

I tried to hide my smile, but I was pleased he had taken such interest in me, enough to ask others about me. I wondered if it was just me or if he had asked about any other girls who had captured his early attention.

"Why did you transfer from your old school? Did you get into some sort of trouble? I don't imagine you did poorly in your grades, and from what I understand, this school's not much closer to your home. You're a pretty good student, right?"

I stopped walking and turned to him. "You know where I live, too?"

"It's not—"

"Rocket science. I know. Since you're asking so many questions about me, why were you home-schooled?" I fired back, hoping Kay's information was correct.

He shrugged. "We traveled a lot. It was just easier."

"Why did you travel a lot?"

His eyes lit with laughter. "We were being chased."

"What?"

He widened his smile. "We're all being pursued by something, aren't we?"

"Very funny. Where did you live before you came here? Why did you come here to this particular town in Massachusetts?"

"Why, why, why. You didn't get a job on the school newspaper and get assigned to interview new students or something, did you?" he asked.

"You're the one who sounded that way first," I replied, my face heating up.

The testier I was with him, however, the more he seemed to enjoy it. His eyes brightened again, and his smile deepened. His teeth were as perfect as mine, his skin just as smooth and blemish-free. Any stranger looking at the two of us could think we were citizens of a future world, a world without illness and disease, a world in which people never lost their youth. I could imagine us paired to have perfect children, our sex the ultimate, the sweetest any man and woman could enjoy. We each would have the power to bring the other into those instant and delicious climaxes the girls were always joking about, assuring our world that we would produce children with flawless genes.

These thoughts changed the surge of heat in my cheeks to a blush accompanied by a tingling around my breasts. I raised my books higher, as if I had been caught half naked. Now I was the one feeling nervous in the presence of a boy, and for the first time, too.

"We'll have to postpone the interview. I don't want to be late," I said, turning sharply away from him and walking faster.

I thought he didn't like the abrupt way I had shut him down and deliberately lingered behind me, but he caught up when we were just about at the classroom door and gently put his hand on my left elbow so we would enter like a bride and groom at the altar.

"Touchy, touchy," he said, bringing his lips so close to my ear I felt as if he had kissed me.

We were the last two to enter the classroom. Everyone was looking at us. The bell rang for class, so I hurried to my desk, forgetting until I sat that Cassie Marlowe had sat across from me in this class. Summer slipped into her seat, glanced at me with those exasperating laughing eyes, and opened his textbook to the exact page we had left off on yesterday, as if he had always been there.

Talk about a new student being prepared from the get-go, I thought. Again, I had the feeling that he could hear my thoughts. He leaned toward me, his eyes fixed on the front of the room as he tapped the page and said, "Peter Murphy clued me in."

I looked back at Peter. He was his usual oblivious self, already reading ahead before the class even began. When did he talk to Peter? I wondered. Peter and Danny weren't part of the group of older boys I saw Summer talking with at lunch or in the hallways between classes. Someone must have told him that Peter was the brightest student in our class. At least he cared about his schoolwork. He wasn't all glamour and flash and another one of those boys who saw school mainly as a playing field for sex and romance.

I desperately wanted to be less obvious about my interest in him and fought to find a comfortable indifference, but I couldn't help looking at him when he looked away. It was impossible to deny it. Yes, he was very good-looking and sexy, musically inclined, and apparently a good student all wrapped into one new boy. He was almost too good to be true, and that alone warned me to remain cautious.

My gaze drifted to Darlene and then to Ginny and Mia, who hid their infatuation with him as badly as they could hide their frustrations. They were all looking at me as if I had done something terrible to them, their eyes sending tiny darts toward me.

"What?" I mouthed.

They all looked away instantly.

Summer turned to me. I thought he had seen it all, but it was actually more than that. He seemed to understand not only how they felt but also how I felt, how troubled and wounded I was. I didn't want to lose my new friends for any reason, and certainly not over him. He shrugged and whispered, "Don't let them bother you. They'll get over it."

I felt my heart stop and start. How could he be so tuned in to everything that happened around him, but more important, perhaps, everything that happened to me? His words of assurance and caution also implied that annoying self-confidence of his again. He had instantly concluded that they were upset because I was getting his attention instead of any one of them.

Arrogance could use him to sell conceit to humble monks, I thought.

The fear I had sensed when I had first seen him returned in waves. That confidence I had when confronting any other boy in this school was under siege. Where was that maturity, that balance and responsibility, that caused my new girlfriends to accuse me of being too old, more like a chaperone? For the first time, I felt vulnerable. Like anyone else, I could be manipulated, tempted, and drawn into doing things I shouldn't do. My parents' warnings now sounded like go-to-your-bomb-shelter alarms.

Get hold of yourself, Sage Healy, I ordered myself. *Don't fall head over heels the first time you get a little attracted to someone.* A little? I nearly laughed aloud at the voice of caution within me. *I think this is already more than a little. Can't you feel the way your body trembles when you're near him? Can't you sense the rising tide of your own sexuality, making those erogenous places on your body tingle and demand the satisfaction that used to come only in fantasies?* I was drifting deeper and deeper into that part of me that defined me as an adult woman. I could sense nothing else. I actually forgot where I was, which almost got me in trouble for the first time.

My teachers were quite fond of me, because I was truly one of the most attentive students in their classes. When they needed someone to provide the answer to a question that would get us moving faster into the assignment, they always called on me. I could sense it was coming, and I was always prepared. So I was genuinely

surprised and shocked suddenly to see everyone looking at me, big smiles on their faces, especially the girls
who always wanted me to stumble and be what they
called "human."

"Miss Healy," Mr. Leshner was obviously repeating, perhaps for a third or fourth time. "Are you
among the living today?"

The whole class laughed, except for Summer. He
just smiled, but then he grew quickly serious, his eyes
urging me to recuperate quickly.

"I'm sorry, Mr. Leshner. That was the Treaty of
Versailles, ending the First World War on June 28,
1919, which ironically was exactly five years after the
assassination of Archduke Franz Ferdinand."

"Thank you," Mr. Leshner said. "Exactly the answer I was hoping to get."

Gleeful smiles fell like late-autumn leaves around me.

That is, except for the smile that blossomed on Summer's face. As if he was responsible for it, he seemed
to be taking more pride in my quick and successful
recuperation than I was. I looked down at my notebook
and didn't raise my head again until the bell rang to end
the class. Everyone rose almost before it had stopped
ringing, just as they did every day at the end of the last
class, to hurry out to after-school activities or their rides
home. Our principal, Mrs. Greene, called it "something
akin to rats deserting a sinking ship."

Summer didn't even stand. He sat there, leaning
back in his seat and looking forward, as if there was
something still happening in the front of the room,
something only he could see. After his long pensive

moment, he tapped his pen, put it in his shirt pocket, and closed his book. I hadn't moved. He wasn't surprised.

"You all right?"

"Why wouldn't I be?"

He raised his hands in defense. "Just an innocent question."

"Something tells me nothing you say, ask, or do is really innocent," I replied.

It brought that pleased smile to his face. The harder I resisted, the more he thought he was conquering me, I decided. "Need a ride home?" he asked me.

"No, thank you. My mother picks me up every day." I immediately regretted mentioning my mother, knowing he had lost his.

"Well, maybe some other time when she's too busy or there's a conflict. I have a car." He stood up.

"You have a driver's license?"

"A car wouldn't be much good to me without it," he said, grinning.

"How old are you?" I asked, also standing.

"It's complicated," he said. "Because of my birthdate, the school I did attend once, before the homeschooling, wouldn't admit me to first grade when I should have been. That put me a year behind, and then, because I was out of the country for a number of years, I didn't get the credits I needed to march along with others about my age."

"So? How old are you?"

He shook his head at my persistence. "I'm seventeen," he said. "But keep it a secret."

"I don't think anything about you will be a secret too much longer," I told him, and started out.

He walked alongside me. "What about you?" he asked in the doorway.

"What about me?"

"Are all your secrets known?"

"I don't have any secrets."

"Oh, you do," he said. "You do. See you tomorrow, Sage Healy," he added, with that know-it-all smile blossoming on his face again.

I watched him walk off to catch up with Jason and Ward, who had just turned into the corridor. They patted him on the shoulders, and they continued on like the Three Musketeers. He made friends as easily as changing from one jacket to another, I thought.

When I reached the school exit to the parking lot, I saw my knot of friends waiting for me, looking like they were ready to pounce on me and pull out my hair strand by strand.

"Well?" Ginny asked first.

"Well, what?"

"Did he ask you out or anything?" Mia demanded.

"He asked me if I needed a ride home," I confessed.

"I just knew it would be you," Kay said. "I watched him all day. Every chance he got, he looked at you."

"What else did you find out about him?" Darlene asked.

"Not much. Just that he's traveled a lot. You all know he's going to be the choral accompanist, right?"

"We heard," Ginny said, the corners of her mouth dipping. "Serves me right for not practicing do-re-mi."

"With Sage around, it wouldn't have helped you," Kay said, her voice dripping with envy.

"I have no idea whether his offering me a ride home means anything. Don't jump to conclusions," I said. "I'm probably not his type." I couldn't believe I was trying to make them feel better by putting myself down. How had it come to this so fast?

"Please," Mia said. "If you're going to play anything in this drama, don't play the innocent one. At least, not with us. He might like that, I guess, but it doesn't work with us."

"You're making too much of this—and of him," I said, now feeling some anger. "If you want to learn a lesson from all this, it's don't be so obvious, and don't let any boy know how much you like him too quickly."

Where those words came from, I did not know, but they all dropped their jaws and widened their eyes.

"Advice to the lovelorn from Miss Perfect," Kay muttered.

"I'm hardly Miss Perfect. Gotta go. My mother's waiting," I said. "Talk to you later."

I hurried out. My mother was there watching for me with the usual look of expectation on her face, anticipating something new, something she feared to learn or had foreseen. I debated whether I should mention Summer Dante so soon, but he settled that question for me when he drove by on his way out of the parking lot. He beeped his horn and waved, a gleeful smile hoisted like a flag of victory on his face.

My mother turned and watched him go. "Who was that?" she asked immediately when I got into the car.

"A new student. He's a very talented pianist and is going to be the accompanist for our chorus."

"Was this his first day?"

"Yes."

She started out of the parking lot. "Do you like him?"

"He's a little annoying," I said.

"Why?"

"He comes off as arrogant at times, but he is very intelligent."

"What grade is he in?"

"Ours."

"And he's driving?"

"It's a long story," I replied, hoping she would end the interrogation. For some reason, answering questions about him was irritating me now. Perhaps it was because of what I had just gone through with my girlfriends, who were so awash in jealousy they could have torn me apart. In far less civilized times, females probably did tear one another apart over a chosen male. Kay did tell me we were all always in competition. I guess I shouldn't have been so surprised.

" 'It's a long story?' People always use that expression when they don't want to tell you something," my mother said.

"I don't know everything about him, Mother. He told me a little. He was denied admission to first grade because of his birthdate, and then, because of his family traveling and his attending foreign schools and then being homeschooled, our school placed him in our class."

"Traveling and attending foreign schools? What do his parents do?"

"He has only his father, who's apparently a romance novelist." I hesitated about saying his nom de plume. Something told me to wait on that, that it would stir up some deeper inquisition and more warnings, and despite how I had reacted to him at the end of the day, I didn't want to be told he was off-limits.

"What happened to his mother? Divorce?"

"I don't know for sure."

"How old is he?"

"Seventeen."

"Seventeen in the tenth grade? That's awkward. I feel sorry for him," she said.

"Believe me, Mother, if there's one thing Summer Dante doesn't need or want, it's anyone's pity."

"Summer Dante? That's his name?"

"Yes."

She was thoughtful for most of the ride home, and when we pulled into our driveway, she turned to me and said, "Be careful. He sounds like he's far too sophisticated for you and your girlfriends."

"I know. But I don't think he's that sophisticated. I think he is really desperate."

She turned and actually smiled at me. "Desperate? Why desperate?"

"I think he hasn't had a chance to have any real friends. He'd hate me for saying it, but I think he's lonely."

She watched the garage door go up and then nodded. "Even more reason to be careful," she muttered.

"You'll have me trembling with fear every time I meet someone who's not perfect in your eyes," I replied with unusual terseness.

She looked at me in annoyance but said nothing. However, I knew the topic would come up as soon as my father came home. When I came down to help with dinner, they were both sitting in the kitchen and looked up quickly.

"Hey, Sage," he began. "Hear you might be fond of a new boy?"

"I didn't say I was fond of him. I said he was very talented musically and very intelligent."

"And lonely," my mother reminded me.

"That's just a feeling about him. Maybe I'm wrong. He just entered our school, Dad."

"Good-looking? As good-looking as I am?" he asked, smiling.

"Yes," I said, so quickly and so firmly his smile froze.

"And what does he think about you?"

"He thinks I'm too touchy, too sensitive, too inquisitive, and maybe even spoiled."

"Sounds like a perfect beginning to a relationship," he joked, but my mother didn't smile.

"Let's get started on dinner," she told me.

At dinner, my father talked about Uncle Alexis and Aunt Suzume's arrival on Saturday. "Aunt Suzume is very interested in getting to know you," he said.

"And I'm anxious to meet her. I haven't met many of your or Mother's relatives," I added. "I haven't even heard mention of many of them."

I did not know where I had suddenly gotten this forwardness and courage, but I did feel aggressive and impatient, if not downright intolerant of all this mystery I had been living with my whole life.

"I don't like your tone of voice," my mother said. My father looked unhappy about it, too.

"I'm sorry. It's just that I'm always hearing the other girls talk about their cousins and relatives, and I have to sit there and listen dumbly. Except, of course, when I can talk about Uncle Wade." *Thank God for Uncle Wade*, I wanted to add, but I swallowed it back.

"You'll meet the members of our families that we consider worthwhile to meet," my mother said. "When it's time."

When it's time? Was this still part of the everlasting test I was living under? I had to reach another goal, gain some other confidence first? "When will it be time?" I dared to ask.

They looked at each other, my mother nodding with that *See, I'm right about her* look on her face. My father didn't nod, but he didn't look happy.

"Stop with all these questions, and help clear off the table," she ordered.

I rose petulantly and did what she said. Neither of them spoke to me afterward, so I went up to my room to finish my homework. Just after eight o'clock, I received a phone call. I expected it to be Ginny or Mia pumping me for more information about Summer, but it was neither.

"Hello," I said, but not with any excitement. I wasn't interested in talking to them about him.

"You sound down. Anything wrong?" he asked. It was Summer.

Persistence and arrogance obviously were born to complement each other.

But I wasn't as upset about it as I would come to believe I should have been.

11

"You got my phone number quickly enough. Is there anything about me you don't know yet?" I asked.

He laughed. "For someone who says all her secrets are known, you sure are sensitive about anyone finding out anything about you, even the simplest things like your name, address, and phone number."

"You're not exactly just anyone," I replied, still holding on to a little testiness. For some reason, that felt like a life raft at the moment. I couldn't get over the feeling that I was swimming in a whirlpool of danger when I spoke to him. The thing was, I couldn't understand why yet.

"Oh, no? Who am I, then? What do you know about me that no one else does?" he asked, with the first suggestion of any worry in his voice. Was there something dark in his past? Was he afraid I had found out?

"The newest student, just one day old, in fact."

"Oh. I see. And that necessitates what sort of expectations? Shyness? Insecurity? Timidity?"

"For most normal people, I suppose."

"Well, now you know something important about me," he replied.

"Which is?"

"I'm not like most normal people. Is that bad?" he quickly followed.

I felt like I was playing verbal ping-pong over the phone, but I couldn't stop. "Maybe I'm the one who's shy, insecure, and timid."

"Something tells me you're not like most normal people, either. Actually, most of the boys in school I've spoken to would never accuse you of being shy or timid. If anything, you've got them spinning on their heels. A few are actually afraid of you."

"Afraid? Why?"

"They think you have devious ways of embarrassing them. Although I haven't seen you in action yet, my guess is you do."

"First, I don't believe any of them used the word 'devious.'"

He laughed. "Free translation," he said. "You don't want to hear the exact words."

"No, I don't. Even if I did have 'devious' ways to embarrass them, I haven't found any of them to be worth the effort, not that it would take all that much effort," I said. Now I was the one sounding arrogant, but it annoyed me to hear that I was the topic of conversation among those boys and that the conversation was mostly negative, even nasty.

"Maybe they're lucky, then." He paused and then added, "Don't be so harsh. All of them are not that bad."

"You can make that sort of judgment after only one day talking to them?"

"They're not that complicated," he said.

"Now I've learned a second important thing about you."

"Which is?"

"You're a little snobby. Maybe a lot."

"And you're not? None of them is even worth taking the time to embarrass them, not that it would take that much?"

I probably should have said good-bye and hung up, but I laughed instead. "Touché," I replied.

"Touché? You don't actually fence, do you? I wouldn't want to end up with a sword in my chest. Do you?" he asked when I was silent too long.

"No. My most dangerous weapons are—"

"Your words. I know. I have nicks and tears all over my ego."

I couldn't help but laugh again. Despite all I thought about him, even the unexplainable fear I felt in regard to him, I couldn't help liking him. At least, he was interesting and obviously very intelligent in addition to being good-looking. That shouldn't be such an amazing thing to think about a boy, I thought. Everyone always complained about girls having beauty without brains. What about boys? The good-looking, magazine-model types of boys in our school didn't have enough brainpower to lift two different adjectives into the same sentence. Even the insults they heaved at one another were trite. If there was a vaccine against airheads, more of them would disappear faster than the girls who were so easily labeled as such.

The more I thought about it, the more I had come to believe that boys, males, men, make the rules, rules even girls accepted willy-nilly, especially my new girl-friends. They were all so desperate to have boys like and appreciate them. Look how easily I got Darlene to change her hairstyle and wear red. Why didn't she come back at me with "If he doesn't like me as I am, he's not worth my affections"? She wouldn't have been that wrong. What about him changing *his* hair-style and wearing what *she* liked?

Was the whole female sex suffering from an inferi-ority complex ever since caveman days?

"All right. Just this once, I'll blunt the end of my sword," I said.

"Promise?"

"No."

Now he was the one who laughed. "I'll have to remain en garde. So, are you going to this party Friday night at Jason Marks's house?"

"Not a definite thing yet," I said, surprised he had brought it up.

"You're meeting your girlfriends at the Dorey Town Mall first?"

"Is there anything you don't know after just one day?"

"I don't know whether you would go to the party with me instead," he said.

I paused.

"Still there?"

"Yes."

"I could come to your house and pick you up, and—"

"No," I said quickly. "My parents don't know I'm going to a party. They think I'm just meeting the girls at the mall."

"They won't let you go to a party?"

"It's complicated right now."

"So then just meet me at the mall? I can take you to Jason's house, or . . . maybe not. Maybe we can do something different without an audience. Better yet, forget the party completely. Why don't we just go out on a proper, regular date? Will your parents let you do that? I can come to meet them first, if you like. I'll put on a jacket and tie and show off my cultured etiquette. I can be Johnny Perfect when I have to be. I'll bring your mother some flowers or a box of candy."

For a moment, it took my breath away just imagining it. This was really the first time any boy was specific about asking me on a date. It wasn't just something like "I'll see you at the party." That implied some hesitation on the boy's part. He'd see me but not necessarily spend all his time with me.

Certainly after the way my mother reacted initially to what I had told her about Summer, she wouldn't leap at granting me permission to go out on a date with him so soon, maybe ever, even if he was Johnny Perfect.

"Have you not ever gone on a proper date?" he asked.

"Not really. Just to a party."

"Oh, so I could make Sage history. I'll bring you a corsage. It will be like going to a prom."

I had to laugh at that, imagining what it would be like for him when he came to meet my parents. They would have to put him through the third degree, not only because he would be my first date but also because they would be nervous about my going out with a boy who had just arrived on the scene. They'd practically X-ray him.

"Well?" he pursued when I was quiet too long.

"I'll have to think about it," I said.

"It's not—"

"Yes, I know, rocket science. All I know about you is that you play the piano beautifully, you've traveled a lot and been homeschooled, you're not like anyone else, and you're a little snobby."

"You know how old I am."

"And I can probably guess your height and weight reasonably accurately," I added. "Just enough for a police report."

"I was right," he said.

"About what?"

"You. You're definitely the most interesting girl in school."

"Oh, you've met them all?"

"Just the ones worth my time. Don't even say it. Okay. Give it more thought. I'll see you tomorrow, and maybe, if you're lucky, I'll let you know more about me."

"I'm holding my breath."

"Not too long, I hope. If you die, I'll have to transfer to another school."

"Thanks for giving me a good reason to live," I said. "Good night."

"You forgot to say 'sweet prince.'"

"Oh, you are so full of yourself."

He laughed again, even though I really meant it. "So poke a hole in my swollen ego and bring me down to earth," he said. "Something tells me you're the one capable of doing it in a way I would enjoy. See you tomorrow," he added quickly, and hung up.

I held the receiver as if I expected him to pick it up on his end because he regretted ending his contact with me. But the dial tone came on.

He was gone.

For now.

My mother stopped by my room before I went to sleep. I had just slipped into bed, knowing I would probably toss and turn for a while thinking about Summer and why he was so difficult for me to understand.

"Who called you? Was that the new boy?" she asked before I could respond.

"Yes," I replied. It would be fruitless, even stupid, to deny it, even though something in me wished I could. In fact, I toyed with the idea of telling her he had asked me out on an official date.

"Did you give him the phone number, or did he get it on his own initiative?"

"His own initiative. Why is that important?"

"I don't want to see you throw yourself at anyone too quickly—lonely, talented, or whatever."

"Believe me, I didn't throw myself at him, Mother. The other girls drool over him. They're so obvious. I think he likes me because I'm not."

She nodded. "That's good."

Wait on mentioning any possible date, I told myself. *You have to do this slowly.*

She started to turn away.

"What about you?" I said.

"Me?" she asked, turning back. "What do you mean, me?"

"Did you drool over Dad?" I didn't know where I had gotten the courage to challenge her like that. Maybe I was still riding on my testiness with Summer. For a moment, though, I wasn't sure whether she was going to chastise me for being so forward or break out in laughter. I held my breath.

"Hardly," she said. "If anyone drooled, as you say, it was your father. If you noticed, you'd see he still does," she added, with the thump in her voice on "does" that indicated this was the last word to be spoken on the subject, and walked out of my room.

I lay back on my pillow, a little amazed. This was the first time I had driven my mother into speechlessness. It also made me think about something and someone other than Summer. What were my parents really like when they first met? They never talked very much about their romance or their wedding.

I tried to imagine them years younger, flirting with each other, going on their first date, liking and finally loving each other more and more. I recalled the pictures in the file drawer that I had seen of them. They did look happier and more carefree. Uncle Wade had certainly given me the impression that they had been.

When did people begin to change in a dramatic way? Was it only after some event, something that hit them like a sharp slap in the face and forced them to become more responsible, so responsible that doing spontaneous fun things like I hoped soon to do was impossible, even a bit frightening? Or did it just come with age when you crossed a line in time, when you woke up and looked at yourself and suddenly realized that you were very different and, in fact, everyone was expecting you to be different? Some were even depending on you to be different.

Maybe that was why my parents had those pictures locked up in a cabinet and not on the shelves. It was too painful to look back and remember and then realize what was gone. I always wondered about movie stars who had to see themselves in films when they had just started out. Those people were so different from the way they looked now that they probably looked at the films as if there was someone else acting in the parts.

And yet when I looked at those old pictures, I didn't see very dramatic physical differences in my parents. They were still as young-looking as they had been. They just behaved differently, as far as I could tell. They'd had a real glow about them that I didn't see as much now.

It was all so confusing, just like my many inexplicable visions and memories. Despite having what my uncle had called my third eye, I wanted to be far less complicated. I'd trade it in a heartbeat to be as simple and as lackadaisical as my girlfriends. I didn't want to feel more mature. I didn't want to be considered a chaperone. I wanted to be no more and no less than any girl my age. Was that terrible? Did it mean I wanted to be bad and irresponsible, not see the outcomes, and take risks? Did I want the freedom to make mistakes? Was that a stupid thing to want?

Before I fell asleep, I thought more about Summer. Despite what I had said to him, he really was far more difficult to understand than any other boy I had ever met. There wasn't one previously who could prevent me from envisioning just what it would be like to be with him. It was as easy as reading ahead in a novel and realizing the ending.

Should I try to get my parents to let me go out on a date with Summer? Or should I avoid all that, let my father take me to the mall as planned, but then leave the girls and go off with Summer this Friday? That would be something of a risk, wouldn't it?

"Yes," I whispered to myself, "a wonderful risk." I could see myself lying some more to my parents. "I'll meet him. I'll take the risk."

There were no voices coming back at me. No dark shadows in the corners, no whispers floating into my ears. Something had silenced them all. I had no one to depend on but myself.

And I was happy about it.

Anticipating the morning anxiously, I pressed into sleep and welcomed the dreams just waiting to be born, dreams in which Summer and I were lovers, the kind of lovers who really didn't need anyone else. Friends were like discretionary income. We didn't depend on anyone else. It was almost as if no one else at school existed. With him playing the piano, I did suddenly become the lead singer. His music magically enriched my voice. I was blossoming in ways I couldn't have imagined.

The sunlight through the windows nudged me gently, but the moment I realized it was time to rise, I practically leaped out of bed to get ready for school. Today I would dress better, make sure my hair looked richer, more alluring, and wear my favorite earrings. I spent twice the usual time in front of the mirror, trying to envision Summer's reaction to me, but there was still something that kept him out of my vision, out of my third eye. There was no predicting. He was almost . . . invisible. In fact, right now, I even had trouble remembering his features, except for those eyes. His eyes were familiar in a strange way. For a moment, I thought about them, tried to realize what it was, but finally gave up and went downstairs to have breakfast with my parents.

They were always up ahead of me. Sometimes I wondered if they even slept, even though they never looked tired.

My father sat back, nodded, and smiled.

"What?" I asked.

"You look very pretty today, Sage, not that you don't always. Special day?"

My mother watched me and waited, her eyes full of that familiar suspicion I had learned to live with, to have beside me daily like a second shadow.

"Not really," I said. I prepared some breakfast for myself and sat across from them.

"Are you sure?"

"Maybe she's trying to impress someone," my mother said.

"Oh," my father said. "Could that be it?"

There was something about the way the two of them were speaking that made me believe they had rehearsed.

"I hope I impress everyone," I said.

"Touché!" my father cried.

I smiled, recalling Summer's reaction to my saying that.

My mother smirked. "We're not in some sort of contest here," she told him, and he lost his smile quickly. "You get a phone call from this new boy and then dress to make yourself more attractive. Coincidence?"

I couldn't recall ever blushing in front of them, but I knew I was blushing now.

"I can't wait to meet this boy," my father said.

"Do you want us to meet him?" my mother asked.

I should have leaped at the opportunity, but I hesitated. There was something in her eyes that told me she would do just as I feared, run him through an examination that would resemble a Homeland Security clearance. He would surely flee, and I would be even more embarrassed in front of my girlfriends once he brought the story to school.

"I've really just met him myself," I said. "I don't know if that's necessary yet."

"He called you," my mother reminded me.

"Maybe he's called other girls, too."

They looked at each other, my father more pleased with my answer. He smiled. "I remember my first crush."

"Crush?" my mother said.

"Well, I wouldn't call it much more. I was only five at the time," he replied, and I laughed. He and my mother laughed, too, and for a few moments, at least, I thought we were finally acting like a normal family.

My father volunteered again to take me to school. I knew he was hoping to catch a glimpse of Summer, but when we arrived in the parking lot, he was nowhere to be seen. I did see his car already parked.

"'Bye," I said, and reached for the door handle just as my father reached for my arm to stop me.

"I love seeing you excited and happy, Sage. I want you to have the best possible teenage life. I know you're a responsible person, and I'm proud of that. Just beware of how easy it is to lose a grip on yourself."

I nodded, and then he did something he didn't often do. He leaned toward me to kiss me on the cheek. His cautioning and his kiss did slow me down. I had been ready to charge into the building and seek out Summer immediately. Secretly, I hoped he would be waiting at my locker.

"Thank you, Dad," I said, and got out.

He didn't drive away quickly like my mother usually did. He sat there watching me enter the school. I looked back and waved from the doorway. Then he turned and looked in the direction of Summer's car. Or I imagined that was what he was looking at, for how could he have known which car was his? I watched him drive off and went inside.

The girls were waiting for me at my locker. Kay was holding out a paperback novel. I had forgotten. They all had copies of the same one, *Reflections of a Desperate Heart* by Belladonna.

"I thought it would be funnier if we all had the same book," she said.

I didn't want to take it. Now that she actually had done it, I thought it was childish, and I didn't want to look childish to him. But I knew I couldn't refuse without causing a stir. One of them was sure to accuse me of not wanting to take the chance of annoying him.

"Keep it prominent on top of your books like we are," she instructed.

"We'll keep them there all day," Mia said. "Of course, he might ask only you about it."

I put my jacket into the locker and organized my books for the day. "I can tell you now what he will probably do," I said after doing as they had instructed.

"What?" Darlene asked, smiling in anticipation of my saying something outrageous.

"Ignore us," I told them. Disappointment bordering on anger flashed across their faces.

"Maybe this will be one time you're wrong," Ginny said.

I shrugged. "We'll soon know," I told them, and we started for homeroom.

"We'll all walk by him," Kay commanded. "Try not to look at him."

Walking past him meant we all had to take a different route to our desks, walk up a different aisle once we entered the room. Kay wanted to be first. I fell behind so I would be last. I was planning on shaking my head like someone who had been made to do something silly, but Ginny turned out to be the one who was right. I was wrong. He didn't ignore us.

He had expected us.

On top of the books on his desk was a copy of his father's novel *Reflections of a Desperate Heart* by Belladonna. I couldn't help smiling. My girlfriends gathered at the back of the aisle, all looking shocked and devastated. I was going to laugh, but Kay turned furious.

"You warned him!" she accused. "You spoiled it."

"No, I didn't. How could I? I didn't know the exact book you would buy, did I?"

Realizing that, she lost some of her fury. "But how—"

The bell rang for us to be at our seats.

"He might have seen you buying the books," I offered as we separated.

All the other students in the room who had realized we were carrying the same novel were looking at us curiously, especially Peter and Danny. I smiled and shrugged at them. *Let Kay explain it*, I thought, but I wanted to know the truth. How *did* he anticipate what we were planning to do? Had one of the other girls given it away somehow, maybe talked about it with someone else, and he had overheard? How clever he was not to mention it during our phone conversation last night. He was definitely complicated, just as I had first thought, complicated and clever.

The second thing he did that surprised me more than any of the others was that he ignored me. I now was afraid that what I had told my parents was true, that he might just have called each of us last night and promised to meet us all or something. What a joke that would be on us. Somehow I would feel more taken in than any of them, however.

He got up to leave when the bell rang and immediately joined Nick, Greg, and Ward. I joined the girls, and we fell behind him and the others deliberately. I was so tempted to ask them if he had called any of them, but then I would have to confess that he had called me. I wasn't ready to do that.

"I guess you're right," Kay said. "He probably spotted me in the bookstore, and I didn't see him there."

"It was still a funny idea," Ginny insisted. None of us was keeping the novel prominent anymore, however.

"I'll probably read it now," Mia said. "It looks sexy."

"That will be the first book you read this year," Ginny quipped.

"Look who's talking. You're the one who gets summaries from Peter," she fired back.

"You're just jealous."

"Right. One of these days, Mr. Madeo is going to realize you didn't read the assignment."

"Not unless you tell him," Ginny said.

"I don't have to tell him," Mia replied.

"What's that supposed to mean?" Ginny said, stopping.

We all stopped. Mia looked to Darlene and Kay for help and then turned to me when she wasn't getting any.

"Probably it means that Mr. Madeo isn't as unaware of what goes on in his classroom as you think," I offered. "He has a way of smiling wryly when you give an answer, Ginny. You're looking at notes Peter gave you and reading them verbatim."

"Verbatim?"

"Exactly how he told you. Everyone has his or her own way of writing, speaking."

Ginny looked at the others, who were all looking at me.

"Do some of the homework yourself," I said. "Put things in your own words, at least."

"You know something you're not telling me," she said.

"Do you?" Darlene followed quickly.

"Mr. Madeo is going to ask Peter about it," I revealed. Moments after I had given her my advice, it had flashed before my eyes. Peter would confess.

"How do you know? How can you know that?" Kay demanded.

"I see the way he looks at him after Ginny answers a question or hands in a paper or test," I said. "Don't worry about it. Peter will simply stop helping you. Mr. Madeo won't change any grades you've received."

"You know," Kay said, her eyes still narrow and dark with suspicion, "you scare me sometimes."

No one else said anything.

They started walking, and I did, too, but I was a little behind them, and my heart was pounding with fear and disappointment. The disastrous result of our prank had put them all in a foul mood, I told myself. They would look for any way to take it out on someone. I had just stuck my head out too fast. They'd get over it, I told myself, but I didn't foresee it. I just hoped it.

Summer continued to ignore me between morning classes and even in class. Maybe he was waiting for me to make the first move, but my mother's warnings were louder than my desire to give in. He was just playing games with me, I thought. I tried to be angry about it, but his occasional quick glances, flashing those deep black, enticing eyes, kept me too fascinated to ignore him.

The girls continued to be cool to me, Ginny most of all. Everything I said either got no response or a quick monosyllabic yes or no, sometimes just a grunt.

I wondered if they would still want me at their table at lunch, but I didn't have to concern myself about it. I had lost track of Summer between our last morning class and my entry into the cafeteria, but he was suddenly at my side when I was in line.

"Let's start the hens clucking," he said. "That table near the window," he told me, nodding at it. "Just the two of us."

A part of me wanted to ignore him as he had been ignoring me all morning and go directly to my girlfriends' table, but it was as if I couldn't turn away, as if I was in his magnetic field, firmly held. I didn't say yes or no, but that didn't matter.

He remained at my side. We got our food, and then he took my tray and started for the table. Despite the plates, glasses, and books, he looked incapable of spilling or dropping anything. Smoothly, he crossed the room, avoiding all eyes, and sauntered comfortably to the table. I followed, my head down. I felt the small smile on my lips and the amazed and envious glares from my friends and other students. He waited for me to sit and then sat himself.

"It's always better to surprise people, don't you think?" he asked.

"Is everything a game to you?"

"Game?" He thought, opened a container of milk, and nodded. "I suppose most everything but not everything."

"Okay. How did you know about the book prank?"

"A little bird whispered in my ear," he said.

"I'd like to meet this little bird already."

"Something tells me you have," he replied. He looked over at the table of boys gazing our way with fat, licentious smiles smeared over their faces. They were poking one another and muttering sexual innuendos. Never had they looked more immature to me. It was Summer who was making me see it, too.

"I have? What is that supposed to mean?"

"You're more like me than you care to admit. Right now, at least. I think it frightens you."

"What do you know about me? Why do you say that? And how am I like you?"

"Questions, questions. Isn't it better when the answers come slowly, naturally?"

"You can be quite infuriating," I told him, and began to eat, chewing harder than usual. I saw the laughter in his eyes but ignored it.

"Okay. I saw Kay buying the books and figured it out. It wasn't— "

"Rocket science. Come up with something new. You're starting to get monotonous."

"Oh!" he cried, holding his hand over his heart. "That's the cruelest cut of all. To accuse me of monotony. It could drive someone like me to suicide. Would you want that on your conscience?"

"So don't be monotonous," I said, and he laughed.

"Exactly what I would have said. See? We *are* alike."

Are we? I wondered.

Most of my life, I felt different from everyone else. There was never anyone I really thought was very similar to me. I didn't want to be thought of as different, so different that being a close friend to me was next to impossible. And yet Summer seemed to make friends easily. That was one of the things that attracted me to him. I wondered how he was able to do it, to be so self-confident and, yes, superior and still be liked so easily and quickly.

"I don't know," I said.

"Oh, I do," he replied, and then he unbuttoned the two top buttons of his shirt and turned to me to show that he was wearing a medallion. He held it up.

There were two dragons on it, facing each other, exactly the way they were on the ring Uncle Wade had given me.

12

"I had forgotten that I had this," he said, tucking it back under his shirt and buttoning up. "Seeing your ring reminded me. My father bought it for me years ago."

I continued to stare at him, my mouth slightly open.

"What?" he asked, smiling.

"You forgot? How could you forget while you were making such a big deal of my ring when you saw it, telling me what it meant? Why didn't it remind you then?"

"What's the big mystery? I put it away a while back and forgot about it, but when I put it on this morning, it felt like part of my body that had come back to life. It's like you and that amber necklace. From what I understand, you've been wearing it since the day you were given it and probably don't think about it, just like it was part of your body. Why do you wear it so often, anyway?"

"It brings good luck."

"You really believe that?"

"My parents do, and that's what's important. Don't change the subject. That medallion is quite a coincidence, don't you think? I told you my uncle found this in Budapest. Where did your father get that?" I asked suspiciously. "Or did you happen to find it yourself in some store, like yesterday, and come up with this story?"

"Absolutely not," he said, now looking indignant. "It's just as I said. My father gave it to me. I didn't think about it until last night just before calling you."

"So where did he get it?"

"I never asked him. It was one of the many things he bought me after my mother died," he added, and started eating.

Now I felt bad. "Oh. I'm sorry. How did your mother die?"

He kept eating, looking at the boys. I thought he wasn't going to tell me because it was too painful for him and he was still a little angry about my accusation, but he put his sandwich down slowly and turned to me. "Drunk driver," he said, patting his lips with a napkin. "It wasn't your typical death by drunk driver, either. She wasn't driving. She was walking across a street, and he went through the red light. I was almost with her. I was five at the time. She usually took me along whenever she went shopping, even if my father was home. She always wanted me with her, and going anywhere was exciting to me. That particular day, I fell asleep on the sofa, and she didn't wake me to go."

"I'm sorry," I said.

"That I didn't go?"

"No, you idiot."

He laughed, and as quickly as wiping a blackboard, the dark, sad moment disappeared. "Can I say how much I love the fact that I can't intimidate you?"

"You can say it," I said. "It had to be a bad time for you and your father, especially with you being so young."

"Yes. My mother was cremated. Her ashes are in an urn in our living room right now. We've never gone anywhere without her. I think you'd appreciate this. I wouldn't tell it to anyone else."

"What?"

"I talk to her, talk to the urn, and when I do, I see her as clearly as I would if she were actually standing there. I remember every little thing about her, every movement in her face, her eyes, the tiny dip in her lower lip when she was very thoughtful, and, most of all, the wonderful scent of her hair. For me, she's never dead. She put me to sleep every night when I was little, and she still does now."

I felt tears come into my eyes.

He smiled.

"Don't feel sorry for me," he said quickly. "I should be the one who feels sorry for you. You have a heavier cross to bear. Both of your biological parents are dead to you. I don't care how good your adoptive parents are to you, good deeds don't replace blood and heritage."

"What makes you so wise?" I wasn't being smart.

I was really interested. For most of my school life, my classmates resented me for being too wise, too grown-up. How was he getting away with it?

He shrugged. "I know what I know. So do you," he added, and started to eat again.

"What do you mean, so do I? How do you know so much about me after just one day and one phone call? How I think, what I know, and what I want?"

"Maybe it's all just lucky guessing," he said. "Besides, you don't want me to make it too easy for you by telling you, do you? It's the journey that matters, how you get there. Anyone can get there." He looked over at our classmates. "Most just stumble into it. They don't have their eyes as wide open and don't make the right choices because they knew enough to make them. If they do, it's pure luck. So, speaking of right choices, have you decided what we should do Friday night? Should I make it formal and come to your house, or should we just meet?"

"I'm still thinking about it."

"Good. As long as you're thinking about it, I still have a chance. I won't pressure you," he added. "I don't think I can anyway, not you."

"Why not?"

"You don't do anything you don't want to do," he said. "Neither do I," he added, before I could ask him how he knew that, too. "We're birds of a feather."

"So we should flock together?"

"See? I knew you'd get it."

Both of us ate silently. I was still struggling with my usually successful vision of the future, but he remained impenetrable. When he went into deep silences, it was as if he had left his body. That was something I had been accused of from time to time, especially by my mother. "Where are you?" she would demand, shaking me back from wherever I was. Of course, I'd be too afraid to say.

When the bell rang to end lunch hour, Summer took my tray to put it on the shelf. I waited, but he surprised me by turning around and looking like he was surprised I was still there, and then, like someone brushing someone off, he said, "Don't wait for me. I'll see you in class and at chorus."

"Thanks for the warning," I told him, now feeling a little indignant and embarrassed. I hurried out to join my green-eyed girlfriends, who had been loitering behind to watch us.

"Sorry," I said. I meant I was sorry that I didn't sit with them at lunch, but it was obvious they took it differently.

"Sure, you're terribly sorry," Mia quipped. "You're suffering terribly every minute with him."

"Did you find out about his father's novel?" Ginny asked.

"Yes. It was what I thought. He saw Kay buying copies in the bookstore."

"And?"

"He thought it was funny."

"Did he ask you out this weekend?" Mia asked. She was always one to get right to the point.

"He's trying," I said.

"What's that mean?" Kay asked. "Trying?"

"He wants either to come to my house to pick me up or have me meet him at the mall Friday night when we all meet to go to Jason's party and maybe just be with him."

"So why is that trying?" Darlene asked. "Sounds like a clear invitation to me."

"I didn't say yes yet."

"To which one, him picking you up or meeting him at the mall?" Kay asked.

"Either."

"You mean you might not want to be with him at all?" Ginny asked, her voice soaked in incredulity.

"I'm not sure. That's all."

They all wore the same amazed expression now.

"The one girl he chooses has to think about it," Ginny said, shaking her head. "Maybe he's not as sharp as we think."

The others nodded. I could see that made them feel better about not being the one Summer had gone after first. We started walking again. I remained a step or two behind, struggling to foresee where all this was going. Now I was sorry I had wished I didn't have a third eye. Maybe, because I was ungrateful, it had disappeared, and I was just as vulnerable as the others.

Peter and Danny were talking just outside the classroom. They were arguing about a new smartphone app. They paused when I broke away from the girls and stepped up to them.

"Hey," I said.

"Hey," Peter said. "We saw you with the new guy. What's he like?"

"Don't you know? You helped him with where we are in history class."

"Huh?"

"Didn't you?"

"I have yet to exchange two words with him," he replied. He looked at Danny, who shrugged. "What's this about?"

I turned and looked for Summer. He was lagging behind with some of the boys. They paused when a senior boy, Ned Wyatt, came hurrying up the hallway past them. He was a good fifty pounds overweight and often bullied by other boys. They called him a mama's boy and had made up a song about him to illustrate how overly protective his mother was. They often tracked behind him and sang: "Ned cannot play hardball; softball yes, hardball no." It usually drove him to tears.

I saw how they were all looking at him now, smiling as Jason sang the song. I was surprised to see Summer join in with them. Ned tried to ignore them. He looked back once, and then his legs inexplicably twisted as if they had turned to rubber, and he fell forward, his books splashing on the floor, his glasses leaping off his thick nose, and his pens and pencils rolling away. There was a roar of laughter from everyone in the hallway. He struggled to get up, but it was as if the floor beneath him had turned to ice. He slipped and fell repeatedly. Other students stopped to watch him, until Mr. Hardik, who was about six foot four and easily more than two hundred pounds, came out of his science classroom and literally lifted him up. Mr. Hardik shouted at the others to get to class.

I looked at Summer. He smiled at me as if he expected I would be just as amused by what had happened as everyone else seemed to be. It gave me a chill. I went into the classroom and got to my desk quickly, trembling a little from the confusion I felt. Someone who had suffered so much emotionally should have more compassion for others, I thought, but then again, maybe the tragedy had embittered him and he was just good at keeping that hidden most of the time. I wasn't sure whether I should feel sorry for him or annoyed at him.

He didn't try to explain anything when he came into the room. We didn't talk; in fact, he didn't look at me, and he was with the boys again between classes. By the time I arrived at chorus class, he was at the piano, playing as beautifully as yesterday, only now he was running through the numbers selected for the performance as if he had been playing them all his life. Mr. Jacobs stood by watching him and listening with more wonder on his face than I had ever seen on anyone's face. It was as if he had stumbled upon a true prodigy who was only his to employ and enjoy. He had found gold.

I took my seat quickly and observed how every other girl in the class was just as mesmerized. Again, for reasons I couldn't understand, I was more annoyed by it than pleased for Summer. He looked like he expected no less than adoration, and that arrogance was starting to wear on me. My girlfriends would never understand.

When we got up to sing, I was shocked when Mr.

Jacobs said he wanted to make a change with two of our numbers. His change was to replace Jan with me to sing the solo parts in both numbers. I looked at Summer. He held a tight smile. I started to protest, but Mr. Jacobs insisted I do it, and we began. Jan looked devastated. Afterward, when we were leaving the room, I told Mr. Jacobs it wasn't fair to replace Jan so abruptly.

He had started to chastise me for telling him how to run his team when I fixed my eyes on his and, using the same concentration I had when I willed my father's file drawer to close, willed him to stop. Suddenly, he did stop lecturing me. He blinked his eyes rapidly and then looked at Jan, who had lingered behind, despondent. He nodded to me.

"Yes, well, maybe I'll have you do a solo in a different number, one that we're not using a solo for yet," he said.

"Thank you," I told him. Jan had overheard and was smiling again.

When I looked at Summer, he seemed furious for a moment and then smiled and shook his head at me.

I turned and started away.

"You can be very convincing when you want to be," he said, catching up to me. "Are you always that successful so quickly?"

"I don't know what you mean," I said, a little nervous, because I, too, was impressed with what I had done.

"Maybe you don't realize yet how effective you can be."

"All I did was point out how wrong he was to replace Jan like that."

"You're better than she is."

"I don't think so. I don't think he really thought so, either," I said. I paused and looked at him. "Speaking of convincing people quickly . . . I suspect that you somehow convinced him to do it in the first place."

"All I did was point out the obvious."

"Right," I said, "the obvious."

"I was just thinking about what's good for the chorus."

"Of course. I'm sure that was your only reason."

He laughed. I continued walking, and he caught up again. "I see. You think I'm trying to endear myself to you quickly so you'll go out with me Friday night."

"The thought crossed my mind."

"Now, do you really think I'm that conniving?"

"Let's just say I have my suspicions." I stopped walking and looked at him with disapproval.

"What now?"

"That wasn't nice ridiculing Ned Wyatt earlier. Looks to me like you're being influenced by the wrong boys."

"It was all in fun."

"At someone else's expense. I thought you would have more compassion and understanding," I said.

He looked at me oddly for a moment, as if the entire idea was something he'd never expected to come from my lips. His expression changed quickly. "You're right," he said. "Sometimes I try too hard to make new friends. I haven't had all that many opportunities to have friends, don't forget, so I probably do make mistakes, compromise my values, and kiss up too much. You're not the first one to notice. My father's bawled me out for it a few times, too."

Because he sounded sincerely remorseful, I walked slowly so we could continue together to our last class of the day. Something else came to mind, however, and I thought that since he was being so honest, I should bring it up.

"By the way, I spoke to Peter a little while ago," I said, before we reached the classroom.

"Peter, Peter . . ."

"Peter Murphy, the boy who supposedly clued you in on where we were in the history text?"

"Oh, right. Peter."

"He said he never spoke to you about it. He's hardly spoken to you at all, in fact."

"That's true."

"But you said he showed you where we were in the textbook."

"I saw where he was and figured it out, so in a sense, he showed me."

"Cute explanation," I said. "But you were giving me the impression you had made friends with him quickly, weren't you?"

"Guilty."

"Why did you do that?"

He shrugged. "I was told you liked him."

"I do. He's very bright and a lot more decent than most of the boys in this school." I gave him a disapproving look, the way my mother would give one to me.

"What now?"

"You don't have to pretend untruths to impress me, Summer. Just be honest. You're picking up bad habits quickly in your new school. Or maybe you always had them, and now you're passing them around."

"*Moi?*" he joked.

I nodded and continued walking.

"Listen, Sage, if you really want to know, it's Jason who's the instigator in that group," he said, when we saw them all pushing and shoving on the way to their last class.

He paused to watch them, so I stopped, too. I could believe what he said about Jason. I was the one who had warned Mia about him.

"If he is, he should get his just rewards," I muttered.

"That's possible," Summer said. "Maybe sooner than later."

I looked at him with surprise. He was staring at the boys with angry eyes. As they passed the stairway, Skip Lowe suddenly lost his balance, as if his left leg had turned into butter, and he hit Jason on his right shoulder with his left the way a football tackler might. The blow pushed Jason to the top step. He tottered for a moment and then fell awkwardly to his left, tumbling down the stairs. Everyone nearby screamed. I shot forward and looked down. Jason had broken his landing with his left hand, and from the way it looked and the pain he appeared to be in, I was sure he had broken his wrist. His friends shot down the stairs to help him to his feet, Skip included. He was apologizing profusely, claiming he didn't mean it. He claimed his leg had just given out on him.

"I swear. I don't understand it myself!" he shouted.

Jason continued to grimace in pain. Some of the other boys helped him make his way back up the stairs, with Skip following, his head down.

Summer stepped up beside me. "Happy?" he asked.

"What?"

He nodded at Ned Wyatt, who had come to see what had caused the commotion.

"Poetic justice, right? Ned Wyatt can have the last laugh."

Teachers were rushing out to see what was happening. More students gathered. Mr. Jacobs was charging down the hallway. Jason was very important to the basketball team, and the season was going to begin in two weeks.

"Come on," I heard Summer say. "We'll be late for class."

I looked back at the scene at the bottom of the stairway and then at Summer.

He smiled. "What?" he asked.

"Nothing," I said, catching up, but deep down in my stomach, I felt as if I had swallowed an icicle whole. I felt a dark cloud swirling around me. Something very strange had just happened. I was sure of it.

The bell rang just before we entered. Half the class was still out in the hallway. The tumult wasn't subsiding quickly. In fact, the shouting and screaming got louder. Mr. Leshner hurried to the doorway to look out and then hurried out, so those of us who had taken our seats rose to look out into the hallway, too. Nick and Ward were infuriated by what Skip had done "accidentally." They were claiming he was jealous of Jason's position on the basketball team and had deliberately shoved him down the stairway. Ward claimed he could see it was deliberate. Other students were standing by watching the verbal argument metamorphose into something physical.

Summer stepped up beside me. I saw the way he narrowed his eyes and tucked in the corners of his mouth, forming a strange, wry smile. Skip broke free of the boys who had been holding him back and punched Ward in the face hard enough to drop him to one knee. Nick shot forward and tackled Skip. Everyone was shouting, some cheering them on. It took Mr. Leshner, Mr. Hardik, and Mr. Taylor to pull the three apart. They were directed to go to Mrs. Greene's office, and the crowd was told to go to class. It broke up slowly. Mr. Leshner headed back, and we returned to our desks.

"Get in your seats," he ordered.

"See?" Summer said.

"See what?"

"Be careful what you wish for, because you might get it," he said, then smiled and opened his textbook.

For a long moment, one of those times when I would certainly be accused of leaving my body, leaving the here and now, I wondered if somehow Summer was right. Maybe I had done something.

Luckily for me, Mr. Leshner determined it was necessary to quiet things down by giving us an assignment of reading, followed by the questions at the end of the chapter. There was no verbal give-and-take. Everyone was into the textbook. Gradually, I came back to reality, and no one had noticed I was gone.

When the bell rang to end the day, most of the kids were hurrying to find out what had happened to Nick, Ward, Skip, and Jason. In less than fifteen minutes, more than half of the varsity basketball team was in trouble. Mrs. Greene was very strict about physical violence in the school. It almost didn't matter who was responsible. Whoever participated was suspended for ten days and put on serious probation. Privileges like being on a team could be revoked.

"Mr. Jacobs is going to be in a state of deep depression," Summer said when we started out. "But no worries," he added as we stepped into the hallway.

"What's that mean?" I asked.

"Now Jason will definitely be left home and will have his party."

"I don't think that's at the top of the list of things to be concerned about, Summer."

"It's all relative," he said as we continued walking toward the building exit. "What makes one person happy can make another unhappy. What's good for some is bad for others. There is no good and evil. There's only happiness and unhappiness."

"I don't want to believe that," I said.

He shrugged. "So don't. That's my point." He

smiled and paused. " 'Why, then, 'tis none to you; for there is nothing either good or bad, but thinking makes it so.' "

"That's from . . ."

"*Hamlet*," he said, and then he leaned over, and before I could pull away even if I wanted to, he kissed me quickly on the lips. "That was good. I'll call you," he whispered, and hurried off.

I stood looking after him and brought my fingers to my lips.

It was as if his lips were still there, still gently touching mine and sending tiny sparks rolling from the base of my throat, around my breasts, and down to the pit of my stomach, where they gathered and filled me with the sort of warmth I had felt only in fantasies.

"What's wrong with you?" I heard Ginny ask as she and the others came up behind me. "Did you have a fight with him or something?" She watched Summer hurry out of the building as if he was being chased. I didn't understand his quick exit myself.

"Nothing," I said.

"Jason definitely has a fractured wrist," Kay said. "Marge Lungen told me Mrs. Mills took him to the doctor. He'll probably miss the whole basketball season."

"And he could have used that to help get him college financial aid," Darlene said.

"Nick and Ward could be suspended for ten days, and there's only two weeks till the first game. They might not be able to play for at least a month, if they can play at all," Ginny said. "We saw their parents arriving just a few minutes ago."

"They knew what could happen," I said.

"Excuse me," Darlene said. "That's it? 'They knew what could happen'?"

"Well, didn't they? You guys were the ones who told me how strict Mrs. Greene could be. Didn't you call her the Iron Lady, Mia?"

"That's not the point," she said. "We should feel sorry for them and for the school. Maybe you haven't been here long enough to appreciate it."

"You've got your boyfriend, so maybe you don't care about anything else," Kay said.

"Of course I care about the school, and I do feel sorry for them, but—"

"But they knew what could happen," Mia mimicked.

They were just looking for reasons to go at me, I thought. Summer had quoted Shakespeare. So could I.

" 'O, beware, my lord, of jealousy! It is the green-eyed monster which doth mock the meat it feeds on,' " I said, and walked ahead, leaving them behind wrapped in stunned silence.

13

From the look on her face and the way her eyes shifted from me to the school building, I could see that my mother sensed something was wrong the moment I got into the car. I knew I would be forced to explain and hoped I could get away with half the story.

"What is it?" she asked as soon as I closed the door. "What's happened today? Something has," she said quickly. "It's written on your face."

I shouldn't have been surprised or hoped I could hide what had happened. I knew that with anyone else but my parents, I could conceal any emotion or thought with a false smile or a blank expression. There was no blood connection between my mother and me, but she was often so in tune with my feelings and thoughts that I believed our hearts beat simultaneously. It was why I always feared lying to her. No other eyes could read my every gesture, the slightest movements in my mouth, or the shifting of my gaze as quickly and accurately as she could. It happened so often that I could understand why someone would question the fact that I was adopted. The bond between us was more like the bond of a child and her birth mother, who could say, "She was part of me. I know when she's upset, angry, or afraid."

"There was a fight in school just before the last period. One of the star basketball players fell down a stairway and fractured his wrist, and three others started punching and wrestling. They're all on the team, so everyone's upset because they could be suspended and prohibited from playing for a month or the whole season."

Any other mother would have been satisfied with that response and prodded no further, but not mine. "And?" she said, driving away. "There's something more than that bothering you, Sage. I can see it's something more personal. What is it?"

"I annoyed my new girlfriends by saying the boys knew what the consequences could be for fighting in school. I didn't mean I was happy about it," I quickly protested. "I just meant they should have realized the consequences and restrained themselves."

"Not everyone sees the future as clearly as you do," she said, sounding like it was a sin to do so. She thought a moment and then smiled. "So now they don't want you to meet them Friday night, is that it, these new best friends of yours?"

"I didn't say that. I just said they were annoyed with my tone of voice."

She drove on in silence for a while, and then, when we stopped at a red light, she turned to me. "Did you have anything to do with the fight?"

"What?"

"Did you instigate it, egg them on, do anything I will hear about later, Sage? You might as well tell me now. I don't like those sorts of surprises."

"Absolutely not. Why would I do that? How could I do that?"

She smirked as if I had asked a very dumb question. "You didn't claim to see some terrible thing in any of their futures caused by one of them and tell them? You weren't whispering in their ears about ugly visions?"

"No," I said firmly. "I would never do that."

"You didn't do that at your old school?"

"That was different. The boy was trying to get me to like him. I knew what kind of boy he was. The girl he abused just didn't want to be embarrassed about it, so she accused me of spreading stories about her. I don't deliberately hurt people, Mother."

The light changed. She was silent again for a while. "What about the new boy you're so fond of?" she asked.

"What about him?"

"Was he part of the ruckus?"

"No. He was with me watching it all happening."

"With you? So he is showing you more attention than he's showing any of the other girls?"

"It's only his second day," I said.

"You're not answering my question."

"I suppose he is."

She nodded, a knowing smile sitting comfortably on her face. "And because of that, from what you told me about the reactions other girls have to him, there is some jealousy fomenting. Right?"

"I guess so," I said.

"You should have anticipated it. What happened to your amazing foresight? Is it blinded by your own emotions? Your hormones starting to scream?"

"My hormones?"

"You know what I mean, Sage," she said. "Don't play dumb with me."

My mother and I had yet to have what anyone might call a mother-daughter conversation about sex and boys. It was odd in a way. She was so in my face about everything else. I knew it wasn't because she was a prude. It was more like everything else that happened to me. She was waiting to see how I would react, how I would turn out, and what I would do. Sometimes I felt confident that she was determining if I was going to be worth the effort involved in her taking on a more motherly relationship with me. Sometimes I felt as if my parents had just brought me home from the orphanage yesterday.

"I don't know. Maybe," I admitted.

She looked at me and nodded. "That's good. The more aware you are of your own weaknesses, your own vulnerabilities, the stronger you will become. Peer pressure especially can smother good instincts. Judgments are clouded. Self-control starts to slip away."

"Did something similar happen to you? I mean, your best girlfriends liking the same boy and resenting you for attracting more of his attention? Is that why you're saying all this?"

"No," she said sharply. Then she thought a little more and added, "Not all my friends liking the same boy. Well, perhaps one or two others did. No boy I knew was so attractive that he captured every heart. He sounds . . . too good to be true. Maybe there's too much fantasy going on. When you and your girlfriends get your feet back on the ground, it could be a hard landing. Be careful of getting too close to him too soon."

"You make him sound like a disease," I said.

"Just be careful," she said. Then she added, "Maybe of yourself more than him."

I guessed having him come pick me up wasn't the better idea right now, I thought. I didn't say anything, and she said nothing else until we got home, when she reminded me about Uncle Alexis and Aunt Suzume's visit on Saturday. I didn't know why she thought I might forget, but it was clear that she was just as intense about my meeting them as my father was. In the back of my mind, I thought this was another one of their tests for me. I was beginning to feel like I couldn't breathe in this house without their measuring how much oxygen I used.

What if Uncle Alexis or Aunt Suzume didn't like me? Could I be treated any worse? I didn't think the fear that I could be rejected and turned out of this family ever left me. Maybe it never would. Thinking about it made me nervous, so I went right to my homework.

Just before dinner, Ginny called me. I answered the phone first, expecting it would be Summer, but I was happy to hear from Ginny.

"You were right," she began, and then gave me one of her giddy little laughs. "Everyone's just a little jealous of you right now."

"A little?"

"Well, Mia might have bought a voodoo doll with your name on it."

"What?"

"I'm kidding. Anyway, I told them to back off. What happened in school isn't your fault, and you're really right about those boys anyway. They should be more mature and responsible. They were suspended for a week and put on probation. The Iron Lady didn't take them off the team, though. It's not fair. Why should they be treated like princes or something just because they can dribble and throw a basketball into some hoop?"

"Exactly," I said, surprised. Could it be that I was having a good influence on at least one of them?

"Anyway, I just heard from Jason. His parents actually feel sorry for him. They're still leaving, but they didn't put up any resistance to his staying, and get this. They said he could have a small party if he made sure everyone behaved and there was no drinking or drugs."

"What are they, ostriches?" I asked.

"What?"

"Do they bury their heads in the sand? They really believe that he'll keep anyone from drinking or doing drugs?"

"What's the difference to us? Let them believe what they want. A party's a party," she said. "Everything is set. We'll meet at the mall at six. We're going in two cars to Jason's, unless you're going to make other arrangements," she added. "Will you?"

"I'm not sure," I said.

"That you'll go to the party? Or go with us?"

"That I'll go with you or—"

"Summer? That's all right. Why shouldn't you? I know he's been invited. Are you going to have him pick you up?"

"No."

"Well, are you going to tell your parents about the party now?"

"No," I said firmly.

"What's with all this no? Why is it such a big deal suddenly? They let you go to my party, didn't they? And you were an obedient little girl coming home when they told you to. You didn't drink anything or take anything. Huh?"

"It's complicated," I said. "For right now, I'd rather they didn't know."

"See? Either they bury their heads in the sand or we make them deaf and dumb. What's the difference? Same results. Later," she said, and hung up.

I held the receiver for a few moments. Should I wonder why it was so important to her that I was still going to the party?

It was as though I could still hear what was going on at the other end. She wasn't alone when she had called me. I could envision the other girls beside her, and I could feel dark vibes. She was just a little too nice and understanding. They were planning something, something that would make me quite unhappy.

All through dinner and afterward, I couldn't help but be nervous anticipating Summer's phone call. My mother didn't bring up anything more about him. I was sure she had told my father about the incident at school, but he didn't mention it. If anything, the two of them were quieter than usual. They had that look that told me they had made some decision concerning me. Neither spoke about it. It was like waiting for the second shoe to drop.

When dinner was finished, I began to help clean up, but my mother told me to leave it and go do my homework. This was unusual, too. I had the sense that they wanted to be alone as soon as they could. Something was definitely bothering them, or they were arguing about something, and they didn't want me to know what it was. I couldn't believe it had anything to do with what had occurred at school or my budding little romance with Summer, but I didn't know what else it could be. What I didn't anticipate was that it would have something to do with spirituality, their spirituality.

While we celebrated Christmas every year with a tree and presents, there was really nothing in our lives that resembled religious beliefs similar to those other kids and their families had. I never asked why not. For me, my parents' religion appeared to be built around their superstitions, like Dad putting that knife under the front steps and my mother hanging the wreath of garlic on the front of our house. I never heard either of them mention going to any church when they were younger. Whenever my mother used the word *god*, I had the sense that she wasn't talking about the same sort of god my friends worshipped.

A little more than an hour after I had gone upstairs, my mother called to me to come down. When I appeared at the top of the stairs, she told me to come to my father's office. Nervously, I hurried after her. It was rare that we all gathered in his office, but whenever we did, it usually meant something very serious, like the time they announced I would be moving to another school.

"In anticipation of his visit, Uncle Alexis sent us a gift today," my mother told me at the doorway. "Your father wanted to hang it and display it properly before we showed it to you and before Uncle Alexis arrived."

She stepped back, and I entered the office. Dad had moved some of the paintings to create a wide available space for the gift. They both stood back to watch my reaction.

Hung on the wall behind my father's desk was a very large cast-iron circle with a five-pointed star in the center, also shaped with cast iron. I stared up at it, mesmerized. Suddenly, a beacon of images began flashing at me like some lighthouse on a rocky shore. Similar circles and stars appeared, some with candles burning around them. The visions became more and more intense. One circle began to spin, and as it spun, it moved closer and then farther away, fading before coming closer again and once again fading. I felt dizzier and dizzier. I brought my right hand to my mouth after I uttered a desperate "Oh," and then all went black.

I last remembered my body sinking into a pool of warm, sticky, muddy gook. I panicked as my head began to sink into it, and I woke on the floor, flailing about with my arms like someone submerged in quicksand, reaching out to grasp anything to prevent her fatal descent.

"Easy, easy," I heard my father say. He grabbed my wrists and stopped my wild swinging.

Gradually, I calmed, and the room stopped spinning. I looked up at the two of them gaping down at me. "What happened?" I asked. I could feel the pounding in my heart begin to slow and my heartbeat becoming normal again.

"You fainted," my mother said, but without sympathy or concern. She flung the words at me. It was more like I had done something forbidden or insulting.

"Why?" I asked as my father helped me into a sitting position and then to my feet. He guided me to the small leather settee across from his desk. I was afraid to look up at the cast-iron circle and star and kept my eyes fixed on the floor.

"We're not sure," my father said, sitting beside me and still holding my hand.

My mother didn't look at all unsure. In fact, she looked angry at me for fainting.

My father took my pulse and felt my forehead. "How are you feeling now? Nauseated, dizzy?"

I took a deep breath. Remarkably, I had no after-effects. It was as though I had imagined fainting. It had come and gone so fast it felt like I had imagined it. "No," I said. "What happened to me?"

"It doesn't necessarily mean something bad," he replied, more for my mother than for me, I thought. She creased her lips and looked at me as though she was anticipating something more.

"I wasn't feeling sick at all before I came in here," I said.

"We have no doubt that there's nothing physically wrong with you," my mother said.

I took another deep breath. How could she be so sure? Shouldn't they take me to a doctor? "I don't understand what happened."

"Don't think about it," she said. "Just look at the pentacle again, and tell us if there is something about it that disturbs you."

"The pentacle?"

"That's what it's called," my father said. "Some believe it's a tool of great power and protection."

"We do," my mother said. "You might as well tell her straight off."

"We do," he admitted. "It's very special for us because of its religious significance."

"Like a crucifix?"

"Exactly," he said, finally smiling. "Go on. Look at it again."

Slowly, I raised my eyes and, holding my breath,

studied it. I was frightened, but this time, nothing happened to me.

My father smiled and nodded. "She's all right with it," he told my mother.

She shook her head. "I'm not sure," she said.

"I am," he insisted, and then turned to me and smiled again. "Let me explain it to you. Each of the corners of the star in the center means something, Sage," he said. "At the top point, we have spirit, power, and on the right of it, we have air, love. Below that is fire, knowledge, and across from it is water, wisdom. And above that is earth, truth. It should be comforting to look at it and to understand it from now on," he concluded.

I glanced at my mother. If she looked at me any more intensely, her eyes would be inside me. "Well?" she asked. "After hearing all that, is there anything about it that disturbs you now?"

I shook my head. "I don't know what would. Nothing sounds terrible to me."

"Perhaps that there is only one point of the star at the top instead of two?"

My father looked at her and then at me, anticipating my answer.

"No. Why should it?"

The soft smile returned to his face, but my mother still didn't look satisfied.

"Why did I faint?" I asked. "I told you. There was nothing wrong with me before I came in here. I ate well at dinner, didn't I?"

"Yes, that's all true. So why did you faint?" my mother mumbled.

My father shot her a look of annoyance and turned back to me. "I've seen it happen before, and so has your mother. She knows very well what the reason probably is. You had a religious experience," he said, "an epiphany. Do you know what that is?"

"I'm not sure," I said. I knew the definition of the word, but I still didn't understand what it had to do with the pentacle.

"You had a realization, an awareness of something so powerful and wonderful and strong that for a moment, it overwhelmed you."

"Or burned her," my mother muttered.

This time, he just ignored her. "Here," he said, reaching for a small box on his desk. "Your great-uncle sent this along with it for you."

My fingers were trembling, but I managed to unwrap the box and open it to see a small pentacle made of gold on a gold chain.

"You can wear it now instead of the amber necklace. I mean, you could wear the amber necklace, too, if you want. Whatever pleases you," he said, fumbling for the right way to say it.

I took it out of the box and held it up. "This is part of our religion?" I asked.

He smiled and nodded. "Yes, it's part of what your mother and I believe. Think of us as spiritualists. The pentacle tells us we have the ability to bring spirit to earth. We told you what the five points represent. The five-fold symmetry is uniquely part of life—the human hand, a starfish, flowers, plants—you find five everywhere. You'll discover more examples now that we made you aware of it. We decided you're old enough to learn about it all, but slowly, of course. We don't want to overwhelm you with too many new ideas and thoughts."

I looked at my mother. She was still studying me hard. What was she waiting for me to do? Refuse the necklace? I undid the clasp and started to put it on.

My father moved quickly to help. "There, now," he said when it was fastened. The pentacle lay a few inches below the base of my throat. "How does it feel?"

I touched it. "Cool," I said.

"It will warm up," he assured me.

"Maybe it will become too warm," my mother said. "Let us know if it does."

"Why . . . how could it do that?" I asked.

"It won't," my father said confidently. He stood and looked down at me. "We decided that you need spiritual protection now. You're traveling new roads, some of which will lead you deeper into yourself. You need more guidance, and that will give you more confidence and keep you from straying off the true and safe path. Okay?"

"Yes," I said.

"You don't have to discuss our beliefs with your friends. Our spirituality is personal. We share that part of ourselves only with those we can trust to know us well. Understand?" my mother said.

"Yes."

"She's fine," my father said, looking at me. "She understands."

"We'll see soon enough," my mother said. "Go on and finish your homework."

I rose and started out. When I looked back, they were both staring at me, and it seemed as though they were holding their breath. I went upstairs quickly to look at myself in the mirror. Maybe because my mother had put the thought in my head, the pentacle seemed to grow warmer, but it never felt hot. For a few moments, I was mesmerized by it, by the way the gold twinkled. I even thought I saw it spin. I was so hypnotized by it that I didn't hear the telephone ring, so I was surprised when my father called up to tell me it was for me. This time, it was Summer.

"Hey," he said. "Sorry I had to run off at the end of the day, but I just remembered I had to meet my father for something. Any news about the combatants?"

"Suspended and put on probation, but they weren't removed from the basketball team. I'm sure missing practice time won't go over too well with Mr. Jacobs. We'd better be prepared to see him depressed and cranky in chorus class."

"Such is life," he said. "You bend with the wind, or you break."

"So you're a philosopher, too?"

He laughed. "I try. Look, I don't see the point in having to go through days and weeks of getting to know each other before we can see each other socially after school. You and I can know someone pretty quickly if we want."

"Why do you keep saying you and I?"

"There's a saying that's true, especially for us. It takes one to know one. You're one."

"One what?"

"Person with exceptional insight. Besides, I get the feeling you're almost as much a newcomer as I am. You're still feeling your way around with this crowd. We should do it together. I know I respect your opinion already. You'll get to respect mine, too. What do you say? Should I come by to pick you up?"

"No," I said quickly. "I've got to prepare my parents more."

"Now I can't wait to meet them. They sound like refugees from Victorian England. So what about meeting me at the mall, and we'll go to the party together, okay?"

Oddly, my fingers went to my new necklace. I touched it as I thought. My hesitation annoyed him.

"I mean, if you go there with your friends and the party isn't what you'd like it to be, you'll be stuck. With me, you won't be."

He was right about that. "Okay. My father is dropping me off at the mall at six."

"I'll be waiting," he said. "See you tomorrow," he added, as if he wanted to end the call before I changed my mind.

After he hung up, I sat and thought for a few moments. Was it possible that we really were alike? Was he just quicker at discovering that? Was it snobby to think like this, to think he and I were so different from everyone else that we were almost in our own world?

This all left me with a greater interest in him, a greater desire to know more about him. In a strange way, I was thinking that the more I learn about him, the more I might learn about myself.

I didn't think anyone I had met was as concerned about knowing herself as I was about knowing myself. They were who they were, and that was it. Most of them felt comfortable in their own skin, but I was still searching for my identity, waiting for the day when I would hear my real name. Sometimes I felt like I was wearing my face and body the way someone else might wear a costume. Who among my friends ever looked at herself deeply in a mirror, concentrating on her eyes as if they were two windows through which she could see her true self?

Who stood there asking herself, "Who are you?"

And who actually waited for an answer?

14

The following day, the girls were outwardly just as friendly to me as they had ever been, gathering around to thread and tighten the knot that made us special. They included me in all their personal intrigues and problems. I sensed who was at fault but kept my opinions to myself. From the way she was lording over them with her controlling looks, I could see Ginny had persuaded them to be nice to me again and wanted to be sure they were, but I still wasn't getting good vibes. I didn't like the way they exchanged smiles behind my back when they thought I couldn't see them, not that I was around them as much as usual. The moment Summer appeared, I broke away.

"Going my way?" he asked, winking at the others.

"As far as the next class for now," I said, and we walked off. I didn't want to look back at the green pool of envy, not that any of them should have been surprised.

Summer and I were spending most of our free time

during the school day together now. We would walk together to classes and sit together at lunch. Since I had agreed to meet him Friday night, I wanted to know as much about him as I could, as did he about me. Even though my personal history was nowhere as interesting as his, he was very interested in it. I was surprised at how many questions he had about my parents. I was embarrassed to admit that I didn't know as much as I should about their past and their families.

"Maybe they're ashamed of them," he commented. It was the first time I ever thought about that possibility, but it did start me wondering. After all, what other possible reason could they have for not being willing to talk much about their parents and grandparents? I didn't want to dwell on it, so I made him talk more about himself.

I particularly enjoyed his descriptions of places he had been with his father after his mother had been killed and the things they had seen in Europe and elsewhere. When he spoke about it, he had the far-off look of someone who could easily recall and relive the beauty he had seen and the good times he had enjoyed. His voice softened and warmed, drawing me closer to him. He was so descriptive and visual that I felt I was accompanying him on his journey back through time.

"Every summer since my mother died, we took a small villa in the south of France or on the Amalfi coast in Italy," he told me. "We went to wonderful restaurants with flowery patios, enjoyed the soft, sandy beaches and the refreshing Mediterranean, and especially enjoyed walking through the colorful and active streets at night, listening to all the languages spoken, seeing the fashionable women and men. The laughter was melodic. It was different."

"You make it sound wonderful."

"It was. It was like I was living in a movie. My father is a very handsome man. I could see the women, even those with other men, startled by his good looks, smiling flirtatiously, and moving on like children being tugged away from the playground, gazing back at us until they disappeared around corners or into restaurants. One summer we went to Greece, and one spring we went to South Africa on a safari. I have some fantastic pictures to show you one of these days."

"I can't believe how much you've traveled."

"My father's books are sold in so many countries now. He had people meeting us everywhere."

"But who was teaching you, homeschooling you, all this time?"

"He was, of course. Wait until you meet him. My father is an amazing guy. He's an expert in just about every subject and speaks four languages."

"My parents can speak French, Italian, Spanish, even Portuguese," I said. "And it doesn't seem to matter that they don't use them much. Whenever there's an opportunity, they do."

"Same with my father. He can learn a new language quickly."

"What about you?"

"I speak French well enough, and Spanish."

"And your father can teach you math and science?"

"Do I seem far behind the others in our class in any subject?"

"No."

"There's your answer," he said.

"But really, what about friends all these years? It sounds like you weren't anywhere long enough to make any, and being homeschooled, you didn't have the same opportunities to make friends."

"I managed," he said. "When I wanted to, that is. Although it might look like I'm trying to be friends with everyone here, I'm quite selective when it comes to that. I know the difference between an acquaintance and a friend. Besides, who are you to talk, anyway? You're more than fifteen years old, and from what you've told me, you haven't exactly been a social butterfly. In fact, it sounds to me as if you've been locked up like the Lady of Shalott in the Tennyson poem we read in class yesterday."

"It's not quite that bad."

"But close," he insisted. "What are they, from another century or something?"

I didn't answer. I wasn't going to disagree with him.

"You're really confusing your girlfriends," he continued.

"Why?"

"From what you've told them, they know how little social experience you have, but they're impressed with how you handle the boys and the advice you hand out to them about their little romances."

"Who told you all that?" I asked suspiciously. Was

one of them actively trying to damage my relationship with him before it had really gotten started? "And don't say a little bird," I warned.

"I overhear them talking. Mia, in particular, likes to raise her voice when I'm anywhere in earshot. Besides, I can see all that for myself anyway. I don't need any of them to point out what's real and what's not."

"Mr. Know-It-All."

"Not Mr. All but Mr. Enough," he replied. His eyes sparkled when he smiled.

"Why is it I believe you're not kidding?" I said.

"Neither of us is when it comes to ourselves," he replied. "That's what I like about you, your brutal honesty."

"Brutal?"

"Well, I suppose for most people, any honesty is brutal. I don't care as long as it doesn't create new problems for me with you," he added.

Did I blush? Was that my heart beating harder but happier? Or was my mother right, and it was merely my hormones, subdued until now, finding their voice inside me. This is how it should begin for any girl, I thought, really learning about each other first; only for me, it was happening faster, peeling off the layer of protection with which we all cover our personal and intimate details.

Was it happening too fast? How could you tell? If I ever needed a warm mother-daughter talk, I needed it now, but I was afraid even to suggest it, afraid of what new scrutiny and suspicion it would bring. I was living under a microscope as it was. No, the only way I could navigate through this new sea of passion and emotion was to make the most I could of my time with him and be as careful as I could be.

Even though Summer spent much more time with me now, he didn't ignore the friendships or, as he put it, acquaintances he had made. Whether he wanted to impress me or not, he seemed to be influential in getting Nick, Ward, Skip, and Jason back together, brokering a truce. He had them laughing and hanging out together again in a matter of days. When I complimented him on that, he shrugged and said, "It was easy. They're like little children, Sage. It still takes longer for boys to grow up. You can't get better evidence of it than watching them in action."

"Well, listen to you, Mr. Enough."

He laughed, but again, I couldn't disagree with him. He was certainly right about the other boys. Still, I wanted him to show more humility, but it was difficult to get him to be modest about anything. He had claimed I would be the one to bring him down to earth. I wondered how could I do that. Where were his weaknesses? He was already excelling in all our classes. In history, Mr. Leshner and he practically were having private conversations. He had a way of challenging the text and the lessons in a manner that amused Mr. Leshner and in some instances had him being the one to rethink facts and conclusions. It was the same way in science, and on two occasions, he caught our English teacher making grammatical errors, but he was clever enough not to look smug about it.

He always couched his corrections in a question, pretending not to be sure himself.

I sat back and observed him more and more, trying to be as objective about him as I could, not because I was, as my mother might accuse me of being, sexually fascinated with him. That was true, but it wasn't all that was driving me. I was learning from him, learning how I should behave, because he was right. In so many ways, we were alike.

When Friday came around, I was more nervous than I had been before going to Ginny's party. I still didn't have the courage to tell my parents the truth about the evening. I was afraid they would forbid it more now than ever because I had held back the truth until practically the last minute. All their suspicions about me, about my true nature, would be justified. Summer sensed my anxiety. Even in this short time, he was better at reading my feelings than I was at reading his. Was it because I wasn't as sophisticated?

"You're worried about your parents finding out you're not really going to a movie with your girlfriends, aren't you?" he asked after we talked again about how we would meet at the mall. I was sure he could hear it in my voice and see it in my face.

"A little."

"More than a little."

"Okay, a lot. I'll get over it," I added, annoyed at myself for being so transparent with him. I certainly wasn't with any other student, or any teacher for that matter.

He put our conversation on hold when class began, but he obviously didn't stop thinking about it.

"They don't follow you around, do they?" he asked as soon as the bell ending the last period had sounded and we were on our way out.

"No, of course not."

"Are you sure? From what you've told me, they sound obsessive and unreasonable. I mean, since you told me about their problems trying to adopt before, I understand them being nervous about you, but you've been with them long enough for them to know who you are."

"I suppose so," I said.

"I mean, what have you done to make them think you're not a good girl? I'm really curious now."

I was too embarrassed to mention the one other time I had lied to them when I denied looking into my father's filing cabinet. He would surely think something that insignificant would be silly even to mention. Besides, that wasn't what kept my parents nervous about me.

"There is something I haven't told you about myself," I said. I hesitated. Would this drive him away from me?

"If you keep me holding my breath, I'll die at your feet."

"Right. Ever since I can remember, I've had memories and dreams about things they assure me I could not know or have seen."

"That's it?"

"Isn't it enough?"

He smirked. "Maybe we really are reincarnated, or maybe you heard something or just glanced at something and it sank into your subconscious. Please. A child's imagination? They found that to be something negative? Sounds to me like they have some serious problems of their own. Listen. If they stifle you, they'll be sorry," he predicted. "They have to learn to trust you, too. It goes both ways, or it means nothing."

"I know." These were exactly my thoughts, especially now that I was older and wanted to enjoy more independence, or at least as much as my girlfriends did.

"You simply have to break loose, Sage. You can't be afraid to bend their rules sometimes. It might be the only way to get them to let you be yourself. Actually, we bring up our parents almost as much as they bring us up."

"Yes, Mr. Enough."

He didn't smile. "I mean it. Stop worrying. We'll have a good time," he promised. "And your parents won't be the worse for it."

"I'm not worrying about them."

"Well, you don't have to worry about yourself. You'll be the better for it. You'll see," he promised. He kissed me quickly, and like always, just before we arrived at the exit, he left me to rush out. Sometimes he went somewhere else in the building to do something he had forgotten. Was it because he didn't want my mother seeing us together since I had told him more about my life at home and how it would be wiser for me to bring him into my parents' lives gradually? Was he trying to protect me or protect himself from losing the opportunity to be with me? I knew he wanted our night to be special, and I had grown closer to him, but I still was afraid I was falling into a trap. He was so much more sophisticated than I was, or at least he seemed to be. Maybe he would move on to another one of the girls once he was satisfied with having had me. He was still looking at them, smiling, flirting. How I wished I'd had some other experiences before having met him so that I would feel I was on more solid ground and have more confidence.

The moment he left, the girls flocked to my side.

"What's he doing, rushing home to start preparing for tonight?" Kay asked, looking at Summer hurrying out. By now, they all knew I was meeting him at the mall and he was taking me to the party. "Washing his car and buying you a corsage?"

"Buying new clothes," Darlene said.

"Shining his shoes," Mia added. "After all, you're his first date here."

"I'm sure he realizes it's just a house party," I said, "and not the senior prom."

"It's not just a house party," Ginny said. "It's going to be a great house party. Jason has a great house."

"Four guest bedrooms," Mia added with a licentious smile.

"And a finished basement with a bar and an old-time jukebox," Kay added. "Bring your dancing shoes."

I walked out with them. "Don't let him talk you into going anywhere else instead," Darlene warned. "You'll miss a terrific time."

"We can see he's pretty much yours," Mia said. "Don't worry about any of us stealing him away. Everyone's already tried that. Right, girls?"

They all agreed and laughed. Ginny and Kay hugged me, and then I watched them walk away in the parking lot. Despite all the friendly words and smiles, those bad vibes were back. As always, it was difficult, if not impossible, to predict my own future, so I didn't know exactly why I had these feelings. I stared after the girls, trying to pierce the swirling dark clouds between us. My mother sounded her horn, shaking me out of it, and I hurried to the car.

"Looks like they've forgiven you for winning the new boy's heart so quickly," she muttered. "Don't deny that you have, either. He's called you every night this week. Right?"

"I guess," I said.

"I'm not a fool, Sage. Don't try to make it seem so innocent. I'm sure he's meeting you at the mall and will go to the movie with you," she said. She looked at me for confirmation before she started driving us away. "Well?"

"Yes." I didn't see the harm in confessing that much. In fact, I thought it would ease her fears if I was that honest.

"Don't go anywhere else with him," she warned. "If this little romance continues, your father wants to meet him properly."

"Okay," I said. I could feel the trembling in my voice and expected she would sense it, but she didn't or she didn't want to say anything, which stirred up even greater fear. What if she sensed what I was planning to do and was just waiting for me to do it? What if Summer was right to suggest that she or my father would follow me?

"Give her enough rope, and she'll hang herself," I could imagine her telling my father.

When we got home, I went up to my room, ostensibly to do my homework so I wouldn't have so much to do over the weekend. What I really wanted was to stay away from both of my parents until I had to leave. I was always afraid they could look at me and read my most secret thoughts.

When I began to dress to go out, I found myself taking more time about my choices, not because I was looking for what might make me more attractive and sexier but actually just the opposite. I wanted to be careful not to overdo it. I knew the moment I stepped off the stairway and turned, my mother would be scrutinizing everything I had put on. To her, every decision I made carried deeper significance, some hidden purpose.

In the end, I decided to wear the violet sweater she had bought me with a pair of jeans. I was hoping what I had read about the color violet was true. I wanted my imagination to be at full strength and any obstacles to that removed. I needed my third eye tonight more than any night, I thought.

I put on my black leather jacket my parents had bought me for the fall and wore both the pentacle necklace and my amber necklace and the matching amber earrings my father had bought me two weeks after my birthday. I had pinned my hair up and wore just a brush of lipstick.

"You look very nice," my father said before my mother had a chance to say anything negative or critical, but I did think she was happy about my choice of the sweater. Ever since the day of the pentacle revelation, they were keen on my feeling and doing something spiritual, something with what they called positive energy.

For a moment, I thought my mother was going to come along to the mall with us to watch me meet up with my girlfriends and be sure everything I had told her was true. She followed us to the doorway but then stopped. I didn't want to look back and show her how nervous I now was, but she seized my right arm to turn me toward herself. She looked intently at me. Did she finally realize the truth? Was she going to accuse me right now and stop me from going out? I tried desperately not to look guilty.

"Every decision you make in your life is another link in the chain that connects you with the spiritual good in the universe, Sage," she began. "And remember, a chain is only as strong as its weakest link."

I nodded. She looked at my father.

"Don't worry. She's a good girl," he said.

"Famous last words," she muttered, and turned away from us. We left.

"Why is she so suspicious of everything I do?" I protested after my father and I got into the car. "Did something terrible happen in her life, something she caused?" I guessed I was learning the bad habits from my girlfriends—put your parents on the defensive every chance you had.

"No. Of course not. She's only looking after your best interests, Sage. She really cares about you, as do I."

I was silent. Those were basically the same words Uncle Wade had used to explain her. Maybe it was true. Maybe Summer was wrong. Maybe I should have trusted them with the truth and not deceived them.

"Uncle Alexis and Aunt Suzume will arrive at about ten tomorrow," my father told me as we drove to the mall. "Your mother is going to prepare a very nice lunch."

"Are they staying for dinner?"

"No. They're visiting with some friends they haven't seen in quite a while."

Of course, I wondered why they weren't staying with us after all these years without seeing my parents, but I didn't ask. He talked a little more about Uncle Alexis but was still very vague with the answers to more of my questions about his family and his growing up. The suspicions that Summer had put in my mind seemed to be justified more and more. There was something in their past, something about which they were both ashamed.

"Have a good time. I'll be right here at midnight," my father said when we'd pulled up to the mall's main entrance. He gave me a quick kiss. I looked quickly to see if Summer was standing outside, maybe loitering in a shadow, but he wasn't in sight. I wouldn't have thought he would be waiting with the girls for me.

Where was he? What if he had changed his mind or for some reason couldn't come at the last minute? Should I go on to the party with the girls?

"Okay. Thanks, Dad," I said, and got out. I started toward the mall as he pulled away. Before I reached the door, I heard the car horn sound behind me and saw that Summer had pulled to the curb.

He was leaning out of the passenger-side window and beckoning. "No need to go in there!" he shouted.

I looked to see if the girls were gathered just inside waiting for us, but I didn't see them. My father's car was gone, so I started for Summer's. He got out and opened the door for me. He saw the way I continued to look around, searching the parking lot and the entrances to the mall before I got in.

I didn't see my father's car, but I had a strong feeling of being watched. There was a shadowy silhouette of a man to my right, just past the corner of the mall, but I was confident that wasn't my father. Whoever it was resembled a statue, unmoving.

"Hey, c'mon. What? Do you think your father circled around to see if you were going off with me or something?" he asked.

"It crossed my mind."

"He didn't," he said.

"How can you be so sure?"

"I just am. Trust me," he said, and we started away from the mall. The silhouetted man I had seen was gone.

"Trust you? How can you be so certain?"

"I don't know. What I do know is when I put my

mind to it, I can sense things other people can't," he said. We pulled out of the mall parking lot. My father's car was nowhere in sight. Summer paused at the first stop sign and smiled at me. "And so can you," he said.

"How do you know that?"

"I sensed it," he said, smiling. "I'm right, right?"

"Sometimes," I admitted.

How much more about my secret self should I reveal? I wondered. I glanced at him. He looked so content with himself. If he had that third eye, too, how was he so comfortable about it? What did he know that I didn't? I was caught between wanting to know his secrets and being afraid to reveal my own. There was no way one would come without the other, I realized. Perhaps I could do it in baby steps.

"Speaking of sensing things, I've had some bad feelings about my girlfriends and Jason's house party," I confessed, and waited anxiously for his reaction.

He stared ahead, his eyes so fixed on the traffic I wondered if he had heard what I said. "Tell me about it," he said, still holding his gaze on the street ahead.

"There's nothing specific. Whenever they talked about the party, I felt . . ."

"Danger?"

"Yes."

He nodded. "Girls can be wildcats. Let's see what they have in mind for you."

"Oh, that's nice. Really makes me want to go to the party."

He laughed. "Don't worry. I won't let anything happen to you," he said confidently. He reached for my hand, pressed his fingers softly over mine, and drove on, as if he had lived here as long as I had, meandering through side streets confidently and arriving at Jason's home so quickly that I wondered if the girls were there yet.

I asked him. "Maybe we should wait for them. We left the mall so quickly."

"No need. They came directly here," he said. "They didn't go to the mall first."

"What? How come?"

"The only reason they were meeting in the mall was to give you a cover story."

"When did you know this?"

"Ginny told me yesterday. She claimed she wanted to confirm that I was bringing you to the party."

"Well, why didn't you tell me?"

"I saw how spooked you were as it was and didn't want to make you any more nervous. What's the difference? You don't need them now. You have me," he said, and shut off the engine. "Well? Let's see why this is such a great party."

He stepped out. I hesitated, and he came around and opened my door.

"Madame," he said with a Shakespearean bow. He reached for my hand, and I stepped out.

I looked at the very large two-story colonial house. It was in a very upscale residential section of Dorey, with each home having a good acre or more of property. There were custom homes on the street, some Victorian and one or two more modern ranch-style, all with elegantly manicured lawns and hedges, double and even triple garages, and, like Jason's parents' home, with elaborate stonework and sidewalks. We could hear the music seeping out of the house but dissipating enough so as not to alarm or annoy the nearest neighbors.

Summer took my hand, but I didn't move.

"What's wrong?" he asked, seeing how intensely I was looking at the house.

How could I tell him that I saw a very dark shadow sweep in and settle on it? Would he think I was insane? Would he find it amusing and annoy me with ridicule?

Maybe, Sage, you should find out before you go any further with him?

"Something very wrong is going to happen in there," I said.

He looked at the house. "So? It won't happen to you," he said. He smiled, and I looked at him. He was so confident.

"What do you know?" I asked him. I was ready to ask him how he knew as well, but he shrugged.

"I know you and I are going to look out for each other," he said. "That's all that matters. C'mon," he urged, and we headed down the walkway toward the front door.

15

I felt like I was stepping through a fog when Summer opened the door to Jason's house and we entered. He expected the door would be unlocked. He didn't press the buzzer or knock. We paused in the wide entryway. No one came rushing out to greet us, but Summer behaved as though he had been here before. He moved us quickly down the short hallway and turned to the right. Just like at Ginny's home, the music flooded every room and hallway, but unlike Ginny's party, Jason's gathering was small. There were only ten of us. Ginny, Darlene, Mia and Kay sat with Todd, Jason, Ward, and Skip in the living room.

No one was dancing. Bottles of bourbon and vodka with an ice bucket and glasses were on the large, black marble oval table. I didn't see any food, not even chips or peanuts. Surprisingly, no one was smoking anything, but everyone had a drink in his or her hand. Jason sat on the corner of the large circular tan leather sectional sofa and had his fractured wrist resting on a pillow on a small table in front of him. He had his other arm around Kay, who was leaning on him. The others sat together on the remaining portion of the sofa. They all looked very relaxed, almost bored, which I thought was strange. None of my girlfriends said anything.

"Sorry we got started ahead of you," Jason said. "Make whatever you like," he added, nodding and waving at the bottles on the center table. "We're ordering in, Chinese. The menu's on the table, too. No one was sure what you drank, Summer. I thought you once mentioned drinking vodka. There's also rum and gin at the bar, and tequila. Choose your poison."

"Thanks," Summer said.

I squeezed his hand tightly and stayed back.

"Oh. If you want a soft drink, Sage, there's an opened carbonated lemonade on the bar," Jason added with a wider smile. "We all know you have to be extra careful tonight."

I started toward it, but Summer still held my hand quite firmly and didn't move, anchoring me to the spot. "So this is it?" he said, gesturing at the bottles and glasses on the table. "Nothing happier and stronger than alcohol?"

"No one had anything for tonight. You?"

"Sure," Summer said, which surprised me. "I always come prepared. It's good manners."

All of them finally smiled. He let go of my hand and stepped forward to kneel at the table. Everyone leaned over to watch him take a small, flat white box out of his right pants pocket and put it on the table. He looked up at them, turned to me, winked, and then opened the box to reveal a dozen small pink pills.

"These are the latest and the best," he said.

"What is it?" Ward asked.

"Some people call them Smiles for obvious reasons," Summer replied.

"I've heard of those," Jason said. "My cousin in Chicago told me about them. Where'd you get them? They're not easy to get. They're illegal to manufacture, sell, or possess."

"I have a trusted source," Summer said. "These live up to their reputation. I can testify from actually experiencing them, more than once. They give you a great kick. I can guarantee that they'll get the party kick-started."

"Did he tell you about this? Are you going to take one?" Ginny asked me.

"Sure I told her, and sure she is," Summer said, answering for me. He plucked one out of the box and held it out for me.

I looked at it in his palm and then at him and saw him wink again. He was up to something. Maybe the pills were nothing, but he wanted to see how they would react if they thought they were something special. It would be a good joke on them, and from the way they were acting toward me and the fact that they hadn't told me they weren't going to meet me at the mall first, I was happy to see a joke pulled on them.

Trusting him, I took the pill out of his palm.

"Well, that's a surprise," Darlene said. "Must be your influence, Summer. I would never think Sage would do any drug, happy or not."

"Oh, you'd be surprised. Everyone has secrets," he replied. He picked up the box and offered a pill to everyone. Everyone took one.

"Can you take it with alcohol?" Mia asked.

"Sure," Summer said. "You won't want much more vodka or whiskey after, anyway."

"You'd better take it with your soft drink, Sage," Ginny said, taking hers. "We don't want anything weird to happen to you since your parents don't know you're here."

"Very thoughtful and considerate," Summer said. He took one of the pills and poured himself a little vodka. "Bottoms up," he said, and everyone joined him.

Then he walked me to the bar. Even if what he gave them was a joke, it still made me nervous to participate.

"I don't want to take this," I told him, sotto voce.

"Don't," he whispered. "Don't drink any of that lemonade, either," he warned. "Pretend to. It's bad stuff."

I looked at the lemonade. There was no way to tell by its color. How did he know what was in it? I wondered. Obviously, they had been planning to have fun at my expense and had spiked it with something. With our backs to them, I did just as he said. I poured some in the glass, brought it toward my mouth, and put it back on the counter. He took my hand again and fingered the pill he had given me. Then he put it in his pocket.

"You don't need this now," he said. I was surprised he didn't whisper.

We turned to look at the others.

Only a minute or so had passed since he had given them the pills, but they all had the same stupid smile.

"No wonder you called them Smiles," I told him, loudly enough for them all to hear, but none of them reacted. They held their smiles and stared at us. "They look like they're hypnotized," I said, more loudly. Again, no one reacted.

"Well, it can have that effect," he said. "You might say it's the only effect."

"What?" I looked at him, a surprised smile on my face.

Then I looked at them again. Nothing had changed; no one had moved. They seemed frozen in time, no one even blinking.

"What's going on? What's happening to them? What did you give them?"

"I knew they were out to do you harm," Summer said. "It wasn't the original purpose of this party, but it quickly became their intention. There's enough Ecstasy in that lemonade to set you on fire." He nodded at the glass on the bar. "You would be in quite a lot of trouble with your parents when your father picked you up later, and from the way you've described them to me, I wouldn't see you for years except at school. Couldn't let that happen," he added.

I looked at the others again. There was still no sign

any of them had heard anything he said, nor had any of them moved an inch since they had taken the pills Summer had provided.

"What is in that pill, and how come you aren't reacting to it like they are? I saw you take one."

"Mine was what is referred to as a placebo. It's shaped and colored the same way, but it's just sugar."

"Where did you get the rest of them?"

"I picked them up in Europe. Don't worry. It won't harm them permanently. In fact, when they wake up, they won't remember anything."

"When they wake up?"

"Don't they look asleep, even with their eyes open? Did you ever see a more vulnerable group of idiots?"

"What are you going to do, Summer?"

"Well, what do you want to do? They were going to hurt you, Sage!"

"Let's just leave," I said. "If you're sure they'll be all right."

"Can't just leave. That's a waste of all my efforts," he said. "Besides, they'll not have learned anything, and they might just come after you in some way again."

"I can take care of myself."

"No offense, but you wouldn't have taken care of yourself too well tonight if I hadn't been with you," he said.

I looked from the gang to the bar, where the drug-spiked lemonade remained untouched thanks to Summer. I couldn't disagree with him.

"Besides, this is a party. They like to party. So let's let them party."

He went to the music system and turned up the volume. Then he went to each one of them and whispered something in their ears. I stood back watching. One by one, they rose, moving very slowly, just like someone who was hypnotized, and to my shock and surprise, they all began to undress.

"Summer!" I shouted as the boys began to take off their pants and then their underwear. "What are they doing?"

He smiled. "It's just your typical nudist party," he said.

Even Jason was struggling to get out of his clothes. I shook my head and backed away. The girls were moving just as quickly to get undressed.

"I can't believe you're getting them all to do this."

"It's nothing special," he said. The girls were nearly naked. Neither Darlene nor Mia had been wearing a bra.

"Stop them."

"They'll stop themselves," he said. "C'mon. Let's not let them ruin our evening."

"What?"

He took my hand and started me toward the front door.

"But . . . when will they stop?"

He looked at his watch. "Give them another fifteen minutes. Maybe they'll enjoy one another more," he said. He opened the front door.

"But are you sure they'll be all right afterward? I mean . . ."

"Depends what you mean. They'll be plenty

embarrassed, and they'll wonder what happened, but no one will be able to explain it."

"They knew we were here, and you gave them the pills."

"What pills?" he said, smiling. "They won't remember us even being here."

"How can you be so sure?"

He held his smile.

"You've done this before?" I asked.

"A few times," he said, "but never with more glee," he added, and led me out.

The music was so loud now that we could hear it clearly all the way to his car.

"Where are we going?" I asked.

"Let's get something to eat. I'm starving. I know a better pizza restaurant than the one you were supposed to go to in the mall," he said, opening the car door for me. I looked back at the house, and then, as if I had been tapped on the shoulder, I spun around and looked back down the street. Once again, I thought I saw the silhouette of a man in the shadows.

"There's someone there," I said, nodding in the silhouette's direction. "Watching us."

"Where?" He looked and shook his head. "Naw, that's not anyone. It's just a small tree."

I looked again. The silhouette was gone.

Of course, the first thing I thought was that it had been my father.

"Stop worrying so much. I'll be sure to get you back in front of that mall by twelve." We got into his car.

"When they regain their senses, they'll wonder

why we didn't show up, even if you're right and they forget we were there, Summer."

"So what? Simple answer is you and I decided we wanted to be alone for our first date. They'll buy into that. No worries." He started away.

I looked back at the house. The girls would be devastated, I thought. "Will they all wake up at the same time?"

"Practically. No one will wake up early enough to cover himself or herself up from the others. I can guarantee you that."

"Really? So where and when did you do this before?"

"What's the difference? Stop worrying about them, Sage. They were out to get you tonight, and I told you, promised you. I'm not going to let you get hurt, now or ever," he said and drove on.

I wasn't sure whether I should be grateful or upset. Despite what they were planning to do to me, I couldn't help but feel bad for them.

Summer laughed. "I can't wait for the story those girls give you tomorrow, if they decide to tell you anything at all," he said. "Can you?"

"Yes."

"Relax," he said. "You didn't do anything to them. I did, but don't you tell them. Believe me, they wouldn't be this concerned about you."

"When did you know about all their planning to hurt me tonight?"

"Almost as soon as they concocted the idea," he said. "I've got amazing hearing."

He laughed again, and we drove on in silence for a while. Did he have amazing hearing, or was there some other way he had found out? When did he over-hear them? He was with me almost every moment of the day.

"C'mon, stop thinking about them," he said, see-ing how deep in thought I was. "We didn't do them any permanent harm."

"Oh, I think those girls will carry that for a long time," I said.

He shrugged.

"Imagine what you would have carried for a long time if they had succeeded and gotten you into big trouble with your nervous-wreck, obsessive parents," he said.

He was right, I thought, but still . . .

He made a few turns and brought us out onto a street I had never been on. Right on the corner was a small Italian restaurant called Mamma Mia's. He parked right in front of it.

"How did you find this place?"

"My father found it. He's like that. He'll scout an area for days locating the best of everything. Wait until you taste the pizza here. Everything's made from scratch and fresh. It's the closest thing to pizza in Eu-rope that we've had."

It wasn't until we got out and approached the front door that I realized this was the first time I had been to any restaurant without my parents. He smiled and kissed me on the cheek before he opened the door. I knew I looked at him strangely, because I thought, although it was nice, it was so unexpected. Why kiss me then and there?

"Couldn't help myself," he said, reading my thoughts in my eyes. "I could kiss you all day. I want you to feel good about this night, Sage. I warn you, I'm going to work at it."

I laughed, finally relaxing, and we entered the small restaurant and went directly to a booth as if it had been reserved for us. When the waitress came to hand us menus, he shook his head.

"No need. We'll have a Margherita pizza and two Cokes. We'll share a house salad," he said quickly. "They're pretty big," he told me. As soon as she left, he reached across the table for my hands and put his around them. "There's no reason we couldn't have had a date like this from the start and avoided all that back there," he said.

"Maybe we will next time."

"I don't know. I'm not confident. You haven't even been permitted to sleep over at a girlfriend's house until now, right?"

I nodded.

"I don't care how you excuse it. There's something wrong with them treating you like a serial killer or something." Suddenly, he let go of my hands and sat back.

"What?"

"I didn't notice until now that you had on two necklaces. I can't see what's on the second one. You have it under your sweater."

"Oh. It's a pentacle," I said, pulling it up to show him.

He nodded.

"Do you know what it all means, each star corner?" I asked.

"Yes. Where did you get that?"

"My great-uncle Alexis sent it along with a wall-sized one. He's coming to visit us tomorrow. Actually, I've never met him or my great-aunt," I said.

"You have one weird family. So your parents are into that sort of thing?"

"You mean spiritual stuff?"

"Yes."

"They are. But your father bought you something spiritual. You're wearing that double dragon piece."

"My father's into lots of things, but he doesn't take anything that seriously. He thinks most religions are full of superstitions. Are your parents superstitious, too?"

"About some things," I said. "Yes."

The waitress brought our Cokes and salad with some bread.

"Bread's homemade," he told me. "The olive oil is from some family vineyard."

"You know everything about this place?"

"My father asks lots of questions. He uses everything in his writing. I'm sure this restaurant will turn up in a novel."

"Do you read his books?"

He smiled. "Not a one. They're too girlie."

"Did he always write romance novels under the name Belladonna?"

"As long as I can remember. Great salad dressing, isn't it?"

"What? Yes."

"So what are some of your parents' superstitions, besides black cats and walking under an open ladder or something? Anything unusual?"

"I don't like talking about them like this," I said. "It feels funny, like I'm betraying them or something."

"Betraying them? Jeez, they really do have you shackled. It's not right. You should be soaring. You could easily be the most popular girl in the school. If you keep a bird's wing tied to its body, it'll never fly, and you can fly, Sage."

I nodded slightly and ate some more.

"That's it. I've made a decision," he said.

"What decision?"

"I'm making you my cause. I'm determined to help you free yourself of your bondage."

"Oh, it's not that bad," I said. "I wouldn't call it bondage."

"Believe me. I've been around, Sage. It's that bad," he said. "There are girls two years younger than you in our school having more of a social life."

The waitress brought our pizza. It looked delicious.

"We'd better wait until it cools a little," I said.

He ran his hand about an inch over it. "It's fine." He looked at his watch. "Eyes are opening back at Jason's," he said with glee. "I'm almost sorry we didn't stay around to see."

"I'm not."

I put a piece of pizza on my plate. It looked like it still should be too hot, but when I felt it, it was just right. It was the best pizza I ever had eaten. I told him so.

"I won't ever disappoint you, Sage," he said with such confidence that I couldn't help but be impressed.

"I hope not," I said. Something kept me from matching his words and making the same promise.

When we were nearly finished, he looked at his watch. "This might sound nuts for me to suggest. I should be monopolizing every minute with you."

"What?"

"We have lots of time yet. How would you like to meet my father? I told him about you," he added quickly. "I don't talk about girls with him much, about anybody, for that matter. He's dying to meet you, and I'd like you to meet him."

"He might be disappointed, Summer."

"I doubt it. We don't have to stay long. I kinda said I would bring you around," he confessed. "I'll get you back to the mall in time. Don't worry about that," he added. "Well?"

"Okay," I said.

He signaled for the waitress to pay the bill.

I wanted to suggest that we circle back to Jason's house to see if the others were really all right, but he was too excited about my meeting his father. They lived in the opposite direction, a good two or three miles from downtown Dorey. Here the houses were farther apart. The area looked more rural, with older buildings and some abandoned or no longer working farms.

"How come you live out here?"

"Dad always looks for the quieter, more remote places whenever we settle down anywhere," he said. "He likes less distraction when he's writing, and he's always writing."

"I guess so. I saw he had more than forty novels published."

"No lack of ideas. Sometimes he works on more than one at the same time. He changes from one story line to another like you and I change television channels."

"Was he always a professional writer?"

"He's always been an entertainer. Let's say that."

"What do you mean? What else did he do?"

"He had a magic act when he was younger," he said.

He slowed down as we approached a two-story Dutch colonial house with dark gray shingles and white frames around the windows. The gambrel roof had double slopes on each side, making it look like a dressed-up barn at first. It had two narrow white pillars on its wide entry portico. There wasn't very much land-scaping, and the grass in front and on the sides looked untended. He pulled up to the single-car garage.

"Magic act? My uncle Wade's a magician!"

"Dad hasn't done magic for a long time. He was already writing and publishing when I was born. This is your uncle who gave you the ring?"

"Yes."

He shut off the engine. "C'mon."

I got out, and he came around to take my hand and

lead me to the portico. It was somewhat overcast now. There hadn't been a moon, but the night hadn't looked as dark to me until now. There was only a small light over the entrance. Most of the windows in the house were dark.

"Are you sure he's home?" I asked.

"He's home. He's probably in his little office and so involved with his story that he's unaware how dark the rest of the house is. There's no one more absent-minded than my father when he's working."

"Maybe we shouldn't disturb him, Summer."

To my surprise, and I think Summer's surprise, too, the front door opened before he reached for the doorknob, and his father stood there, silhouetted against the backlit hallway.

"I thought I heard you drive up," he said.

He reached to the side and flipped a switch for a small chandelier above his head. The illumination flowed down over his coal-black hair, which was cut and brushed in the style of a 1920s actor, with the top brushed to the right and a part on the left. He wore a vintage burgundy velvet smoking jacket, a black cravat, a white shirt, and black slacks. I saw he had on a pair of black fur-lined slippers.

"You must be between chapters," Summer said.

"Yes, perfect timing. So this is Sage? I can see she is even more beautiful than you described," he said. "Welcome." He stepped back.

"Thank you," I said, and we entered the house.

I smelled a familiar scent. "Is that garlic?" I asked.

"Oh, yes. Sorry. I made myself pasta tonight, and

as Summer will tell you, I can be heavy-handed when it comes to the garlic."

"And the red pepper," Summer added.

"The spice of life. Please, come in." His father led us to the small living room on the left.

There was barely any light coming from the small table lamp next to a large dark brown cushioned chair. He quickly turned on a larger floor lamp next to the matching sofa.

"Let me get a better look at you," he said, indicating that I should sit near the lamp.

Summer led me to the sofa, and we sat.

"Can I get you anything to drink? Had dessert?"

"We're fine," Summer said. "Mamma Mia's," he added, as if that would explain everything.

His father nodded, smiled, and sat across from us. He crossed his legs and folded his hands on his flat stomach. On his left hand, he wore a silver ring with three strands of woven gold in the center. It seemed to seize the light from the smaller lamp and glitter. His face was in some shadow, but I had seen that his eyes were an interesting and unique shade of gray. He had my father's kind of handsome, symmetrical facial features, only his face was narrower, his chin a little sharper. I thought he was a little taller than Summer, not as broad in the shoulders, but with a more regal stature and a mature elegance. Even though it was the first time we had set eyes on each other, there was something familiar about him. It was as if he had been in my dreams more than once, a stranger introduced to me in sleep, faintly recalled and always fascinating.

"As I understand it," he began, "this is a forbidden date tonight."

Surprised, I looked at Summer.

"I always tell Dad the truth," Summer said.

"My parents are very careful about my socializing," I said.

"Why? Did you do some terrible things in the past? Come home late, get into serious trouble, use drugs or drink too much?"

"No, none of those things," I said.

He shrugged. "What makes them so concerned? From what Summer tells me, you're a perfect A-plus student, in the chorus, and well thought of by your teachers."

Where should I begin? I thought. Should I talk about the way my parents had reacted to my stories and dreams from the time I was able to talk? Should I tell him about their fear of my biological father coming to snatch me away? Should I bring up their failure with two previous children? "I'm hoping they'll change and become more relaxed about me," I replied instead.

"So I don't have to worry about you leading my son into a life of sin?"

I glanced at Summer. He was smiling, but his father still looked serious.

"I think the devil will be quite disappointed if he's looking for help from me," I said, and his father laughed.

"She's bright," he said.

"Summer told me you were once a magician," I said.

"Yes, in my younger days." He leaned forward. "Does magic interest you?"

"I have an uncle who's a magician. He travels all over the world performing."

"Yes, the Amazing Healy."

I looked at Summer. I was sure I had never told him Uncle Wade's stage name. "How did you know that?"

"Oh, I still have an interest in the profession and keep up with the stars of magic. Do you do magic tricks now, too?"

"Me? No. Hardly. My uncle doesn't give away his secrets."

"Nor should he ever," Summer's father said.

"I am fascinated by what my uncle can do, however."

"I imagine so. Summer also tells me that you and your girlfriends had copies of one of my novels."

"That was supposed to be a joke on Summer, but he beat us all to the punch."

"Yes, he can do that," his father said. "Well, if you still have the book and read it, let me know how it was. I value comments from young, beautiful women more than the comments I read in reviews."

"Okay," I said.

"Well, you two probably have things you want to do, and I have to get back to a young woman whom I have in such a depression over a lost love that she is threatening to kill herself."

"Oh."

"Don't worry. There's a knight in shining armor

about to come into her world and save her from un-happiness. He's even going to help her see how much potential she has and free her of all those things that keep talented people from enjoying their talents," he added as he smiled and rose.

I stood up, too, and so did Summer.

"I do hope you will come see us again," his father said, crossing to me. "Perhaps your parents will relent and permit you to come to dinner, or maybe Summer will figure out a way to get you liberated long enough."

I was a little surprised at what he was giving his approval to: deceiving my parents.

He could see the shock on my face. "Sometimes the ends justify the means. I am a believer in that. Nice to have met you, Sage. I love your name." He reached for my hand and brought it to his lips. They felt more than just warm on my skin. When he raised his head, his eyes locked on mine, and I felt like something within me, something more than just my heart, was caressed by something within him. It was almost over-whelming, making my head spin just a little.

He looked at Summer and then turned and walked out of the room.

"What a charmer," Summer said. "I can't tell you how often he has embarrassed me into being more polite than I had ever intended to be with some of the girls I introduced to him."

"That's not a bad thing," I said.

He laughed. "Let me show you my room. I have a surprise for you." He took my hand, and we walked out of the living room and up a short stairway to the second floor. His bedroom was the first one on the right. He turned on the light first and then stepped back for me to enter.

I stepped in and stopped quickly.

There on the wall, facing his queen-size bed, was a photograph of me that measured at least four feet by five feet.

16

His room wasn't very big, even compared with mine, which I always thought was smaller than most of my classmates' bedrooms, especially from the way they described their furniture, televisions, closets, and computer desks. However, houses of this vintage normally didn't have large rooms or high ceilings. Maybe that didn't matter as much to boys. He certainly didn't look embarrassed or ashamed, neither of it nor of my blown-up photograph.

I was surprised that he had nothing else on any of his walls, no sports posters, no posters of singers or movie posters, nothing. It was as if he had just moved to America. The room was spartan, with an old, dark cherry-wood dresser that matched the bed's headboard. There was a large, dull yellow, saucer-shaped light fixture overhead and light brown hardwood floors with no area rugs. The closet was on the left, and there was one nightstand on the right side of his bed, with a square-shaped clock on it and a small lamp that also looked like a refugee from a thrift store. The bed itself was neatly made, with two large pillows and a light blue spread. There were two windows, both with their dark blue curtains closed. I wondered where he kept his books and did his homework. I imagined there were motel rooms that had more character and certainly more furniture than his room.

"I know it doesn't look like I have much right now. I haven't half unpacked my things," he explained. "In the past, Dad's packed us up and left where we were almost before I could settle in. He gets a feeling for an area quickly. Before you ask, he likes it here."

I still had my gaze fixed on the picture of me. In it, I had turned around in class and was looking at him, probably, but I didn't recall him snapping my picture, either on a smartphone or with a camera.

"When did you take that picture of me?"

"The first day I was in school," he said.

"I didn't see a camera."

He walked over to his nightstand, opened the drawer, and took out a camera that was so small it could fit in the palm of your hand. "Neat, huh?"

"No. Sneaky," I said. "Why did you do it and then blow it up so big?"

"I have this thing for real beauty when I see it," he replied. "I like waking up to your face," he added without the slightest hesitation. "I go to sleep with you and wake up with you."

I knew I was blushing.

He sat on his bed and looked up at me. "I want to

know more about you, Sage. I want to really get to know you."

"I've told you everything. I haven't had as exciting and interesting a life as you have."

He shook his head.

"What?"

"I don't believe that."

"Why not?"

"You're holding back," he said. He reached out for my hand. I didn't move. "I won't bite. I've been accused of many things but never of being a vampire."

I stepped forward, and he clasped my hand and gently pulled me to him. We kissed. It was the longest kiss of my life. My whole body seemed to swirl, but in more of a panic than I had anticipated. Until now, his kisses were quick pecks on my lips and my cheeks. This kiss seemed to have fingers reaching deeply down inside me and touching places that slept comfortably in the sanctity of my youth. It was as if the sleeping sexuality within me was ambushed, roused, unprotected. His hands slipped down my back and over the crests of my buttocks, pulling me even closer and then turning me so I fell beside him on his bed. In an instant, he was over me, straddling me and then bending closer to kiss my forehead and trace the side of my face to my neck with his lips, lips that were so hot I thought they would burn my skin. Instead, they broadcast waves of heat down to my breasts and the base of my stomach.

I felt myself start to weaken, my resistance starting to crumble beneath the erotic weight of his hands, his longer kisses, and finally the full pressure of his body against mine. It was all happening so quickly. I felt myself surrendering. But the alarms that sounded and the hardness that came to my rescue surprised even me, for there was a strong part of me that had wanted his advances, had craved his affection, and I thought had prepared willingly to surrender. From out of a dark place that I didn't know existed inside me, I could feel and hear a great *NOOOO*, and I pushed up on his chest, practically lifting him completely off me.

He stopped, surprised at my strength and my refusal to continue. "Hey," he said, rolling onto his right side, "I thought you would want this."

"I do, but not so fast," I said.

He smiled and nodded. "You think I'm out to nail every pretty girl in school and began with you, is that it?"

"In the garden of suspicions, that one has flowered," I admitted.

His smile widened. "How could I get a reputation like that so fast?"

"How else would you explain the rush?" I asked.

"Okay, okay. I was told to expect that you'd be different," he said, and sat up.

I sat up, too. "Who told you that, Summer? Who told you that I would be different?"

"Never mind. I'm not complaining. If you want to know the truth, I kind of like it. You're the first girlfriend I've had who's been able to resist my charms," he added, half kidding. "I love a challenge."

"You didn't give the rest of your girlfriends one of those pills on your first dates with them by any chance, did you?"

He laughed and brushed down his pants. "No. Never needed anything but my own animal magnetism and good looks." He stopped smiling and reached for my hand again but held it more gently this time. "I didn't mean to rush you. You underestimate your own charm and good looks and overestimate my power to resist."

"Oh, clever. Now blame me," I said, rising.

He continued to hold my hand and sit there looking up at me, his eyes and his smile subtly changing from amusement to a suddenly deeper perception. "You need to realize and accept that you are head and shoulders above everyone else in that school, Sage. What applies to them doesn't apply to you. You're special."

"Why do you keep telling me that? There are other girls who have grades as high as mine, girls who do more extracurricular activities, have more friends and certainly more boyfriends."

"I'm not talking about any of that."

"What are you talking about, then?"

"Your power to anticipate the future for others, even somewhat for yourself, and . . ."

"And what?"

"To persuade and control other people."

I started to shake my head.

"No," he said. "I saw what you did to Mr. Jacobs that day."

"What day?"

"The day you persuaded him to put Jan Affleck back to sing the solo part he wanted you to sing."

"All I said was—"

"What you said wasn't enough to change his mind, Sage. He wasn't going to do it. He even resented your telling him how to run his chorus, and then . . ."

"Then what?" I asked. Inside me, I knew the answer, but it was something I had never recognized, something I had been afraid to recognize.

"Then you did what you do, and he changed his mind. You focused on him. You transmitted your will, and he easily surrendered to it, and quite abruptly, I might add. Even I was surprised. It happened in the blink of an eye, didn't it?"

I stared at him.

"You've done that before, haven't you?" he asked. I started to shake my head. He let go of my hand. "That's what I meant when we first came in here, Sage. That's what I meant when I said I really wanted to get to know you, when I said you were holding back. What else have you done? Who else have you controlled?"

"This is silly talk, Summer," I said. I looked at my watch. "I'd like to start back to the mall."

"What if I told you I've done similar things? Something told me that you suspected that, too."

I stared at him. Could that be true? Was that why he said so often that we were alike? I was tempted to tell him more. Holding these secrets close to my heart was a lonely, scary thing at times.

"Your adoptive parents suspect all this about you, too, don't they? That's why they're so hard on you, try to keep you so confined and under their control. They are afraid of you. Am I right?"

"This is crazy," I said. "You're frightening me."

"Okay, okay. Maybe I am rushing things. I'm sorry. I really like you. I was only trying to help you realize you shouldn't be afraid of anyone or anything, and if anything, you should be permitted to grow, to enjoy your powers, not resent them or be afraid of them."

"I don't have powers," I insisted.

"Call it what you like. It's nothing to be ashamed of. That's all I'm trying to say."

I looked away. "I don't want to talk about this," I said.

"Okay, let's go," he said. "I'm sorry. Please don't be upset with me."

I looked at him and nodded. "It's all right. Right now, I'm just worried about . . ."

"Everything," he said, and smiled. "So am I." He took my hand and led me out of his room, shutting off the light and closing the door. "Please don't tell my father I said any of that to you. He's been on my back lately about not making friends and having what he calls 'normal relationships' whenever we do settle down somewhere."

"He should understand how difficult that is for you because of how much he moves you two around."

"Exactly," Summer said.

When we reached the bottom of the stairs, his father called to us.

"Let's say good night to him," Summer said, and we turned to continue down the hallway to a room on the right. His father sat at a large, dark oak desk with a single lamp throwing just enough illumination for him to see what he was writing. I was surprised to see he was writing in longhand and not on a computer.

His face was cloaked in shadow, but he leaned forward into the light. "Leaving?"

"Yes," Summer said.

"I wanted to say that I really do hope we'll see you again soon, Sage. I have a selfish motive to confess," he added. "Summer can tell you. I like to read some of my new manuscripts to young women whenever I get the chance. I both enjoy and learn from their reactions. Many times I have changed things in one of my books because of a young woman's reaction, and I think, from what Summer's told me of you and from what I can tell, that you can be of great help to me. If you don't mind, that is."

"No. I'd be happy to do that when I can, Mr. Dante," I said.

"Oh please. Don't call me Mr. Dante. My given name is Roman," he said.

I hesitated to ask, but it was just too heavy on my mind not to. "Roman Dante is a beautiful name. Why not use that instead of Belladonna on your novels?"

"Ah . . . see? She's asked an excellent question, Summer. She's a jewel. So," he said, turning back to me, "what do you know about that name, Belladonna?"

Should I tell him about my adoptive parents, their

heritage? "I know what it was used for and how dangerous it was—it is," I said.

"Yes, and that is love. Everything has another side to it, Sage. Never lose sight of that," he said. "Besides, I can't use my real name. I've got to be mysterious now. My readers are drawn in by that romantic darkness. Do you know anyone who is like that, who needs that?"

"My uncle Wade," I said.

"Ah. Magic. My old love. And you understand why. See? You'd better treat this girl well, Summer, or I'll be very upset," he said.

Usually, when someone said something like that, they were kidding, but the tone of his voice and the little I could see of his face reflected what sounded more like a real threat.

"Will do," Summer said. He reached for my hand. "We've got to go, Dad. I don't want to get her into any trouble."

"Oh, right. That business about your parents being worried about you, perhaps a little too much." He shook his head and sighed deeply. "Parents. Do you know how a fencing instructor instructs a new student, Sage?"

I did, but I didn't know how I knew. I said nothing and shook my head.

"Hold it like a bird. Hold it too tightly, and you will crush it. Maybe you should gently remind your parents about that."

"Yes," I said. "But my father is a very clever man. He'll remind me of the second part of the instruction. Hold it too loosely, and it will fly away."

He laughed. "Perhaps when it's your time, you will do just that," he said. "Fly away." He turned back to his pad.

When he moved his head, there was just enough illumination to reveal the wall on the right. Summer was starting to lead us out of the room, but I caught a glimpse of what I was sure was a smaller but definite pentacle. Only this one had two star points at the top. Or at least that was what I thought. I didn't have time to look back. We were on our way down the hall and out of the house quickly now.

"My father wasn't kidding about reading his writing stuff to young women," Summer said. "He says I'm of no use to him when it comes to that. I don't have the right sensitivity. I wouldn't say it, but I'm happy he spares me. You girls are definitely a different species."

"How is he so successful at getting into the feminine persona?"

"He claims all writers have to have split personalities, more yin and yang," he said as we crossed to his car.

"He said that? Yin and yang?"

"Sure. Why?"

"Nothing. My parents believe in that."

"A lot of people do, Sage. No surprise there," Summer said. He opened the car door for me and hurried around to get in. "So you're supposed to have seen this movie tonight, *Ruby*, correct?"

"Yes. Ginny was supposed to give me the novel to read just in case my parents asked about it, but she somehow forgot. Maybe not so *somehow* now that I know their real goal for tonight."

"Don't worry about it. I saw it. There's this Cajun girl who lives with her grandmother. The grandmother doesn't like her husband anymore because he sold Ruby's twin sister to a rich Creole man from New Orleans who is really her father. It's not until she's dying that she tells Ruby about her and advises her to go find her real father, and she discovers her twin, who's the exact opposite, a spoiled rich girl who will become jealous about sharing her father's affection. I love the voodoo business in the story," he continued, and he told me the whole plot before we reached the mall.

I was half listening, because I couldn't stop thinking about the pentacle I was sure I had seen in his father's office. When we arrived, I hesitated before getting out and asked him, "Does your father have a pentacle on the wall in his office? I thought I caught a glimpse of one."

"Someone gave him one, yes. He has a lot of unusual gifts. I think he was given that by a baron or something in Hungary when we were staying in Budapest for an international publishing event."

"Hungary? You're sure?"

"As sure as I am about anything he tells me."

"I didn't get a good look at it, but it looked different from the one my parents have."

"Did it? I guess these things are different in different countries. Let's go inside. We have a little more time. I'll buy you an ice cream or something."

We got out and started for the mall. Before we walked to the main entrance, I heard my name called and looked to the right. Ginny and Mia were standing there, smoking cigarettes.

"What are they doing here?" I wondered aloud.

"This oughtta be good," Summer said. "Remember. We were never there."

I didn't believe they had forgotten that, but the second we were upon them, Ginny asked, "Where were you?"

"Oh, we got sidetracked," Summer replied quickly. "Actually, I wanted Sage to meet my father. You know, the author you're all reading." Both Ginny and Mia looked uncomfortable at that. "How come you two are here so early? Didn't you enjoy the party?"

"No," Mia said quickly, too quickly for Ginny, who nudged her.

"It was boring," Ginny said. "We decided to come here to see if you two were still here or something."

"Well, we've returned. I was going to buy Sage an ice cream. I'd love to buy one for you girls, too."

"An ice cream," Ginny said dryly. "That's your big night."

"We did go for pizza, and then I took Sage to meet my father," he said.

I was uncomfortable with the way Ginny was looking at me, but I didn't reveal anything in my face.

She shrugged. "Might as well have an ice cream," she muttered. "Apparently, there's nothing better to do."

We started into the mall.

"What would you call something better?" Summer asked her. He held my hand, and they walked beside me.

"If you don't know, I'm not going to tell you," she said, and he laughed.

Of course, I was full of questions I couldn't ask.

What happened when they realized they were all naked? How long did it take to get dressed? What did the other girls do? What did the boys do?

Summer bought our cones, and we sat at one of the tables in front of the ice cream store. The mall was thinning out. People had already left the last showings of most of the films at the movie complex, and the restaurants, even the pizza place, were nearly empty.

"Who was at the party?" he asked.

"The usual suspects," Ginny replied, and she rattled off the list of boys and the other two girls.

"Sounds like a small party. Maybe that was why it was boring," Summer said. "Didn't Jason have anything to liven it up for you?"

Neither girl responded. They looked at each other, and then Ginny offered a quick, sharp "No."

"Well," Summer said, looking at me, "I think I'll be on my way. It's good the girls are back and can go out of the mall with you when your father arrives. That way, he'll believe you were all together."

"I don't see what the big deal is. Why does she have to hide the fact that she was with you instead?" Mia demanded.

"She won't much longer. Everything good takes a little time. You're not the sort of girl who rushes into things on the first date, are you?" he teased her. I squeezed his hand under the table.

"At least I *have* a real first date," she replied petulantly.

"I must say I'm really surprised," Summer said. "Wasn't there anyone at the party you liked?"

"They were all immature idiots," Mia said.

"Boys will be boys," Summer replied.

Mia turned away, and Ginny looked down.

Summer stood up.

"Okay, good night, girls. I'll call you tomorrow, Sage," he said. He leaned over to kiss me but kept his eyes open to watch Mia's and Ginny's faces. Then he smiled and walked off.

"Did you have a good time with him?" Mia asked immediately.

"Yes."

"What's his father like, then?"

"He's charming," I said.

"Charming?" She looked at Ginny. "Who calls anyone charming, for God's sake? Is he sexy, as sexy as Summer?"

"He's elegant, mysterious, very handsome, and yes, sexy," I said. "I would call that charming."

She looked disappointed.

"So why did you two leave the party so early?" I asked, recalling what they had intended to do to me. "Something happen that upset you? Someone get too drunk and throw up, or what?"

Neither spoke, but they looked more devastated.

"What?" I pursued.

"We were drugged," Ginny said.

"Drugged?"

"Jason must have put something in our drinks."

"What happened?"

"If you dare tell anyone . . ."

"Jason probably will," Mia said sadly.

"No, he won't, or we'll describe him in centimeters," Ginny said, making it clear what she meant.

Mia smiled and nodded.

"So what was it?" I pursued.

"All of us went into some hypnotic state or something. When we became conscious again, we were all naked."

"Naked?" I was so good at sounding surprised that even I believed it. Summer would surely be proud of me, I thought.

"We were drugged with something new. All the boys must have been in on it. They must have stripped us and then gotten undressed themselves as a practical joke. They claimed they didn't and put on this almost convincing reaction of shock and surprise, but how else could it have happened?"

They looked at me for an answer.

"Well?" Mia asked. "You seem to know everything else."

"You're right," I said. "How else could it have happened? I suppose you're right not to believe their reactions."

"You're damn lucky you weren't there," Mia said, but more mournfully than as if she was happy for me. She looked ready to cry. I was sure she had, that they all had.

But I wasn't thinking of that. I was thinking about the spiked lemonade they had planned for me to drink. "Yes," I said. "Damn lucky."

17

When my father drove up to fetch me, Ginny and Mia made me promise them again that I would never tell what had happened to them at the party.

"Especially don't tell your parents," Ginny said. "My parents find out about this, and I'm dead," she emphasized, her eyes wide with fear but also with a clearly unveiled threat shot in my direction.

"No one will find out anything from me, Ginny," I assured her, but then I looked at Mia. "But someone will talk too much," I added, with the firmness of any prediction I had ever made. She knew and felt it, too. "Night," I said, and got into my father's car.

"How was the movie?" he asked immediately.

"It's a great story," I said, and I repeated it almost word for word the way Summer had related it to me. It took almost the entire trip home.

"Your mother tells me you probably met this new boy at the mall."

"I did," I said. That wasn't a lie. I had met him at the mall, only right after my father had dropped me off.

"When are you bringing him around to meet us?"

"Soon," I said.

"Remember, tomorrow your great-uncle and great-aunt arrive."

"I have it marked down on my right palm, and I won't wash tonight," I said.

I thought it was funny, but he gave me a nasty look. "Sarcasm doesn't look good on you, Sage."

"I'm sorry," I said quickly.

"I know it's in fashion with you kids today, but I think it's a clear way to show disrespect. Some parents ignore it. We won't."

"Okay, Dad," I said. "I'm sorry."

I had never heard him sound so furious. Something was changing. He was nervous about something. I could sense it. He was quiet the rest of the way, and so was I.

My mother was waiting for me with her questions just as she always was when I returned from somewhere. Tonight it was where did we eat? When did we go to the movies? Who was there? What did we do after the movies? And most important of all, did I notice anyone in particular watching us, watching me? The more she asked, the angrier I could feel myself getting. Summer and his father were right. My parents, especially my mother, were obsessive and unfair. Look at how much trouble the other girls had gotten into, and yet look at how much freedom they had.

"I don't know why you're continuing to treat me this way. You're making me feel like some sort of criminal. I didn't go out stealing. I just met friends. I want to have friends, and I want to have a good time, too!" I cried. "Why do I have to be treated like I'm on parole or something? What have I done to deserve it?"

Hot tears burned under my eyelids. I could feel the heat in my face. It was as if a bomb had gone off. The silence that followed was shattering. I thought even the windows had rattled.

My parents didn't move, didn't breathe. Neither of them had ever seen me this way. I was surprised at my outburst myself, but I didn't feel bad about it. I had almost used Roman Dante's analogy and talked to them about holding the sword too tightly and crushing the bird, but I didn't. I didn't want to start my mother questioning where I had gotten that idea. I had never taken fencing lessons, so she would go on about another one of my inexplicable memories and tell me I hadn't improved at all.

"Too many parents don't take enough interest in their children's activities," my mother said very calmly, but it sounded like a weak argument. I could see she knew it, too.

My father finally interceded, telling her that I should get to sleep. "Alexis will be here late in the morning," he reminded her, but he made it sound like all her fears and concerns would be alleviated once my great-uncle Alexis and Aunt Suzume arrived.

She relented, nodded, and sat, still looking a little stunned. I said good night and hurried up the stairs.

The moment I closed the door, I felt a great sense of relief but also the weight of my emotional roller-coaster ride from the moment I had met Summer to just now, when I'd finally escaped my mother's third degree. I was exhausted. It took me only minutes to get into bed, but I didn't fall asleep quickly as I had expected. Instead, my mind began to play back images like a slide show on the closed lids of my eyes.

Once again, I saw the dumb, stunned looks on the faces of the girls and boys at Jason's house after they had swallowed Summer's pills. It was truly as if their brains had been shut off. Their eyes were as glassy as the eyes of the dead, stone-cold still, blind to everything in front of them. After he had whispered in each one's ear, I once again saw the way they began to undress, slowly at first, moving robotically, and then suddenly in a frenzy to beat everyone else to nudity. When I had looked back from the doorway, the girls were already totally naked, and the boys were catching up and turning to face them. No one was touching anyone else. It was as if they had been turned into statues.

The silhouetted man I had seen in the dim light began to haunt me, too. He floated in and out, and then, in what was more like a nightmare vision, he was sitting right beside me in the pizza restaurant. I opened my eyes, and for a moment, in the glow of light seeping through my curtains, he seemed to be there in my room, standing just inside my door, looking at me. He had no face. I leaned over to flick on my side table lamp, and the image evaporated.

"Don't be afraid," I heard my voices whisper. "Sleep is your escape."

I shut off my lamp and lay back. *Think of something pleasant*, I told myself. Summer's long kiss came to mind, but I shook it off. I wasn't aroused the way any other girl surely would be. I wasn't preparing to fantasize about making love to him. I was hurrying to go through the darkness of sleep to find another place, a comfortable, safe place in which I could curl up and forget. I heard another voice, soothing, loving. It came from a woman shrouded in a memory so old and thin that it was difficult to imagine her face. Her voice was enough. In moments, I was warm and comfortable and asleep.

In the morning after breakfast, I helped my mother prepare what would be a much bigger lunch than we usually had on weekends. Usually, we had a big breakfast, but today we had a small one. It was more like a day for a holiday luncheon. She had bought a turkey to roast. We made homemade cranberry sauce, creamed spinach, and sweet potatoes. My mother was a good pie maker. She always prepared her own crust and had a secret recipe for her mincemeat pie, something I knew was traditionally served during the Christmas season in England. My father once let slip that her recipe went back to the thirteenth century, handed down by her ancestors, but then she would answer no questions about her ancestors.

The first time I remembered eating it, I thought I had eaten it many times. My parents swore that wasn't possible. My mother made it only on very special occasions, and my father said he could count on the fingers of one hand when they were. But it was like any of my other inexplicable memories, still true to me despite what he or my mother said.

Uncle Alexis and Aunt Suzume arrived a little before eleven. The first thing I thought was that a great-uncle should look much older than he did. Aunt Suzume looked only a little older than my mother, if that. My father treated them both with great deference. Someone would think that members of a great royal family had come visiting. I could see the adoration and respect in my father's face when he greeted them. They weren't embarrassed by it. In fact, they looked like they had expected the adulation and reverence.

Uncle Alexis was a little taller than my father and did have a stately and imposing posture, offering his hand with the august manner of someone imperial, almost pompous. Aunt Suzume was barely five feet tall, with exquisite facial features and a pearl-like sheen to her complexion. It was a face that looked lifted off a delicate, flawless cameo pin, and yet, despite her diminutive size, she, too, seemed to have been brought here in a royal horse-drawn carriage.

Of course, I understood that older relatives were supposed to enjoy some veneration and honor because of their age or wisdom or successful lives of which the family could be proud. Unlike most of my classmates, I had no grandparents who could visit and leave behind some pearls of wisdom that would help guide me to a more successful life. That was the way it should be. Sometimes I had the sense that it once was true for me. It was simply another inexplicable memory of things past, a memory better kept to myself.

"Well, now," Uncle Alexis said when I was introduced to him, "so this is the wonder girl who has captured everyone's attention."

I looked at my father. Wonder girl? Captured everyone's attention? Except for Uncle Wade, whose attention did I capture? My parents weren't treating me like some wonder girl. What was I missing?

"She's very, very beautiful," Aunt Suzume said, smiling at me. "No one exaggerated about her."

Again, I was surprised. When were all these wonderful things said about me, and by whom?

My father took their coats and led everyone into the living room. Uncle Alexis was wearing a dark blue suit and a light blue tie. Aunt Suzume was in a navy-blue sleeveless lace sheath dress. Although there were strands of gray in it, Uncle Alexis had a full, thick head of hair, brushed back but not as trimmed as I would imagine someone of his age should have his hair. Aunt Suzume's ebony-black hair was pinned in a French knot. She wore the most interesting gold teardrop earrings. They seemed to pick up a bluish tint when she crossed the room. She wore a gold watch and a white gold wedding ring with diamond specks that looked like they were baked into it.

They sat together on the settee, not an inch apart. Mother brought them each a glass of her homemade elderberry wine and set a bowl of mixed nuts on the table. Dad sat in his favorite chair, and I sat on the matching settee facing my great-uncle and great-aunt.

For a moment, no one spoke. They were studying me so intensely that I shifted uncomfortably and looked at my father.

I was expecting to hear them talk about old relatives and family memories, but it was as if they had seen each other frequently and not years and years ago the way my father had described. It was quickly apparent to me that they were not interested in my parents and what they had done since they had seen them. All their attention was focused on me. Why?

"You're in the school chorus, we understand," Uncle Alexis began, after taking a sip of his wine.

"Yes."

"What instruments do you play?" Aunt Suzume asked.

"I don't play any," I said.

They didn't look like they believed me. They glanced at my parents for confirmation. I looked at them as well.

"She doesn't play the piano?" Aunt Suzume asked my mother.

"No. Not yet," she said.

Not yet? Years ago, when I was only six, we had dinner at the Blacks' house. There was a piano in the den, and while everyone was talking in the living room, I wandered in, sat at it, and began to play. Moments later, everyone was in the den watching and listening to me. It was a while before I realized they were all standing behind me, but as soon as I did, I stopped. Then Samuel and Cissy Black applauded, but my parents didn't.

"How long has she been taking lessons?" Mrs. Black asked.

"She hasn't," my father said. "Ever."

"Well, she has a natural ear for it. I've heard of that," Mr. Black said. "You should think about having her study with someone. You might have a musical genius on your hands."

My mother indicated that I should get up quickly and come to her. We went to the dining room, and nothing more was said about it until we got home, and my mother seized me by the shoulders in the entryway and told me never to do that again. I was not to play anyone's piano. If they wanted me to study piano, they would arrange for it when I was older, but they never did, and I never sat at one and played again.

"The piano?" Uncle Alexis asked my father now. He shook his head. "That was a little bit too much caution, don't you think?"

"We had reason, if you'll recall," my mother said.

Caution? About what?

Uncle Alexis nodded, sipped some more wine, and turned back to me. "Tell us more about yourself, Sage. What are your favorite subjects in school?"

"I suppose English, history. I do enjoy being in the chorus. Actually, I like math and science very much, too."

He smiled. "Your thirst for knowledge knows no bounds," he said. He looked at Aunt Suzume, and she smiled.

"Do you still have dreams about people and places you've never seen?" she asked.

I looked at my mother and then at my father. I couldn't help it. I felt as if I had somehow been betrayed. Ever since I had been sent to a therapist, those things were never discussed, certainly never with anyone outside of our small circle, which only included Uncle Wade.

"Tell them the truth," my father said sternly. For the first time, I wondered if they were really who my parents told me they were.

"Yes, that happens occasionally," I replied, "but I don't speak about it to anyone." I looked at my parents. Was this the answer they had hoped to hear?

"And these strange memories, they are usually about people being punished, burned at the stake, stoned, whipped, things like that?" Uncle Alexis asked.

"Not just that sort of thing, no. I remember being at ocean shores, riding in horse-drawn sleighs, being at prayer events with lots of candles and chanting. Things like that," I said. "I could go on and on about it." They wanted me to talk? All right, I'd talk. They'd be sorry.

Uncle Alexis smiled. "That's not necessary, dear. We also understand that you are in the prognostication business, a modern-day soothsayer."

"I promised my mother I wouldn't do that anymore."

"But you were successful as a prophet?" Aunt Suzume asked.

"Maybe not all the time," I said.

"We understand why your mother might be a little nervous about such things, but you need not be ashamed of anything with us," Uncle Alexis said. He had finished his wine. My father rose quickly to pour him another glassful. "Thank you, Mark. Your uncle Wade thinks you are quite an extraordinary young lady," he continued.

"I'm very fond of Uncle Wade. I'm sure he exaggerates a little," I added.

Uncle Alexis widened and softened his smile.

"Modesty. That's good," he said. He looked at my mother, who shifted as if she was uncomfortable. "And you have excellent school grades and have never gotten into trouble at school or outside of school?"

"Maybe I haven't had enough opportunity," I replied.

For a moment, I thought my father and mother would tell me to go to my room or something. They looked as displeased as they used to when I said things that embarrassed them in front of their friends during my younger days.

"What do you mean?" Aunt Suzume asked.

"I haven't gone out much. I've been to a party, and I've met some friends, but I really haven't done all that much socializing."

Uncle Alexis nodded. "Your parents have been careful. That's not a bad thing."

I didn't reply. Why weren't they changing the subject? Why was it all about me? "Where do you live, Uncle Alexis?" I asked, hoping to change the subject myself.

"Oh, we're in transit at the moment. We've lived abroad for many years, but we're thinking about returning to Boston. Wherever we are, we hope you'll come visit."

"Of course I would," I said. I wanted to add that I would go anywhere since I hadn't been anywhere. "What did you do as a profession?" I asked. I wanted to make it clear that I was told little or nothing about him or my great-aunt.

"I was a doctor, a therapist," he replied.

"A very, very successful one," my father added.

I almost asked him why he hadn't sent me to see him years ago, but Uncle Alexis quickly added that this was when he was living abroad.

"And you had no children?" I asked. I knew my mother wouldn't want me to be so direct and inquisitive, but Uncle Alexis didn't seem to mind.

He smiled, in fact. "I've had many children," he said. "All clients. I specialized in child psychology."

"But—"

"No. We were married late in life, and we didn't have any children of our own," he said.

I caught a movement in Aunt Suzume's face, the way her eyes looked down. They weren't telling me the truth, but I would never dare say it.

"Your great-aunt Suzume was a well-known opera singer in Japan in her youth," Uncle Alexis said. "She was very dedicated. It took a great deal of persuasion to get her to think of me with as much passion."

Everyone smiled. Aunt Suzume looked a little embarrassed, suddenly like a little girl to me. I could hear her singing.

"I need to get to our lunch preparations," my mother said. She rose and looked at me, and I rose, too.

"I will help," Aunt Suzume said, but my mother wouldn't hear of it.

"We're fine. You enjoy your visit with Mark," she insisted.

Aunt Suzume didn't put up any argument. She nodded, and then my mother and I left to go to the kitchen. The others retreated to my father's office. I heard them go in and close the door.

My mother worked silently. I could see she was in deep thought.

"I like them," I told her.

She looked at me as though I had no right to say it. Then her face softened, and she nodded. "Of course you do," she said.

I began to bring things out to the dining-room table. I thought I heard what sounded like chanting coming from my father's office. I started toward it, but my mother called to me, and I returned to the kitchen. This time, when I brought something to the dining room, there was no sound coming from my father's office.

There was a change when we all sat at the table. I was relieved that the conversation was no longer centered around me. Uncle Alexis described some of the places they had been and talked about connecting with old friends. I was surprised at how many my father remembered or knew. Both Uncle Alexis and Aunt Suzume raved about my mother's cooking and especially about the mincemeat pie.

"I haven't had it so good for a very long time," Uncle Alexis said. And then he put down his knife and fork and leaned forward toward me, looking suddenly very hard and serious. He spoke as if we were in the middle of a sentence, a sentence that had been hanging in the air just waiting to be brought back to our ears. "And all these predictions you have made and you say you no longer make, were any meant to hurt someone, to make them sad or tired or give them any sort of pain, whether it be physical or emotional?"

"No," I said. "It was to help them prevent any of that. That's why I wasn't happy about being told never to do it," I said, my voice firm, even snappy.

I didn't look at anyone else. He didn't flinch or blink until I leaned toward him.

"Who are you?" I asked—more like demanded.

His eyes began to widen, and a tight smile spread from his lips and into his cheeks.

"Sage!" my mother cried.

Uncle Alexis put up his hand. "I apologize," he said. "I can't keep the therapist quiet inside me. Too many years of practicing. Can you tell me one thing, one very good thing you did for someone because of your visions, your premonitions?"

I looked at my parents. They were of one face, frightened. I sensed it. This was probably the most important question of all.

"There was a girl at school whose father was sexually abusing her," I said.

He nodded, his face full of anticipation.

"She had bruises. I had visions about her, and I left

a note with the school nurse. I didn't sign it with my name, but it was enough to get her to investigate. The police were brought into it, and the girl was taken out of our school. She's in a special school being counseled."

He sat back, nodding softly.

"You never told us about this," my mother said.

"I was afraid to, because of how angry you get whenever I mention anything like my visions."

"It's all right," my father told me.

I nodded. Then I looked at Uncle Alexis again. "Who are you?" I asked, a little more fervently this time.

"Who do you think I am?"

"I don't know . . . yet," I said. "But I will."

He started to laugh. Aunt Suzume smiled. My father smiled, too. Only my mother kept her face solemn, her eyes still awash with concern.

I rose and began to clean up. Everyone just watched me, but I no longer felt timid or nervous under their watchful eyes. I didn't understand why, but I sensed a new strength in myself. It was as if I had leaped years ahead. I had passed some test, and although I wasn't sure what it was or what it meant, I felt a sense of accomplishment.

They returned to their conversations about people I had never met or known. I listened with half an ear. My mind was racing with too many other thoughts. I was loading the dishwasher when my mother stepped into the kitchen to tell me they were leaving. I followed her out to say good-bye.

Uncle Alexis took my hand into both of his and

smiled. "Please forgive me for being so inquisitive, Sage. You brought me back to my younger days, when I was very involved in my work."

"I don't know if that's a compliment or not," I said, and he laughed.

"You don't need a therapist," he said. "You will be fine."

He hugged me, Aunt Suzume kissed and hugged me, and then they said good-bye to my mother. My father followed them out.

I thought my mother was smiling at me. It was as if she had been caged in ice, and it was all cracking up around her and melting away. She surprised me by putting her arm around me.

"Thanks for helping with lunch and doing all the cleanup, Sage," she said.

I knew I was beaming.

We paused when the phone rang. She looked at me.

"It's for me," I said. The vibrations were clear.

"Did they say anything to you after I left you at the mall last night?" Summer asked as soon as I said hello.

"They think Jason drugged them and all the boys were in on it. Ginny made me swear I wouldn't tell what they told me, but this is not going to be a secret well kept under lock and key."

He laughed. "I agree. There's trouble in River City."

"Pardon?"

"A song in *The Music Man*. I saw the show in London years ago."

"Oh. Yes, Monday will be very interesting. Every-one will be wondering why no one is talking to each other."

"Except us. We won't be wondering, and we'll talk to each other."

"Will we?"

"I want to see you tonight."

"Tonight?"

"I want to do what we did last night but without any subterfuge. No hiding, no deceit, just a boy and a girl going on a dinner date. Ask your parents. I'll come to meet them."

The very idea made me tremble. Before I could say anything, he rattled off his phone number.

"I don't know about this," I said. "I mean, they hate my pulling anything surprising on them and—"

"Use your powers of persuasion the way you used them on Mr. Jacobs," he insisted. "I have faith in you," he added, and then said good-bye before I could tell him that was something I would never do to my parents, even if I was able to do it.

18

As it turned out, I didn't have to rely on any powers of persuasion. I had no doubt that if things had not gone as well as they had with Uncle Alexis and Aunt Suzume, my parents would have said no immediately, but it truly was as if a page had been turned, a door opened, and chains unlocked.

"Where does he want to take you?" my mother asked.

"Just to dinner, so we can talk and get to know each other more."

She looked at my father.

He shrugged and smiled. "As Uncle Alexis says, Felicia, we've got to let her grow up," he said, almost in a whisper.

"Young people grow up too fast today. They don't know it, but they miss the best part of their lives, innocence," she said.

"Innocence has become a luxury in this world, Felicia. You know that," he said.

"Too well," she said. "Tell him to come in and spend a few minutes with us," she told me, which was her way of saying yes.

"Thanks, Mother," I said, and went to call Summer.

He picked up almost before the phone rang. "I knew you could do it," he said before I told him.

"How did you know they would say yes?"

"I believe in you, Sage. I believe that whatever you want to do, you can do, as long as you want it enough."

"Blind optimism," I said. "Okay. You'll have to come in and spend fifteen or twenty minutes under the bright lights. What time will you arrive?"

"Six thirty. Don't worry. I'll be Johnny Perfect."

"Don't be too Johnny Perfect. They'll see you're trying too hard to please them and that you're being false."

"Okay. I'll just be myself, reasonably well behaved. Don't worry. Rather, yes worry," he corrected.

"Thanks."

"No. That means you want to be with me so much that you'll be on pins and needles praying I go over well."

"I've got to warn you," I said, annoyed at how right he was, "my mother can smell arrogance, and she's allergic to it."

He laughed. "See you at six thirty on the dot."

After I hung up, I went about choosing what to wear. I really didn't have the variety of fun clothes the other girls had. I had to improvise again, matching a blouse with a skirt first and then going back to my one pair of designer jeans. When I looked at myself in the mirror, I decided I wasn't making enough of a fuss over a dinner date, wasn't making it seem as special as it should be, so I put on a dress, the last one my mother had approved of. It was a slip-on, rhubarb-colored, soft wool-blend sweater dress with wide ribbing at the V neck and additional ribbing at the cuffs and waist. It fell to midthigh, which was probably a little high for her taste, but I believed the thing that got her approval was the dress being labeled an angelic dress. How could you criticize angels?

She bought it for me almost two months ago, and at the time, it was a little looser at the hips and in the bodice. When I looked at myself in the mirror, I realized that the changes I thought were subtle in my body suddenly looked more pronounced. My bra felt tighter, and my cleavage was deeper. I ran the tips of my fingers along the sides of my neck and then to the base of my throat. There was something richer about my complexion. There was a slightly rosy tint above my breasts. It was almost as if it had happened overnight. I wasn't upset about it. If anything, it made me more self-confident.

I let my hair down and watched how softly the strands floated to my shoulders. Even my hair looked thicker, more radiant. I felt it to convince myself that I wasn't imagining it. Was it terrible to be so pleased with and enamored of yourself? When do you cross the line, become narcissistic and in danger of being your own worst enemy? Somehow I was sure I was wise enough to handle my budding maturity. I hoped that wasn't overconfidence.

I decided to wear only my pentacle this time and no earrings. Of course I wore the ring Uncle Wade had given me. It was almost a part of my finger by now. I touched it, recalling Summer's matching pendant. Then my eyes were drawn back to my image in the mirror, and suddenly, a strange thing happened. Summer's face seemed to emerge out of mine, his smile soft and tender but his eyes full of lust. I actually stepped back and caught my breath. The image disappeared quickly, but I felt a little shaken.

You're thinking about him too much, I told myself. *You're too worried about pleasing him, attracting him. It's becoming dangerously close to an obsession. He's your first boyfriend, Sage Healy. Get hold of yourself. You'll only embarrass yourself. Find something else to think about.*

I had gotten myself ready far too early anyway, putting myself into an even more nervous state. I was worrying too much about how my parents, especially my mother, were going to react to him. I could easily imagine her having a change of mind and telling me I couldn't go out with him after all. It wasn't something I foresaw the way I saw events that involved other people. It was just a palpable fear. I tried submerging myself in homework to keep from thinking about it, but every few minutes, I looked at the clock. I decided I would go down at six fifteen, and the moment the clock's hands indicated it, I leaped out of my chair, brushed my hair once more, ran my hands over my dress to make it look smooth, and hurried out.

My parents were in my father's office, but they heard me and came out. They paused in the hallway and looked at me.

"I must say, you know how to make yourself attractive without making it too obvious," my father said. His sincerity took me by surprise, not that he hadn't given me compliments in the past. It was just the expression on his face. He looked like he hadn't realized a girl like me actually lived upstairs. My mother said nothing. She just nodded, which I took to mean she approved of what I had chosen to wear.

"Thank you, Dad," I said.

"I'm glad you're wearing your pentacle."

He looked at my mother, who bobbed her head almost reluctantly. I wondered if this was a good time to mention that Summer's father had given him a pendant similar to my ring and that his father had a pentacle on the wall in his office, too, but I held that back, afraid my mother would see something wrong or strange about it.

"She really is growing up fast," my father said.

"Too fast," my mother muttered.

I saw the way they looked at each other. My father had that appeal in his eyes, that way of asking her to remain calm. How long did she want it to take? How could I be so far behind and still have any friends my age? Why couldn't she realize that?

I went into the living room to wait for Summer. My mother went into the kitchen to begin preparations for their dinner. My father followed me and sat in his favorite chair. I was too nervous to sit. I stood near the window that faced the front.

"So this boy is a good student, I take it?" he asked.

"What? Oh, yes, very good, very well read considering he was homeschooled for so long."

"Homeschooled? And this was because . . ."

"He and his father traveled so much."

"That's hard on someone so young," my father said. "You told your mother recently that his mother was killed in a car accident?"

"Hit by a drunk driver while she was crossing the street. He went through a red light."

"Tragic. Have you met his father?" he asked.

Before I could respond, I saw Summer drive up.

"He's here," I announced.

My mother heard me and came in from the kitchen. She stood beside my father, both of them full of anticipation. I watched Summer get out of his car and straighten his clothes, brushing down his pants and then checking his hair in the side-view mirror. It brought a smile to my face. He looked so handsome, in a dark gray sports jacket, black tie, and black slacks. Surely he'd win them over, I thought.

He started for the front steps and stopped as abruptly as he would have if he had walked into an invisible wall. He actually backed up, rocking on his heels for a moment. I brought my hand to the base of my throat and was unable to hold down a troubled "Oh."

"What is it?" my mother asked, stepping toward me and the window quickly.

I shook my head and looked out at him again. He wasn't moving. He was just standing there looking at the house. He brought his right hand to his temple, his left hand to his forehead, and looked down. What was he doing?

"Well?" my father said.

"Something's wrong," I told them, and went to the front door. He was still standing there with his hand on his forehead when I stepped out. "What's wrong, Summer?"

He looked up at me and shook his head.

"I don't know. I just got dizzy for a moment, dizzy and a little nauseated," he said.

My parents came up behind me.

"What is it?" my father asked.

"He isn't feeling well," I said.

I started down the stairs. My father followed, but my mother remained in the doorway.

"Hey, what's up?" my father asked.

"Sorry, sir. I just got very dizzy."

"Well, come on in and have a glass of water. Sit for a while, and let's see. Maybe you're coming down with something like the flu."

Summer looked at my mother. He saw something in her face that displeased him and shook his head. "I'm sorry, Sage," he said. "Probably best if I just go home."

"Well, you shouldn't drive," my father said.

"No, I'll be fine." He backed up, spun around, and quickly got back into his car.

"Let us call your father first!" my father shouted to him.

"I'm fine. Sorry," he said. He started the engine.

"Summer!" I called.

He looked out at me. "I'll be fine," he said more confidently, and then he smiled and backed out. He acted like he couldn't get away from us fast enough. It was as if a hurricane had passed right in front of our house and was gone in seconds.

"What was that about?" my father asked as Summer drove off.

I stood there looking after him and then turned and looked at my mother. During all of the occasions when she was upset with me or with something that involved me, she had never appeared as terrified as she did now.

My father saw it, too. "Felicia?"

"Come back inside," she said, and looked ominously in Summer's direction. "Now!" she screamed.

Both my father and I moved quickly to the steps. She backed into the house and closed the door as soon as we entered.

"What?" he asked her. "What's wrong?"

"Didn't you feel it?"

He shook his head.

"Feel what?" I asked.

"Didn't you?" she asked my father again.

"He probably just has the flu or something, Felicia. You're overreacting." He placed his hand on her right shoulder. "Relax. Calm down. The boy looked very nice. Maybe he is shier than we think—or," he added, looking at me, "than Sage thinks."

She shook her head but looked like she was calming down because of the gentle way he spoke and stroked her upper arm.

"It's all right," he kept saying.

"I'm okay," she said.

"What is it? What's going on?" I asked—more like demanded. "What made you so upset?" I asked her. "I'm the one who should be upset."

"Go up and change," she told me, "and come down to help with dinner. Start on a salad."

I turned to my father. He rolled his eyes and nodded. I looked at my mother again and saw she would countenance no opposition and no more questions. Her face had that cold, stony look, a look that had frightened me to the bone since I was a little girl. Disappointed but very confused now, I headed for the stairway and then hurried up to my room, closing the door sharply behind me and throwing myself on my bed.

What had happened to my first real date? It felt like it had been scooped out right from under me. All the excitement, the anticipation, was crushed in a few moments. The whole world seemed to spin on its head.

Was my father right? Summer had a flu? Was he simply ignoring it to keep our date and it just got worse? And why would that upset my mother to such an extreme? Did she think he had been irresponsible? What else could it be? He certainly looked sick. His face was pale when I first stepped outside. He did appear to recuperate quickly when he got into his car, however.

I doubted Summer was shier than I thought or than they had anticipated. I couldn't imagine him getting cold feet when it came to meeting my parents, no matter how hard I had made it sound. Yet if he wasn't really sick, it had to be something like that, something like stage fright. My mother's reaction made me wonder what I was missing. What was it she saw that made her think it was something else, something threatening? What did she mean by "Didn't you feel it?" Feel what?

I changed into a pair of jeans and a sweatshirt, then slipped on a pair of sandals, still feeling terribly confused, even a little frightened because of how quickly everything had changed. I left my hair the way it was and hurried downstairs. There was no one in the kitchen or the living room. I realized they were both in my father's office with the door closed. It sounded like they were arguing, but their voices were too muffled for me to make out any words clearly. I didn't want to be caught listening in on them, so I returned to the kitchen and gathered the dishware and silverware to set the table before I started on the salad.

They were unusually silent when they came out. My mother went right to work on dinner. I stood beside her making the salad. Less than an hour ago, I'd had no idea I'd be doing any of this. Of course, I couldn't stop thinking about it. It had been very important for Summer to be able to take me out on a real date tonight. There was no way he would have backed out of it unless something serious had happened.

A terrible new thought occurred to me. Maybe it wasn't just the beginning of some flu. Maybe he had a terrible pain in his head. Maybe there was some health problem that he had not yet revealed. It frightened me. Could he be seriously ill? Surely he realized how shocked and disappointed I had been. He would have to tell me the truth.

I kept expecting the phone to ring with him calling with some explanation, but he didn't call before or during our dinner. The whole time, I was poised to fly at that telephone. My parents were talking about something else, but I wasn't listening. I thought they had put it all out of mind by now, so I was surprised to hear my father suddenly insist that I let him know what had happened to Summer.

"As soon as you find out," he added, and looked at my mother, who just ate as if she already knew the answer. Right now, I hated her for that look, that arrogant assurance that she knew more than either my father or I knew or could ever know.

"What did you mean before when you asked Dad if he had felt it, Mother? Felt what?"

I thought she would become angry again at my cross-examining her, but instead, she looked at me curiously and sat back. "You didn't feel anything unusual?"

"I was concerned about Summer. It was certainly unusual for him to drive all the way here and, moments from entering, stop and get sick. Is that what you mean?"

"Not just that, no."

"Well, then, what?"

"It's not something I can explain. You have to either know or not," she said.

My father looked down and shook his head gently.

What was she talking about? I searched my memory to find something that might have interested her and perhaps me, too, something else besides the shock and disappointment I had felt, but nothing came to mind.

"Why can't you explain it?"

"Let's not talk about it anymore until we find out something substantial," my father insisted. From the way he was looking at my mother, I knew he meant that for her, not me.

I really had no appetite now, but I forced myself to eat enough not to be criticized, and then, when it was time to clear off the table, I rushed at the opportunity to escape this funeral-like atmosphere.

"You know," my father said, coming into the kitchen after me, "perhaps you shouldn't wait to find out. Perhaps you should call his father to see how he's doing. I feel I should have. Do you have his phone number?"

"Yes," I said.

I was nervous about doing it, but I went to the phone in the kitchen and called. Summer's father answered on the third ring.

"Mr. Dante, it's Sage," I said. "How is Summer?"

"Summer? I thought he was with you," he said. "Why? What's happened?"

"Oh. I . . . he said he wasn't feeling well right after he pulled into our driveway. I thought, I mean, I just assumed he went home."

"What was wrong?"

"He said he felt dizzy, a little weak. My father thought he might be coming down with the flu. Now I'm worried."

"Well, don't panic. He's a very independent and resourceful young man. The moment I hear from him or see him, I'll have him call you."

"Please do," I said. I stood by the phone, thinking. Where would he have gone? Was he in trouble? Did he go off the road?

My father waited in the doorway. "Well?" he asked.

"His father said he didn't come home."

"Really? Now I do feel bad about not calling him immediately." He thought a moment. "Is his father calling the police?"

"The police? No. As a matter of fact, he didn't seem at all concerned," I said. "Even after I explained what had happened."

"That's odd," my mother said, coming up behind my father. She had been listening to our conversation.

"Maybe he's just embarrassed. He might have felt better and didn't know what to do. He knew he couldn't come back because you'd both be concerned about my going out with him now." I spoke quickly, like someone who was desperately trying to find an explanation that would satisfy them.

"Maybe he did feel better," my mother said coldly. She looked at my father. "Once he left here, that is."

Did she believe he was that shy? Was that what she meant?

"Kids today," my father said. "Who can understand them? Maybe it's better not to try."

She shook her head. "You always were the one with his head in the sand, Mark," she told him. "Even when something is right before your eyes, obvious, black and white. I heard the alarms."

"Stop it. You have nothing to go on."

What were they talking about?

"Have you met his father?" my mother suddenly asked me. "You have, haven't you?" she followed quickly.

"Yes," I said. "He introduced me to him."

"Where? Where?" she shouted before I could think of an answer other than the truth.

"His house," I said.

"You left the mall with him last night," she said, nodding, and looked at my father.

"Sage, how could you do that?" he asked.

"It was just a short visit," I said, but I knew that wouldn't justify or explain it in a way that would satisfy them.

"Mark," my mother said, filling the sound of his name with alarm. She stepped closer to him. Her eyes were full of panic, wide, blazing.

My father's own expression changed to become more like hers. "What is he like?" he asked, obviously fighting to remain calm.

"He's very good-looking, elegant, and devoted to his work, his writing. He was very nice to me."

"Where do they live?"

I described the area. "It's an older house. He hasn't done all that much to it. Maybe he's thinking of getting something more substantial. It's not very big, cozy, but—"

"Maybe he's thinking he won't stay long," my mother interrupted. "Was there anything else about him that struck you as different, odd?"

"Odd? No," I said. "I could see that he and Summer have a close relationship."

"What did he ask you about us?"

"About you?"

Was I going to tell them how not only Summer and his father but all my friends thought they were too strict with me? Was I going to mention the way to hold a rapier so as not to crush the bird? I was sure that would all just add fuel to this fire that was burning around me, around them.

"Yes," my father said. "About us."

"No. He told me about his work. He was very complimentary. I think he works so much out of loneliness."

They stared at me.

"It's just a feeling," I added.

"Then what did you do?" she asked.

"Returned to the mall to wait for Dad. I was with

the girls, who waited with me," I said, looking at my father.

"Yes, that's true."

"Nevertheless, you disobeyed us. We specifically told you not to go anywhere else."

"I know, but—"

"Don't ask to go anywhere for a month," my mother said.

"A month?"

"You were quite disobedient. Just go up to your room and do your homework, Sage. I'm disappointed in you," she said.

I looked to my father for some reprieve, but he just shook his head.

"This isn't fair," I muttered, and ran out of the kitchen and up the stairs, practically charging through my bedroom door and then slamming it hard behind me. For a moment, I just stood there, fuming. I could feel the tears building in my eyes. I closed them to press the tears back. I would not cry. I would not moan and wail and sulk like a child.

I took a deep breath and held it.

Something made me open my eyes slowly. It was a warmth, a glow washing over me.

He was standing there, right before me, smiling, and I wasn't imagining it.

19

"How did you get up here?" I asked in a whisper.

For a moment, I thought I *was* imagining it, that my powers of visualization were so strong that I could not only imagine him in a mirror but conjure him up right before my eyes. As if he knew I was questioning reality, he leaned forward to kiss me quickly on the lips. It was like a firecracker snapping me out of a daze. My heart began to race as the realization set in. I listened keenly for any sounds to indicate that my parents were rushing up the stairs because they knew he was here.

He simply smiled and leaned forward to kiss me again. I pushed him back.

"Stop. How did you get up here? How long have you been here?"

"Not that long. I slipped in the back way while you were having dinner," he said. "I learned a long time ago how to walk on a breeze."

I moved him and myself farther away from the

door. "Are you insane? If they find out, I'll never ever be able to see you again."

"Except for in school, you won't for a month anyway, if your mother has her way." He went to my bed and sat, still smiling calmly.

"You heard all that?"

"Every syllable."

"From up here?"

"Well, I was hovering on the stairway for most of it. They're like jailers or something. I'm surprised you're as stable as you are, having lived under the same roof with those two all your life. I bet you can tell me plenty of weird stuff."

I looked at the door. "I'm so frightened that they'll hear you and find you in here, Summer."

"They won't. I'll fly under the bed if they come to the door. Don't worry." He looked like he could fly. He didn't look sick and pale anymore.

"What happened? Why did you get so sick out front when you came for me, and where did you go? I called to see how you were. Why didn't you go home or at least call your father and tell him what happened?"

"I really felt a lot better after about ten minutes, but I knew I couldn't come back. They wouldn't let you out with me after what had happened, so I circled around for a while and then decided I just had to see you, to be with you. It was going to be our night, a real date. I knew how disappointed you were. It was all my fault, and I couldn't stand the thought of that."

"You should have called to let us know how you were."

"Wouldn't have done any good. Even if I said I felt wonderful now, they wouldn't have let you out and maybe not even let me in, thinking I might give you the flu or something. One look at both of them, and I knew what it would be like, what it will be like. I saw the way they were looking at me. *Here's the boy who's going to steal away our little girl.* You'll always be a little girl to them. You're never going to reach your potential until you're free of them, Sage. I know it was nice that they adopted you, but you might have been better off growing up in an orphanage."

"No, Summer. Don't say that."

"Okay. This is a realization you'll have to come to yourself." He leaned back on my bed and gazed around. "This room isn't you," he said. "It lacks imagination. Any other mother would have done much more with the curtains, the walls, and the furniture. Most mothers and fathers dote on their daughters, adopted or not."

"Look who's talking. You practically live in a barracks," I replied.

He started to smile and then stopped. "You're right. We're both in the wrong place."

"What do you mean? What place?"

"We don't belong here. This town's too small, too provincial. None of the girls you hang with or the guys I've met is in the least interesting. It's like they were all cut from the same cloth, clones. The last original thought they had was their first. There's nothing to challenge us, no discoveries to make. We need to be where we can breathe, explore, and experience so much more. I know. I've been to places like that. I know what's out there for us."

"So why did your father bring you here?"

"To meet you, of course."

"Very funny. Listen," I said. "You've got to go. You've got to leave before they come up to go to bed."

"Impossible. They'll hear me, and it will be worse. They'll think this was our plan all the time. They'll accuse you of conspiring and me of pretending or something. I'll stay here until they go to sleep. It will be easier, safer. Go on. Get yourself ready for bed. Act as if I'm not here. Don't mind me," he said, then kicked off his shoes and lay back on one of my pillows.

"Summer."

"Shh. I'm sleeping. Remember? I wasn't feeling well before, so I need my rest." He closed his eyes but kept that tight, small smile sitting on his lips.

I looked at the clock. My parents might not be up for more than an hour. Maybe it would be better if I prepared for bed and turned off the lights. There would be less chance of them stopping in. I went into the bathroom. I was never filled with so many conflicting emotions. It was exciting to think of him being in my room, lying in my bed, but my blood felt like it would run cold with fear, too.

I washed, got undressed, and slipped into my nightgown. When I stepped out, he was still lying on my bed, but he had folded down my blanket and moved to the other side. How did he know what side I usually slept on? He patted my pillow.

"Better put out the light," he whispered.

"You're going to make a lot of trouble for both of us," I warned.

"Hope so," he said, smiling. Then he turned serious. "You're very beautiful, Sage. You have a glow I've rarely seen in a girl. I'd risk everything to be with you."

"You have," I said.

I turned off the light. My curtains were open, and the light of the new moon penetrating the gauzy clouds in the night sky gave my room the surreal look of a dream, full of shadows, changing all that I was familiar with into the props of some magic show. It made me again question the reality. Was he really here? In my bed waiting for me?

"Come to bed," he whispered. My feet felt glued to the floor. "Don't make me raise my voice too loud by begging."

"Shh," I said. He had already raised his voice too much for my comfort.

I went to my bed and sat. It still felt unreal. Summer was in my bed?

He reached for my hand. "Actually, this turned out better. Don't you think?" he asked.

"No. Hardly."

"I'm the first boy you've had in your room, aren't I?"

"First I've had in the house."

He tugged me to come closer. I listened and then lay back. He moved closer and kissed my cheeks, my forehead, and the tip of my nose before kissing me long but softly on the lips, his hands moving over my stomach to my hips. I think he was as surprised as I was at how quickly my body tightened and hardened.

"Relax. It's all right," he said, bringing his right hand up to my breasts. He slid my nightgown off my shoulder and kissed me on the neck, his lips then grazing over my collarbone and then down to my increasingly exposed breast. In the soft moonlight, his eyes were radiant, shimmering.

He kissed me again, and the sweet taste of his lips was mesmerizing. My lips were magnetically drawn to his for another kiss, but then I pulled away.

"Summer, don't," I said. There was a twirling sensation going on in my stomach, a sensation I had never felt but still recognized as an alarm sounding inside me. Was it warning me about myself, my own desires, or against him?

"If I plead, I'll get too loud, and then they'll hear us," he warned.

"You're blackmailing me."

"No. Just helping to convince you of something you want yourself," he said, and he brought his lips to my now fully exposed breast just as we heard my parents coming up the stairs.

I pushed him away. "They're coming up. They might open the door. Go into the bathroom," I said. "Quickly!"

Reluctantly, he slipped off the bed and started toward the bathroom.

"Wait. Your shoes," I whispered. He scooped them up and retreated just as my parents stopped at my door.

I held my breath, waiting. I could hear the handle

turning, but then my father said something, and the handle stopped. I heard them move off to their own bedroom. The house became quiet, but I didn't move or call to him. I wanted more time to pass to be absolutely sure that my mother didn't change her mind and return to say something. Finally, impatient, he stepped out of the bathroom.

"Well?" he said.

I put up my hand to keep him from moving or speaking and then got up and went to my bedroom door. I stood there for a moment listening, and then I opened it slightly and looked out into the dimly lit hallway. I closed the door. When I turned, he was standing there, ready to embrace me again.

"No," I said firmly, putting my right palm against his chest. "You've got to go. My mother gets up during the night. I've heard her many nights come by my room and stand just outside my door listening. Sometimes she peeks in."

"Now, when you're this age?"

"Yes."

"Why? What does she expect to find you doing? Or does she think you might sneak out or something?"

"I don't know. It's her way. It's always been. Please. Go out the way you came in. Be very careful."

"I'm going home pretty frustrated," he said.

"We'll be together again soon. I promise," I said.

"I don't trust promises. Never have. Promises are excuses for excuses, mostly to put off reality or ignore it. Make no promises, and you'll disappoint no one.

That's a lesson I've learned the hard way." His face was in the shadows, but I could sense something about it that wasn't pleasing. He wasn't only frustrated. He was angry.

"Please," I pleaded. "Just go. This is so dangerous."

"Ridiculous. You shouldn't be living here anymore. You shouldn't be with them."

"It's too late for that sort of thinking, Summer."

"No, it's not," he insisted.

"Please," I begged again. "I'll work on them. I'll get permission to see you sooner on a date. I'll be remorseful. My father will feel sorry for me and convince her to relent. It's worked before. That's not a promise; it's a real plan, okay?"

"Sure," he said, soaked in pessimism. "Work on them. Scheme. Make plans. This time, it's different. I can see how far that will get you when it comes to seeing me."

"All I can do, Summer, is try. Please. Give me the chance."

"All right. I'm not going to let you fail, but let's not worry about the future right now. Let's enjoy the moment. I don't have to leave just yet. Like I said. Give them a chance to fall asleep," he said, surprising me by taking my hand. "It'll be safer." He tugged me back toward the bed.

"No."

"I want you, and you want me. Forget about them for a while. Think about me," he said. "Think about us." He sounded as if he was trying to hypnotize me. "Me . . . and you . . . together."

My resistance did weaken. He was drawing me closer, and as he did, he grasped my nightgown and began to lift it over my head. I tried to stop him, but it was as if my arms were strapped against my sides. In a moment, I was naked, and he embraced me, kissed me, and moved us onto the bed, but when he began to undress, that swirling alarm not only began again in the pit of my stomach but this time shot up through my body with an electric speed, shocking my heart, tightening my throat, driving me quickly to a panic like none I had ever known in life or in any of my strange, unexplainable memories.

"No!" I cried, and now, with not only a return of my strength but an even greater strength, I practically lifted him away from me and got up. I quickly put my nightgown on again and stepped away.

"What's wrong?"

"You must go. This is too dangerous. They'll keep me locked up for a year and not a month."

He sat up and shook his head. "It's okay. They've gone to sleep."

"It's not okay. I'm not comfortable this way. It will be no good for either of us."

"All right," he said, this time seeing and hearing my determination. "I'll go, but you have to promise to meet me at the lake next to your house tomorrow afternoon at two. You'll find a way to get out. Tell them you need fresh air or a walk. Just come. Will you come?"

"Yes," I said.

"You're not saying that just to get rid of me, are you?"

"I'll come. Go," I said.

He moved to the door. I opened it very slightly again. He still wasn't wearing his shoes, which I thought was smart.

"Kiss me," he said. "Or I won't go. But kiss me like you mean it."

"Blackmail again?"

"Whatever gets me there," he replied.

I kissed him. I tried to kiss him the way he wanted me to, but it was either because I was standing in a pool of cold fear or something else, something that began reviving that twirling in my stomach again, but whatever it was, I couldn't kiss him the way he had hoped I would. I knew he wasn't satisfied the moment my lips lifted away from his. "I'm sorry. I'm too nervous."

"Naw. You just need more practice, that's all," he said. "I'm an expert. Lessons begin tomorrow."

I stepped back. He slipped through the door and did move amazingly quietly, sliding through the shadows to the stairway. I kept the door open to listen, expecting one or more of those old steps to creak. They always did, but for some reason, somehow, they didn't. At first, I was afraid he might not have even begun to descend. Maybe he had changed his mind and was going to return to continue to blackmail me into being passionate. I waited and waited and finally felt confident that he had gone down and left the house.

I released a hot held breath of trepidation and closed the door. For a moment or two, I stood there reliving it all. It still felt more like a dream. Had he really been here? Had we almost made love? All my life, I had distrusted things I saw, because too often my powerful imagination was able to conjure up things, people, places no one else would see or remember. Why couldn't this have been another example of that? I half hoped it was.

But when I returned to bed, that doubt died a quick death. It wasn't simply the sense of him having been there. It wasn't the scent of his aftershave or his hair. It wasn't the creases in the pillows or the warmth still under the blanket.

It was hard, metallic.

I felt it and then put on my lamp to look at what I had in my right hand. I had his pendant. He had left it behind. He wanted me to be sure he had been here and that I had almost given more to him than I had to any other boy. I thought it was his way of telling me I would, and not because he blackmailed me into it. The pendant left behind was another symbol of his confidence, his often annoying arrogance.

But that didn't make it any less true.

I had wanted to give myself to him. What kept me from doing so was not the fear of my parents overhearing us and finding him in my room. It was something else, something inside me, a shrill voice coming from a place I had never been. It was quiet now, for the moment satisfied, but it was no longer asleep. To be sure, it wasn't simply every girl's guardian of her virginity, her natural reluctance to be too easily won. It was more.

And as I lay there thinking about it, I realized that

it wouldn't be long before I understood completely. It was a thought that should have brought me comfort, should have helped me ease myself into a restful sleep, but it wasn't doing that. It was sending me back through time to a place I had no reason to recollect, a place somewhere in some eastern European village, where the church bells were being sounded with an intense sense of alarm. Candles were being lit in every house. Parents were checking on their children. Door locks were being rechecked. Something terrible was sweeping down from the cold, dark north. There was a parade of villagers carrying torches through the main street of the village and singing hymns. They formed a wall of light and stopped whatever it was from entering their world, their hearts, and their souls.

Children slept peacefully. Dawn was never more welcomed.

I saw and heard it all before I could feel my body soften and accept the embrace of welcomed sleep, a dreamless sleep. I had no idea where the images of those frightened people had come from and where they had gone, but I was grateful they had left.

When the morning light pushed the darkness aside, I rose slowly and took longer than usual to dress. I gazed at myself in the mirror, thinking I still looked half-asleep. It was as though I had traveled for days through endless nights to get to the new morning. Cold water on my face helped, but every muscle in my body was complaining. I started down the stairway like someone descending into a dark pit, and when I stepped into the kitchen, my feelings didn't change very much. Of course, my parents were up and waiting, as usual.

From the way my mother was looking at me when I moved to the table, I half expected her to say, "I know he was in your room." There was so much accusation in her eyes. My father glanced at me and then looked down at his newspaper. I was surprised he didn't say good morning.

"Why didn't either his father or he call you to tell you anything last night?" my mother asked the moment I sat. "And don't tell me he was too embarrassed. His father knew about our concern. You called to see how he was. They don't sound like very reliable people. I'm hoping you will open your eyes and avoid this boy now."

"Avoid him? Why?"

"He's not right for you."

"That's not true. How could you know that from looking at him once? You just don't want me to have any sort of social life," I countered. "Maybe you want to turn me into a nun."

My father raised his eyes from the newspaper, looking just as surprised as my mother at how aggressively I had come back at her. "Sage," he said.

"I'm sorry, Dad. She's so eager to have my blossoming relationship with Summer die on the vine."

"I gave you permission to go out on the date, didn't I?" she said.

"Reluctantly," I muttered. "And no, you couldn't wait to restrict me to in-house arrest for a month."

"It's what any good parent would do. You should

appreciate our concern for your welfare. Too many parents are too self-absorbed to concern themselves with their children and then wonder why they go wrong."

"I've always been wrong," I said, almost in a whisper. "I don't know why, but in your eyes, I've always been a bad seed. Why didn't you fulfill the threat you always used to frighten me, that you would return me to the orphanage? Maybe you wouldn't be as miserable as you are."

"Stop it, Sage. This isn't like you at all," my father said.

"I don't care. I can't help it," I said, and started to cry. The tears surprised me, too. Usually, I was good at keeping things locked up, tears falling inside me and not streaming down my cheeks. "I'm not hungry," I said, and shot up and out of my seat.

"Sage!" my father called after me as I charged up the stairway. I didn't turn back.

Something had changed in me. It wasn't only my courage to be defiant. I wasn't running up to my room to sulk like any other teenager. Something bigger had exploded within me, something that had been pent up and building for a while now. Oddly, I didn't feel like a mop soaked with self-pity. I felt stronger. It was as if my tears had unlocked someone else inside me. Everything felt different; my vision, my hearing, all of my senses were sharper, stronger. I was like someone hallucinating after taking a mind-altering drug. I seemed to grow taller, giving me a different perspective about everything around me. I had awoken in a dollhouse and would soon crash through the walls, the floor, and the ceiling.

After another moment, the room began to spin around me. I realized that I was falling into the same sort of swoon I had experienced when I first confronted the large pentacle in my father's office. I was having trouble breathing. I gasped and then managed a cry, before I felt myself sinking to the floor. It was odd. I wasn't falling. I was oozing down onto it, forming a puddle of myself. I was grateful to lose consciousness.

When I awoke, I was lying in my bed. For a few moments, I stared up at the ceiling. The room wasn't spinning, but my mind was fumbling with thoughts, stumbling through a fog. It all began to clear, and I realized I had passed out again. I turned and started to sit up, expecting to see my parents standing there.

They were.

But they weren't alone.

Moving toward me on the right was Uncle Wade, and moving up on my left were my great-uncle Alexis and my great-aunt Suzume. All of them seemed to have the same eyes, black, the pupils swirling. My parents stepped forward to the foot of the bed. They were all staring at me as if I had metamorphosed into a giant butterfly or something.

"What happened? Why is everyone here?" I asked.

"Because it's time you knew who you are," my father said.

20

"Who am I?" I asked in a deep whisper.

My heart was pounding. All my life, I had been anticipating this day. Even though I never fully expressed it to myself or anyone else, I knew it would happen. What I didn't know was whether it would result in my being sent away. I had grown up under a cloud, a threat that thundered in my mother's every angry glare or comment and my father's suspicions and disappointments, from the first day I could talk and tell stories about my dreams and visions. Having been adopted provided trepidation and insecurity enough. I didn't need that added layer of doubt and fear.

"You're one of us, the Belladonnas," Uncle Alexis said. "Not full-blooded, but nevertheless one of us. We know that now."

One of them? That sounded like more than just being in a normal family. Who were they? I looked from face to face and stopped on Uncle Wade's. He smiled and stepped forward to take my right hand into his.

"I think," he said, "in your heart you always knew."

I shook my head and looked again at my parents, who did seem different. They seemed more mellow, like two people who had come a long way and now could relax. The tension I had always seen and felt wasn't there. What did all this really mean? I turned back to Uncle Alexis.

"Is your uncle right?" he asked.

"Yes. I felt something. I've always felt different, but I don't know what it means exactly when you say I'm one of you. Am I now an accepted member of this family for some reason?"

"Yes, you're an accepted member, but we're not just any family, Sage. We are all Wiccans. We were all born into it. You were born of a mother who wasn't one of us, but your father was. You're not the first who was born this way. Some have joined us; some have not. Your parents had the responsibility of bringing you up to determine if you would be one of us or not."

"Wiccans?"

"We're often referred to as witches, but that belies our true meaning and purpose because of how the word 'witch' was used to denigrate people with spiritual power and vision. Religious leaders thought we were heretics, children of the devil, when we have always been just the opposite. We do no harm, and those few of us who do evil know that they eventually will suffer three times as much," he said.

"We tried to bring you along slowly, a step at a time. Your parents already have introduced you to our spiritual beliefs," Aunt Suzume continued. "In our religion, our god and goddess complement each other. Think of yin and yang."

"Our doorbell," I said, looking at my mother. She smiled and nodded.

"We will teach you more about us, about yourself, now," Uncle Alexis said, "but we've always known you have inherited much of what we are. Those visions and memories you've had are real. We believe the soul is reincarnated over many lives in order to learn and advance spiritually."

"They weren't simply mad dreams?"

"Oh, no. They were paths leading you back to your true heritage, your true self. The powers that you've observed in your uncle Wade and have begun to experience yourself are what we call white magic. Wade uses it to make a living," Aunt Suzume said, smiling at him, "but, like us, he uses it to heal, to protect, and to fight negative powers. You have never used your visions to harm anyone, but you have used white magic to help someone, haven't you?"

"Yes," I said, my voice barely a whisper. "I told you about this girl. Her name is Cassie Marlowe. She was being abused by her father. I used the pen Uncle Wade had given me to alert the school nurse," I said, looking at him. "More white magic?"

Uncle Wade nodded and smiled.

"I suspected the resulting handwriting style was the style of the man who first owned it. It was clearly not mine, a perfect disguise enabling me to remain anonymous."

"Exactly," Uncle Wade said. "I knew you would use it for a good purpose one day."

"You've always tried to help others, to make them happy. You've demonstrated humility, concern, and compassion," Aunt Suzume said.

"How do you know all this, know that I've done more?"

"We know the way you know things that are beyond others," Uncle Alexis said. "We have never been very far from you."

I looked at my father. "You told me Uncle Alexis was away and you hadn't seen him for a very long time, when he was always nearby."

"We told you what we could when we could," he said. "We were worried about moving you along too quickly and frightening you, Sage. We tried our best to be proper parents to you, proper Wiccan parents."

"Who is my biological father? My birth mother?" I asked. I looked at Uncle Wade. Was he my real father? Was that why we always seemed more connected?

"Your biological father is an outcast," Uncle Alexis said. "He is not part of our coven, our family, anymore. He was corrupted, drunk on his powers. He bewitched your birth mother, bewitched many women. To escape us, he took on another identity. For years, he has been on the run from not only us but also from other Wiccan families."

"But he has returned," my father said.

"For you," my mother added.

"This was the man you were always warning me

about, questioning me about whether I had seen someone watching me, stalking me?"

"Yes."

"Why didn't you tell me all this years ago?"

"We weren't sure how you would turn out," she
said without blinking an eye. "We had to discover if you
would be more like him or more like the rest of us."

I looked at Uncle Wade. He had been trying to tell
me some of this in his way. It was why he was always
telling me to be more patient with my parents. My latest conversation with him returned to me, especially
my confession about what I had discovered in my
father's office.

"The two other children you took in . . ."

"Were also of mixed blood," my mother said. "But
we were able to quickly realize that they weren't going
to be like us. We couldn't keep them."

"Were they my biological father's children, too?"

"No," she said quickly. "In their cases, it was the
mother who had gone wrong."

"A terrible disappointment to us," Uncle Alexis
said, shaking his head. "Every family has one or two,
but we've had three."

"Where are those children now?"

No one answered. I nodded. Some things needn't
be spoken for me to hear the answers.

"Where I might have gone?"

Uncle Wade nodded first.

"Why are you telling me all this now? Why
today?"

"Because, as your parents just said, he's come back for you," Uncle Alexis said.

"Why now? Why did he wait so long?"

"He's not stupid. He planned well," Uncle Alexis said. "If it weren't for your parents, he might have succeeded."

"Taking you away with him would be a great victory for him over us," Aunt Suzume added.

"Where is he right now?"

"You know," my mother said. "You've met him."

I felt my heart stop and start. My right hand fluttered up to my throat. I started to shake my head. It couldn't be. They had to be wrong.

"Don't worry. He won't be here long," my father said.

"How did you know he was here?"

"We weren't sure until yesterday," my mother said. "When his son couldn't overcome what we had placed in front of our house to protect us from evil spirits, we knew his spirit was among us. His son has followed in his path because he was brought up with him. I'm sorry."

"Summer's not evil. He can't be."

"Think," my mother said. "Has he used what powers he has inherited to harm others?"

I couldn't swallow for a moment. My lungs seemed to seize up. What was done to poor Ned Wyatt, Skip pushing Jason down the stairway, the fight in school, what he had done to the girls and the boys at Jason's house—all of it came rushing back at me. He used his powers to do all those evil things. I understood why I was so suspicious, but I wouldn't see it because he was sincerely interested in me.

"I believed he was in love with me," I said. "I have strong feelings for him, feelings I can't deny."

"You have to deny them. He's your half brother," my mother said. "Don't tell us you never sensed it?"

I looked at her. Yes, I had sensed it. I had sensed it last night. That was what made me resist. How much did she and my father really know? Did they know he was here? Did they let it happen to see what I would do? Their faces seemed to be saying yes.

I shook my head. "This can't be."

"It is," my father said. "It can be, and it is."

A new hope occurred to me. "But does Summer know who I am?"

"Yes," my mother said quickly, too quickly.

"We're not absolutely sure," my father added in a softer tone, "but most likely, yes."

"I can't believe this."

"You must," Uncle Wade said. "You must accept that what we are telling you is the truth. We never lie to one another."

"Don't be nervous," Aunt Suzume said with a warm smile. "Don't be afraid."

"There is much for you to learn now about us, about yourself," Uncle Alexis said. "You will be part of our family. We'll teach you how to use your powers and your wisdom for great good. You'll have special responsibilities, and you will swear to obey our rules and our laws and follow our beliefs. Above all, you will swear to protect us. You can begin now by accepting all we have told you. It's a joy to have you," he added.

I looked at my parents. Never before had they looked as happy and as loving as they did at this moment.

"I'm sorry I've been so hard on you," my mother said. "We had to be sure you are what you are."

"How are you so sure now?"

"We know you haven't used your powers for evil, but we also know you are in a dangerous place now, with your father and his son trying to win you away. Both your father and I sensed that this was a crisis, and Alexis decided it was time to bring you into our family to have its protection," she explained. "The temptation is too great."

The mysteries and secrets I saw as flies caught in cobwebs in our house began to break free. I understood now why my parents did not want me telling stories about visions and dreams. There were things that had to be kept hidden so as not to bring unwanted attention to them, to us all.

"Those things I found in your office filing cabinet, Dad, those pictures and documents."

"What about them?"

"They were real, weren't they? They weren't jokes you and Uncle Wade created."

"Yes, they're real."

"How old are you?"

"We're both old enough to be beyond our Wiccan powers. They weaken with age, but not for the first hundred years or so," he said. "That's why your mother and I foster children who are questionable. It's our responsibility to the family now, how we can still contribute to the Belladonnas. But you must believe me when I say you have been different for us. We do love you, Sage, love you no less than if you were our biological child."

I looked at everyone's face and saw how they were all studying me and my reactions. Was this the final test? The truth and how I would accept it? Would I still refuse to accept it? Would I flee?

"What exactly will happen to me now? Am I to leave? Live with someone else?"

"No, no. You'll continue as you are," Uncle Alexis said. "And as I said, you'll take your place among us, and in time, you will completely understand yourself and what good you can do. It will be different now that you know all this, but you have the wisdom of ages in you, and we're confident you'll be someone of whom we can be proud."

"What about my father and Summer?"

"You must not worry about that," my father said. "What needs to be done about them will be done."

"And my mother, my birth mother?"

"What about her?" Uncle Alexis said.

"What happened to her?"

"Nothing bad."

"Where is she?"

"She has her own life, her new family. She's fine. We made sure of that."

"Does she know what happened to me?"

"No. She doesn't even remember giving birth to

you," Aunt Suzume said. "It was for the best. It had to be. We only use our powers for good, and it was good for her to escape your father and what he had brought."

"Me. He had brought me!"

My outburst surprised them all, and for a moment, no one spoke.

"If we didn't do what we had to do, she wouldn't have survived. She wouldn't have the good life she has now. It's okay," Aunt Suzume added. "You don't have to worry about her."

"But I can't stop thinking about her. I want to know who she is. I want to see her."

"She wouldn't know who you are. You'd frighten her," Uncle Alexis said.

"I don't have to tell her who I am. I want to know who *she* is."

No one spoke. I knew this was an unusual situation for them, a situation my biological father had caused. It was untested ground, but I was willing to test it.

"It's what I want," I said firmly. "If I'm going to live with the truth now, I want the whole truth. I want to know exactly who I am. I won't swear to anything. I won't accept anything less."

They all continued to stare at me, and then Aunt Suzume broke the heavy mood when she smiled. "She's a lot like me when I was her age," she said. "Stubborn and determined."

"All right. We'll see what we can do," Uncle Alexis said. He looked at everyone else. "Let's let her rest.

She doesn't realize how tired she is and how all this has affected her."

"Alexis is right. Just rest," my mother said. "Later, we'll all gather for a celebratory dinner and for the rituals that will bind you to us and us to you. Every day from now on, you'll learn more and more about us, what we believe, how we help each other, and how we can help others. Nothing more will be kept from you. I promise."

Uncle Wade stepped forward again and kissed my cheek. "Now you will be another magician in the family," he said.

My father kissed me, too. "I always believed in you, Sage, always."

They all turned and walked out slowly.

I lay back on my pillow. Uncle Alexis was right. This confrontation was mentally and emotionally exhausting. My head felt like my brain was overflowing, pouring thoughts and images out so fast it made me dizzy. It was like overeating and waiting for it all to digest. I closed my eyes and drifted off, but not for long. Something getting very hot stung me and woke me. I had left Summer's pendant in my bed. Slowly, I picked it up and looked at it.

Could I just forget him despite what I knew about him? My father wasn't as confident about what he knew and didn't know as my mother was. This pendant didn't just turn warm. He made it turn warm, I thought. He was calling to me. I rose slowly and went to my window. It was nearly two o'clock. I had promised to meet him at the lake. If I did, would my new extended family think I was betraying them? Was it possible to do anything they wouldn't know about?

I looked toward the lake. The partly cloudy sky was playing hide-and-seek with the sun, but the rays made the water a dazzling silver. A lone crow flew close to the water and then turned into the forest as if something had frightened it. The breeze strengthened and seemed to shake the trees. Just as suddenly, it stopped, and all looked still, more like an oil painting framed in my window.

My father had said I shouldn't worry about Summer or his father. "What needs to be done about them will be done." What did that mean? Was Summer already gone? What about the pendant and what I had just felt? I strained to look closer at the lake. *He's there*, I thought. *He's waiting for me. He has to be.* He was just as much a victim of his father as I was. Yes, he did bad things, and he was far more capable of doing them than I was, but I must have seen something good in him to care about him even now, even after I had heard the truth.

I stepped out of my room and listened. Everyone was in the living room talking. What was it Summer had said? He walked on a breeze? I imagined it, imagined myself doing it, and descended. Softly, I opened the rear door and slipped out. Then I hurried around the house and toward the lake. Half of me hoped he would be there, and half of me hoped he wouldn't. I followed the path Uncle Wade and I had taken when we had our little talk not so long ago.

Farther along, there was a place on the shore that jutted out a bit into the water. The narrow land looked like a natural dock. To the right, the forest had a thicker patch of trees and bushes, but the leaves had dried and fallen, creating a rug of dark orange and brown. I waited and listened. Foolishly, I had come out without a jacket or a sweater, and the cooler air stung my cheeks. I hugged myself and was ready to turn back when I heard him say my name.

I turned and saw him standing at the edge of the woods. He wore a black sweatshirt with the hood up and had his hands in the pockets.

"I knew you would come," he said, stepping toward me.

"Do you know who I am, who we really are?" I asked. I had no time to build up slowly to my important questions. Everything was going to happen quickly now.

He stopped but held his smile. "Of course. I knew who you were from the first day I entered the school," he said, with that cool, confident smile I had at first admired. Now it filled me with dread.

"How did you know?"

"I would have known just looking at you, listening to you, and seeing the way you looked at other people."

"But that's not the way you knew," I said.

"No." He stepped closer.

"Our father told you, didn't he?"

"Yes, but what difference does it make now?" He reached out to touch me, and I stepped back.

"What difference does it make now? We have the same father, Summer."

"That's why we're special people, Sage. The rules that apply to everyone else don't apply to us."

"Not that rule."

He didn't lose his smile. "You'll get over that," he said. "We're the prospective parents of the wonder generation to come. What we can do, what we can see, will be nothing compared with what they will do and see."

"Your father's told you lies. He seduced your mother, just as he did mine. He's not a good man."

"No. He's a great man."

"You're wrong. He's hurt you deeply, taught you all the wrong things to do and believe. You used your gifts to hurt people, Summer."

"Please. You can't feel sorry for them. Besides, what I did was for you."

"Me?"

"To protect you, to keep you close, and to win you to me. It's right that we have the power to enjoy each other. We deserve whatever we can get. They don't matter. *We* matter."

"I can't think like that."

"That's because you were brought up by them," he said, nodding at our house. "They're stuck in the old ways. They'll die out. You'll see. We're the future."

"Is this what your father has been telling you?"

"I told you. Our father's a great man with great vision. They're jealous of him. That's all. They know he doesn't need them, and they can't tolerate it. You belong with him, with me."

"No. The family is what keeps us strong. I know that now. Your father's alone, and you'll be alone."

"Not if I have you."

"You won't," I said.

His smile changed quickly to a grimace of incredulity. "You can't really want to stay here, be with them, after all they've done to you, Sage."

"They did what had to be done. I believe in them."

His incredulity turned to raw anger, his eyes reddening, his lips taut. The bones of his jaw and his cheeks pressed up against his skin. I could feel his rage flowing out of his body, but I held my ground. I locked my eyes on his. I had grown stronger. He couldn't make me back down, and he knew it.

"We're going," he said. "We won't be back. My father won't let me return."

"Then don't go. Come inside the house with me, and meet those who can help you, change you, make you a part of the family."

"Part of that family?" He shook his head. "You're a terrible disappointment, Sage. You'll make my father see me as a failure. I was supposed to bring you into *our* family."

"He's the failure, and you'll be one, too. I can see your future. It's dark and full of unhappiness and pain, but you can change it."

He shook his head. He looked like he was going to cry now.

"Summer, please, listen to me."

"No," he said, stepping back. He looked up at the house. "I'm going. You'll be sorry. No one will love you like I do."

"Yes. Someone will," I said.

"You can't see your own future."

"I can see his. He's out there for me."

He turned and started back toward the forest. Before entering it, he looked back at me. Then he looked toward my house and started to run deeper into the woods. I watched him disappear in the trees, run into a shadow of himself, as if his body had been vaporized. I took a deep breath and started back to the house, pausing when I looked up and saw them all standing out front, looking my way. That was what had made him run, the sight of them gathered, the power of their combined energy sent in his direction. I walked faster toward them. They waited for me, but no one was smiling.

"Why did you meet him?" my mother asked immediately.

"To see if you were right that he knew who I was. I had to know for certain. I won't live with doubts. Not anymore," I said, with a firmness they recognized and appreciated.

"Well? What did you learn?" she asked.

"You were right, but it isn't all his fault."

"He is what he is now," my father said.

"We can't change that," Uncle Alexis added. "It's beyond our powers. Many things are. You'll learn the limits."

Yes, yes, I thought with exhaustion. *I'll learn everything*. I looked back at the woods. "Where will he go?"

"Where he has already gone . . . into the darkness," Uncle Alexis said. "It's where he would have taken you, too."

"Despite what you're saying, I want you all to know that I can't help but feel sorry for him."

"That's the goodness in you," Aunt Suzume said.

"Soon he'll feel sorry for himself, too," my mother added. "Come into the house now, Sage. We have things to teach you, things for you to do."

She held out her hand. I glanced one more time at the forest shadows, then took her hand and started to walk with them.

I suddenly stopped. "Wait," I said, letting go of her. "I have something else to do first. I'll be right there."

They looked at me a moment, and then Uncle Alexis nodded at the door, and they all went inside.

I went to our garage and got a shovel. Then I walked fifty paces toward the north and stopped to dig a hole in the ground. Instinctively, I knew how deep it had to be. When it was deep enough, I reached into the pocket of my jeans and took out Summer's pendant. I dropped it into the hole and covered it with dirt and small rocks forming the shape of a pentacle.

After I patted it down, I looked out at the lake and the woods. The crow had come back. It was flying its own patterns over the water, feeling free and alive again. When it reached the farthest end of the lake, it looked like a large dot moving through the air. I glanced back at the covered hole.

"He's gone," I whispered to the breeze that embraced my words to carry them off. "He's gone for good."

Silently, I walked back to the house to join my family and become one of them forever.

Epilogue

I stood off to the side in the girls' section of the department store and watched her with her two daughters, one fourteen and one ten. There were clear resemblances to me in her, I thought. Our hair was the same color. Our noses and mouths were the same. She was very pretty, and so were her daughters. I was confident that in time, I would look more and more like her, and what in me that resembled my biological father would retreat into some small, dark pocket of my very being, never to resurrect itself.

My adoptive father and Uncle Wade were standing off to the side like two mother hens. They had come with me, expecting that all I would do was look at her and then turn around and go back with them, but I wanted more. I approached her and her daughters. They were sifting through a rack of blouses.

"The fashions change so quickly these days," I muttered as I sifted through another rack close to the one they were at.

She turned to look at me, and her daughters did the same, but the girls quickly went back to their perusal of the blouses.

She smiled. "Which is what makes it harder for the mothers of girls who are too eager to grow up," she said.

"That doesn't change even when they grow up."

"No, I suppose not. I like what you're wearing."

"Thank you. I like what you're wearing, too."

"I want to try this on, Mom," her older daughter said, holding up a mint-green jeweled sweater.

Our mother looked at the price tag. "Just like Tara to pick out the most expensive one on the rack," she said with a smile.

"Tara? You're a fan of *Gone with the Wind*?" I asked, and she laughed.

"I'm surprised you're aware of that. Most teenagers these days haven't seen it or read it, but Tara will someday, won't you, Tara?"

"Just to stop you from nagging me about it," my half sister said. I smiled at her, and she laughed. She reminded me a lot of myself at her age.

"Go on. Try it on," our mother told her, and she and her sister headed for the changing room.

"What's your younger girl's name? And don't tell me Scarlett."

"No. My husband wouldn't put up with two from the same novel. She's named after his mother, Grace."

"Sweet. They're both very pretty."

"Thank you." She looked at me curiously for a moment. "Have we met?"

"No. I'm just visiting an aunt in this town. I live in Massachusetts."

"Oh. I have a cousin in Boston."

"I'm in a smaller city, Dorey," I said.

"What grade are you in?"

"I'm a senior now."

"How wonderful. These are the best years of your life. Don't rush them," she advised.

I shrugged. "We don't listen. Someone once said that youth was wasted on the young."

"George Bernard Shaw."

"Oh, you know."

"I'm a community college English teacher," she said. "I don't volunteer that information," she told me, leaning toward me to whisper as if we were sharing a state secret. "As soon as people learn that, they watch how they speak. Some *don't* speak."

I laughed. "I know exactly what you mean. I had an English teacher who would pounce on anyone who left out a consonant, like saying 'mou-in' instead of 'mountain.'"

"Exactly. Where do you hope to go to college?"

"Probably somewhere in California, like Occidental or UCLA. Maybe Stanford."

"What do you want to study?"

"Humanity," I replied, and she laughed. "The arts."

"Something tells me you're going to do well. What's your name?"

"Sage," I said.

She blinked her eyes. "I almost named my older daughter that. I mean, it came to me, but my husband thought it was a little too different. He was wrong, of course. It's a beautiful name."

"Thank you."

I looked off to the right. My father and Uncle Wade were moving closer. Both looking very concerned.

"Well, I guess I had better go look for my aunt," I said. "It was very nice meeting you."

Tara came out of the changing room and stood in front of the mirror.

"Oh, she looks good in that," I said.

"I know. I'm not ready for what's coming."

"Yes, you are," I said. I knew. I knew she would be a wonderful mother and a wonderful grandmother for both her daughters' children.

She looked at me strangely. "You sound so confident when you speak about the future, Sage. You have a fortune-teller's eyes," she said, and out of some instinct that no woman could subdue no matter what, she leaned forward and kissed me on the cheek before turning away to go to her children.

For me, it was as if I had traveled through time and for a moment lived and understood the life I would never have.

I didn't cry. I didn't even feel sad.

We had touched.

And really, that was what was most important after all.